The Shadows' Apprentice

Book 1

By K. L. Alexander

First paperback edition April 2022

Book design by Kim Dingwall
Edited by Sarina Cornthwaite & Fiona Wadsley

ISBN/SKU: (978-1-7387079-0-4)

Acknowledgments

Thank you, Lord, because I never could have thought about this.
Thank you to my friends and family for believing in me.
Thank you, Sarina, for making this jigsaw puzzle into a novel.
Thank you, Akilah, for your pestering on description, and Deniqua on your *seed* of involvement (which grew into a forest).
I thank everyone for taking the time to read my story.

And thank you, mommy, for being there from draft one.

Prologue
WAR

"The heart is deceitful above all things, and desperately wicked:
who can know it?"
Jeremiah 17:9, KJV

The doors crash open with a force that threatens the rusted hinges.

"The rebels have lost!" the soldier cries, panic in his gasping voice. A boy gets a closer look at the man; there is a broken arrow in his back; the boiled leather armour offered no protection against its metal tip.

The soldier collapses onto the aged oak floors, creating an echo that stuns the room into silence. Not even the cold winds of winter whisper as they slowly drift in through thinly covered holes in the wall behind them. A young girl is the first to shriek in terror. Then the panic begins, and more people awaken from their stupors as reality sets in; babies wake in the arms of their mothers, their own pitiful wails joining the chaos; some people begin to board up the drafty windows; a few people race to the back of the large house looking for another exit, one not blocked by a soon-to-be dead man. Better to take their chances in the wilderness, in the forest with its ferocious beasts, rather than face the monsters of men. In one corner, a group of young maidens sob into each other's arms; just moments ago, they were laughing and singing songs of hope and victory. Any remaining rebel soldiers who stayed behind try to gather the attention of those panicking with no success.

With no exits in the back, many men and women scramble over each other and the dying solider to reach what they believe is freedom. Others cry, 'What will we do?' but no one responds with a sensible answer. Amidst the chaos is one boy who also feels the waves of panic and fear, but does what no one else will; he stops and breathes. That's all he can do.

The boy called Nick ducks under the arms of the soldiers flailing for attention and direction. He's pushed by the crowd, shoved by one of the larger men trying to escape, and even gets knocked to the floor by a thin woman who races past him. He almost gets stepped on, but scrambles up, ignoring the pain in his arm, and continues to push through; crushing a doll under his feet.

It's not his fault he's so small. A lack of food and a lot of wondering if you'll live to see tomorrow will do that to you. He is well below average for a boy his age; fifteen, often mistaken for a child of eleven. He goes by many names: 'a boy who is still growing' from the women, 'breakable thing' from the men, and 'twig' from his cousin. The most creative, in his opinion, is 'talking fishbone': a title graciously given to him by his father. The 'talking fishbone' pushes through the last group of people and crouches beside the fallen soldier, more battered and out of breath than before. He grabs the soldier by the leather vest, his small hands fighting to get a grip, and pulls with all his strength (which isn't much), and begins moving away from the chaos, leaving a trail of red in their wake. His best and only friend skulking in the corner quickly grabs the medicine woman racing past, dragging her to the injured soldier. The medicine woman is better than no one, because their rebellion doesn't have any of the academy-trained doctors found in cities.

"Make sure you can save him," Nick commands, his voice cracking with nerves.

The woman kisses her teeth, unimpressed by his attempt to be authoritative. "Boy, can't you see that the man is at death's door? He just said that the rebel army, your *father's* army, has fallen! We need to move!" She gets up and hurries out with the other people, knocking over her medicine bags. She doesn't bother picking up her bag as she flees with the crowd, choosing life over replaceable medicine.

He wants to call after her, but the words die on his tongue. He was never good with words. As he turns away and looks at the ground, a deep feeling of helplessness begins to crawl up his throat. He hates it. He can see from the corner of his eyes that

Kaius, his friend and a gentle giant of sorts, wants to comfort him, but before he has the chance, a powerful voice rings out.

"People!" His cousin Braawen's voice echoes out to everyone. By some miracle, people begin to stop and listen once more. "I know that we are fearful, but we mustn't lose our heads! The Emperor's army has not arrived yet. Pick up your things and let us hurry to the next base." He points towards the packed supplies at the side of the house, and as usual, takes credit for something that Nick has done. Kaius rolls his eyes and Nick bites his lips hard enough to taste iron. But he doesn't care about glory right now, he only cares about getting as many people out of here as possible.

Everyone remaining obediently makes their way towards the supplies, fear, hope and loss as their only motivators. Nick leaves the soldier for a moment to help distribute the supplies. The night before, while everyone was talking about the new world order that they would make and how they plan a better life after the war, Nick and Kaius carefully divided and packed food, blankets, and other supplies for the amount of people in their little group. It took them all night, but it was worth it. Soldiers scolded them for their lack of faith, but Nick's father always told him to always prepare for the worst. After all supplies had found homes in the arms of the desperate, Nick returns to the soldier slumped against the wall, still bleeding.

"Come on, Kaius, let's try to bring the man with us." Nick states.

He pretends not to hear his friend's mumbled response. "I—I don't think... I don't think he'll make it."

"Well, we have to try," Nick insists. "It's the least we can do. The man did make his way here to warn all of us, after all." He picks one of the man's arms up and slings it over his shoulder, wordlessly directing Kaius to take the other, which he does rather reluctantly. He can't see why his friend is complaining. Kaius is rather tall and has a little muscle on him. The few muscles Nick has can barely hold his own bones together, but he still manages to lift the man.

Just as they begin to move forward, an explosion blows apart the doors and windows, sending the two boys and the man flying.

In hindsight, it was a good thing they took the dying man with them.

His body took the deadliest blow.

Chapter 1
Lost

Three months after the five-year rebellion of the Kingdom of Availa finally ended, the leaders of the rebels were put into cells while the woman and children were put into indentured servitude. Some took their lives and their children's lives, but many more chose to live. The Kingdom of Availa became one of the many kingdoms to be consumed by the Andromendor Empire.

The Night Emperor, ruler of the Land of Andromendor came and defeated the rebel leader Markus in single combat. Now, the Night Emperor and his brave council could once again rule the Empire in peace and harmony.

Or so Nick has been told.

From what he could recall, Availa *was* a powerful country, such that even the Empire respected it. Yet, the kingdom had been steadily getting worse under the rule of their fallen King. From what he could remember, his father began a small stand after an increase in taxes; his stand grew into a rebellion. Things escalated quickly to the point where the Empire became involved. Then they had to fight the Empire. It started with a fight to lower taxes and turned into a fight for independence. They lost that fight.

In Nick's opinion, if anyone cared to hear it, the late king of Availa was a fool. From what he heard through the rebels, they were fighting against the throne, whether the King of Availa or the Night Emperor was sitting on it. They no longer cared about nobles and royalty. Nick's people stood for their home and family. He asked his father if he would take the throne once this was over; his father laughed and said maybe. Nick remembers his mother glaring at his father.

Everyone wanted to fight in a war, but no one asked the big questions. *What happens after? Who is in charge if not the King?* The late King had no legitimate heirs, just bastards. Not that it mattered. Anyone with the Availian royal family blood was killed by the Night Emperor himself. Everyone in the country heard about the massacre of the royal family, and all those in the castle. The dynasty that lasted over one thousand years, gone in a single night. That night would be forever known as 'the Night of the Silenced'.

People whispered about that horrible night, even within the rebel camps. People said that as the city was attacked, the screams and sounds of the destroyed buildings were blocked by royal knights and imperial soldiers fighting against each other. Even the most seasoned warriors ignored the cries of pain from their fallen brethren. However, no one could forget the sounds that emanated from the King of Availa's castle, which paralyzed everyone in their tracks. Swords froze in mid-air and shields lowered as the city went silent. The inhabitants stopped running; even the crying and injured stopped as they heard the sounds. They all remained quiet as they heard the blood-curdling cries of the people in the castle... and the abrupt silence that came afterwards.

Now the Empire's flag flies proudly across Availa, replacing the roaring lion with a black and gold dragon.

Nick is in a holding cell. It didn't take long for the soldiers to come and find him in the remains of the rebel house. Many people actually survived the bombing... except for the wounded soldier, of course. He felt the man go cold on him, as Kaius screamed in pain. A woman in black uniform leaned over them and Nick passed out as rough hands pulled him up. Now he's here, a prisoner in his own land; thankfully, he's not alone. In the cell with him were Kaius, Braawen, and Braawen's best friend Lorcan. Braawen and Lorcan sit on one side while Nick and Kaius sit on the other. All the occupants in the cell wish that they were anywhere else but together.

The first week in this nightmare of a situation is hell. Braawen and Lorcan yell and fight with the guards. They shout saying that they will never break, that the remaining rebels will come to their aid. However, their taunts make it more difficult for Kaius and Nick, with the guards giving them less food and dirty water.

By the second week, the guards have had enough, and beat the living daylights out of Braawen and Lorcan. Nick has to swallow his pride many times that week to get clean water so that he and Kaius could clean the other boys' wounds. Nick tears his clothes for bandages and gives what little of his food he can spare to his cousin

Finally, near the end of the month, both Braawen and Lorcan begin to behave themselves. They still glare, but Nick tells them to ignore the guards.

"This is the coward's way," Lorcan spits. "We should fight to the very end."

Braawen smiles, "I agree. We should ambush them when they give us our meal and—"

"Fight every single guard?" Nick interrupts him. Kaius remains silent, mumbling prayers. Braawen and Lorcan glare at him now, causing him to fidget in his place, but he swallows whatever fear he has in him. He just wants them to realize the situation that they're in. "If you fight a guard, you get beaten, which is something that neither I nor Kaius want to deal with again. If you kill the guards, you will die, and so will everyone else in the prison," he explains slowly, hoping they'll understand.

Lorcan scoffs. "A warrior's death."

Nick doesn't even bother to hide his eye roll. Normally, he would remain quiet around the two, but he wasn't planning on dying because of their stupid warrior code.

"Tell that to the little children, and the rest of the men and women here." Nick takes a deep breath, hoping that whatever courage he has in him lasts. "What will your people say if your actions bring about the deaths of innocent children?" he asks Lorcan. "Your warrior code is meant to protect as well."

Lorcan glares at him but remains silent.

"And you, Braawen? How would your father feel if you lead such a terrible massacre? Which is what it will become if you kill a guard. I bet that he would be disappointed, even devastated, at the news." His cousin's eyes narrow at him, but he doesn't say a word. "They have orders from the top to kill, so they will not hesitate to end us."

"Then what do you suggest?" Braawen grits out.

Nick sighs. "Wait and gather whatever strength we have. With the way things are going, we will be waiting for a while."

"For how long?" He could hear his cousin's teeth grinding.

"Until we're safe, or safer, at least. I don't have to tell you how 'safe' we are. It would be best to keep our identity a secret. Let no one know that we're Archers."

He can see the curses ready to leave his cousin's lips.

"Think, Braawen," Nick hisses, startling everyone in the cell, "We could be used as leverage against our fathers, or worse, killed." Realization dawns on his cousin's face. "Right now, we hide in plain sight and keep silent."

A heavy silence falls on the cell. Four young boys fearing for their lives and the lives of their families. Unbeknownst to the other three, Kaius sits quietly in his corner watching the whole conversation, praying. *Oh, goddess of Earth, please give us strength. Please give us strength to have a strong and wise leader.*

He opens his eyes to see Nick.

The second month, he sees small rays of sunshine, but it's through the sack on his head. The morning they leave the prison, Nick and his companions have chains around their legs and arms. This is his first time having such heavy chains on his legs; he wishes to never experience it again. He can feel the hands of the guards on him, guiding him to another destination. The first thing he hears is his own rapid heartbeat and the cries of other prisoners. The first thing he feels is the cold winds of the North touching his skin through his prisoner's uniform. He is then lifted into a cart and shoved into a cart. He moves his feet to feel solid ground, and smells pine.

He hears a whisper. "Nick?"

"Kai?"

They both let out a sigh of relief.

"We're here, too, you know." He can hear Braawen grumble and Lorcan scoff, muttering a word that sounds like the language from the Plains of Availa.

This is going to be a long ride.

When the wagon ride stops, hours later, all of them are pushed off the cart. Nick can hear shouting and commands from different people. He takes a deep breath to calm his nerves but stops. He sniffs again and smells fish and salt. Before he can guess, his sack is pulled off his head and he blinks rapidly. The view takes his breath away.

He sees the setting sun over the sea. Never would he have guessed that his first time viewing the sea, he would be in chains. Though, at the moment it doesn't diminish the sky's beautiful masterpiece. It seems as though the god of Air blended the colours of the sky to bring peace to a group of enslaved people. It's a mix of purples, and blues fading from orange, leaving a warm and gentle hue. The noise fades as his ears focus on the calming waves and the sounds of the seagulls flapping their wings.

"Nick." His friend's voice brings him back to reality and the sounds of the sea are overcome by the shouts and screams. He looks around him and sees that people are being forced onto large dark ships. Kaius stays near him as both are pushed back into the crowd. They're at a port, one that Nick's never been to before. He tries to find a sign, only to see that the signs of whatever city this may be are torn off. He knows it's a city, though he hasn't been to many, as only cities have paved walkways. The city itself looks small, yet the port is large enough to hold three vessels.

This could be one of the trading ports, but now instead of food and natural resources, they are trading in war prisoners. He has to stop himself from laughing as he remembers that *he* is the natural resource.

Instead of the fisherman and merchants that he heard ports should busy with, there are soldiers all around. For a moment, the fluttering sounds of the flags above him takes his attention. He looks up expecting to see the roaring lion of his country; instead he sees the guarded black and gold dragon of the Empire. Nick shrinks as he feels the gaze of the dragon on him. He looks anywhere but at the flag; however, the flapping stays in his mind.

Nick turns his attention to a gaping young man, a free man, getting pulled into a house. By the surprise on his face, it might have been a stranger's house. However, he sees more citizens protecting as many people as possible. The other citizens that aren't prisoners close their windows and doors. He looks to the window to see a little girl pop her head up, only to be pulled back by an angry woman who closes the drapes.

With the city dampening his mood, he looks at the sea again; the waves unfortunately, are no longer majestic or calming. A soldier slaps him to get his attention for not hearing his orders. No fuss or snarky remarks are uttered when Nick sees the soldier's hand grab the hilt of his sword. Instead, his body goes weak as the man shoves him towards the ship, hearing the cries and moans of his people.

They are transported onto a ship heading to Andromendor; their voyage will take a month at sea. Nick and his group are put into a small and dark cell; they have to put their knees up to their chests for all of them to fit. The only form of light are the five small glass lanterns surrounding the ceilings, barely giving off enough light to see the person next to them. The journey is terrible and deadly at best. Many of the cells are cramped from the prisoners that they hold.

One morning, Nick can hear coughing, which turns to hacking. There are an increasing number of complaints from the other prisoners. Those complaints turn to cries for help and fear. When a person dies on the boat, the sailors only listen to their cries when the body begins to smell, throwing the body overboard. The prisoners stay locked in their cells, only getting up to go to the second floor to stand and eat for one hour a day. They do not receive any sunlight. The poor conditions allow the sickness and death to spread freely through the ship. Nick thought that he has seen everything from the war, but this torment is beyond cruel and he has to wonder how men can be so twisted. Then he remembers the words his mother would say. *The hearts of men are full of darkness.*

He wishes that they would just throw his body into the sea. He can't swim, but maybe drowning would be better than this. As he looks at his companions in their cell, Nick has the feeling that none of them would see their homeland again. Their land full of forests and fertile lands blessed by the goddess of Earth to feed their people in the summer. He would even miss the cold winds of winter and the snowfalls that purified the earth as a gift from the god of Water. He closes his eyes and leans his head on the ship's wooden board. The board smelt too much like human waste and sea salt. He can remember the smells of oak and maple near his camp, and wonders if the wood used on this ship came from his country. They traded in lumber and timber, and had a good relationship with the Andromendor Empire at first, until their late King.

After the terrible month at sea, they finally make it to their final destination. The capital city of the Empire, Andromeda.

Nick and his group of four unload on the docks. He needs to close his eyes, adjusting to the bright sunlight from being in the dark for nearly a month. However, his ears are working fine; he can hear the roaring crowd of applause for the Emperor before he even can see them.

He looks ahead and the first thing he sees is snow. The white flakes catch his breath. It wouldn't be snowing yet back home. He looks at the cold and pure fluffs of ice that he loves so much. The snow reminds him of the mountains; the snow reminds him of his mother.

His thoughts are interrupted by a snowball landing on his face. He stumbles and narrows his eyes, looking towards the crowds for the first time. There, he sees two children in colourful warm coats and fur hats, pointing and laughing at them. He looks around to see that the people in the crowd are all wearing long, thick coats and leather boots, some going up to their knees. The soldiers acting as a border wear black coats and fur hats, more sombre than the bright, happy citizens. The longer coats have simple, geometric decorative patterns while their boots remain a somber black, grey, and brown. Nick sees vibrantly dyed scarves and other accessories with even more colorful designs.

I forgot that they get Winter first. Availa is more in the South, anyways. It's so cold. He shivers. For the first time, all the boys have no problem huddling keeping each other warm. The meagre clothes that couldn't even make them sweat in the summer were too thin to keep any warmth in. He had half a mind to believe that the soldiers wanted to kill them off sooner. However, before they could receive any warmth from each other, they are pulled apart and chained at the neck, arms, and legs. The chains from the arms and the neck are so short that they have to keep their hands close to their neck. There is also limited movement in their legs. The four are pushed back together and Braawen's chain knocks Nick's head, gaining a small chuckle from his cousin.

He quickly glances around to see how everyone in his group looks. In three words: alive, but terrible. They are all still a head taller than him, besides Kaius, who is still the tallest; but now, he isn't the only skinny person.

All of their hair is cut short, almost bald. Braawen's golden locks that had made the girls fall for him were cut short by one of the guards to de-lice them. His hair is almost brown from dirt, his face hollow and pale from the lack of food; his lips are chapped from the lack of water; his eyes, once bright blue, are now black and baggy from the screams and cries of the other captives; his muscular arms are lacking. Nick worries about his cousin's silence. The one that was bright and arrogant is still a bit arrogant, but his light is almost gone. He needs his cousin to be strong. The gods know Nick can't inspire people or give them hope.

Lorcan's sheared auburn hair has a mix of brown as well. His tan skin is pale and bruised from sleeping next to the iron bars on the ship, and his face is hollow. However, his almond-shaped, golden eyes, a trait only the people of the wild plains possess, dart from one end of the crowd to the other. Kaius isn't any better. If Nick was a small talking fishbone, his friend is a scarecrow. His earthy skin is normally darker, but the lack of sunlight actually manages to lighten his skin. Little curls are growing on his head, but his large green eyes are sparked in fear.

Nick's own dark brown hair is cut unevenly, and his slightly hooded, almond-shaped blue eyes take in the state of his body. He almost gasps as he looks down at his legs. He didn't think he could lose any more weight. He's a walking skeleton.

They are pushed forward and are now walking in a line with the other war prisoners. He can't make out anyone he knows, but they are all in a sorry state. As they walk, he can see more the people cheering with roars of applause, getting louder as they enter the city.

The city is beautiful with its stone buildings; some seem to tower high with six windows above each other, while others have pillars suited for temples, but seem to hold places of business now. It is easier to walk on the paved stones compared to the dirt-covered roads throughout most of Availa. Although even the stones in Availa could not compare to the large flat stones that they traverse on now. The street is wide enough to fit two carriages, and more than wide enough to fit the war prisoners and their guards atop horses on either side.

As they walk along the freshly shovelled snow, Nick's legs ache from not walking in over a month and his soles hurt from his poorly-made shoes. He sees someone fall ahead of him. Instead of helping the man up, one of the guards cuts the chains off the man and commands the prisoners to continue to walk, so they trample over him. Nick tries his best to not fall. If he does, he knows the people will just walk right over him. Gods know they did metaphorically.

A terrible way to die, especially after all I've been through, he thinks. He would have thought of more things until he sees a person around his age amongst the crowd, a red fruit in their hand. Before he could come up with a reason why, the fruit lands on the left side of his face, splattering juice and seeds all over his clothes. He sees Lorcan, who is next to him, dodge another thrown fruit. Even Kaius ducks in time, barely missing a fruit. Nick looks up and sees that Braawen is indeed smiling now. Instead of getting angry, Nick tentatively licks a smear of fruit on the corner of his mouth. It's a little spoiled, but still better than the meagre oats they've been eating.

They come at a stop at the edge of a large platform, much to the mercy of everyone. However, if Nick knew the reason why, he would have begged the guards to keep moving. What he sees next knocks the breath out of his lungs. *His father.*

His father is kicked behind the knees by a soldier wearing all-black armour, with the dragon of the Empire emblazoned on his chest. The once strong and proud rebel leader falls hard on his knees. The sound elicited a roar from the crowd in the square, yet Nick ignored them, focusing on the man he calls Father.

The man who used to stare down at his son looks around to see the people that he once led a rebellion, now in servitude. To the side of the square is a large black pavilion with the sign of a gold and black dragon. There, the Night Emperor and his men were watching. They couldn't see the Night Emperor, but he could see them.

His father's gaze stops at the one person Nick hopes he cares to see. Blue eyes meet blue eyes. Nick sees his father's eyes widen in recognition. There he is, the strongest man Nick has ever known in his life, kneeling. Nick looks his father over and sees the journey did not treat him well either; he has also lost weight and muscle; and his face is also bruised and pale. Before the guards commence the executions, he looks at his father one last time.

Amongst the roaring crowds and the soft whimpers and cries of his people in chains, Nick speaks his last words to him; barely a whisper.

"Goodbye, father."

He isn't sure that his father can hear him, but the nod his father gives him is enough. Then he sees his father's eyes widen as the guards walk to the war prisoners and begin to separate them. Nick and his group are pushed on one side, along with more children. Panic resurfaces as children cries for their parents, while parents are trying to reach their children but are hit or forced back to stay on their side. He can hear the cries and goodbyes of loved ones, as they realize that they would probably never see each other again.

How can these people be so cruel as to separate a child from their parents?

The hearts of men are full of darkness.

Nick stays close to his group, even as they are taken away from the square. Perhaps the Emperor didn't want them to see the executions, or he wanted the adults to suffer more. How many believe they are going to be killed? Nick walks with his head held high; if he was going to die, he would do so with honour. It would make his mother proud, and maybe even his father, for once.

It's always the children that suffer from the mistakes of the parent, Nick can't help but think bitterly as the children around him sobs. Lorcan, Kaius and even Braawen have tears in their eyes. Nick blinks his own tears away as he sees that a little girl of six is thankfully not in chains; she is holding onto the clothes of an older boy a little younger than him, with the same hair as the girl. The boy is chained, but keeps telling the girl called Noel that it will be okay.

Nick has to turn his head. *We're just children.*

The journey to their new destination is a sombre affair, with a mix of cries of sorrow from the children and commands from the guards. The young children and young adults stick closely together as many of the citizens of the empire mock them. This time even Nick feels his walls crumbling, as his body begins to slow down. Kaius at one point has to knock him to keep him moving.

As they march, the only mercy that Nick notices is that the guards are slightly gentler with the youths. They even slow the pace of their march and stop the citizens from throwing anything at them. Nick doesn't know if it's to show mercy or to let them freeze faster. However, with an hour of added marching, Nick can't feel his toes. He's used to cold weather, he lived in the cold mountains before all of this, but this cold is different from the mountains. The mountains bring back long-forgotten feelings of home, familiarity, and safety. Here, the cold only feels like death. Honestly, he just wants to fall over and be done with it. Yet, at the commands of one of the guards, Nick slowly lifts his head, rubbed raw from the chains. In front of them, set apart from the beautiful buildings of the city, is a grey fortress with high stone walls and gates. The building looks imposing and many of the children cry louder, fearing for their lives. Nick feels fear at first, but the prospect of potentially dying in a warm building brings small comfort.

The four of them sit in a quiet corner. There are guards roaming the hall of over a hundred children. The room is warmer from their body heat as the four huddle close to each other. The children receive better care, now; they each receive blankets, bread, and soup with vegetables, and a hot bath. The bath was a surprise for everyone. He couldn't remember the last time he had a warm bath back in Availa. At home, it was custom that people bathe in separate rooms to have privacy. Even when the rebels took a bath in the lake, they would spread out to not be seen. Yet here in Andromendor, all the children are brought in groups to a wide room with a steaming hot pool of yellow greenish water that smelt of salt and herbs. All the children are stripped, then pushed into the water.

Nick and his friends try to go into a corner by themselves. He closes his eyes for modesty's sake, but even that was thrown out the window when all the boys had to dry themselves and change together. He kept his back to the wall the whole time.

"Look at them squirming like little girls, no.... worms are a better description!" The guards surrounding them are laughing, pointing, and mocking them.

Nick can even see his cousin blush and his eyes fill with anger.

Braawen clearly wants to start a fight, but Nick grabs his arms. "Remember, hiding in plain sight," he whispers. He receives a glare in return, but his cousin remains silent.

The four of them keep their heads down, hiding in plain sight, listening for any information that can help them. But on the third day, they hear from the guards that Braawen's father was executed.

He was hanged.

Braawen goes into a rage and says that there was no way that his father died like a common thief.

Nick groans. *So much for hiding our identities*.

"Oh, an Archer!" His laughter grows. "Of course, he wasn't hanged like a common thief. He was hanged, drawn and quartered!"

Nick tries to comfort him afterwards, but Braawen swats him away.

"What would you know about having a father?! You don't understand what I'm going through! I loved my father and he loved me!" His cousin snaps. "Yours didn't even want you!"

Lorcan and Kaius hesitantly look between the two. Nick just glares and remains silent, not even trying to deny it. He decides to comfort himself, as he too, feels a great loss at the death of a kind uncle.

There is no mention of Nick's father until the end of the week.

After all of his father's friends and closest advisors are killed, the Night Emperor makes sure to set an example to other people who think of rebelling.

"There has been news, children!" a guard yells, a cruel smile graces his lips. All of the children turn to him, but Nick can't help but feel a pit of despair in his stomach.

"The rebellion leader Markus Archer has been executed by the command of the Night Emperor." The guard didn't say how he died, but the fear in the room was palpable. Only quiet whispers spread throughout the room. The guard finished his announcement and made his way to the four, looking for Braawen.

The guard stops and whispers. "I know he was your uncle... would you like to hear more? I don't want the other kids getting scared, but since he was your family, I thought that you would want to know." Braawen looks at Nick who nods.

"What happened to him?" Braawen asks in a hushed voice.

The guard kneels and whispers to them all. "Nasty way to die. He was flayed, then put on the rack to have his bones dislocated. Then he was whipped with clawed irons that tore through his muscles. He was healed before he could die. Oh no, the Emperor didn't want him dead yet."

Nick's stomach turns as he listens to the sweet satisfaction in the guard's voice.

"Then, he was chained up by his arms at the city gates and exposed to the elements where people threw fruits and stones at him, all while the Emperor watched and ate his meal."

Even some of the children near them look on in horror. However, the guard ignores how quiet the room is getting. "It took him until the next night to die from the exposure from the cold winds. By order of the Emperor, the body will remain there until nature takes its course." The guard shakes his head and stands up, leaving the four of them wide-eyed.

There should have been more rage or mourning at the news of his father's death. Braawen, Lorcan and Kaius look at Nick, wondering if, for the first time in their lives, Nicky the fishbone would actually use his backbone and fight, but he keeps his expression neutral.

Marcus Archer was a great leader, fighter, and a great soldier.

But he was a terrible husband and father.

Instead of crying, Nick rubs his back and feels some of the scars that his father put on him. He believes it's ironic that his father was whipped; he would pay gold to see that. He pushes his thoughts back as he sees the scar on his wrist. This one wasn't from his father. This one was because of his mother. As he rubs the scar, he thinks of her; she wouldn't approve of his thoughts.

"Don't worry, guys." They can barely hear him, but he doesn't face them. "It's like Braawen said." He can feel the stinging of the scars on his back. "My father didn't want me anyway."

Braawen looks down, ashamed for once. Lorcan sighs and leans against the cold stone. Kaius looks like he wants to say something, but after a few failed attempts, he gives up.

Nick doesn't know why he is surprised by the brutality of the Night Emperor. He remembers when his father and his men captured one of the Emperor's generals. The man looked like a silly thing, almost begging them to just end his life. Everyone ignored the strange behaviour and his father sent a message demanding that the Emperor surrender, or he would cut off a piece of his general and send it to him every day.

The Emperor sent a fast reply and requested that the first cut be the general's head.

Nick looks around, seeing what little hope the children held onto die. Everyone in here suffered, because of the rebellion. He was an orphan because of this stupid rebellion. Mother was killed by the King's men. Now Father, by the hand of the Emperor.

Though he didn't have the best father, he did have the best uncles. Nick's face takes on a hopeful look. Uncle Tys, his father's youngest brother, wasn't mentioned. Nick realizes that he may still have an uncle alive, maybe two if his mother's younger brother is alive as well.

Three days later, the door opens again for a new arrival. There stands an older woman with silver hair and black eyes, standing tall under her fur-collared black coat. She shrugs it off and hands it to one of the two guards in black armour behind her. She wears an all-black military uniform, with a pendant with a large purple gemstone around her neck, which stands out against her practical uniform. She scans around the room as the children quiet down under her glare.

"Are all of these children from the ages of ten to sixteen?" Her voice sharply cuts through the air, leaving no room for questions.

"Yes, Lady Swan." One of the guards spoke.

Her eyes narrow as she scans around the room. "Good. Children, my name is Lady Adele Jamila Aisha Swan. I am one of the four council members under the Night Emperor. We are looking for talented children to be a part of the Emperor's studies. Only those who pass the test will move on to a better life."

The children were either too scared or too shocked to show any real emotions.

We've all seen too much death to care. Nick thinks to himself.

"Those of you who do not pass... will be put into servitude, or worse..." She lets that last word linger in the air.

The guards start grabbing the children in groups of four. The four boys huddle closer together, trying to disappear into the walls.

"I'm not joining our family's killers!" Braawen spat.

"But your Uncle Tybalt is still alive out there. We heard nothing about his capture or death. Maybe we could do some damage inside the Emperor's circle?" Lorcan whispers.

"Are you mad?!" Kaius hisses, tired of the situation all together. "How can we, four boys, Nick age fifteen and the rest of us sixteen, do anything?! We're war captives, in case you haven't noticed! So please shut up!"

The three boys are shocked. Lorcan is about to speak, but Kaius puts up his index finger, stopping anyone from speaking. "Before you open your mouth, think about what you're going to say, because all you do is talk shit and glare! Nick and I don't feel like dying!" He huffs, out of breath and glares hotly at Lorcan and Braawen, challenging them to speak.

Nick turns his attention from the staring contest to the woman, now leaving with three groups of four. They need a leader.

We're Archers. Nick can hear his father's stern voice. *Archers lead!*

He thought about Braawen at first, but Nick can see that Braawen would not be the best leader. Braawen was willing to sacrifice people for a warrior's death. The boy couldn't even keep his identity a secret. They were the only Archers.

Maybe this budding courage within him, is from the stress of their capture. The death of his father and the fear consuming all of them make his mind turn. Perhaps Nick has just gone mad. But whatever this madness or bravery was, he had a crazy idea. However, some of his craziest ideas brought terrific results.

"Well, Kaius, you know what they say, 'If you can't beat them…'"

"Join them?!" Kaius looks at him in disbelief.

"Not, quite," he hisses. "Become their new leader!"

Chapter 2
Judgment

The four boys are one of the last groups to be taken. They are brought to a hallway of plain grey stone. In front of them are two black armour guards standing near the only doors in the hall. The guards look more like statues than humans. Each boy walks into the double oak doors separately. His cousin goes in first and then comes out with more men in black armour taking him away. Braawen looks stoic. The same is done to Lorcan, who fights and pulls against them. Kaius whimpers as he's dragged out. Nick burns with dread when it's his turn.

He stands in a room with the woman, Lady Adele Swan, who sits behind a long black and grey table flanked by two other men at her right and left. One of them is an older, robust dignified man wearing a military uniform with a purple collar. His chest puffs proudly, showcasing five army medals on his uniform that shine bright, and multiple ribbons of what must be some sort of distinction. His greying moustache is impressive, but not as impressive as his full head of grey hair. The other man is thinner and wears dark blue robes. He looks to be the youngest of the three of them, with long black hair and bangs that cover one of his eyes. The large window behind them showcases the greying sky, which brings no comfort to his mood. They all look at him, and he sees that Lady Adele doesn't look too pleased with the boy in front of her.

"Ha!" the uniformed man barks. "Lady Adele, just send this skeleton to the mines. I do not think we should even waste our time testing him."

Nick swallows hard, praying that he would not be sent to the mines. He knows he wouldn't last.

"No." Her reply was sharp.

"But why?" the man mopes.

"Because," the other man to Lady Adele's right speaks. "The Emperor ordered for **all** children to be tested, and we will do just that."

"But—"

"General Herald, what the Emperor commands shall be done. We've wasted enough time entertaining your idea." Lady Adele's voice swiftly ends the words of the General.

She turns her attention to the boy in the room. Nick tries not to shake, he really does, but it's so cold.

She looks over him once again and clears her throat. "What is your name, boy?" She asks, though he is surprised to hear her voice is softer.

He blinks slowly. "Nickolaus, my lady and lords," he whispers tentatively.

She nods. "Do you have a last name, by any chance?" A small smirk graces her olive skin.

He doesn't hesitate. "Westmore." He uses his mother's name; best leave his father out of this.

"Well then, Nickolaus Westmore, can you tell us how old you are?"

"I'm fifteen, my lady."

Lady Adele's eyes widen as she looks him up and down in surprise. All three of the adults have looks of disbelief written across their faces.

"You are quite small for someone who claims to be fifteen. Are you sure you're not younger?" The man in the dark blue raises his eyebrows as he looks at Nick.

Nick shakes his head, eyes unfocused as he thinks on the past year. "War can do that to a child," he slowly replies,

He can see the General draw his eyebrows together as he examines him again. The man's old grey eyes seem to pierce Nick with his gaze, evaluating him, but then he just hums and sits up straighter.

Lady Adele sighs. "We need to know your age to know which school to place you in. Can you please step in front of the circle?" She motions to the centre of the room.

There's a large, freshly-hewn stone on the hardwood floor. Nick can't tell what kind of stone it is. *Just another reason I can't be sent to the mines—I couldn't identify stones of importance for the life of me,* Nick thinks. He doesn't want to start learning now.

Within the block he sees five circles, with strange markings etched on the outer circle. They almost remind him of the runes of his mother's people. He doesn't want to step in, but his choices are limited as the guards in the room walk towards him. He steps in slowly, praying to any god who listens to keep him from dying just from standing on it. He takes a deep breath to steady his nerves. The stone glows white as soon as he is standing in the centre circle. He almost jumps back, but one of the guards behind him holds him in place, before leaving him in the circle alone.

"Now, we are going to test your potential. The magic circle will test your talent in magic sensitivity. If you do possess some *seed* of magic, then you can move on. If not, well… we can put a skeleton to work." Lady Adele's smirk became much more predatory.

Nick swallows.

"How this will work is that you will feel either pressure or a tingle. The circle will change colour based on what you feel. If you feel nothing, the circle will remain white. Do you understand?"

Nick nods. "W-when do we start?" His voice shakes.

"Oh, child," the General laughs. "We started as soon as you entered the circle."

His eyes widen as he begins to panic. *That's not good.*

"Unfortunately, we can't give you any direction, other than to feel around the room, feel deep inside you, feel—"

"Jacques, enough of your dramatics! Just let the boy fail or pass," the General barks. The man in the dark blue just glares at the man and turns his attention back to Nick.

Well, at least the one in dark blue gave me a clue. He wants to snap at the old man. *The old man probably wants me to fail,* he thinks bitterly.

However, he couldn't focus on that, as he can see that he's running out of time. Nick closes his eyes and feels around the room for anything, but finds nothing. His mind is going around in circles, and he feels around the room again until he feels something. It's something colder, like a breeze. He focuses on that until he opens his eyes to see white and the faces of three unimpressed people. He wants to roll his eyes. It's just a cold breeze. He closes his eyes again and feels for something, anything!

Then it hits him. Why try to feel for anything, when he should be feeling for any*one*? Lady Adele Swan mentioned that she was a part of the Night Emperor's council. *All his men and women should be able to use magic, right?* Nick thinks hopefully. She must at least have some semblance of magic in her, or at least on her. He envisions her in his mind and sees the gem on her neck. As Lady Adele's about to say time's up, he opens his eyes to see the outer circle turning yellow.

He smiles and even feels something else. However, instead of focusing on the other thing, he praises all the deities. *Thank you, gods!*

"Why does the boy look so happy? It's the weakest level!" The General's voice booms. "Even children at the age of five in our region can get into a higher level. My grandchild of five is in Orange, for deities sakes!"

"But he's not from our region." Jacques states, though he, too, seems unimpressed but Nick doesn't care. He likes this man so far; he seems to be the only one sticking up for him.

"It's still a seed," he mumbles.

"What?" Lady Adele's voice is sharper than ever.

Nick's face goes even paler. *I really need to shut up,* he moans inwardly, asking himself why he said that.

Her voice is colder this time. "Repeat that again."

Leave it to my mouth to get me killed. He gulps. "Pardon, I said: it's still a *seed*."

Silence, then the General suddenly booms with laughter that echoes around the entire room. Even two of the guards are trying hard not to snicker.

A playful smirk graces Jacques' tan face. "He has a point."

The General stops laughing and turns to Lady Adele. "The boy may be a skeleton, but he definitely has some guts. Let him pass. I will train the boy and have him gain some muscle to go with his balls."

Nick's eyes widen at the inappropriate language.

Lady Adele nods as the corner of her lips quirk upwards. "It is indeed a *seed*. A very small one. Take this boy to the Equinox house."

Two of the guards in black armour grab him and when he is off the circle, he sees some of the runes glow. He looks at the three judges, but they do not notice the glow. As they drag him out the room, Nick yells a thank you before they shut the door.

The three judges look at each other.

Jacques smiles. "What a nice boy, he's the only one who said thank you."

"Because he's grateful," the General states in a more sombre tone.

Lady Adele only nods and waves for the guard to bring in the next child.

Chapter 3
Equinox House

Nick is practically carried from the room, through the maze-like hallway and out the doors. He closes his eyes as the sunlight hits him, blinking enough to see that the sun has gone back into the clouds, leaving the snow to fall. The soldiers nudge him towards the simple yet brightly painted wagons, which remind him of the wagons of his childhood in the country.

The soldiers gently place him in the last wagon, a bright yellow one which holds four other children. He sits in a corner and looks around, watching as the other children file into different wagons. After the yellow was orange, then red, then blue and lastly purple. They begin their journey when the purple wagon is full, which holds only two children. As he looks around his wagon, he can see the two boys and two girls, are all sitting apart from each other. One of the boys is sickly pale and has not ceased coughing since the trip began, but once he looks up, he has the brightest green eyes that Nick has ever seen. The other boy across from him is quiet and shaking, yet Nick wonders if he starved at all on the ship. The boy must have been fat, for he was still round, yet there were bouts of his stomach rumbling. Each rumble makes the chubby boy blush harder; the blush almost matches his small, brownish red curls.

Ignoring both the boy's stomach and his own, Nick turns his attention to the girls in the cart. One of them keeps her head down and her dirty blonde hair blocks her face. She crosses her arms, which are littered with scratches, over her legs. The other girl's head is up, her eyes darting around. There were times when she will look him in the eye before quickly looking elsewhere. Her short, dark blue hair looks darker against her pale skin. Her hair was tangled in knots. Her small eyes have bags under them, and her chapped lips continue to mumble *Torosan* while biting her nails.

Everyone looks like they're at their breaking point, and Nick may just jump off the wagon if he hears that boy cough one more time. He takes deep breaths, as he has no idea what's in store for him. The only thing he can remember is them mentioning a school. He would prefer a school over the mines.

I always wanted to go to school, he tells himself.

Nick breathes out and watches his breath in the breeze. He pulls his legs up closer to his body to stave off the cold. He knows he'll be warmer if he snuggles with one of the other children. Unfortunately, he doesn't trust any of them, and he fears that if he makes a move, someone will attack him. Even the round one.

He looks to the road and sees that they have exited the city and are entering a forest. The trees are tall, but the road is still paved. After a quiet moment, he looks at the wagons ahead. There are more kids in the red wagon; he counts nine, and smiles as he sees a familiar face amongst them. It is Lorcan, sitting on the edge of the wagon but still huddling in to get some warmth. He wonders if Lorcan is looking for anyone he knows. That thought ends when their eyes lock onto each other. Lorcan gives a grin, it's the most welcome Nick's ever received from the teenager. Lorcan points to the orange wagon next to Nick's, and tips his head towards the purple wagon in front of them.

In the wagon in front of him, Nick sees Kaius, whose head is on his knees. *Poor boy must be crying,* he thinks. There were twelve other children in there with him.

Ahead of the empty blue wagon is the purple one. Nick was a little jealous. The two children there have blankets to keep them warm, while the rest freeze from the cold. His bitterness dries away as there is one hope that he sees. There, in the purple wagon, looking to the side, is his cousin Braawen.

On a snow-covered hill, he can make out the black silhouette of a building surrounded by what looks like trees. As they get closer to the building, the forest begins shining a dull blue. Nick's eyes widen as he realizes that the lamps aren't gas light, but are instead, powered by electro rocks. Nick's only heard about electro rocks from Kaius. However, seeing them amazes Nick.

He always imagined what going to school would be like. He'd seen what some of the academies have looked like from the outside, but never went in. This building that he sees, passing the black gates in front of him should not be called a house. The vast estate had five floors and a clock tower. It appeared that more of the building went around behind it. The building's black corner stones seem to absorb the light and the central tower features a huge arch window beneath the clock face.

As they enter the courtyard, all the wagons take turns unloading the children. Nick's cart comes last as two soldiers open the side doors. The sickly, pale boy is the last to exit and makes a loud thud against the ground, not moving. Nick rushes over to the fallen boy, passing the chubby boy, who just looks away. Nick gets down on his knees and turns the fallen boy over. He brushes the hair out of the boy's face to reveal two dull green eyes. Nick sits there for a second, not even feeling sick being next to a dead body. The guards pull him up and one of them pushes him towards the building, while the other drags the dead boy away.

As Nick turns his head towards the building, he faintly overhears the guards.

"This boy was better off dead anyway," one of them states, as their footsteps and the dragging sounds of the body move farther away. Nick wonders if they'll give the boy a proper burial, then quickly shakes his head free of that thought. It's nonsense to think that. They didn't even give them blankets to keep warm.

Only the strong can survive. His father's voice enters his mind. He pushes it back as he looks at the double dark solid wood doors with carvings of dragons eating the sun and moon.

He gulps. *I should have prayed harder on which school the gods were to send me to.*

He enters the building and holds in a gasp. The building is grand on the outside and the inside is no different. In fact, the interior is full of rich and intricate designs that have his eyes wandering all over the front foyer. The walls are a light grey with different black patterns on each walls, some with moons and others with suns. The grand staircase that branches off to different levels of the school grabs his attention with its polished dark oak railings and an emerald green carpet on the steps.

The foyer easily holds all of them. He watches as the children are separated into different wings. Nick sees five doors on each level, yet the sixth level has no door, just a wall. He watches from the ground floor as his cousin and a girl head towards the upper floor, the fifth. A tall man gripping a cane and wearing black and purple greets them with a large smile.

Lorcan gets shuffled into the mid-levels towards a short old woman, her skin as dark and rich as the fertile earth of his homeland, and her silver hair in a tight bun. She wears an outfit similar to the tall man's, but in red and black, and a smile graces her face as well.

Kaius glances worriedly at Nick as he and the other children are brought through the doors of the main level. The instructor is a young woman in her mid-thirties with wild red hair. She wears orange and black, grinning eagerly.

All that was left was himself and the other three surviving children, who are shivering. They look at each other, their expressions mirroring their fear, worry, and pain. They hear the sound of heavy boots banging on the wood floors of the building and a shadow looms over them. Nick turns around and sees General Herald. The old man changed his outfit into a yellow and black uniform, similar to the others, but still wears his five medals.

"Hello, children." He gives a feral grin. "Come! I will show you to your rooms. Then we train early in the morning. No buts!" he yells, and heads to the main door they came from outside.

The children look at each other and follow the man outside, coming off the path of the building and into the snow. They walk until they see a set of metal cellar doors. The doors make a creaking sound as the General throws them open.

"That sound will get fixed tonight," he booms happily.

They descend into the basement and Nick thinks that the door is the last thing that should be fixed as the lights are turned on. The lights are white this time, but dim. They enter into a dark and cold section of the school that goes deeper underground. There are cobwebs and cracked walls that differ from the splendour he saw upstairs. Around them is the smell of mold and dust. He hears a girl shriek at the sight of the spider, and turns to see that it's the girl with the dark hair.

"Get used to them, girly," the General chuckles as he leads them towards two yellow double doors that have seen better days. The faded doors open to a larger room. The General walks in and the children follow behind just enough for the doors to slam quickly behind them, causing everyone to jump.

The man clears his throat. "Don't worry, the door does that. It keeps the warm air in."

As Nick's heartbeat slowly returns to normal, he stands still and can feel that the room is, in fact, warmer. He turns to see five beds, which have seen better days. They are dirty and springs are poking out of them, but to the children, it was a bed. A bed instead of the floor; Nick would weep with joy if not for the situation that he is in. There are also pillows to lay his head on and not just clothes rolled into a ball. Each bed has a small table and dresser on one side, with a desk and a chair on the other. The warmth comes from a little fireplace already lit, and on the side of the room is a larger table and chairs, with bread and fruits.

"Your night and day clothes are in your dressers, while your school uniform will be handed out later. Your desk will also have school supplies, and grooming tools such as hair pins and combs." The General then points to the door. "There are three showers that you all have to share down the hall. Remember to turn off the lights at night. You'll only be eating in here tonight. Tomorrow you will be eating in the feasting room, where you will meet the other students. I know you all are hungry and cold, so I will explain more tomorrow. I also recommend that the lot of you drink these." He takes ten vials from his pockets. Nick doesn't know how he managed to fit all of them in. Each of them takes two vials: one red, the other blue.

"The red one will help heal whatever wounds you have sustained on your travels. It's not that strong, but it will help with the bruises and the cuts." He demonstrates by taking a knife from his shadow which causes everyone to gasp. Nick takes a step back from seeing such dark magic as the General cuts his arm. The man takes the extra red vial and chugs it down. He shakes his head and makes a bitter face. "Nasty stuff, but it works." He shows the children his arms and they are amazed to see that there are no cuts.

"The blue one helps you sleep. I want you all to take it. I will know if you don't, and I will be cross." He glares at the children as they all nod. "Good!" he yells. "I expect you all up by morning at dawn. Eat and sleep, I will put you all into shape." Without further explanation, the man stomps off. He opens the yellow doors and walks out, slamming the doors shut behind him.

At the slamming of the doors, the children run to the bread and fruits, making themselves a plate of food before settling next to the fire. Nick brings the blankets down from each bed and hands them out before getting his own plate of bread and fruits. He grabs his blanket and takes a seat next to the chubby boy. It's hard to break old habits, he was always the last to eat during the rebellion.

"So," the chubby boy breaks the silence. He has a similar accent to the people near the capital city of Availa. "How did you guys all get here?"

"Failed rebellion in the South, you dolt! *Boko*!" The girl with dark blue hair snaps, mumbling the last word. "Sorry," she quickly apologizes. "Just …just trying to take all this in." She quickly pulls on her hair a little. "One minute you're farming, and the next, you're in chains. All because my brother was dumb enough to join the rebellion." She scoffs. "Now my whole family has to suffer the consequences of his actions." Then she goes back to biting her nails.

"Damn. Well, I was a part of it, but not by choice. I just didn't like the old King that we had. My father was the baker for the King." The boy rips off a chunk of bread with his teeth, and his frown shows he deems it crappy. "One day, one of his apprentices gave the wrong thing to the King, and my father as the chef baker took responsibility. So, the King took his head."

Everyone in the room stops eating and looks at him; even the blonde girl raises her head a little.

"So, yeah," the boy continues. "I'm kinda in a weird position, where I'm happy that the Empire overthrew and killed the King and his family, but not so happy that all of us are forced into this. Like, why couldn't we have a truce and the rebels take over the country?"

Because no one wanted to lead. Nick holds his tongue at the unspoken words. His tongue has gotten him into enough messes today.

The boy continues, not seeing the bitterness in Nick's face. "I'm sure that Markus could have been a better leader than the King. The King killed all the good leaders, like Lord Jameson and General Hiver. I mean, Markus did a good job leading the rebels."

Nick stiffens at that comment the other boy makes as he eats his apple.

The blue-haired girl raises one eyebrow. "Was that before or after he lost the war?" The chubby one just shrugs and continues to eat. The girl turns her attention to the other girl, who goes back to looking down at her food.

"What about you, blondie?" The blue-haired one asks.

The blonde girl looks startled at first, then sighs and tosses her hair up, showing her face. Nick uses all his self-control to not wince like the other boy and stare like the blue-haired girl. There is a long and hard scar cutting across her face from her bottom of her left eye, across the corner of her right lip, and down to the edge of her face on her right side. It looks like someone full of hate and anger carved it.

What enemy did she face? And how did she survive?

The girl licks her lips. "Got caught by the Night Emperor's guards as me and my family were trying to escape. Didn't make it, now I'm here." She lowers her head again, playing with the grapes in her bowl.

They sit in silence. Realizing that the girl wouldn't say anything else, they turn to Nick.

"Okay, skinny one, your turn," the boy says.

Nick clicks his tongue. "I was a part of the women and children hiding when the final battle started. We tried to run when we heard that the battle was lost, but then there was an explosion. My friend and cousin are here. So that's not so bad."

It's horrible, he wants to say. His uncle was killed brutally, his other uncles are probably being hunted down, and he was far away from his homeland. Right, and his father is dead as well.

"Wait, your cousin and friends are here? Which rank did they get?" the chubby one asks.

Nick looks confused.

"He means colour," the blue-haired girl explains.

"My best friend is in Orange."

"The one above us," the boy munching on an apple says.

"My other acquaintance is in Red." The others nod. "And my cousin is in Purple."

The blonde girl stops playing with her grapes. He looks around to see that the other boy's mouth is wide open.

"What?" he asks.

"Skinny, Purple is the second-highest rank a person can be in. They could become generals when they complete their training. Damn, it sucks that you're in the lowest level." The other boy shakes his head.

Of course, he's in one of the highest levels. Nick wants to speak to whoever oversees his fate and demand to know why Braawen is always better than him. "No one will know that we're cousins. We don't look alike."

"Lucky," he hears the blonde girl mumble.

"Well, I am tired," the blue-haired girl announces. "By the way, my name is Takara."

Chubby says his name is Bhaltair, and the blonde one states her name is Rohana.

"Nickolaus."

Chapter 4
Stranger

Nick imagines it is late when they all go to bed; there is only one small window near the ceiling to let the slow setting sun stream in. The group of children take their time in the showers, washing the day's filth and stress away. Each of them enjoy the surprisingly hot water, and for the first time in a long while, Nick can feel his body relax. Even though they are in a foreign land, they each take turns leaving the showers to protect each other's privacy. Rohana takes the longest.

When Rohana comes out drying her hair with a towel, each of them look at their vials with suspicion, too afraid to drink them. After a few minutes of silent debating, Takara shrugs and drinks the red vial.

"Eugg!" She sticks out her tongue with a grimace. As if by magic, the scrapes on her hands and her fingernails began to fade away, leaving a healthy glow. Even her hair shines a little from the firelight. "I'm still alive and well. I feel great, actually."

They all swiftly follow her example and take a drink. Almost instantly, they begin to feel better, physically at least. Nick looks at his wrist and sees that the scar is still there. He feels under the nightshirt he's wearing, disappointed that the scars on his back are still there. *At least the bruises and scratches from the ship are gone,* he tells himself.

All of them hesitate to take the blue vial until they remember what the General said.

Nick sighs. "What's the worst it could do? Kill us?"

They all share similar looks of unease before picking up their own vials. As if a quiet countdown occurs, they swiftly swallow down each blue vial in unison. The silence that follows is heavy, and the feeling that hits them even more so. They feel the effects happening quickly as they take to their beds. Nick can feel the springs already piercing his back as his body collapses onto the bed. He slowly closes his eyes and wonders if the floor would be a better option, however, he remembers that he has to be grateful. He has food, a warm room, and a bed. His night clothes aren't itchy, and he even has slippers.

Oh deities, I sound like a pet.

Before his eyes close, he looks to his right—Bhaltair is already out. Before he could ask if anyone else is awake, his world goes dark.

Nick's eyes snap open as he's jarred into an immediate state of awareness. There's yelling and screaming all around him. He can smell burning wood.

I have to leave, he tells himself. Nick quickly crawls off his bed. He can see the smoke coming from his door and feels the heat rising all around. He climbs on his bed and opens his window. As soon as the window opens, he can feel the bitter cold winds and snowflakes enter his room. The chilling relief does not last; the heat begins to suffocate him anew. He looks around and sees his bag, grabbing it from the foot of his bed. He looks back at his blanket. He wishes that he could take the blanket that his mother made for him. But he isn't a baby, he's a big boy. He just turned eleven. He didn't need it.

He climbs out the window and runs out of the house. He turns to see that his home is on fire. His house isn't the only one; the fire has spread to many houses that are hopelessly ablaze. Yet, no one worries about the houses as soldiers begin attacking people. From where Nick stands, he sees that the men and women destroying his home are wearing the royal crest of Availa. His own King was attacking his people.

Nick runs as one of them spots him, looking for his parents. He turns the corner to see his father is fighting and winning, while his mother has just stabbed her spear in someone's chest. Nick sees someone about to strike his father from behind and reacts quickly. He picks up one of the rocks from his house and throws it with all his might. The rock hits the man's skull and he collapses. Nick's father turns to stab the man with his sword and nods at his son.

Then two archers face them, one pointing at Markus and the other pointing at him. Before Nick can move, they release their arrows. A shadow leaps in front of him, pushing both of them to the ground. Nick can hear the screams of his father. He turns his head to see that his father has an arrow in his leg, but more men arrive and slaughter the archers before they can fire again.

Nick can't move his legs and when he looks down, all he sees is long dark hair.

"Mommy?" he asks. He tries to shake her off, but cries when he feels a blinding pain in his wrist. He sees a lot of blood coming from his wound and his eyes start to blur. The last thing he remembers is his Uncle Malcolm crying over his mother when he picks her up. There's an arrow sticking out from her chest, her eyes closed. He would cry if he didn't feel so lightheaded. Warm hands wrap around his wrist.

"Stay with me, Nick!" He hears Uncle Tys calling out to him. "Stay awake!" His uncle turns away, but his warm hand stays firmly in place. "We need a medicine man! Please, some…" Nick's vision fades.

· ☾ ·

Nick sits up gasping for air. His eyes wander around, quickly assessing where he currently is. The room is dark and sharp compared to the cold and fluffy snow from his dream. The raging fire is replaced by the small glowing embers of the hearth. He rubs his hand on his face and slowly breathes out a huff. He remains still, recounting the day in his mind.

Just a dream, he tells himself, trying to steady his breathing. He looks to the small window below the ceiling and sees that it's dark outside. *Just a memory.* He coughs a little and walks over to the large table, pouring himself a drink of water. Everyone around him is still asleep. He envies them.

He can't and won't sleep again, however, he's tired... no, exhausted. Bhaltair releases a deafening snore, his robust belly rising and falling. Nick looks to his left and right; no one else seems to mind. At first, he thinks that Takara is awake, but at a second glance, Nick concludes that she must move in her sleep a lot. In the short amount of time he watches her, she moves a total of three times, each flinch more violent than the last; she almost looks like she's being hit. Rohana's once blanket-covered head is revealed in the dim firelight; her eyes are firmly closed, and her cheeks are wet with tears.

Not comfortable with watching people sleep, Nick's tired eyes sees the boots next to the door and grabs a pair. They're a little big, but he'll make them work. He wraps his blanket around himself tightly, walking as quietly as he can towards the doors. He slowly opens one of the doors, then slowly closes it behind him, leaving the three to slumber.

There are no creaking sounds as the metal doors that lead to the outside world open. At least the school seems to be efficient in that. He feels the icy fresh breath from the god of Air greeting him as a long-lost son. Taking a step out and gently closing the door, he turns his attention to the sky, seeing a clear blue night. Everything seems peaceful, like his whole world hasn't been destroyed. As though his life is insignificant to the cosmos.

As he walks, all he can hear is the crunching of his feet in the snow and the wind blowing in the trees. There are a few guards on duty, but Nick is used to sneaking into places. Being the smallest one in the group, he was 'volunteered' on many stealth missions. He did his duty during the rebellion by sneaking past guards and scouting for useful information. His inability to stand out in a crowd proved beneficial during this time. He preferred scouting over fighting on the front lines, where he would surely have died. His cousin said that it was the coward's way, not that Nick really cares what that boy thinks. Slipping past these guards is child's play.

He realizes that the building is much larger than he originally thought as he walks along the snow-covered path. After a few paces with nothing but the sound of his shoes in snow, Nick spots an opening at the edge of the building, a small silver gate with a shovelled path. On the gate's surface is an insignia made up of a silver crescent moon and stars. It's smaller and looks older compared to the large gate at the entrance. It's almost like a hidden gateway. There's a sudden pull of curiosity towards the gate, one Nick can't resist, and against his better judgment, he reaches out and pulls. Nothing. He sighs and pushes instead; the gate gives way without the slightest screech, the hinges so well-oiled that not a sound follows.

It's always good to know your way around a building, his uncle Tybalt's voice whispers in his ear. *Especially in enemy bases. Know the way in and out, know more than one entrance and exit. Trust me, there will always be one.*

Nick walks past the gates and looks to see that none of the guards have done anything to stop him. They didn't even notice him.

As he walks along the path, it opens onto what he believes may be the back of the school. The stone walls are covered with large ornate windows, balconies and greenhouses full of plants he can't identify. He continues to walk along the path, passing by snow covered hills and green bushes layered with snow. He stops at a rather large frozen lake, the ice giving off an unearthly feel. A closer inspection at the edge of the lake reveals nothing but a dark forest to the side where the path continues.

The area that he's exploring seems peaceful and brighter than the black silhouette of the school behind him. Everything is still. For a moment, there is nothing but silence, then he lets out a great scream, ripped from the deepest part of his core, one he was holding in. He doesn't care who might hear. It's a short scream, shorter than he thought it would be. For so long, the feeling had coalesced in his chest and that scream felt like a release, an end to his growing madness. Silence falls once again.

Nick looks out to the lake, then up to the moon. It looks peaceful... How unfair. For a moment, he thinks the only way to stop the torment of tears from falling is to squeeze his eyes shut. Then they snap open. No one is here, no one came running for him after he screamed. No one will judge him; his father certainly can't. He begins to sob, which grows into a cry, then to wailing. Tears stream down his gaunt face and snot rolls down his chin.

He mourns the lost lives of all the people he knew and didn't know. He cries for those who lost their lives in battle. He cries for the kind commanders and his father's advisors. For the first time, he cries for his mother. If there were anyone around to hear, they'd note this cry as crucially different from its predecessors. Longer, quieter... and yet, filled with so much pain.

He even cries for the death of his father. At least the man was his blood.

As his tears begin to slow and his mind begins to clear, a feeling of lightness penetrates deeper than he imagines. He freely takes a deep breath in, wishing that he was able to do so many years ago. He breathes out and it feels like chains are falling from his mind, like a fog clearing as he slowly breathes in and out. Then another feeling appears. He doesn't know what it is exactly, but he feels something, like a tingle in the air. It's on his neck, it's so pronounced that he has an urge to reach for his neck trying to get the tingling off. The feeling is behind him, like soft hands pulling him, guiding him. Afraid to turn again, he tries to ignore it, but the more he does, the more he can feel it. He begins to hear a small voice whisper:

Turn.

He hears them. For the first time it isn't the voices that he knows. It's not his father, his mother, nor his uncles. These voices, so strange yet so familiar. Voices blending together, like a crowd of people trying to get his attention. He almost thinks he's finally gone mad, but the feeling is not imaginary.

With one last deep breath in and out, he turns around slowly, tightly gripping the blanket he took from his bed. The forest is what he sees first, but as he looks further past the shadows, he sees something else. He tries to make it out; it seems like a small figure. Curiosity gets the better of him, but as he walks closer, he can feel the tingling sensation and the pressure increase.

As he takes his first steps off the path, the pressure builds to a point where his ears begin to ring. The sound of the snow under his feet is muted. He feels like he's fighting something, fighting a wall that he's trying to break through. The pressure now trails a path down his back, lighting a fire in each of his scars, before spreading to his knees. He takes smaller steps and harsher breaths.

Why is it so hard to breathe? he thinks, as he continues to move forward. The shadows around the trees get darker, but just as he feels that his legs are about to collapse, something gives. He takes that one last struggling step and stops as though he broke through a wall. He takes deep breaths and the pressure on his leg retreats back up to his neck now, relief flowing through him as the pressure subsides.

He closes his eyes and opens them to see a man. He has to blink again, because he can't believe what he's seeing. There wasn't a man there moments ago. Yet, sitting in the snow, with a black cape covering him from his neck down to his feet, is a man. All that is showing is his head and hands. His hands have black gloves with dark yellow stitching in patterns that Nick doesn't recognize. The stranger's handsome face is pale, and both his eyes and hair are so dark that they're almost black. The stranger looks like he could be in his late twenties or early thirties, give or take. He also looks quite comfortable in the snow.

"Well." The stranger's deep voice vibrates through Nick's very being. The pressure is building again. The shadows of the trees grow against the light of the moon.

Nick blinks, too stunned to speak.

"Come closer, boy." The stranger makes a waving motion with his hand and almost as though he's in a trance, Nick gingerly walks closer. When Nick is but a few paces away, the cloaked man looks directly at him.

Nick swallows and gathers what little courage he has remaining. "Good evening, sir," he croaks out, voice raw from his earlier emotional release, followed by a shiver that he isn't sure is from the cold.

The stranger nods his head. "Good night to you as well. Such a polite lad, but can you tell me why you were screaming your lungs out? It shocked me, and I am a man that doesn't surprise easily." His voice is soft yet commanding, though there is nothing but a small smile on his face.

Numbness. That is a new feeling for Nick. There is nothing but numbness and tingling in his hands, and the muscles in his legs begin to weaken. Something in him tells him that this man is dangerous, and he must be wise with his words.

"Only if you tell me why no guards are coming out after hearing a child scream?"

There's a moment of silence in which Nick questions all his life's decisions. Maybe it's the circulation to his head being cut off from the numbness, but he doesn't understand why he still has no self-preservation after living through a war!

The stranger chuckles, causing Nick to relax a little. The man doesn't seem offended, though Nick knows many people would be annoyed. Before Nick can ask if he offended him, the stranger stands up, causing Nick to take three steps back. The man is tall, and Nick finds himself craning his neck up to keep the figure in his view. At first, he thinks the man might attack him, yet all the stranger does is gracefully walk past, him towards the lake. Nick cautiously follows him to the edge, trying to leave a safe distance between the two. Even though something tells him the safest distance between him and the man is out of the Empire.

The stranger turns and gives a wider smile. He has white, straight teeth, and the wind gracefully ruffles his dark bangs from his eyes. "The guards are used to hearing screams, cries and shouts. The only time a guard will come is if someone yells 'guard' or *teems*. The suffering of children to reach their gifts is a regular occurrence here." The stranger says, pointing to the school. He says it so nonchalantly, as though such a thing is normal.

Nick looks back at the school in horror, then back at the man.

"Oh, come now," the man drawls, glancing at him, almost hiding a smile. "Don't look like that. Some of the students do it to themselves or to other students. If you don't believe me, you'll see it soon." There's a pause, as though Nick should think on what's been said, perhaps a warning. "Now, answer my question on why you screamed." His voice sounds deeper, almost a growl.

Nick shuffles a little. "I yelled to get my sorrow out. I wasn't allowed to mourn the death of my family and friends. For my mother." He sighs, not knowing why he's opening up to a complete stranger. "I wasn't allowed to cry for my mother, I had to be a man. But whenever I asked questions about a mission, I was a boy again who shouldn't question his orders. I was a boy when it suited them, but a man on dangerous missions. But... I'm just a child that watched his whole world burn and I couldn't cry about it then. So, I screamed."

"And sobbed," the stranger remarks, adding salt to Nick's already wounded ego. So far, this is getting to be one of the most embarrassing nights of his life. First, from the nightmare of the ever-haunting death of his mother, that he thought he had buried deep in his mind. Now he has a stranger taunting him.

Nick swallowed hard. "Yeah..." he whispers.

The two are quiet as they look at the moon.

"It's okay to cry," the stranger assures Nick, surprising him. "I do it sometimes, it... helps."

Nick looks at the man. His black hair is cut but his eyes, dark eyes turning red as he looks out into the distance. Nick is amazed at the changing eye colour and wants to ask, but the stranger speaks first.

"How did you get in here?" The man asks, with a questioning look.

Nick shrugs. "I came in through the gate. It was open."

The stranger lifts one eyebrow. "I mean how did you get past the guards?"

He shrugs again. "I'm a forgettable person."

"Hah!" The stranger barks out a laugh. "Really? I find that unbelievable. Well, it's been a long time since I have laughed like that, but it is best that you don't stay too long here. I, too, shall make my way back.

Though, if you really want to impress me—and you will want to—come back tomorrow around this time. I'll be here." With that the man turns away.

"W-wait!" Nick stammers getting the stranger's attention. "Why aren't the gates locked? Aren't they afraid that someone will try to run away?"

The man turns again and smiles. "Where would you go? You all can run, but you won't be able to hide. The world out there is cruel, especially during winter. The cold winter winds will kill you quickly in these lands. No one will offer you shelter, and no one is kind to beggars, not even the slums. But here," he gestures to the school. "This place will give you food, shelter and an education. If you want to leave, it will be one less mouth to feed. That is why the gates remain open. This can be a haven to some, but out there will be hell." Nick hears a soft chuckle. "The gates are open—it's your choice."

Without another word, the man turns for the final time, cape fluttering in the winds; as the boy watches the stranger leave through the silver gates in the distance.

What a strange man, he thinks as the man is gone. Now it's just him and the moon. The pressure is completely gone, and Nick drops his body into the snow. He looks at the lake and before he can stop himself, he is once again sobbing at the memory of his fallen people.

When Nick starts to lose feeling in his feet, he stands and begins to give the last rites to his people. It's not perfect; he doesn't have the instruments, the candles or the bells. However, the boy has a voice and by the deities, he uses it. Once complete, he heads back feeling a little lighter.

He passes through the gates but then stops dead in his tracks. There's a lump on the ground, surrounded by dark red that colours the beautiful snow. He cautiously moves closer and realizes that it's not what, but whom. The guards he snuck past lay on the snow, blood pooling out from their bodies. Nick's eyes widen and he swiftly checks the bodies to see that they are indeed dead. He doesn't stick around long, turning instead towards the shovelled path to make his way back into the basement.

He closes the doors gently and sees that the rest of the children are still asleep. He jumps into his bed breathing heavily and praying to whomever is listening, gods or not, that he will not be held responsible. But then he stops that thought. He's a skeleton in the lowest class, he couldn't kill those guards. He pulls the covers over his head and shivers.

Just sleep, he tells himself over and over. *Wait, could it have been that man?* Maybe he shouldn't meet him again, but what if he doesn't, and he comes looking for him?

"Oh, no," he whispers, but then realization dawns on him.

He didn't mention anything about my size.

Chapter 5
Student

"Another lap!" Herald yells at the running children. During the run, Nick tries his best to encourage the others. He receives a few glares from Rohana, but he pulls her up when she trips on a snow-covered root. The slap he receives informs him that he should not touch her unless expressly told otherwise. Takara, on the other hand, gladly takes his hand whenever she trips. He also has to encourage Bhaltair when the other boy feels dizzy. Nick himself is tired; his weakened muscles have him stopping more than once. There are even times when he's lagging behind Bhaltair. Poor Bhaltair picks him up once his body collapsed from the cold, but even throughout the pain, he pressed on.

I may be the slowest, and the last, but I'm not stopping, Nick vows. He knows that stopping could mean death.

As they run around the school, he can't help but look around and notice how different it looks during the day. As the sun shines on the school, it reveals the care and detail in every stone placed. Unlike the midnight moon, the sun turns the monstrous carvings into works of art. The windows shine with no cracks, unlike Nick's previous home. He looks up the higher levels of the school, towards the balconies and windows, and wonders if the other students feel like royalty looking down on them. The craftsmen must have spent most of their time on the top levels of the school. He can't wait to see them up close. In fact, as he runs, he catalogues all sorts of ways that he could climb the walls and pipes.

As they wheeze along the way, he thanks the deities that they are almost done. He knows from running towards the black clock tower that they are approaching the centre of the school. He looks up at the tall tower, which would have an amazing view. He wonders how to climb it when the black stones appear so smooth.

He sighs as they pass the tower and run towards the silver gates of last night. He guesses that old habits are hard to break.

As they finish their final lap, Nick wonders if he should have been the one that died on the wagon instead of that other boy. His lungs burn and his legs can no longer support even his tiny frame. The muscles that hold his bones can no longer deal with the run, but Takara pulls him along.

He and the others were awakened early in the morning by General Herald yelling at them to get dressed. Nick's mind immediately went into battle mode as he rushed to get dressed. He was the first one finished, and he could see the others struggling to complete their task on time.

"Why are you just standing there?" The General turns his attention to Nick. "Spread your bed!"

Without a word, Nick quickly spreads his bed, beads of sweat falling on his blanket, as tears fall on Bhaltair's.

The yelling continued even as they ate in the feasting room, causing both Bhaltair and Rohana to choke from chewing faster. They could all hear the snickering and laughter from the other tables. Nick's stomach was in knots, and he could barely drink the water in front of him. Takara looked like she was about to throw up her slice of bread. Luckily, the man seemed to takes breaks between yelling while they ran.

As soon as they finished, the man found his voice again and began screaming at them to get off the damn ground and drag themselves into the school.

Rohana is gasping for air as she collapses on the entrance steps. Bhaltair doesn't even make it to the door. He's still on the path to the main steps. Takara kneels on the cold steps, gripping Nick's hip as he leans on the door frame for support. He can feel the pressure on his neck again, but before he can think on it more, he's pushed off the door and to the ground by the General. Takara comes down with him as the General makes his way past them.

The man turns around and gives them a disappointed look, shaking his head. "Come children, this is just the beginning." He's grinning ear to ear as he leaves towards one of the hallways.

One after the other, the children struggle to make their way down the hallway. As they walk, there are other students watching and laughing at the Yellows.

"Waste of space, if you ask me," an arrogant female voice reaches his ears. He turns to see a older blond girl wearing a uniform with a short, clasped cape in red.

The boy beside the girl with blonde hair and a similar red uniform looks down his nose at them. "Rejects like them should just go to the slums."

Nick turns to see that Rohana is glaring at them. One of the girls shrieks as she sees the scar on Rohana's face.

"So barbaric," the girl whispers.

Another girl wearing orange laughs. "Maybe that's why their country got conquered." Her mouth spills more condescending remarks as they pass her.

Bhaltair's throat bobs as he swallows the cries that threaten to escape, putting his head down to hide his quivering lips. Takara's eyes frantically begin to look around as the students point and sneer at them. Her hands begin to shake, and she feels pins and needles on her arms again. Without thinking, she grabs the closest person's hands. Unfortunately, it's Rohana's but she shakes it off, not wanting to be touched. Not wanting to be here. Nick just focuses on moving forward. These remarks aren't original. He's heard worse, and he looks past the judgmental glares, ignoring the demeaning words that pass through his ears. He looks to the open door ahead, has the one person whose words matter to him. The General flashes them another grin under his moustache as they approach him. The man then walks into the room.

"At least wait for us," Nick mumbles.

The first thing that Nick notices are the old desks and dark wood floor. Every one of their steps makes a slight squeak compared to the stone floors of the hallway. Nick looks down and believes the floor could be maple from the very little grain, though it looks like they stained it dark. Pity, he liked maple for its light colour.

Each child plummets to their wooden seats. The wooden desks and seats are a far cry from the splendour of the rest of the school. Nick's desk has names carved into the surface and dark green paint, chipped away to being almost non-existent. At least the windows are rather larger, five of them providing what little natural light there was on such a dismal day.

General Herald watches them, listening to the heavy breaths of each student mingle with the mocking voices of the students outside. He decides to give them a small mercy and shuts the door. He gives one last look at the tired students before he grabs the chalk and starts drawing circles on the black board.

Bhaltair squints at the drawings. "Are you teaching us magic?" Bhaltair asks innocently.

The General stops and throws the chalk at Bhaltair, hitting him square in the face. "When you dodge or catch the chalk, I'll teach you magic! Right now, the lot of you are useless to the Emperor. A five-year-old child could beat you in a Shadow duel. Heck, my little Greta can wipe the floor with you!"

Bhaltair seems to deflate even more in his seat.

Their teacher stands tall and looks over the four red-faced children. "You four have until Spring to show that your *seed* of sensitivity to magic can actually grow to something useful. By the end of the three months, you should be able to move into the Orange circle." He points to the chalkboard.

"Right now, you are in the weakest and lowest level of magic. If you can't go up another level, you leave. Those are the rules. Most Yellows don't even make it into this school. If a person can't rise out of Yellow during their years in Solaria House, then they would need a very special reason to come here. Lucky for you lots, *you* all are a special reason."

The General looks at the children, who squirm in their seats. "Equinox House," he continues, "is a school to help develop your skills and magical abilities. Children are sent here to study from age fourteen until age eighteen when they can be used to further the Empire. So far, only a very small percent of people can use magic. By magic, I mean the only one that exists—Shadow magic."

"There are no other forms?" Takara asks.

General Herald smiles. "Nope. We've tried and looked into light, water, earth, air, and fire magic. We've evev looked for magic that goes past the elements. We hoped they were real, but it is not the case! As of now, Shadow magic is the only one you should give a damn about! It is the only magic to exist." His face remains confident in that statement. "Let me explain to you the basics." He rubs his hands together eagerly.

"Shadow magic is a powerful force that allows wielders to command the shadows. And you lots, are Shadow wielders," he motions around the room. "Shadow wielders are highly regarded in the Empire, no matter the circumstance of your birth. Even you sorry lot will get food and shelter here. After you graduate, if you do well here, you will be able to go anywhere in the Empire."

Nick couldn't believe it. The rest of the rebellion children in the higher circles seemed to be treated better than the four in this class. From what he remembers from this morning, he's table had food, but the other tables looked better. He didn't understand why. Aren't they all shadow wielders? Nick knows his goal to become their new leader is getting further and further from him each day. However, if he could become their leader, he would have them re-examine how Yellows were treated. In fact, he would try to help all people. It wasn't fair that certain people were treated better. It reminded him too much of the society back in Availa. The second-class citizens. He shivers, trying not to think too much about it.

He abandons his thoughts on becoming their new leader, and returns to the General's explanation on Shadow magic.

"Shadow magic allows a person to use the darkness around them against their enemies. You can use an object's shadow as puppets and attack them. The shadow can also be used to travel great distances." He looks at the shadow of the desk and with a sharp wave of his hand, the shadow obeys and turns into sharp claws that puncture the walls. Bhaltair and Rohana, the two closest to the walls, almost jump from their seats. The General just grins as he moves his hands quickly against the wall and the shadow returns to its original form as a desk. The only evidence left are the small holes in the walls. The demonstration leaves the class in a mixture of awe and fear.

"A stronger attack is called Shadow Slash. I can't use that attack inside the school. It's that deadly. If I did use the spell, it would have destroyed the wall... and part of the school," the General adds sheepishly. "It's an attack that many shadow wielders use, especially in the Purple circle. You will come across that attack in duels. So, heed my advice, just dodge the attack. Nothing can block or break a slash, understood?" His voice thunders around the room, all heads nod. "Good, because the stronger the wielder, the stronger the attack. I've seen people cut in half and buildings destroyed. However, it's a quick and silent killer. A good attack for wielders that go on silent missions."

"Like the Shadow Assassins?" Rohana asks, and Nick can surprisingly detect a hint of reverence.

"Ah, you know about them! Good! I'll let them know you're interested!" The General grins as Rohana shakes her head quickly. He chuckles at her response. "Don't worry, scar-faced one, they protect their own, and would treat you as family. Very good people, even better at gaining information and killing." He ends still smiling.

"Sh-shadow assassins?" Bhaltair mumbles.

General Herald waves his hands dismissively. "We'll go through the different sects you can join next month. Right now, we focus on today!" He claps his hands, looking even more eager as his students begin asking more questions. "This class used to be a punishment for me, but then I found out that I was good at breaking students and pressuring them into something valuable or worthless."

Nick gulps, not liking the General's methods. At the moment, he would be easy to break.

He points to the board. "There are six circles." He points from the outer circle to the middle. "Yellow, the 'Beginner Class' is the lowest level, normally a child by the age of five is at that level as they awaken their powers. Eighteen is the latest a power will awaken. It's rare to awaken your powers later, very rare, so you four need to improve greatly if you want any sort of respect from the students and teachers. As you heard from your little walk here, you can guess how your stay will go if you do not improve. There are many here who oppose letting in Yellow users at this age. So, you lot better prove them wrong!" he yells, causing Bhaltair to pale.

"The next level is the one above you, Orange. It's also known as the 'Common' Class, mainly because many people seem to be at that level. Still low in the circle, but considered tolerable compared to Yellow." The General shrugs.

Great, Nick wants to roll his eyes. *I guess Yellow is the stick you measure yourself against.* He remembers that Kaius is in Orange and wonders what his friend is learning right now.

"After that comes Red, the 'Classic' Class. Red is the middle ground for shadow users and is widely seen as the most acceptable level to be in. If you wish to get into higher positions, you better rise to that class. Some of the rarest Yellows make it to Red, it just proves that it is not impossible. So, if you all can make it to Red before you graduate, then you should count it as a great success."

Nick looks at the ring, it's where Lorcan is right now.

"Blue," the General continues. "Also known as the 'Advanced' Class. Many of the Nobles are in this ring, the 'Blue' bloods of society. Ahead of Blue is Purple, also called the 'Elite' Class. That is a special ring for special people, and I am not just saying that because I'm in it." He winks at the class.

"Very few people get into this level, and many hold positions of power. Talented individuals are generals and advisors to the Emperor. However, you sorry lot are far from it. But maybe you all can prove me wrong." He slams his hand on his desk causing Takara to jump. "Purple has a whole society of their own, which includes rules, edicts and culture. You want power?" He looks at the class. "Then you get in Purple. You want the world to respect you—and trust me, they will—then get in that circle." He taps his finger on the board with the word Purple. "I cannot stress it enough. I have seen people just take a Purple's word for granted without any background check. I've done it. All of the Purple students' words will be above yours."

"That's not fair!" Bhaltair raises his voice. The class looks at him in surprise at such an outburst.

The General doesn't reprimand him; instead, his smile widens.

"Good, feel that anger. Hopefully, it can fuel you lot into getting into higher classes. It isn't fair, that I will agree with you, but that's how it works. Now, I have never used it against someone else, but let me tell you twits something." His eyes darken as he looks around the classroom. "The Purples here will eat you alive. Do not go against them. Very few people, if any, will be on your side. You are in the lowest Class. If you want to get back at them, rise above them. Remember every joke and insult that they throw at you. Use it like a weapon. Prove them wrong!" His thundering voice echoes in every corner of the room.

There is silence before his teacher continues. "Those children are special. Now, you have to prove to them why you should be here. You may be special to your magicless friends, but here, you are nothing." He spits.

The word nothing bites into Nick like someone carving out a pound of flesh from his body. He's heard that word thrown at him so many times, but the effect is still the same. *Special.* He wants to roll his eyes. *Of course, Braawen's in there. Braawen is always the special one.* He hates to admit it, but even he sees his cousin as more important than himself.

The General continues with another simile. "The most important people are in this finale circle. They are the rarest and have the most envied positions." He points to the centre and last ring. "Black, the 'Legendary Class'."

The room seems to get colder just at the mention of the name. Nick looks around the room as he feels a tingle on the back of his neck, but there's no one else in the classroom except for them. Nick turns his attention back to the General.

"Black is the smallest and hardest group to get into. Many Purples have tried hard to get into this group, but even I have failed. There is only one person who is in this group presently, the Night Emperor." The General's smile slowly dims. "I have seen with my own eyes the great and terrible things he has done. Have you all heard of the Night of the Silenced?" he asks, voice lacking the thunder.

"Who hasn't?" Nick replies, as each of them nods. Bhaltair's skin is like porcelain, blue veins becoming visible on his flesh. "It made the Night Emperor a legend, but is everything that happened that night... true?"

The General looks at them, slowly taking a seat on the chair for the first time. A soft chuckle is all that sounds in the room. "I was there that very night. I was outside the castle when I heard screams and the crashing of glass. The screams were..." He sighs and shakes his head. "Let's just say, when there was a sudden silence in the castle, no one in the Capital city dared to make any noise that night. It was surreal. Everyone, even the horses were quiet, like a spell was cast on us."

He looks at Nick, older grey eyes looking into blue serious ones. "Let's just say the rumours are true and that I am happy to be on his side. But back to the lesson!" He rises from his seat. "We can talk more about the Night Emperor later. Now, there are myths about what this class can do and they are at the top of the circles. Once a Black, you will have everyone's ear, including the Emperor. They are the only people that can travel into the shadow lands and tame the great shadow beasts of legend."

A sense of unease settles around the room, in contrast to the loud quick beats of Nick's heart.

"Now!" The General slaps his hand, startling everyone. "Let's leave the circles for a moment and focus on the magic that you four are blessed with: Shadow magic can help you use the darkness around you, but very, very few people can use the darkness inside of them as a weapon. Those people are in the Blue to Black level. Using the darkness and hate inside of you can not only increase your strength and intelligence, but your overall will to survive or the drive to kill your enemy. Rarer is the skill to use your opponents' shadow against them. However, a Purple—a very powerful Purple—can enter and exit through someone's shadow with the approval of the person's knowledge. We use it on our allies, not our enemies. Blacks, however, do not need your approval. They can do whatever they want with your shadow. It's a useful skill, but I've only seen the Night Emperor use it. So, enough on that." He waves his hand dismissively.

"So, there are three levels. The first uses the shadows of the environment, Yellow to Red. The second uses the darkness inside yourself, Blue to Purple. The third uses another person's shadow against them, only Black. Remember what I'm going to say next: knowing the darkness inside you can help you become more powerful."

Nick narrows his eyes as he reflects on his own actions; he doesn't really have that much inner darkness.

The General continues: "It is very rare for someone to start out using positive emotions to control the shadows around them. It's possible, of course, but it's much easier to connect with the darkness in your heart. Channel that anger you lot have right now to plan, execute, and achieve your goals. Once you have that down, you won't have to rely so much on your anger. Right now, you lot should be focusing on your body. The better the body, the better the hold of magic. Now, we will focus on strength, endurance, and agility."

He looks at each of the students. "Bull!" He points to Bhaltair. "You'll turn that fat to muscle. Cows are meant to be eaten or sent to the mines." Bhaltair gives a faint nod.

"Nightshade." He points to Takara's dark blue hair. "You'll focus on endurance." The poor girl doesn't even have time to react when the General moves onto Rohana.

"Scar-faced one." Rohana glares. "Fine. If you make it out of Yellow, I'll call for the scar removal." That almost puts a smile on her lips. "Ice, then, for the one eye colour I can see through your bangs. Focus on agility."

Then he gets to Nick. The General gives a wolfish grin as Nick gives a slow but nervous smile back. "Guts, focus on all three." Nick's smile vanishes. "Right now, you're just a skeleton. I need you to get some muscles to hold up your balls." He blushes, trying to look anywhere but the man in front of him. "By Spring, your seed better be a harvest or more because I, personally, will kill you trying."

Nick personally wishes he could go back to the testing circle of when he first met the General and slap himself for talking.

The General strides over to the front of the classroom. "Remember, children—there are also weaknesses in the shadows. Light is a major weakness for the shadows. If light is strong enough, it can overpower the shadows. Light rooms are used to stop shadow wielders from using their powers. Too much light isn't good." He turns and writes light on the black board under weaknesses.

He then writes Shadow Blocks on the board. "Shadow Blocks are stones that cannot be affected by the shadows. All Shadow Magic is neutralized by them. However, Black circle users can affect the stone, though even their powers are weakened. But…" He lets it draw out. "That is a very rare weakness, so rare that you don't have to worry about it."

They all nod.

"Great," he sits up straighter. "One must also know that mentality is important to shadow wielders. If a shadow wielder does not have a clear mind or is afraid to confront the darkness in their heart, they shall not move into their potential. Their minds can become a stumbling block, a prison even. Even Blacks are affected by this. Lastly is pride. Pride can be helpful, but too much of it can stop people from hearing the shadows clearly or altogether."

He closes his eyes and snaps his fingers. "Right, I forgot about one weakness. Again: you cannot wield another person's shadow. You can travel through it, but you can't bend it to your will. Only the person of that shadow can mess with their soul. Not many people know this, but your shadow is a part of your soul, your darkness, and that is why it is so important to accept it. Controlling your shadow is in the higher levels. It is easier to control or take a non-living shadow to bend to your will. The only people who aren't affected by this are the Blacks."

Nick raises his hand and the General motions for him to speak. "So, the more powerful you get, the more you can control your own shadow?"

The General smiles. "Yes, but you have to remember it's your shadow, a part of your soul. The way to improve is to know yourself, your strengths and weaknesses. It's based on how truthful you are to yourself. Light may be a weakness to shadows, but casting light on yourself will help you improve."

Nick looks on, slightly confused by that statement as the General gives him a knowing look.

"This will be your introduction week. Lessons officially start next week." The General grins wolfishly. "Welcome to Equinox House!"

Chapter 6
Test

Night falls over the school and Nick is grateful for it. This is only the first day, but his legs are on fire and his stomach wants food! However, they are only allowed to eat after they get their uniforms, which for them is a black long-sleeved tunic embroidered with a yellow emblem of the school on the right of the upper chest. Nick's yellow pants are too big for him at the moment, so a thin long leather belt has to be used to hold them up. His footwear goes from holes for shoes to a pair of rough leather boots that are still a little big.

Takara had to move in between people, almost dancing through a crowd in order to get their uniforms. All of them were surprised as she handed out their uniforms.

"Thank you," Nick mumbles, feeling the coarse material.

She smiles, it's a nice one, and she even looks him in the eyes. "Those students were all crowding around like chickens. It reminded me of the farm back home. I'm used to dancing around things, the chickens and the students here are no different from each other."

From his observation, he sees the different uniforms on display. However, as he looks around, he can only see Yellow, Orange, and Red students he sees wearing the uniform. Blue and Purple students aren't around, so Nick only has the uniforms on display to compare.

From the looks of it, the higher a student moved up in the circle, the more scholarly the uniform became. Right now, Nick looks more like a novice for the army than a proper student. His pants were made out of a straw-like material that scratched him with every slight movement he made. He believes that the school could afford more comfortable pants, but they just chose otherwise. His judgment on the clothes seems correct as his fellow Yellows agrees as they adjust various areas of their uniforms, while the other students look surprised and happy with their new uniforms.

He wonders how Kaius will look. Kaius hates bright colours and Nick knows his friend will look at orange in disgust. *Maybe it will encourage dear Kai to move to a darker colour like Red*, Nick thinks. At least he can be happy for Kaius and Lorcan. The Orange and Red uniforms look comfortable and the students actually look like students. The boys like their vests and black dress pants; while the ladies wear dresses. One girl pokes her puffed shoulders while another twirls around in admiration. The higher the circle, the more decorations and shiny jewels are added to their uniforms.

Blues and Purples uniforms hanging on display look amazing. Nick would love the robes; it would keep him warmer than the clothes he's wearing now. Both uniforms have even more intricate designs on their blue and purple vests. purple gems, a stone Nick isn't familiar with, are added to the Purple uniforms as buttons. Their robes seem to shimmer in the light, unlike his dull material.

However, there's another set of robes on display that doesn't shimmer, which makes even the purple uniform look inferior. It is placed on a higher pedestal than the rest, and Nick has to crane his neck to look up to see it. It seems that this uniform catches everyone's attention one way or another. The teacher sees where all their eyes are looking towards and smiles.

"Feast your eyes, children, as this display will be the only time you shall see it in its glory." She glares directly at the Yellow group, and her eyes narrow further as she seemingly stares directly at Nick. "Not that some of you deserve to even look at it." Her tight lips give a condescending smile at the group.

Students crowd around the uniform, pushing the Yellows back further. Nick only got a quick glimpse at the Black uniform, which is locked behind the glass of the display, presumably only opened by a teacher's key. They probably hoped that by displaying this uniform, it would inspire one of the students to reach up to the legendary rank.

The mysterious black material seems to absorb all light. It's pure black, except for a thin line of gleaming silver used to embroider the school's emblem. It is grander than Purple's uniform, with a vest tailored to fit with a black jacket. The robes look incredible as well, as though the sleeves could open or it could become a cape. It even has a hood. The teacher explains that the clothes were created by master craftsmen, the head tailor of the imperial family.

Finally, they can enter the feast room. He expects it to be small, like the rooms the rebels sometimes ate in, yet, Nick shakes his head as he looks at the large hall they eat in. He is able to briefly see Kaius, but the feast room is separated into different tables based on rank. The feasting period, as Nick found out, is the only time that all staff and students ate together. Each of the heads are also present and eats with the students but stays at their class' tables.

"Can anyone eat at different tables?" Nick asks the General.

The General wipes the mash potatoes from his moustache. "You can, but no one wants to. Plus, if you sorry lot try to sit at another table, the tables will fight you or a teacher will send you back," the General states before he goes back to his meal.

Nick takes the time to look around the hall, and deems it to be definitely worth being called a hall instead of a room. The hall has high ceilings with dark blue, purple, and black geometric designs, merging together in a way that makes the ceiling seem larger, creating a lighter atmosphere to the room.

He tears his eyes away from the ceiling to the rest of the room and remembers what the General said about the tables. Purple has one of the better tables further into the hall, and the people there all screamed of talent, arrogance and—dare he say that the General was right—the aura around them just screamed 'cult'.

The students sitting there seem to have gotten better, well... everything. Their purple banner hangs proudly next to black. There are plush seats and the table is adorned with purple tablecloths, delicate glass cups, and a rich variety of foods. It seems that the school spent most of its coins on these students. Nick saw some of them in the hallway on the way to dinner. The fabric used to make the purple's uniform is definitely of a higher quality, reminding him of the dresses and suits he found in abandoned noble mansions.

He can see them point and sneer at his table. The Yellow table is simple and bare, adorned only with a plain yellow tablecloth and a yellow banner on the wall, and their food simple in comparison to the other tables. He wonders what the school calls simple, as the meal has a variety of meats and fresh vegetables, even though it is winter. Even the water in his cup is the freshest water he's ever tasted.

At the table, Bhaltair is put on a high protein diet. The poor boy is forced to eat and drink a slimy blended drink meant to facilitate weight loss. Takara and Rohana are both put on a diet to give them more energy and strength. Takara eats, but Rohana just glares at the Purple table.

General Herald catches her glaring. "Good, Ice, feel that anger and hate. Use it to your advantage to move up the levels. If you can't beat them in Shadow magic, you can at least beat them in hand to hand combat. Shadow Assassins will like you." He grins again.

Rohana glares harder at him. "I'm not hungry. Can I leave?"

"No!" he snaps. "You must eat everything, then we exercise followed by meditation." His voice is calmer at the mention of the word meditation.

Rohana begins eating again, but slower.

Nick can't finish his meal of protein and strange liquid. It's thick and grey, and tastes as good as it looks.

"Guts, better you finish that, because next week, you have to eat two!" his teacher commands.

Nick grumbles as he drinks it all. His meal reminds him of his time in prison. He ate much worse and drank filth-ridden water that could kill a man. However, there was no old General with an impressive moustache drilling them to eat.

He glances up to look at Kaius again, who waves from the next table over. He waves back with a smile, then smiles at Lorcan at the next table, who nods back in reply. He looks to the Purple table once again, where he sees Braawen laughing with one of the girls. He wasn't too surprised to see that his cousin made friends, but did he have to make them so quick?

Nick turns back to his table and eats his food a little faster. He doesn't see the General grinning at him.

Takara looks up and sees the Black table at the very head. If the Purple table looked luxurious, the Black table looked royal. Even from a distance, the large table looks imposing. The table is completely black, with a few gems and embroidered silver swirls scattered across the tablecloth. There are three chairs placed at the table facing the school, as though the Blacks overlooked them all. Takara remembers stories that her parents told her about kings and queens, and she imagines that those chairs could be thrones. However, there is no one sitting there and no food, just really beautiful chairs that she wouldn't mind sitting on.

"General," Takara speaks with her mouth full. "Why is there no one at the Black table?"

The General puts down his large goblet of mead. "Let's see if you remember class this morning. Where is Black?" he asks.

"In the centre of all the circles." Takara answers, spitting out a few grains of rice as she speaks. Rohana glares at her as some of it lands on her bread.

The General ignores Takara's terrible table manners, for now. "Once someone enters the Black circle, they can use other people's darkness as power. Who is the only one who can access another person's darkness?"

Nick responds, "The Night Emperor."

"Correct," the General said. "Until someone hits the Black circle, no one will sit at that table. Same with the uniform, only Black circle students can wear it. One must earn the Black."

"It looks nice, way nicer than Purple." Rohana gives a small smile for the first time.

"They have the best food too. But now you all need to finish eating," their teacher grumbles then turns to Bhaltair, hounding him to eat.

◗

Overall, their first day is uneventful after the meal and when night comes, everyone easily falls asleep with another blue vial.

Except for one.

Nick's eyes snap open at the sound of the bellowing snores. As he throws the covers off him, he stops mid-motion, remembering what occurred the night before. He fights with himself on why it was a bad idea to go, and why it could be worse to not meet the stranger. After successfully debating with all his emotions, he decides to meet the man. His fear of the stranger finding him is greater than staying in bed. It also doesn't help that the dead guards were just removed and replaced without a word.

Nick makes his way around the room grabbing various 'tools'. After going through Takara's desk, he creeps towards the doorway. He quietly opens the doors, slips out, and closes them behind him without a sound. Once he's outside, he sees the moon again, and this time, he sees stars. Silence greets him, but it's different from last night. He knows this silence; it leaves him feeling heavy all over.

People are tense, alert, he thinks. He runs back down and takes off his bright yellow coat; his shirt has a yellow badge, but that's easy to cover with his hands. His pants are yellow though, so he has to be careful as he heads back out. He's cold but moves forward anyway.

Remembering the jog from this morning, he heads towards the silver moon and star gates. After dodging multiple guards, he hopes it's still open. As he looks around the corner, he sees that the gate has two guards, as well as guards along the roofs and corners.

He inhales sharply, wondering why there's an increase in guards now. Then it hits him. He remembers that the stranger wants to be impressed. It seems that just having a few guards and an open gate impressed him enough to increase the security. Nick looks back down at his outfit; the yellow pants are a perfect target.

"I need a new outfit," he whispers. Turning to one of the many school windows, he smiles as he knows where his new clothes will be.

Getting into the school is easy for him. It costs him two fingernails by unscrewing some of the screws and nails. His nails, weakened by malnutrition, break easily; but he's used to damaging his fingers to get into tricky places. The pain means nothing as he places his fingers in the snow to numb his nerves and wipe some of the blood off.

"Just like a mission," he whispers to himself. "You can't fail this; Father would not tolerate failure." Looking around the area, he stays still until the guards move to a different section of the roof. The window opens and his small frame slides through the cracks like a snake, though his cousin likes to tell him 'like a worm.'

He gently closes the window and takes a step, wincing at the small tap that his boots make. Realizing they would be too loud on the floors, he takes them off. With boots in hand, he silently creeps down the hall. His feet are cold, but after many twists and turns, he remembers where the uniform office is. His uncle always told him to plan ahead, and with his 'tools' the hair pins that he took from Takara's desk, he easily fit into the lock. It's just like the ones he picked when he had to sneak into Imperial bases during the rebellion.

"This really is a mission," he whispers to himself, smiling as new-found confidence flows through him.

After a minute of trial and error, a small click rings in his ears as the lock opens. "Beautiful," he whispers and enters the room, closing the door behind him. In the room he sees all the uniforms, from Yellow near the front to the higher ranks in the back. Now, he could use the Red or Purple uniforms as they're dark enough to hide, but he knows what he wants, and he is willing to take a risk to get it. Though when he searches, he realizes that it's not with the rest of the uniforms anymore. A curse is ready to leave his lips until he sees another doorway with a lock. He picks at another lock to get into the back room.

"So, they allow it to come into the open to get people to want that uniform? Well, it works, and I'm just going to borrow it," he whispers mischievously.

This lock clicks open and he sees that rich black fabric, looking resplendent even hanging in a back room. He smiles as he grabs the smallest uniform, locking everything behind him, and leaves the room like nothing ever happened.

After many minutes of searching through hallways and hitting dead ends, Nick finds a washroom. He changes in the washroom and looks in the mirror to check out his new outfit. He admires his black collared shirt, and even fixes the cravat around his neck like a scarf. Even though the vest seems a little big, he believes that it will fit him in time. His jacket is all black with an intricately embroidered silver design on the cuffs. The black emblem of the school is bordered by a thin silver line. His black pants fit him better and the fabric feels like a second skin instead of a straw sack. He chose the boots over the shoes that he saw. These boots are more his size and fit tightly to his legs. The black uniform fits him extremely well, as though he's made for it.

Pride comes before a fall, he can hear his mother's voice in his ear. He blushes and humbles himself when he sees his gaunt self wearing the noble clothes. His self-confidence diminishes as he starts to feel like he's playing dress up, instead of being an actual student. He sighs as he turns from the mirror, placing his yellow boots and uniform in a corner.

He puts on the robe that can clasp as a cape when needed. The robe is made from a thick and rich black material with the emblem on the school embroidered in black threads that reaches below his knees. What he likes best is the hood that is sure to hide his face, and the frost breath of the god of Air. With one last prayer, he opens the washroom window that leads to a ledge. It doesn't go straight to the back towards the lake, but it will work.

Nick climbs up pipes, and jumps and grabs balconies, staying in the shadows. His bloodied fingers are numb from the ice as he grips ledges and metal pipes. He remembers the outer layout from his jog this morning. As he was dying from the run, he put every corner and window to memory. *Well, almost every corner,* he thinks to himself aching from the amount of times he's already hit a wall.

With his sense of direction, he knows that he is close to his destination but it requires him to reach a ledge that he isn't too sure he can make. He grabs onto the wall, and glimpses a guard overlooking the area he needs to cross. He sticks to the shadows and lets them envelop him. He watches the guard turn slightly from the spot he's in and moves quietly towards the ledge. His eyes never leave the guard as he breathes slowly, straining his ears to hear them. Balancing on his toes and praying, he takes his eyes off the guard. He sees that he can dash over to the other ledge. It's thin, painfully thin, but he's thin enough to stand on it. He looks at the guard again, who isn't moving, narrowing his eyes as he sees the guard turning his head fully away from him. He braces for the impact as he jumps and bites, his lip tasting iron as the pain stings on his foot from landing on his toes.

These boots are not made for climbing! Running, yes, climbing? No! he thinks as his toes curl at the tip of his boots. He looks up, seeing the guard turning back but not reacting to anything. Nick stays like that for another five minutes, then slowly makes his way to his destination, walking on eggshells the entire time.

In order to reach the ground, he makes his way to the greenhouse roof and jumps. Sliding down the greenhouse is fun as he falls into a soft pile of snow. His landing makes a little crunch, and more snow falls on him, covering his head. He pops his head out slowly from the snow, looking up to see that the guards aren't stationed in this area. A sigh of relief leaves his blue-tinged lips, and he thanks the deities who are watching over him. Not wanting to waste any more time, he gets up and slowly walks to the lake. There's nothing he can do about the crunching of the snow underfoot, and honestly, he's too tired to care.

The stranger is standing overlooking the frozen lake again, wearing all black, and turns around when he hears Nick approach, right as Nick licks the blood from his lip. When Nick looks up to him, the man looks concerned, or at least that's what he thinks. Although, he knows that can't be right, since they've only just met.

"My boy, what happened to your lip? Did someone do this to you?" The stranger sounds worried as he walks over. Not a second later, the man grabs his chin gently to see the wound.

"Yes, me. I had to bite down on my lip to not alert the guards. Nice addition, by the way," he mumbles sarcastically, which does not go past the man.

The man grins. "You have done well to impress me. I honestly thought that you wouldn't get past the guards." The man reaches into his pocket and grabs a dark blue tin, unscrewing the lid to reveal a white cream, which smells faintly of lemons. "Hold still," he commands as he takes off his gloves and places them in his pockets, and begins to gently dab the cream on Nick's lips.

Nick can feel a tingle and the pain stops within seconds. "Can you do that for my hands too?" He holds up his two broken fingernails and scraped up hands.

The stranger's eyes widen, and he grabs his hands, rubbing the cream on them. Nick has to shut his mouth as he sees that not only are the stranger's nails black, his fingertips are too.

The stranger looks at him and lets out a short chuckle. As the stranger finishes rubbing the cream on his hand, Nick gasps as he sees that all of his nails are fixed, his scratches healed. He wonders if the lemon-scented cream would heal the scars on his back and wrist, but his mind quickly returns to the stranger's hands. Nick wonders if the cream can help him, too.

"I know what you're thinking, and no, it will not work for me. It will take time for this to go away." The stranger explains as he reaches into his pockets and places the gloves back on.

Nick begins to blush. "Sorry, I—I shouldn't have looked." The stranger smiles, and his dark eyes widen as he finally takes in the outfit that he's wearing. "My boy, I did not expect you to steal a Black uniform." Nick wants to protest, but the stranger puts his hands up, stopping him. "I know you stole it. There hasn't been a single student this year who can enter the Black circle."

Nick looks down at the uniform and tries to suppress a smile. "I needed the Black to blend into the shadows." He digs one of his feet into the snow.

The man laughs. "You are an interesting child. You seem very clever and intelligent."

He isn't used to praise. *Praise would just make you big headed*, his father's voice chastised him. Nick just nods, not really believing in it. To him, this is just another mission that his father sent him on. He was pretty certain that his father wanted him dead sometimes. He bites his lips and looks towards the lake. Thinking about his father created an emptiness in him, eating him up and numbing him. After screaming and crying out his sorrows earlier, he managed to release some of that numbness, although, there is another emotion lurking inside him now taking its place. He doesn't like it; he preferred the numbness.

"You aren't used to praise, are you, boy?" The stranger gives him a smile.

No, Nick wants to snap, but realizes that it's a bad idea. "No, sir, and this boy has a name." He stops himself from glaring at the stranger.

The stranger raises an eyebrow. "So, do you mind telling me your name?"

He sees no harm in answering. "Nickolaus. Nickolaus Westmore."

The stranger smiles. "Volodimir."

"Just Volodimir?" Nick raises an eyebrow.

"Just Volodimir to you."

That doesn't sit well with Nick, but then again, it must be a cultural thing in this school. The General said to just call him the General. So far, the teachers here were either called by their first name or title. Before Nick could ask why, Volodimir continues.

"I have to say, I'm hoping that I can see you in Black more often."

"I was told that I had to earn the Black." Nick replies.

Volodimir's smile widens. "Maybe you will. I have high expectations. You should keep it for now."

Nick looks down and feels the uniform again. He likes it, especially compared to the harsh fabric of the Yellow uniform. This outfit actually makes him feel like a student.

"You have passed my test, and I am impressed. Now, listen, I do not impress easily. But I would like to know what class you are in."

Nick licks his lips. "The lowest."

"Yellow?" Volodimir asks, Nick's surprised the man isn't shocked by his answer. "Yellow," he repeats, as he ponders what he's about to do. However, it doesn't take long before his eyes glow for a moment. "You see the path in between the trees? Walk along the path and on the hill, you will see a little cottage. Go there around this time in two nights. I will train you. We will become my student, my apprentice."

Nick blinks in surprise. "Train me? Apprentice?"

"Yes, and you must wear the Black uniform." Nick wants to ask him more questions, but Volodimir turns away and walks towards the forest. "Oh, and Nico?" Volodimir calls.

The name 'Nico' grabs his attention; no one had called him that before.

The man throws a black bottle at him. "Keep this a secret and drink the bottle now."

He looks down at the bottle he caught. The golden rim of the cap shimmers against the moonlight. The small glass bottle is easy to grip and fits neatly in his hand. It's a very nice bottle, Nick wonders what could be inside. He pulls off the cap to see black liquid inside. He looks at the man, whose eyes glow red for a second as a small smile appears on his face.

"It's not poisonous. I already said that you were interesting."

Nick gives a nervous smile and looks back at the bottle with hesitation. *Gods, please don't let me die,* Nick thinks as he closes his eyes and gulps it down, finding it sweet to the taste.

He braces for pain, but nothing comes. Instead, a warmth envelops him as he can feel a mysterious energy come through his veins. The sensation spreads throughout his blood. It's a sensation he can feel within every fiber of his being, from the crown of his head to the soles of his feet. Even though the feeling is strange to him, it is welcome. He looks at his hands and clenches them into a fist; he feels stronger.

As a word of thanks begins to exit his lips, Volodimir is gone, leaving footprints where he once stood. Nick can taste the remnants of the strange liquid on his lips. He thinks that maybe it was medicine, because the pain in his body from the climb is gone. This potion seems to be stronger than the red vials.

He makes his way back to the building through another window, grabs his shoes and debates putting the uniform back. However, he remembers that the man, Volodimir, wants him in this uniform.

He makes his way back to the cellar and finds that very little has changed; everyone is asleep. He quietly changes and places the uniform flat under his mattress and lies down, hearing the snores of Bhaltair. He takes the sleeping vial and as his eyes go heavy, a thought enters his mind.

I didn't ask if Volodimir killed those guards.

Chapter 7
Interest

Volodimir appears from the shadows at the bottom of a hill. Black steps greet him as he climbs up to the cottage up on the hill, surrounded by trees. The cottage looks rather small from the front, but like the school, it holds many secrets. The light from the cottage can be a beacon for others in such a dark forest, but it is an annoyance for him; it means that he has visitors. He sighs, knowing they're waiting for him. Even though he's late, he wants to make this quick.

The door opens to a wooden open space. The heat is the first thing he feels, coming from the roaring fire lit in the back of the room. Candles all around the circular room provide light. The place is welcoming, but Volodimir clenches his jaw as he sees his guests in their seats, and the five head teachers of the school turn to face him, each wearing their respective black robes and coloured stoles. Only the General wears a black military uniform, but still proudly wears the yellow stole on his shoulders. They all nod to him and he nods in return.

General Herald returns to making jokes with Miss Leia, Head of Orange Circle. Her hair is still as wild as ever, and she wears the orange stole around her neck as a scarf. The oldest member of the group, Miss Catherine, Head of Red Circle, wraps her red stole as a scarf as well, smiling while closing her book. He almost feels guilty for stopping the elderly woman from reading, but this is an important meeting. An old woman she may be, but with her great power and endurance, Volodimir knows she'll be staying a little longer as Head of Red. He also knows that she is older than she looks, but her dark skin has very few wrinkles, which she swears is all natural.

The one wearing the blue stole over one of his shoulders is an odd man, even by Volodimir's standards. The young man sits still and observes the rest of his faculty members. He is thinner than most people, with long black hair and bangs that cover one of his dark hazel eyes. However, as strange as he is, Jacques has his uses, and excels at communicating and uncovering the secrets of the shadows. Lastly, is the one wearing a purple stole properly and proudly, Professor Arran. The man sits in his seat like a king, rubbing his short-pointed beard and almost sneering at everyone. Volodimir can see the man's mouth twist, which is quickly replaced with a plastered smile just for him.

Volodimir takes his seat at the head and places the black stole on his shoulders. He clears his throat, gaining their attention. "My apologies for being late. There was something interesting on the school grounds that needed my attention."

Arran gives a small, mirthless chuckle. "Even more important than your punctuality for this meeting?"

Everyone looks between him and Volodimir. All the heads know of the on-going feud between the Black and Purple heads. Arran was certain that he would be the one to bring about another Black circle user and receive praise from the Night Emperor; it was his wish to become the new Black Teacher. Yet again, the man was rejected.

"Let's just say that it may affect the school," Volodimir replies honestly. "I will keep an eye on it for now and write a letter to the Royal Palace that a child managed to sneak past the guards." He can hear the gasps from Leia and Catherine. "Maybe we'll get better guards than the ones you brought on while I fought in a war." He ends with a thin-lipped smile, daring Arran to speak anymore on the matter. That seems to shut the man up.

Leia quickly covers her mouth. Despite her best efforts, the bell-like giggles still escape her lips, causing Arran to narrow his eyes at her. Catherine gives her a soft hit on the leg with her book, but can't hide the smile forming on her lips.

"Can we just start the meeting, please? I'm very tired, as I'm sure everyone else is as well." Jacques's overly dramatic voice cuts the tension. "Though, I guess we can alert the Shadow Assassins that they may get a new recruit."

Jacques just wants this night over with. The last thing he wants to hear is Arran's complaints. He knows the foolish ambition that Arran has to become the Head and leader of this school, the Black Teacher. Yet, Arran's leadership skills and teachings were debilitating at best. Jacques sees the results of Arran's 'teachings' with his students. In Jacques's opinion, the only person suited to teach a Black is a Black wielder.

He sighs. The only Black wielder is the Night Emperor, but he has an empire to run. So, he appoints someone in his place. The last Black Teacher, Alesander, was a good leader in the beginning but had to leave after a sudden 'illness'. Jacques knows the illness to be foul play. He wrote a letter to inform the council of Alesander's 'sudden' illness that prevented him from doing his duties. This was something that Arran should have informed the council about. But why would he? He was practically ruling the school in Alesander's absence.

Jacques was surprised by the quick response. The Night Emperor and Council sent Volodimir. Apparently, the council requested the man and the Emperor approved, though rather begrudgingly. Things improved, in

Jacques's opinion. However, Arran had questioned Volodimir's actions from day one, until the day Volodimir and Leia had to leave for war in Availa. Things became worse again when Volodimir left. When Jacques saw Volodimir return with the General last week, he almost jumped for joy. For the short time that Arran had control, he had free range to do as he pleased... until Volodimir returned. Jacques wonders when Volodimir will lose patience. He can't wait for the day to come.

Volodimir crosses his legs; his presence eclipses the others. They each feel a soft tingle at the back of their necks, bringing everyone to attention. Jacques's mind is brought back into the cabin.

"Let's begin. Are there any potential candidates for the Black circle?" Volodimir asks to start the night. The Night Emperor made it clear to the council and the school that he wished for another Black wielder to be found, and soon.

It's Arran who speaks first: "There are two new members of the Purple circles, the prisoner children from the Availa Rebellion. Even though their background is less than favourable, their potential is outstanding." He beams with pride.

Volodimir nods at the information. "That is unique, for students who have no prior knowledge to be already placed in the Purple circle." He nods and hums. "Please continue to tell me the progress of the two students. May I have their names?"

"Emelie Snowfield and Braawen Archer."

"Archer? As in, the resistance fighter, Marcus Archer?" Catherine asks. The rest of the teachers lean in.

Arran smiles. "His nephew."

The others murmur around each other while Volodimir ponders on this new information.

"To have the resistance leader's nephew on our side, how ironic." Herald laughs.

"But can we ever trust the boy?" Leia asks. "It's not as if the boy can contact anyone outside of Equinox House, but still, I would like to be safe."

Arran scoffs. "Safe? We have 26 children who are war refugees. I believe that their numbers are too small to do anything, especially with a school that has over 300 more students from our Empire. Anyways, I believe that the boy can be... molded to fit into our cause. Even the girl, Emelie, has a similar personality. Leadership, ruthless, and darkness. They see themselves as above others and will do anything to stay that way." He smirks and takes a sip from his cup of tea.

Volodimir nods at the information but narrows his eyes. "Good. Please keep an eye on them. Any others in the Purple circle?"

Arran creases his beard. "Maybe Astor."

"You said that to the previous Black Teacher last time as well," Volodimir states, annoyed.

"Well, he is trying, so there's still hope. But that seems to be all," Arran concludes.

Volodimir resists rolling his eyes. He'll continue to keep a close eye on Arran's teachings for now, and place additional guards to watch this Archer boy.

The others state that there are no students that they see going into the Black, but may move into circles above them. When it's Herald's turn, they all look at him with pity. Except for Arran, who smirks at the man for having the worst students. Herald hates all the looks.

The General straightens himself in his seat after a moment of silence. "I will not lie to you. These are the saddest bunch that you have given me." He cuts straight to the point while others either look away or stiffen. Then a wide smile grows on Herald's face. "And I thank you for it, for it will be so much fun to mold them into something great." His rumbling voice full of eagerness instead of his usual thunder.

Volodimir nods. "I see... tell us why?"

The General grins and leans in closer to everyone. Usually, when Herald was the Yellow teacher, he would just laugh and ask to be excused from this meeting altogether.

"There are four students, and I will work each of them hard to at least make it out of their level.

"The first is Bhaltair. I call him 'Bull'. He's a boy who eats instead of standing up for himself, but I see that I can make him into a man of muscle and strength. I see him using the shadows to make himself stronger and smashing his enemies with weapons of steel.

"The second is Takara, 'Nightshade'. The girl is graceful with her feet and I envision her dancing around her enemies, using shadows to teleport from one place to the other. I want to focus on her endurance to allow her to travel through the shadows and to focus on her mind.

"The third is Rohana, called 'Ice'. That girl has a lot of anger and hate. I think it might be someone in Purple who gave her that nasty little scar on her face. With training and meditation, she could become a spy, gathering information and become a Shadow Assassin hiding in the shadows, waiting to strike. But she needs to work on her agility and use her anger to further her powers instead of hindering her. Once she controls her anger, she can think clearer."

He licks his lips for this one, his body almost vibrating as his smile grows which gets all their attention. "But the one I'm most excited for is Nickolaus. I call him 'Guts'. The boy was sassy during his test, so my first impression was that he needed hard training. He's a skeleton now, very small, but he surprises me by how well he can hide his presence amongst a crowd."

"Another potential Shadow Assassin?" Catherine asks.

"Maybe. But he's focusing on all the skills. The boy has potential, a lot of it. I can see him being a leader; he's clever, and is very good at controlling his emotions. He just needs confidence. But I know that deep down there is a bottomless pit of anger and hate. I can sense darkness in his heart. I felt it briefly in the feast room, but then he swallowed it back down as quickly as it came."

"I remember the boy. Sassy, but a nice lad." Jacques adds. "But if you say there is darkness in his heart, I believe there will come a day when it explodes."

"I hope I will be there to see it." Herald looks delighted at the thought.

"So," Volodimir turns the attention back to him. "All four have great potential?" General nods proudly; he would personally make sure each of them passes the Yellow circle. "Even to go into Black?"

All look surprised and turn back to Herald.

The General shrugs. "Honestly, it has never happened before, I mean... the highest people in the Yellow circle have moved up to is Red." He sighs and leans in his chair.

The corner of Volodimir's mouth twitches up, he already knows who Herald is thinking about. Herald looks back at the group as though he's having a eureka moment. "Guts. It's still too early, but I believe that if I can get him out of the Yellow, he might make it past Red to Blue. But Black, well... I did say he has a lot of darkness."

Volodimir smirks and nods in agreement. *I know,* he thinks to himself. He watched the jogging that the Yellow students did in the morning. All of them were in a sorry state, but there was one who caught his eye. One small boy that encouraged the others to keep moving. Volodimir sees beyond what others see as a poor excuse for a boy.

When they see dirt and mud, he sees soil and clay. Soil in which he could plant a seed that would grow, and not wither. Clay that he could mold.

Chapter 8
Reality

Nick is nervous throughout the day, believing that someone will notice one of the Black uniforms is missing. However, he realizes that no one checks on the Black uniforms, because no one would have the gall to even touch them. The day passes and there is no mention of the missing uniform. He hasn't breathed a word about the clothes under his mattress or about Volodimir.

Today the Yellows are paired with the Oranges for their 'Introduction to Fighting' class. They have their class in a small room that the General has converted into a gym, until the actual training hall meets his standards. Apparently, whenever the General isn't dealing with the four of them, he's the instructor for self-defence and attack class. As the General tells everyone to pair up, Nick and Kaius make eye contact, but before Nick can move, the General grabs Nick's arm and pulls him to his side. Kaius ends up with Bhaltair while he's with his teacher.

After the General goes through a few kicks and blocks that remind him of what his father would teach the rebels, each person practices with their partner. Nick looks at the General, who takes off his coat, leaving him in his yellow undershirt, and Nick gulps when he sees the muscles and the scars on the man's arm. He is drilled *hard*. The General beat him black and blue, and each time he was struck down, he gets back up. His arms were burning, but each punch reminded him of his father's or Braawen's strikes. Nick was used to this sort of training. Members of the Orange and Yellow class pity him afterwards.

After mid-meal break, Nick tells the others that he will make his own way to the infirmary. He limps, trying not to put too much pressure on his injuries even though he feels the sharp stabs, especially on his arms. He ignores the snickers from the other students. He looks down, not paying them any mind and turns into an empty hallway.

I don't think this is the right way, he thinks, looking around and trying to remember where the General said the infirmary was.

You're going the right way... He hears a soft whisper that causes him to turn sharply to the left. But there's no one there. He strains his ears to hear anything else.

Nothing.

He sighs, relaxing his muscles.

"Hi, Nick!"

He jumps and winces as the pain from his arm spreads to his back. The pain can't dim the smile that he gives his friend. He knows this voice very well, so different from the whisper.

Kaius gives an apologetic smile. "Sorry, Nicky. That General beat you hard. What did you do to get on his bad side?"

Nick rolls his shoulders, trying to loosen up his abused muscles. "Nothing. He told all four of us in Yellow that he would push us to our limits. He wants to see us move beyond Yellow or die trying."

"So, this is him helping you?" Kaius asks, then winces when Nick nods. "Damn... then what's him not helping you?"

Nick shakes his head. "I don't want to find out."

During the rebellion, Nick was used to going to a medicine tent, or having the medicine man or woman come to him personally. Going into the medicine tent had a fifty-fifty chance of surviving. Many soldiers, including himself, would take their chances with their injuries rather than risk getting diseases and infection.

However, as soon as both of them open the doors, the smell of alcohol and disinfectant fill the air around them. Nick looks down to see freshly cleaned white tiles. He lifts his head to see a spacious room with at least ten beds, each bed having curtains that could be drawn for privacy. The walls are a brighter shade of grey and there are three large windows, one of which is propped open to bring in fresh air.

"Are you two going to stand there or come in?" A new voice brings him out of his thoughts. Sitting behind a large oak desk is a woman with a sour face, sucking on a candy, careful not to ruin the lipstick she has on. Her light brown hair is braided away from her face, though a few curly stands have come loose.

"Sorry, are you the one in charge?" Kaius asks. "My friend here," he points to Nick, "he needs help."

"I'm Nurse Stewarts, and yes, I'm in charge." The woman scoffs. "And, I have two working eyes, I can see he needs help. Can the boy speak for himself?" She gets up, and Nick sees that she is slim, wearing a dark blue dress with a white apron on top. She puts on a white thin coat and walks over to them, pointing to one of the empty beds.

He sits on one of the beds as the nurse pulls up a rolling stool and inspects him. He's never been to a registered healer. Only medicine people, whose knowledge extends to herbs and sewing wounds.

"Take off your shirt."

Nick blushes. "There's nothing wrong with my back. It's just my arms." He reveals the bruises on his arms.

"I'm a professional, I've seen everything. You don't have to be embarrassed," she sighs.

He just shakes his head, as she sighs again, this time rolling her eyes. She looks over his arms and chuckles.

"This is definitely the work of the General. I'd know these bruises anywhere." She finishes looking over his arms and takes out a vial with a green potion from her pocket. "This will help with the healing. I want you to lay down here for at least an hour for everything to heal up nicely." She rises from her seat on the stool. "I'll be at my desk if you need me."

"Can I stay with him?" Kaius asks.

The nurse chuckles. "Of course! This room is open to anyone, just not after hours." With that the woman makes her way to her desk. Once seated, she takes out a book and begins to read, ignoring the two.

"Nick," Kaius whispers.

"What, Kai?" He settles himself in the bed and notices that these beds were much more comfortable than the beds in the Yellow cellars. *Is everything better than what the Yellows have?*

Kaius moves closer to him, leaning more to his right from his stool. "Lorcan and Braawen aren't friends anymore."

"What?!" Nick howls as he quickly sits up. He instantly regrets it and slowly lays back down, while Kaius winces and holds his left ear in pain at the explosion of sound. "They've been through thick and thin together. What happened?" Nick whispers.

Kaius recovers and removes his hand from his ear. "Braawen. He... I don't know what's going on in the Purple class, but Braawen... He's changed."

Nick narrows his eyes. *Braawen doesn't change for anyone, people change for Braawen,* he thinks to himself.

"How? From what I can see at his table, he's still as arrogant as ever."

"He's more arrogant than ever, and when Lorcan tried to talk to him, he flat-out ignored him and told him in front of his new 'friends' to leave him alone," Kaius sighs.

Nick bites his lips, going over the new information in his head. Braawen is many things, but when he collected a group of friends, he kept them close. He shakes his head and looks back to Kaius. "We should talk to Lorcan to see what he said. Braawen isn't one to just leave a friend like that. Something must have happened in Purple. Maybe he's trying to gain everyone's trust. And... And maybe he knows a way to contact my uncle." Nick bites down on his lips harder.

Kaius looks at him skeptically. "Nicky, it was Lorcan who told me. The warrior can be a bit stubborn but he's not a liar. Lorcan is crazy good at reading body language and knows when someone is lying or feeling pressured. Braawen showed none of those signs."

Nick's about to say something else until he sees another person walking closer to them. Kaius turns around to see the impassive face of Lorcan, his amber eyes ablaze.

A heavy silence falls between the three, and Nick decides to break it with a nervous smile. "So… about Braawen?"

If amber eyes could burn, he would be ash. *Not that I'd weigh any less.*

"Trust me, your *cousin* made it very clear that he doesn't want anything to do with us." The venom coming out of Lorcan's mouth is lethal.

Nick rolls his eyes. "Come on guys, this is Braawen we're talking about. He loved his friends more than his family. I can vouch for that." He gives a sly smile, but the two both roll their eyes in response. "Guys, this is Braawen. He's not cruel."

"Yes, the one who used you as a punching bag," Kaius retorts.

"And took all your ideas and credit for your hard work," Lorcan adds.

Nick glares at Lorcan. "Funny how you knew all that and still gave him the credit." Lorcan shrugs.

Nick quickly changes the subject; there is no need to dwell on Braawen if he doesn't even give a speck about them. "Well, I think I've had enough of talking about the special boy. Does anyone have any idea what's going on back home? What of my uncle?"

Kaius looks at Lorcan and then shrugs. "There isn't much. I don't hear anything from Orange, except for the times when Professor Leia goes on a tangent and talks about the plans they have for Availa. She went on at least three rants before mid-meal."

Nick closes his eyes and tiredly sighs. "Kai, that's actually good information. What did she say?"

"Mostly that the rebel forces are all gone." Both boys' wince at that information. "Your uncle Tybalt is still missing, so there's some good news, at least. The monarchy has been replaced by an imperial governor from their ranks. I'm not surprised that a lot of merchants and low-born nobles from the Empire are flocking to Availa because of the warmer weather and it's a place where many people are seeking their money and wealth."

"And the people who live there?" Nick's voice is laced with anger.

"Second-class citizens, not that there's much to being citizens to begin with. With the awful King we had, then the rebellion, let's just say that not a lot of people survived," Kaius points out. "Plus, it's not like there weren't second-class citizens before." His words are bitter and even Lorcan looks upset, nodding to his words.

"And the people from the rebels were put on ships and sent to this land," Kaius adds, pulling his sleeves over his wrist. "Many have been placed in different workhouses and mines or even spread out across the Empire."

Lorcan nods. "Though, there is a way to become a full citizen. Either they become citizens through marrying a person from the Empire, joining the army, or work in the mines. It's ironic that they have to become full citizens in the kingdom they were born in. I guess some things never change." Lorcan groans and rubs his red hair; which is growing back quickly. "The worst is that the children that were brought here as war prisoners aren't considered citizens of any country. We're 'wards of the state'. We can't be granted our imperial citizenship until we prove our loyalty through hard work, and well... graduating."

Nick puts his hands to his face and groans, dejected about this new reality. "What can we do?"

"What happened to the whole 'I'll become their new leader' thing?" Kaius teases, giving Nick a hopeful smile.

"Yes, well as you can see, I am at the bottom of the barrel!" He snaps. "It makes it a little difficult to become their leader."

Lorcan chuckles.

"What's so funny?" Nick glares.

"You, a leader," Lorcan laughs. The two haven't heard him laugh in ages; no one has laughed, really. However, as the others stare at Lorcan and realize their new reality, it doesn't take long for them to join in the laughter. In a matter of minutes, their laughter produces tears. The tears are overflowing from an emotion deep within, but their laughter seems to mask it.

It's okay to cry, Nick remembers Volodimir saying. He listens to the silence that comes after, his ears picking up the soft chattering of students outside. He looks to the nurse to see that she's already in her office.

"You know what?" Lorcan gives another soft laugh. "If the deities allowed you to be here, then you're here for a reason."

"Who knows? Maybe we'll be next to you as you become the leader," Kaius teases.

"But leader to what?" Lorcan asks. "Your father's broken army, defeated and gone? Or the Night Emperor's Empire, our enemy, our captors, our..."

"Salvation." Nick whispers. The two look at him, shocked. "Don't look at me like that!" He snaps. "This is the reality that we're in! As you so kindly pointed out, there is no rebel army, no way home. We have people who are in chains. It's our job to do the best we can to help them. Whether we want to or not, we represent our people here. We have to deal with the cards that have been dealt. I don't want to start another rebellion! I don't want more innocent people to die."

He lays down and gives a mirthless laugh. "Funny how everyone in the rebellion thought about what to do when they won, but no one asked about the consequences if we *failed*."

Nick's words are brutal and to the point. There's no going back to the life they had right now. If the teachers so much as smell a rebellious plot, they are all as good as dead.

It's Kaius who speaks first, though the boy looks nervous as he tugs on his sleeves harder. "Nicky... You're right, some people didn't think about the actions and consequences of what happens when we lose. But you have to remember that sometimes people will go in too deep, and forget their main objective. Right now, they're teaching us Shadow magic. We're dealing with some very dark stuff, stuff that I know your mother wouldn't be pleased about. What will you do to make sure that you don't lose your way in the darkness?"

Nick thinks about his friend's question. His father had a goal, but what first started out as a peaceful protest turned into a full-out war. Nick could plan and plan all he wanted, but what if someone broke apart his plan piece by piece. What if he loses his way?

He doesn't want to be like his father, focused on his goals and alienating everyone. Markus didn't even realize the consequences of his actions until it was too late. Nick closes his eyes, feeling the scar on his left wrist. The cut that he got when his mother pushed him out of the way to save his life. *A scar of life.*

Remember, Neacel, holding onto hate and anger will drain you. It's best to forgive your enemies and move on. The best revenge is living your best life. Never let darkness consume you. His mother's words enter his mind.

"Remember, the hearts of men can be filled with darkness," Kaius warns.

And desperately wicked, Nick wants to add. He touches his scar.

"I won't forget my way."

I need to talk to Braawen, he's the only family I have left.

However, he doesn't even see his cousin for the rest of the day. Since Braawen is in Purple and Nick is in Yellow, they're on opposite spectrums. It will be rare for them to see each other now.

The rest of the day is focused on more exercising and meditation. Nick finds meditation difficult, as there are too many things on his mind. He slowly opens his eyes to see Rohana's frustrated expression, and Bhaltair is asleep. Only Takara is meditating as the rest struggle.

He wonders how Bhaltair isn't snoring, until something hard hits his head. He groans as he sees a piece of chalk on his lap and the General glares at him once he looks up. "Guts, clear your mind. Bull, wake up!" Bhaltair jumps and comments on how he wasn't sleeping. "Ice, we are meditating, not taking a shit. Only Nightshade seems to know how to meditate."

"Not anymore," Takara whispers.

"Nightshade! You shouldn't get distracted so easily!" The General glares at her. She groans and takes a deep breath, trying to slip back into a meditative state.

Chapter 9
Voices

Darkness falls upon the world as many students drift into sleep. Nick is not one of those people. After he's sure that everyone is out cold, he grabs his Black uniform and slips out the door. Under the lights of the cellar washroom, he feels as though he's changing identities. Yellow to Black, from the weakest to the most powerful. Just looking at his reflection makes him feel different, more confident and dare he say, special. Even the cracked mirror and damp floor of the washroom can't diminish how he feels. A chuckle escapes his lips, but he quickly smothers it. He gives himself one more glance, then turns off the lights.

The fierce winds greet him as the cellar door almost slams shut on his hand. The poor boy has to struggle against the god of Air's wrathful breath to open the door. He finally opens one door and sees a wall of white, sharp winds cutting his cheeks. He slowly closes the door behind him, and grabs the walls to help him make his way to the gate.

It's truly based on the deities' good graces that he stumbles upon the silver gates. He opens the gates, thankful that the building, as well as the trees, provide shelter from the winds. It's when he makes it to the lake that the winds are at full force. He realizes that he's going the wrong way when he steps on the lake by slipping on ice. He walks away from the lake, grateful that the ice is too thick to break. Not seeing anything, he closes his eyes and inhales deeply. He can smell the rich pine from the forest and begins to walk in that direction. As the scent gets stronger, he opens his eyes, but the heavy snow makes it impossible to even see the path to the trees.

Where's the bloody path? Nick asks himself. The snow falls harder, and his eyes can't see much. He puts out his hand and feels the trees. He hears a whisper in the wind and turns around, trying to find the source of the sound.

"Hello?" He calls out. He gets no reply and stops for a moment to wrap his cape tightly around his body. *Where do I go?*

L—left... A soft voice whispers in his mind.

He blinks, thinking that he's hearing things, but the unfamiliar voice repeats it again.

Left... The voice is much clearer this time and he turns around, but sees nothing and no one.

"I had a stressful day, that's why I'm hearing voices," he chuckles to himself, shaking his head. However, he hears the voices again, this time louder.

Left! A cacophony of voices scream, causing him to jump and run left.

As he runs to his left, the voices scream for him to go in different directions. Too afraid to disobey, he does what the voices say and miraculously, doesn't hit a single tree. This worries him as he goes deeper into the forest. The voices finally quiet down and he stops, waiting for the next set of directions. He looks around and sees that most of the wind is blocked by the branches and he's finally able to see the path. Shocked and even more concerned, he whispers a thank you before continuing on the path.

Even with the trees shielding him, the winds are cold and harsh. He follows the path until he sees a little light, almost beckoning to him. He gasps in relief as he comes closer to see a little cottage on a hill. He runs towards the light, kicking snow everywhere, even falling twice over snow-covered roots, at the thought of reaching somewhere warm. As the cottage draws near, he slows down and smiles. It reminds Nick a little of home.

Home. I haven't had a home in a long time, he sadly thinks as he makes his way up the front step. The door reminds him of his house, or what he can remember from it. The door light hanging above him guides his hands to the black, dragon-shaped door knocker. Without the light, he would have missed the knocker as both knocker and door are black. He hesitates to touch the black dragon biting down on the ring; the dragon almost looks threatening, but he will not be stopped by an inanimate object. He knocks on the door with the knocker. The sound coming from the knocker startles him, as its deep echo even causes the winds to fall silent.

"What the -..."

"Come in," says a muffled reply.

He grabs onto the door handle and pokes his head in, feeling the heat assault his face. The cottage is brightly lit from multiple candles on poles and a roaring fireplace in the back. The smell of maple wood and tea causes him to leave all his anxieties behind him as the inviting atmosphere puts a small smile on his face. He slowly steps into the cottage and closes the door, wondering if he should take off his shoes.

"Keep the shoes on and come in." Nick looks to where the voice is coming from and sees Volodimir sitting on an armchair next to the fire sipping from a teacup. "Come sit." The man kindly motions to the seat across from him.

Nick knocks the snow off his boots and takes in his surroundings. The space is so different from the steel greys and dark stones of the school. The wooden walls and various patterned rugs on the floor give this space a splash of colour. He wonders if the maple scent could be coming from the walls. He takes the seat across from Volodimir. Volodimir offers him tea which he gratefully takes. It smells like the chamomile flowers from his aunt's garden.

"I bet you're wondering why I want to train you." Volodimir's voice is calm as the man's eyes leave his cup.

Nick nods. "Yes sir. I—I have a-another question." He fails to keep the tremble out of his voice, but succeeds in not shaking the cup.

"Go for it." Volodimir gives a smile.

Nick puts the teacup down on the small table between them. He rubs his hands on his legs and bites his lips, hesitating to speak, but Volodimir is awfully patient. "Did you kill those guards on the first night we met?"

Volodimir just keeps smiling. "What makes you think that?" He looks at the boy as though he just asked a mundane question.

"Just a feeling, and you and I were the only ones out that night, right?" He asks, unsure now that he thinks about it.

Volodimir puts his cup down on the little table and sits straighter. "Nico, I will bring you no harm, as long as you do as I say. Yes, I did kill those guards. They failed in the simple task of guarding the gate. I even told them to lock it. So, imagine my surprise when you told me it was unlocked."

Nick hears a laugh travel around the room, sinister and foreboding, completely different from cheerful ones he hasn't heard in so long. Nick looks around the room to see the man's smile widen, and he wonders where his voice is coming from; certainly not just from his mouth.

"I reward those who do well and punish those who do not." Nick can see that the man's eyes are evaluating him. "I'm happy to see you in the Black. It looks like it was made for you. I have no doubt that General Herald will whip you into shape." Nick can feel a tingle again, except this time, he can feel pressure on his skin, running along his scars.

Is it my imagination or is the room getting darker? He looks around to see that the room is indeed getting darker. Many of the candles flicker out, and even the fireplace looks like it's giving its last breath before the fire goes out. The only candle left is the small candle on the little table. Nick gulps and steadies his breaths. He looks at Volodimir whose eyes are piercing him, unmoving. *Is the man even breathing?*

Volodimir gets up, causing him to jump and almost knock his cup off the small table. The man is quick as he grabs Nick's wrist, looking into his eyes. Nick can feel something going into his wrist, slowly making its way to his chest. The loud sounds of chains penetrate his ears from nowhere. Breathing becomes harder until it stops altogether as the man inches closer to his face. The last thing Nick sees before the last flame go out are Volodimir's red eyes.

They're in complete darkness and silence. No one moves or makes a sound, not even his own heartbeat can be heard.

"Oh, what anger I see..." Nick hears Volodimir whisper, breaking the silence.

His father and Braawen's faces come into his mind.

"No... no," Nick stammers. *Remember Neacel, no hating.* His mother tsks him. "I-."

"Lies," Volodimir hisses in the dark. "I can see it. Hear it with each beat of your heart. Your heart carries a lot of darkness, hate and anger. Let it out," Volodimir commands.

Something is trying to get in. Something that Nick knows shouldn't be in him. He wants to move, to fight and push back, but... the presence no longer feels invasive. It's almost as though something inside him is trying to reach out too. Like a door, a door with chains slowly breaking. Chains cracking.

Let us out, he hears multiple voices cry in his head. *We want to be a part of you. Please acknowledge us.*

Nick finally finds his strength. "

No!" he grits out, yanking his hand out of Volodimir's grasp, causing the whole room to light up again.

Sweat drips as he struggles to breathe. He grips his wrist where Volodimir held him, still feeling the lingering touch. "What, was that?" He tries not to scream. Despite his reaction, the man still crouched down in front of him has the audacity to have a neutral expression. When he sees that Volodimir isn't going to respond to him he continues. "I felt like something was crawling into me. Like...Like something was trying to get into my chest."

The voices, those voices are the ones I heard, he thinks back to the walk in the woods.

Volodimir looks him over and stands up silently.

"And-And what were those voices?! Why do they keep coming back?" Nick cries.

His teacher blinks, surprised, then a smile slowly curls on his lips. Volodimir makes it back to his seat and crosses his legs. "Nico, you said you hear voices, correct?" Nick nods, wide-eyed and sweating, as the man in front of him looks excited. "This is a good sign. Not many people can hear the voices of the shadows. Some people take years to hear even a whisper. What did they say to you?" The man is all too eager to know.

Nick looks down and closes his eyes. "L-let us out. We want to be... a part of you." He breathes out. "Then they asked me... to acknowledge them." He looks back up to see a wide smile on the Volodimir's face and a gleam in his eyes.

"No need to look afraid, Nico. The shadows don't want to harm you. As they said, they wish to be a part of you. The shadows aren't evil. You have a shadow. I have a shadow." Volodimir picks up the teacup. "This has a shadow." He places it down.

Nick shakes his head. "But it didn't feel right," he whispers. *It felt like something was getting into me. Or was something trying to get out?*

His teacher tilts his head. "Why are you afraid of your own shadow? It's your darkness." Voloimir gives a small chuckle. "I believe that it didn't feel right because you aren't used to having your darker thoughts and feelings surface," his teacher states nonchalantly. "You need to acknowledge that darkness. Once you get past that, many other emotions can flow through, emotions that will help you grow and develop, not just in the shadows, but as a person."

Volodimir can see the critical expression on the boy's face.

"I'm not judging you, Nico. I am just stating the facts. You have a lot to be angry about. Your life has been thrown upside down, and I believe that you may be the last of your family line." Volodimir comes close to him again and kneels in front of him, grabbing his hand gently.

"I didn't mean to scare you. I just needed to test how well your heart could adapt to Shadow Magic." He grips Nick's hand a little harder. "I see great potential in you, Nico, and I would like to help you reach that potential."

Nick looks back at his hand and sees the scar on his wrist. A mere whisper escapes his lips. "Why?"

Volodimir stands up. "Because," he looks at the fireplace which slowly burns brightly again, "when I see potential, I want to make sure that it grows." He turns to him. "So." There is excitement intertwined in his commanding voice. "Do you want to reach your potential? Prove to yourself that you can beat everyone's expectations? Or do you wish to stay as you are?"

Nick looks down at his cup and bites his lips. *I'm going to be their leader!* He remembers the day he said that to Kaius. However, now that he's here, he doesn't know. He can hear the voices in his head, but they aren't the shadows.

You, a leader? The voices of the other children in the rebellion group cry at him. He can remember all the insults and degrading words used to describe him.

Disappointment.

Fish bones, skeleton!

Even the teachers thought that he was a waste of space.

It should have been you. Not your mother. His father's voice runs cold in him. He can no longer feel the numbness, no, this is another feeling. A deep, jaw-clenching feeling; he wants it out, he wants to let it loose.

Nick can feel the anger boiling in him, but he takes a deep breath, then another. The calming techniques that he remembers his mother used isn't working, it's still there, not cold but hot, fiery hot.

You have the potential. Why not take it? Nick shakes slightly. It's the shadows. He knows it is. Funny how the shadows seem to be encouraging him, not his family. Well, there is one friend who believes in him.

Kai, he thinks. *What if something happens to him?* He also remembers Lorcan and the rest of his classmates. They all had lives before his father started this rebellion. He's hit by a wave of guilt. He shakes away his thoughts and replaces them with new ones. *I don't have many friends or family members left. I won't let them suffer. I will be able to protect the people I love.*

He looks his teacher in the eye. "I want to reach my potential... and more. I don't want to be in Yellow or Purple."

Volodimir gives a sly smile. "Oh? So, what colour *will* you achieve?"

"Black," Nick states. His voice does not waver. It's solid, strong, and there is no doubt in his mind that if he wants to survive, he needs to be on top.

Volodimir flashes him another wicked smile. "Then let's get started."

Chapter 10
Special

"Astor," Professor Arran calls out to the boy. The boy's breathing slows down slightly, with only a candle on the small stool in front of him to illuminate his breaths. They are in Arran's private office, late into the night; the only way to guarantee that no one could distract his students during private lessons.

Yet, as Arran circles around the boy, he wonders if tonight is just a waste of time. The more he looks at Astor, the tighter Arran clenches the ruler in his hand. The boy hasn't improved in the shadows, and he begrudgingly admits that Volodimir was right. He did tell the last Black Teacher, Alesander, that Astor had potential. However, after a year of working with the boy, he hadn't improved at all.

Arran sighs dramatically and shakes his head as he stops in front of the boy. He tilts the boy's chin up to get a better look at him. He hears his haggard breaths as blood and snot drip from the student's nose. Both of the boy's eyes are closed, though one is swollen and can't open.

"Fail," Arran spits as he strikes Astor's cheeks with the ruler.

A new bruise begins to form on Astor's cheeks, but he's too busy spitting out blood to feel the pain.

"I—I'm sorry," Astor barely breathes out, his head drooping.

Arran quickly grabs the boy's chin and tilts it back up. Arran can see the boy's grey eye widen, and tears fall further down his cheeks. It only makes him scowl more.

"Pathetic. I've given you every chance. I have given you my time, my energy, and *this* is how you repay me?"

Astor's lip quivers in response.

Arran gives him another slap, disgust written on this face. "You have one more chance, Astor." He can see the boy's eyes look up at him. "Feel that pain, build on it. Get angry and reach out to the damn shadows!"

Astor tries to reach into the pain, but the pain blinds him. He tries to curl his fingers on the armrest, but he can't. A sharp pain reminds him that his professor broke his fingers. He opens one of his eyes. Gods know it hurts too much to open the other. He can barely see or hear his professor's rant when his vision turns blurry. With a split lip and blood coming from his mouth, he whispers, "No more."

Astor doesn't care if his professor can't hear him. He doesn't care if his peers will look down at him. He'd rather be in Blue again with Professor Jacques. Jacques didn't beat him, didn't make him feel like he was nothing.

Help, Astor calls to anyone. He doesn't know why he's not hearing the professor. He wonders if this is what happened to Chloe. She was a year above him but left the school for medical reasons.

Maybe I should warn the new kids? he thinks.

No, he doesn't believe they'll listen to him.

When he tries to move his fingers, he feels nothing. Then he notices that the pain in his eye is gone too. *Weird? It doesn't hurt anymore.* Those are Astor's last thoughts as he slips into the darkness.

Arran sees Astor pass out. He rolls his eyes and walks over to his desk, forcing two dark red vials down his student's throat. The boy gasps and breathes deeply as the healing vials take effect. Arran can't heal everything tonight, but he'll keep Astor out of class until he's fully healed. Arran knows the lemon balms will work faster than the vials, but they are too costly. The vials couldn't heal broken bones fast enough, while the lemon balms could heal in minutes.

"Astor," he waits until the boy can look up at him. "You are to stay in your room for three days. Continue to take the vials. Use the lemon balm if needed. When you are healthy enough, I will allow you to enter class."

The boy looks at his feet and nods.

"Good. This will be our last night, Astor. I will not be your private teacher anymore."

Astor isn't even disappointed, just relieved. *I don't want to be a shadow wielder anymore,* he cries inwardly.

Four days later, Astor DeCorteau leaves the school.

Chapter 11
Wake up

It is only the third day of school when Nick realizes that the school of his imagination will never match up with the school of his reality. Reality is painful... but not as painful as the General's fist waking him up.

Today is the day that the General announces the Training Hall is finally up to his standards. They walk together down the familiar path to the lake, only this time, they go to the east side of the school. The building is separate from the school and one must follow a swept, paved path that leads to the formidable structure. The large rectangular building sits by itself on another hill covered by the trees of the forest. The light grey stones are a stark contrast from the dark greens and browns of the trees. When the Yellow class approaches the entrance, they are greeted by two large steel doors, with bushes and two large windows on either side. The General takes a set of keys from his pocket and chooses a larger grey key that opens what sounds like a set of locks, which shake the doors. As they open, the shaking stops with a click from the top handle.

He turns to them with a grin. "Don't worry, children. This is just to make sure that no one sneaks in here. We don't want any accidents."

He pushes open the doors and motions for them to enter. The first thing Nick notices is three large rays of light that stretch across the vast gymnasium and the gleaming wooden floors. He looks to where the sun rays are coming from and sees three large windows overlooking a small balcony. Looking below the windows, he sees weapons gleaming in the light and a peculiar-looking red door covered in chains hiding in the shadows. He looks around the gymnasium, seeing a large raised platform at the centre surrounded by mats and smaller rings. They remind Nick of the makeshifts sparring rings that the rebels would fight in.

Bhaltair steps in further, stopping at the sounds of the creaking floor. The girls move over more to the walls.

"I wonder why the wall here is made out of wood?" Takara asks.

Rohana looks at the stone wall across from them inlaid with wood. "Design? I'm not sure."

Suddenly, bright lights flood the room. They all quickly cover their eyes as the General chuckles. Nick opens his eyes, slowly adjusting to the artificial light. He didn't even notice that the General made his way over to the light switch; he didn't hear his teacher move.

"This will be where you'll study the majority of your time. Like I said yesterday, your body needs to be fit to hold magic. As you can see, there is equipment all along the walls." The General points to a wall that has all sorts of weapons hanging on it: weapons for short, mid and long-range combat. He even sees a weapon that he's been dying to try. They all walk towards the weapon racks, excitedly talking to each other.

The General walks over to the centre of the room, then loudly clears his throat to get their attention. "The raised platform here is big enough to hold four people. The mats around it are what you'll mostly train on for hand-to-hand combat."

They continue their walk past the mats and sparring rings to get to the other end of the vast building. Along the wall were dark wooden blocks and platforms of varying sizes.

The General points to them and smiles. "These are shadow platforms. We use these to build courses. The training course is not only for running, but dodging and using the shadows to help you get to your destination. However, that will be more advanced training. With my shadows, I can move platforms around the room to create a course that you will all have to run."

"Will it be high up?" Takara asks.

The General sharply turns his head. "Nightshade, you shall use manners! Raise your hand and then address me as 'sir'."

She raises her hand. "Sir?" she almost whispers.

Their teacher smiles. "Yes, Nightshade."

"Will it be high up? I'm afraid of heights," she mumbles, but the General and the rest of the group can hear it all too clearly in the empty room.

Nick can hear the disappointed grunt from the man. "Well, that's something that we will work on. This is also a warning to all of you." He looks at the four of them. "Do not let anyone, besides me, know your weaknesses. Children here will do anything to know your weakness."

They all look at Takara, who nods her head.

Nick raises his hand. "Excuse me, sir?"

"What is it, Guts?"

He inwardly sighs; he hates his nickname. "Why is there a door with chains on it? The one under the balcony."

The General looks over, then smiles back at him. "Good eyes. That door is locked because that is where we keep the shadow weapons. We'll learn more on those later; they are mostly used for Red and above. Under my supervision, you can use regular weapons. However, you all look like you would fall over if my great-grandmother swatted you with her purse." He shakes his head. "And she's 103, turning 104 next week."

"Congratulations, Sir." Bhaltair smiles. "She's so old and yet still strong?"

The General just lifts an eyebrow. "Yeah, she's not going anytime soon." He waves them over. "They always say the good die young. No wonder she's still alive," he mutters.

Throughout the week, they all tour the school, with the General telling them various facts about the school and its resources. They have plenty of resources. They are informed of the various caravans that come once a week to sell different products. There is a small general store with a baker in the school, hair salons, and different merchants from the Empire. Even a priest is available if you wish to worship any of the deities. You could have full advantage of all the facilities of the school... if you had the coins. Which none of them do. Only a priest from the School Temple is free. The school allowed anyone to worship and connect to any of the deities. Yet, Nick knows for a fact, that no one from Availa would want to speak to the priest, or the deities. Why would they? The deities didn't listen to their prayers.

On their first day of their week touring the school, they start outside in the front, facing the clock tower.

"Now, class," the General begins, "I'm sure you all can see that this is the entrance, but the place I would like to start is the clock tower, also known as the Black Tower."

They all look at the towering building and see the arched window below the large clock.

"Any guess as to why it's called the Black Tower?" The General asks.

"Besides the brick being black, I don't know." Nick couldn't stop his mouth. Even the other children snap their heads around to look at him, shocked. He wants to apologize but receives an icy glare from the General. "I—I mean... I don't know, sir." He quickly stammers.

The General nods. "Each floor of the school has rooms that belong to each circle. The cellar is Yellow, the main floor is Orange, the second and third floors are Red and Blue." The General walks closer to Nick and he can feel the large form of the General overtake his small one. Even Bhaltair, who was behind him, steps back away from him.

"Purple, is the fourth floor. The fifth holds the shadow rooms. But the clock tower," the General whispers. "The tower belongs to Black. So, until there is a Black student, the tower remains empty." He glares at Nick. "Does that answer your question?"

Everyone is silent around him. He nods and gulps, swearing to himself that he would bite his tongue off if it ever got him into trouble again.

"Good." The General snaps. "Then let us continue."

As they walk around with their yellow uniforms, the majority of the students they pass either ignore or glare at them. Nick watches Takara edge closer to Bhaltair while Bhaltair nervously plays with his fingers. Rohana stays behind everyone, keeping her head down to hide her scar as much as possible. Nick and Bhaltair were once pushed down a flight of stairs when they were alone. He sees how the children act when the General is around them, they may get a few scathing glances, but they refuse to attack them with the General around. So, Nick stays behind the General.

By the end of the tour, each of them had a favourite place.

Bhaltair's favourite spot is the greenhouse. There are three, but he seems to have taken a special liking to Greenhouse Two, also known as the food house as most of the plants and flowers housed inside are edible. The buildings are made out of iron and glass that have a slightly green tint to their archway structure. When they enter into the large green house in the back of the school, Bhaltair begins to look over as many plants as possible, even pointing out which ones could be used as ingredients in meals.

"See these yellow petals?" Bhaltair points to a smaller bundle of flowers. "If you pick off the petals and wash them, they'll taste sweet. Letting them dry and finely crushing them will create a sugary powder."

Nick looks at the petal and watches as Bhaltair takes a water canister next to the flowers and dips it in the water. Bhaltair puts one in his mouth, then smiles and hands one to him. Nick doesn't like to put random things in his mouth, but he puts the petal on his tongue, surprised by the rich sweetness that comes from it. He's a little disappointed that the petal is so small.

"Where did you learn this?" Nick asks, reaching for another petal.

"My father taught me. He used to add them to Lord Jameson's cakes because the man had a sweet tooth, and Princess Estelle's teas. She loved tea. I heard she could get anyone to like tea." Bhaltair looks around before leaning closer to Nick. "Even the Night Emperor," he whispers.

"Really?" Nick asks as he sucks on his third petal.

Bhaltair shrugs. "Maybe."

"Guts, stop eating the flowers!" The General's voice rings out, getting the two boys to join their little group again.

Takara loves the dance studio located in the school's basement, not far from the Yellow quarters. The way there is much cleaner and well-maintained compared to their entryway. She walks in first and gazes in awe at the chandeliers and mirrors all around the room. The floor isn't the hard cement that they had to walk on every morning, but wood that has a little bounce to it.

She raises her hands and the General nods at her. "Sir, can I come here anytime?" There's hope in those dark brown eyes, something that none of them have seen in her.

He nods and receives a happy squeal from the girl. "But, you have to be here with an instructor. I'm sure that Mr. Apolus will be happy to help."

She stops and straightens herself up. "Thank you, sir."

Rohana slowly enters. Upon seeing her face, she quickly leaves without a word. That day, she asks for a yellow scarf to hide the lower half of her face.

"Remember what I said about weaknesses," the General warns her when he gives it to her.

She nods, wrapping it up to her nose.

Rohana's favourite place is an open courtyard. They enter one of the smaller courtyards full of snow at the moment, but that doesn't bother her. In the centre is a fountain that she believes would look beautiful in the spring. Yet, the ice that surrounds the fountain gives it a cold beauty that shimmers with the light of the sun. As they walk around, Rohana takes a seat on one of the benches under the archways to sit and watch the snow. She claims that as her spot.

Nick favours the library. As soon as the double doors open, he gasps at the tall windows stretching up to the high ceilings. The room towers with books and surrounding a crackling fireplace are tall and inviting chairs. Before he could wander off, he is dragged by the General to face the head Librarian, Ms. Joy Bell, who allows all of them to come during opening hours.

The library may be his favourite place in the school, but his favourite place on the school grounds becomes the cottage in the forest.

Chapter 12
Teacher

At first, Nick is nervous watching the moon rise high in the sky. He's at the entrance of the forest, looking ahead at the winding path. He bites his lips as he looks behind him to the clock tower of the school. It's almost two hours to midnight. He only has five minutes to get to the cottage.

Come on Nick, it's just your real first lesson. Nothing to be nervous about. He nods and runs into the forest, towards his new teacher.

He knocks on the door to the cottage and hears a voice telling him to come in. Once the door is open, he notices that the layout and atmosphere seem different. There are no carpets, just polished wood. The candles are in different corners. The scent of tea is still in the air, however, the new herbal tea on the small table seems stronger than last time. Sitting at the table, wearing an all-black suit with a purple flower on his chest, is his teacher. The man motions for Nick to take a seat in front of him.

"Thank you, sir." He takes off his cloak and hangs it on his chair. He straightens his jacket and sits, his heart beating fast. Volodimir passes him a cup and a few cookies. "No thank you, I'm stuffed."

Volodimir's eyes narrow and Nick quickly changes his mind. He quickly puts a cookie in his mouth and takes a sip of tea. He chokes and hears a small chuckle from his teacher. "What kind of tea is this?" He gulps it down as he swallows down the rest of the cookie.

"Turmeric." Volodimir sips his cup.

"Oh." Nick looks at the orange tea.

"Not into it, are you?" He looks up to see that Volodimir doesn't look offended. He shakes his head. "Well it's good for you, so drink one cup, at least." He smiles.

Nick just nods and sips. The cookie doesn't take away the taste.

"I recently got into tea when it became popular in court. Hopefully one day, I'll find one you enjoy. But we're not here to talk about tea." Volodimir finishes his cup and places it onto the table. He rests his hands over his crossed legs as he stares intently at Nick.

Realizing that they are about to begin, Nick puts down his tea and sits up.

"Now, Nico, I am a very busy man. I also will not lie to you, and therefore, I expect you not to lie to me. I detest **liars**." He spits the last word out with venom.

Nick nods, realizing that it wasn't an option.

"I am also not an easy teacher; I expect over 100 percent from you as you will expect that from me. If I see you slacking or not trying even once, this is over." Volodimir's warnings circle around the room.

He gulps. "Yes, sir."

"No need to call me sir. I have enough people here calling me that. Now, as for your training. I need to know what the General plans to do with you. Don't ask how I know, as a teacher here, everyone knows that man is the Head of Yellow."

With that question out of the way, Nick realizes that Volodimir is a teacher at this school. "He wants to focus on training our bodies."

Volodimir nods. "The General will be good at that. I can start you off with mediation for the first two weeks or more. When you have a bit more muscle, we will move to fighting and weapons. Shadow training will have to be the last. Hopefully, we can do that before the start of the third month."

Nick hides his displeasure by looking down at his hand.

"What's wrong, Nico?" His teacher's voice brings him to look at him again.

"I was just hoping that I could learn Shadow magic, faster?" he asks innocently. "I mean... The General only focuses on warm-ups and hand-to-hand combat. But we came to this school to learn Shadow magic, which I really would like to learn." He doesn't even notice his voice rising, but his teacher does.

Volodimir stares at him, his eyes slightly narrowed. "Do you believe he's wrong?"

Nick blinks, taken aback from such a question. "No... I just think that spending a whole month on exercises would only leave us two months to practice magic, if we're lucky." He gulps. "Are the exercises really that important?"

With a flick of Volodimir's finger, his chair rises with him in it and is shoved hard against the wall, knocking the breath out of him. As his eyes begin to adjust to the dark, he sees Volodimir get up and walks towards him. The closer Volodimir walks towards him, the more he's pushed deeper into his chair, almost as though something is grabbing him, forcing him back. He can feel every scar on his back rubbing against his clothes. Volodimir stops just five steps away from him; he can barely breathe.

When his teacher finally drops his hand, and the room is flooded with light, Nick gasps and grips the chair as he slides down.

"You want to learn Shadow magic?" Red eyes glare at him and all Nick can do is focus on his breathing. "You can't even breathe properly." Volodimir returns to his seat, and with a motion of his finger, Nick's chair flies back in place.

Nick tries to sit up straight again, his body trembling.

The man sighs, more tired than annoyed. "I'm not trying to scare you, Nico. However, your body is in a poor state. That is why the General wishes to focus on the body. Your body stores all your magic; it's a vessel. Right now, your vessel has cracks, holes, and honestly, if I'm being frank, I'm surprised it's holding together."

There's a sharp pain in Nick's chest. He doesn't know why, it's something that he's heard before. Weak body and all the other creative insults the men and women hurl at him. "I know that," he mumbles.

"Then don't question your teachers. Even the great Night Emperor listened to his teachers. Every single teacher here had to go through the process you're going through now. So, heed our advice," Volodimir commands.

"Yes, sir." His head drops down.

Volodimir takes a deep breath and gives Nick a small smile. "I know you're eager to learn, but I also need you to trust me and the other teachers here. No one wants you to stay in Yellow. It will look like a failure of the school and of the General's, and even of mine."

He snaps his head up at that.

"You're also my student now, and I'm going to make sure that you excel in your training. We will meet three times a week. Do not fear, you will have your day of rest. I need rest too. However, we will meet the first, third, and fifth night, two hours before midnight."

"Three nights are more than enough." Nick can't help but smile at the extra lessons.

His teacher nods in agreement. "Now, we will have to work on your meditation. Your mind is as big an asset as it is a weakness. This is also not something to be rushed, but there are still some exercises we can do even now. Come, follow me and bring your cloak."

Nick follows him outside, biting his tongue to keep from asking questions.

They walk through the forest, with only the moon and stars as their witnesses. Nick doesn't mind the walk in the snow; the smells of the forest relaxes his nerves. The oak and maple tickle his senses, reminding him of home. They venture deep into the forest and farther from the school, until they stop at a snow-covered hill. Nick stands silently as Volodimir holds a long wooden pole with a white flag in his hand. Nick would ask about the pole, but he's pretty sure that his answer will come soon. As Volodimir walks up the hill, Nick looks around and sees that it's just them. *It is a very large area for a school, even larger to hide a small body.* He shivers at the thought.

The sound that pierces the still of the night and his thoughts, is the stab of the white flag on top of the hill. His teacher grins as he walks back to him.

"Nico," Volodimir's voice gets his attention. "We are going to play a game tonight."

"A game?"

Hide my body?

"Yes. I know it's cold, but this will hopefully keep you warm as well. Tonight, I want to know your skills on hiding in the shadows. I have no doubt that they're good because you managed to sneak in last time. However, there is one clear difference, the guards aren't going to catch you. I am." Volodimir gives a cunning smile.

Nick nods. *Another test,* he thinks. "Alright, what are the rules?" His body trembles from both the cold and excitement.

Volodimir gestures towards the pole. "All you have to do is grab that flag. I won't use any shadow powers. I will also be hiding in the shadows."

"Is there a time limit?"

His teacher taps his chin as though he's deep in thought. He bends down and pulls out a black hourglass from his shadow. Nick tries hard to not gasp. The hourglass is bigger than the ones he used to play with as a child. Volodimir holds it with two hands, each gripping handles shaped like the body of a black serpent. The only colour that the snakes possess are ruby eyes staring back at Nick. The glass holds red sand on the bottom that shimmers in the moonlight.

"You have ten minutes. When I say go, you go." Nick nods. They wait for a minute and Nick can hear his chest pumping.

"I suggest hiding first." Volodimir's smile becomes even wicker. "Go!" He turns the hourglass as Nick runs behind a tree.

Nick moves from the tree to the bushes, eating snow to hide his breath. He looks out from under the leaves and sees that Volodimir is gone. Undoing his cloak to leave a decoy, he crawls on his belly listening for any sound that might tell him where his teacher is. He quickly moves to the next tree and climbs up, getting a better view.

He stays in the shadows and slows his heartbeats, refusing to make himself known to Volodimir. He recalls how most of the trees look surrounding the area. *The trees here can hold my weight, even the smaller ones up top, but they can't hold Volodimir.*

The dense trees are his saving grace as minutes pass; each step he takes reminds him of the lessons that his Uncle Tys would tell him. *If you go up, Nicky, make sure that the branches don't leave any trails.*

He hears a crack to his right, too close for comfort. He can also see movement in the branches that doesn't match the rest of the wind-blown branches at the other end.

Time, boy, time! He can hear the shadows, but he ignores them.

He's there, his own inner thoughts yell out to him. He leaps down and grabs another branch to soften the blow. He flips to the ground closer to the flag and he can see Volodimir jump out from where he saw the branches move. The man doesn't have his usual grin. The quick glance that he receives tells him that this is a man who's on the hunt. As Nick nears the flag, his chest starts to burn, and his legs go numb.

Am I really that out of shape? he thinks to himself.

Before he could even reach towards the flag, large arms grab him, lifting him up by his chest. He fights, kicking in the air as he hears Volodimir's laughter in his ears.

"I win, you lose." Nick tires out quickly and Volodimir lets him down.

He just plops himself in the snow and sees his teacher looking down at him with a triumphant smile and a flag in his hand. *When did he get the flag?*

"Now, Nico, do you understand why working on your body is important?" Volodimir raises his eyebrows, looking down on Nick while he grins, but helps him up.

"I used to be able to do this for hours." Nick dusts the snow off and huffs.

My time on the ship really did a number on me.

"Can you walk?" Volodimir asks as the man hands him his cloak back.

Nick nods and puts on his cloak, feeling much warmer. He tries to steady his breathing, but as the cold air enters his lungs, he coughs. With his chest burning and legs aching, he begins to move. He doesn't want to stay here any longer than necessary.

As they walk, Volodimir takes slower steps to not tire out the boy. "You did well in hiding, but you forgot one thing."

"What?" The boy looks confused and cheeks red from the cold.

"The timer." Nick gasps. "I had to make a sound to get you to move, you were one minute past." Volodimir chuckles.

All Nick can do is groan, as his teacher pats him on the head.

"Let this be a lesson. You were so focused on me and the flag that you forgot the timer. Remember, Nico, don't be too focused on one aspect of your goal."

He nods as they make their way to the cottage and his teacher smiles.

"Good. Nico, I can't wait to see what you'll become."

Chapter 13
Classes

Nick is an opportunist, not optimistic, but even he is hoping for a good first day in classes. What kid wouldn't?

Their first official week is an interesting one. The first thing given to them is a class schedule. Nick is used to some schedules and time limits; that's how he was able to survive in the rebellion. However, their schedule is strict and the General won't have them skipping classes. Mornings consist of classes that focus on the shadows, after everyone breaks their fast. The first half of the morning is spent with the General building them up physically, and the other half in a classroom is still with the General to learn more about the Yellow circle.

Then comes mid-meal where the school gathers and eats. Bhaltair hates this time of day. He always looks longingly at the other tables' meals but is wise enough to not complain. He started to once, and the General shut him down with a slap that made it hard for him to chew.

In the afternoons, they learn different subjects, such as sciences, mathematics, the arts, and history. Since the Yellow class is so small, they are placed together with the Oranges, and because of the war children's lack of education, they are all put in the same classes.

Nick is excited by the prospect of a science class, but he can tell that his other classmates are less than ecstatic. The science room is large, with vast windows and desks. In the back is an area that is separated by glass, containing all the experiments and lab equipment. The children take a minute to look around the room, and Nick and Kaius wander over to the lab section.

"It's been so long," Kaius whispers. Nick stays on his right side and just pats his friend's back. "I can create so many things. Do you think they'll let me build anything?" he asks.

"Why don't we ask the teacher?"

They both go to the teacher, a broad-shouldered, red-haired man with eyes too purple to be natural. Kaius is too afraid to ask, so Nick does it.

The teacher laughs. "Not yet. We have to do a test on lab safety."

Kaius narrows his eyes. "But I know lab safety," he pleads. "I've been in a lab and even worked in a lab. My parents were inventors."

The teacher chuckles again. "I'm sure they were, but here you will have real equipment. Equinox house supports the sciences and arts as much as the shadows. Hopefully, you'll learn. But if you use anything to try to hurt or cripple the Empire...Well," he smirks. "One student going missing won't cause too many problems."

The threat is clear enough as both boys run back in their seats and wait for everyone else to return to theirs.

"Now students," the large man starts as he puts on orange gloves for his hands. "My name is Mr. Teslan. I will be your science teacher. My goal is to improve your thinking, not just test your knowledge." He grins. "I want to show you something fun first."

Mr. Teslan takes out a container and smiles as he lights it. Explosions lights up the room in colourful blazes and cracking sounds erupt throughout the classroom. The container shoots little fireworks of dazzling purples and greens. It would have been a beautiful demonstration of the beauty and fun of science, but despite Mr. Teslan's best intentions, the teacher overlooked something extremely important about his class.

A high-pitched shriek is heard above the fireworks and gets the class moving. The students scream at the display, and some look on in fear running as far back in the classroom as possible. Kaius and Nick dive under the table as soon as the first crackle sounds. Nick holds Kaius's head down as he covers his ears tightly.

The cries of the children alert one of the teachers next door. A woman in red runs in, calming down the students along with Mr. Teslan. The rest of their classes are postponed. Nick's first day of school became his shortest.

After that incident, the war children are placed on a watch list to ensure that there would be no self-harm. None of the students in the room recovered quickly and Mr. Teslan uses quieter experiments from then on. From what Nick is told by Bhaltair, the Black Teacher had a talk with their science teacher. It's not until the next day that he sees Kaius again, finding his friend in a side hallway, tucked in a corner on the stairs, hiding from the world.

"How are you doing?" Nick asks Kaius, but his friend doesn't respond. Nick taps him, and Kaius jumps. Both look startled, though Nick is the first to recover. "I said, how are you?" he raises his voice.

Kaius rubs his left ear. "I—I'm good, good, you?"

Nick nods his head. "Have you heard? Our class is the school news. Apparently, we 'overreacted.' I would go over the other things they said about us, but..." He takes a seat on the stone steps next to him.

Kaius just shakes his head, pulling his sleeves to cover his wrists, where a tattoo of a sun is placed. "They're just being idiots about it. I bet that none of them have ever had to deal with a bomb going off or buildings falling on them." Kaius looks to the windows. "I hope they have to join the army." The tone of his voice goes darker, his green eyes narrowing. "I hope they get a taste of battle and freeze. I want them to hear the sounds of bombs going off and people dying around them. Then I want to know if they can still sleep or if they can tell the difference between a firecracker and a bomb."

Nick just stares at his friend, shocked at such dark thoughts and words. This isn't the friend he knows.

"Don't think like that, Kai." Nick shakes his head. He doesn't want his always optimistic friend to go down that path. "I wouldn't want anyone to experience that."

His friend gives him a sharp look. "Well, there are some people that should experience it. That way, they'll learn." Nick just leaves it. There's a bitter taste in the air after that conversation.

The incident in the science labs makes it mandatory for the war children to speak to a councillor one on one once a week. For the Yellows, that person is the General himself. However, after the first talk, it becomes a blessing in disguise. Nick actually doesn't mind talking to him, as the General is a person who has experienced war firsthand. His teacher was able to also share his experience in war and that he and his wife adopted a few children as their own. Even with the General's talks, many students were still on edge. Nonetheless, there were other students that needed medication. Kaius and Bhaltair are a couple of them.

When Nick enters the cottage for his second lesson, he isn't expecting the rich aroma of tea and a blanket on his chair. As he sits, his teacher pours tea for himself and asks if Nick would like a hot chocolate. He hasn't had that beverage in ages and happily sips a cup as his teacher wraps the blanket around him. It leaves him a little on edge as to why his teacher is being so kind, but that little act of kindness leads to him being very cozy. If only he knew it was a trap. He isn't expecting Volodimir to also play a role as his councillor as well.

"I may not be the first person you wish to talk to about your reaction during Mr. Teslan's class."

Nick rolls his eyes. *Of course he heard about it.* Though he wished he didn't.

"No, I thought that belonged to the General, but he turned out to… actually understand war and its effects."

"Well," Volodimir's voice sounds so soft compared to the first lesson. "I am also available. I did my share of fighting in many wars. I even fought in the war with Availa. But I'll be here to listen and talk only if you wish."

Speak with him. He will listen. The voices of the shadows sound soft. The last time he ignored them, he was wrong.

Nick sinks deeper into his chair as Volodimir puts marshmallows on the small table, encouraging him to take a few. The tea that Volodimir drinks smells like flowers. Nick recalls the most beautiful flowers he'd seen were in a garden, flowers that he knows are long gone now, along with the smiling red-haired woman and the scent of strawberries.

"I remember that my favourite snacks before the war happened were strawberries."

He stops as he sees Volodimir's eyes go wide as his teacher looks at the tea pot. With no warning, his teacher picks up the tea pot and throws its contents into the fire, startling him.

"Wait one minute." Volodimir grabs his cup and dashes through a door behind him.

Nick just looks at the wet logs and the embers that still try to burn. *It's only been two official days of school and the whole school hates us even more.* He wraps the blanket tighter around himself as he pushes down the uncomfortable feeling inside him, closing himself off from the world.

Do not worry, the shadows reply. *You will look back on this day and see how far you've come.*

He just gives a rumble at the back of his throat that's supposed to be a chuckle. He closes his eyes and curls up in the chair. He lowers his head to his knees, thinking of his life before the war. He remembers his aunty, Braawen's mother, who had red hair and vibrant green eyes. She had a beautiful strawberry garden. He could almost smell the juicy fruit from his memories. He takes a whiff of the air, recognizing a familiar scent. He snaps his head up from the blanket to see Volodimir pouring a cup of tea from a new teapot and offers it to Nick.

Nick cautiously takes the cup that his teacher gives him and watches Volodimir place the new black teapot down on the table. His teacher takes a cup and looks at him, encouraging him to take a sip.

He looks at the cup with the red liquid and sniffs it. He knows it's bad table manners, but Volodimir doesn't seem to mind. He takes a sip and has to cover his mouth to muffle a sob. He doesn't know why he's reacting like this; the tea tastes like strawberries. However, even as he covers the muffles with his hands, his eyes begin to water.

"Nico." His teacher's voice is soft. "This is a safe place, you can cry. Now what happened to the strawberries?" he asks, taking a sip of tea.

Nick sniffles and surreptitiously wipes his nose on the black sleeve. "Oh, deities," he mumbles as he puts down the cup and takes off the jacket. He sits with his legs crossed on the chair, throwing the blanket over his legs as he takes another sip of the strawberry tea.

"Gone." Nick's voice is barely a whisper and he shakes his head, his eyes glazed over with tears. "Burnt down. The King raised the taxes again and Markus, in his anger yelled, 'Enough is enough', in the tax office. I was there in my mother's arms as she tried to calm him. But…" He sighs. "His words were heard in the office and outside. Other people started to agree with him, and one thing led to another. The day after, Markus led a protest in our village. None of us would have guessed that it would be the day that started a movement."

Nick takes another sip of tea. "Months later, Markus began gathering more people to his side; my 'parents' joined. People even came from other villages to 'hear the words of the people'." He just rolls his eyes.

"I remember the fear in my mother's eyes as she walked alongside my father during a protest. It was her idea for it to be peaceful. But things grew and later on, more and more cities were fighting rather than protesting. By the end of the year, it was an unorganized rebellion. The first year, many children were sent to fight, after a group of men and women raided one of the King's Wheat Houses that stored the grain that was to be sent to the capital. That's how I saw my first fight. We won that and many more."

Nick takes an even bigger gulp. "The victory was short-lived. Let's just say that the King had enough. After two years of fighting, he decided to hit Markus where it hurt. He attacked Markus's village, and unfortunately, I lived there. He burnt down my village, my home, and sent soldiers to kill the protesters. My aunt's house and gardens burnt with her in it. My mother…" He can feel a tear run down his cheek. "My mother died… protecting me."

Volodimir takes out a handkerchief from his chest pocket and hands it to Nick. "Any parent would want to protect their child," he hears Volodimir say.

Father didn't see it that way, Nick wants to say, but doesn't.

"After that, there was no turning back. The rebellion truly broke loose. At eleven, I lost my home, family and my childhood. I am luckier than most. I was eleven, turning twelve, but there were children that were younger than me. I should count my blessings and not complain."

"Don't do that!" He can hear Volodimir snap.

"Do what?" He rubs the rest of the snot from his nose.

"Don't diminish your suffering. It's good to acknowledge someone else's pain. However, your pain and experience are unique to you." Volodimir places his cup down. "You've been through a rebellion that turned into a war. You made it through all that, and you will make it through this." He walks over and gently kneels down, taking Nick's hand. "Whenever you want to talk, any night, we will talk."

That night turns out to be a good night for him. They continue having nights dedicated to talks or relaxation once a week. The cabin always feels warmer and comfier on those nights.

Chapter 14
Month

A month passes and Nick and his friends experience many different things in the Equinox House.

One night when Nick came back from an evening lesson, he saw Bhaltair staring blankly at the wall from his bed. He tapped his friend's shoulder and Bhaltair just turned to him and whispered, "I can't take the vial. I don't want to sleep."

Nick was tired from his night training, but nodded his head. "Want to go for a walk? It's nice outside. I-…" He pointed to the door. "I just came from one." Bhaltair nodded wearily. Nick could tell that Bhaltair wasn't alright; the boy didn't even notice that he was wearing his Black uniform. Nick quickly changed and waited as Bhaltair quietly put on his clothes.

The two went for a night walk. Bhaltair didn't say anything, and Nick was too tired to hold a conversation. Their comfortable silence was suddenly broken by a screaming student, and the yelling of *teems*.

Volodimir wasn't kidding when he said that children would hurt each other to move up a circle. Over the past month, there had been three cases so far.

During this first month, Nick was balancing his studies during the day and his training with Volodimir at night. Nick found out that despite some kind moments, Volodimir did not lie about being a harsh teacher. He pushed Nick to his breaking point more than once. The first week, Nick had to focus on his meditation, which Volodimir had stated was shit without hesitation. He still struggled with meditation but excelled in concealing himself in the shadows. He stopped ignoring the shadows and listened to what they had to say. His teacher helped him greatly with focusing on the shadows' voices, though he told him that he had a natural gift with them.

Sometimes they gave him advice to help with his training, which he shared with his classmates that also helped them improve. The shadows would always whine and say that their advice was meant for just him, but they stopped complaining when he told them he wanted all of his friends to succeed with him.

He can remember the first time he tried to help Rohana, who snapped at him. They were rock climbing one day and Rohana had fallen for the sixth time.

Help her, he could hear them say.

He could help her, but this was Rohana, the girl who still couldn't open up to them.

You know you can, they said to him.

He sighed and kindly gave her pointers. He received a middle finger in response. Her reward was that she fell for the seventh time.

She laid on the floor until he came into her line of vision, holding out his hand.

"When I first fell, I fell into sheep dung." He gave her a small smile.

Maybe it was a trick of the light, but he could have sworn that he saw a smile. She took his hand, and Takara had to run over and help him pull her up. Nick wasn't skin and bones, but his muscles were still lacking.

When they got Rohana off the floor, he could see her gaze at his arms. "Well, if what you say works. I can show you some exercises for the sticks you call arms." She gives him a nervous smile.

Takara laughed, realizing that the icy girl was trying to be nice. Nick gave Rohana a huge smile picking up on the attempt. Their moment was broken by Bhaltair's scream of pain from getting thrown out of the sparring circle by the General.

"Get up, Bull!" the General yelled at the student moaning on the floor. "My Elena is old and could still box the teeth out of you!"

The Yellow group have slowly become close friends. They have to be close when the whole school looks down on them. Even the teachers in the hallways would give them disappointed looks or sneers. The only teachers Nick sees who don't care are the General, Miss Leia, the head librarian, and Nurse Stewart. The nurse isn't a teacher, but with all the injuries that they received from the General's training, Nick was learning a thing or two from her on healing.

As for the students, there are a few people who still remain his friends. Nick is still close to Kaius and even Lorcan, but he spent most of his time with the Yellows. He still hasn't talked to his cousin, who was always with Purple students. He could never get close to Braawen, so he tried to find other methods to communicate with him. They all failed, so he focuses on his training and strengthening his body instead. The faster he gets stronger, the sooner he can help his uncle and people.

Throughout the dark days, there has been light. They were improving and it was starting to show. Nick's complaining about knee pains forced him to go to the nurse. The nurse told him that it was normal and a good thing, for he was going through a growth spurt. He was finally getting the nutrients he needed to grow. At the end of the month, Rohana got chalk and Takara pushed Nick on the wall where they measured his height; they did the same for Bhaltair, turning him to his side and measuring his stomach.

By the end of month, Nick had grown slightly taller and Bhaltair's stomach had gotten smaller.

Bhaltair's fat was melting off and his arms were getting muscular. Nick found out the hard way when he sparred with the boy and ended up with a broken nose. Takara beat them in long distance jogs and started jogging at night in the forest for 'fun'. Sometimes Nick would join her, but if he went too slow, she would go on ahead. She also is the best dancer in their class and Mr. Apolus had reluctantly commended her on her talents. Her dance skills are useful for fighting as well. Rohana is the fastest runner, which earned her a little prize in the form of a pudding. She began to open up more to them about her distaste for the Purple circle.

Nick didn't think that he was improving much until he noticed that he doesn't have to put his belt in the farthest hole, and he can no longer fit into any of the smaller places to hide. His friends agree that he has the fastest reaction time and is the best at dodging hits. It annoys General Herald when he spars with him, but Volodimir said to use that annoyance against his targets. Finally, General Herald managed to rile Nick enough for the boy to hit him. He was so happy that he landed a hit on the man and he would have screamed with joy if it weren't for the General using that opening to throw him straight out of the fighting ring.

When he told Volodimir that he had managed to hit the General, he saw the joy on his teacher's face.

"It seems that your meditation is getting better. I think you can also do some sparring against me," Volodimir replied.

Nick's confidence is at an all-time high, and he thought that since his teacher is smaller than the General, it shouldn't be that difficult. He would find a way to take him on, so he happily agrees. He regretted that decision and ended the night with a broken arm. He had to drink a number of vials from Volodimir to heal in time for daybreak, making it back just in time for the General to wake them up for their morning jog.

As the morning class begins, each of them takes their regular seats while the General writes 'Final Exam and Spring Festival' on the board.

"Now, students," he says and turns to them with a huge smile. He glances around to see the red cheeks of his students, believing they are from the cold. "Congratulations on surviving your first month."

The four of them clap and cheer for themselves.

"That means you have two months until the Finals and Spring Festival," the General continues, raising his voice to be heard over their cheers, "The Finals are the last exams of the year. This is a school, and we want you lot to succeed academically as well. Then, it's the Spring Festival."

Bhaltair raises his hand. "Spring Festival?"

"Yes, Bull. As I said in the beginning, you have three months to prove that your seed can grow. You are not expected to stay in the Yellow. By the end of the third month, I expect you all to move to Orange. In order to move up a circle, one must complete the spells in their level. However, it is very rare for a person to use a higher spell without completing their level. Using a spell higher than your level can result in death."

He pulls a chart down in front of the board that has the shadow techniques from Yellow to Purple written across it. Nick quickly takes out the ink from his desk, copying down the chart.

"These are all the shadow techniques and spells. I'm only going to explain the Yellow and Orange skills," the General begins as he sits on the corner of his desk. "To master Yellow, you all must master Shadow Jump and Shadow Walk. These two spells allow a user, like myself, to go from one end of the room..."

He stops and drops into the table's shadow causing everyone to gasp. He comes out of the desk's shadow behind Takara, causing her to jump, before vanishing again.

"To the other." He smiles as everyone looks back at the desk to where he is now. "Now that, students, is Shadow Walk. That spell can allow you to transport yourself in small distances, while Shadow Jump allows you to traverse long distances."

Nick looks at the board then back at his sheet. He writes the difference between the two, but stops as he looks at the board again. He raises his hand.

"Yes, Guts?"

"Um, sir... where's Black?"

Everyone turns to look at him and even his teacher looks stunned for a moment until he grins.

The General chuckles. "Well, Black is a class that likes to keep their mysteries to themselves."

"But, there's a Black Teacher... right?" Nick heard of the Black Teacher once and it seems that no one talks about them, almost as though they're afraid they might summon them.

"The Black Teacher here is really a Purple. They're a very high-ranking Purple, though, so don't look down at them. I'm sure that you'll hear more about them. However..." He grins and walks over to the board and points to 'Ghost 1'. "There is a reason why it's called Ghost '1'."

"There's a Ghost 2," Rohana said.

"Yes, Ice. The Ghost 2 is for the Black circle. Legend says that it allows you to possess a person. The Black user can stay in the person's body, while the original owner can do nothing but watch. Stronger users can control the body completely, causing the original owner to not remember the experience. However, the Night Emperor, an excellent Black wielder, has said that the spell allowed him to experience a person's memories."

"That's an amazing spell!" Bhaltair exclaims.

The General only laughs. "Another interesting technique I heard the Emperor mention is 'Nightly Calm', which can allow the Black wielder to control the emotions of those around him."

"How?" Nick asks. "How is that possible? That sounds impossible."

"Yes." The General chuckles again at their surprised faces. "That's why they're called Legendary."

Chapter 15
Education

One day, Yellow and Orange share a class on the civics and theories of the Empire, taught by none other than Miss Leia. Her wild red hair is everywhere. Her pair of purple goggles act as a hair band to stop the curls from falling on her face. They helped as much as Nick fixing the relationship with his dead father.

Nick sits next to Kaius, who is beside a girl named Laura, who has vibrant green eyes and dark green hair. She becomes a member of Nick's friends through Kaius. She came from Availa as well, but from a different province than the boys.

"Students," Leia starts, pushing the hair from her face. "Today, we will talk about some of the roles that you can go into after graduating from school."

She turns to the chalk board and writes down: *Yellow, Orange, Red, Blue,* and *Purple.*

"We will begin with Yellow and Orange. I'm sure you've heard that Yellow are 'Beginners' and Orange are 'Common'. Yellow and Orange circle users may not be very powerful in connecting with the shadows, but they can still be useful for the Empire, in civil service jobs and administration. Some even go into regular work with people that don't have Shadow magic. The sky's the limit, except for the areas that need one to be a Red user or higher."

Kaius whispers to Nick, "So, all the powerful roles."

Nick nods.

"Reds are known as the 'Classic.' It's a middle ground for shadow users and seen widely as the most acceptable level to be a part of in order to get higher positions. Most Red roles are used for businesses and exploration, as they have the skills needed and a focus on combat. Many go into the army and become commanders of smaller troops."

She then points to Blue. "Blues, the 'Advanced' class are normally in politics. The majority of the noble houses belong in Blue. Many nobles go by the term 'blue bloods' and some commoners in Blue can be elevated in social rank. Nobles do love a Blue."

Her smile starts to wane a little at this point. "There is another group that uses a lot of Blues: the Shadow Assassins. Many who are not of noble blood go to the Shadow Hallows which is the main house of the Shadow Assassins."

Many of the students around them seem to pale, and some even look to the shadows to see if an assassin would jump out.

Leia continues talking, ignoring the frightful looks of her students. "The Shadow Assassins follow the orders of the Emperor and are the most elite spies that the Empire has to offer. If you wish to join, they will happily accept you; sometimes they actually 'claim' a student, sometimes by force. They start training you as soon as you graduate. I, personally, don't know how many are in their order, but I would guess a good few from the amount of sister branches across the realm." She giggles. "They even made a new one in Availa."

Of course, they did. Someone needs to make sure to watch the people. The Emperor would want to have his shadow over the land. Nick sighs.

Leia sees that the room is getting quieter, so she decides to tell them about the good things associated with the Shadow Assassins. "However, with that position comes power. If you become a Shadow Assassin, even those in Purple will respect you, as your orders will come from the Emperor himself. It doesn't matter if you're a noble or a commoner, if the Shadow Assassins tell you something, then you best follow them." She twists in her seat. "But the Shadow Assassins are good to their own. No matter what level you are in the organization, you will be protected." She then gives them a cunning smile. "But be warned, once you enter the Shadow Assassins, your only way out is death."

Everyone in the room knew of the Shadow Assassins. Their stories became legendary in Availa, especially when the rebel army collapsed an entire building on some of them, and it only slowed them down.

As the teacher continues to speak, Nick remembers the cold and dark night that he met a Shadow Assassin.

Nick's mission was to find out if the Shadow Assassins were actually coming. He didn't want to go, but his father slapped him and told him to man up because Archers were not afraid of death. However, at the mention that a Shadow Assassin had been sent to kill him, the brave Markus went into hiding.

Nick made it into one of the enemy bases and hid for over a week, starving himself to fit into smaller places. He finally saw one of the commanding officers speaking to a man wearing a silver skull mask and an all-black cape. The man took off his mask to reveal an ordinary face, though there was a scar on his right eye. His eyes rivalled the Archer blue.

Nick watched as the commanding officer angrily asked why the Shadow Assassins couldn't just kill the rebel leader and called them useless.

Nick gasped as the man was thrown against the wall, the Assassin's tighten his grip on the officer's head. Even outside the window, he could hear the officer's cries of pain. Nick heard many things that night as he drew closer to the window.

"Remember this," the Assassin hissed. "We follow orders from the Emperor. He thought that you and your men could handle this rebellion. For crying out loud, the people turned against their King, and the rebel leader turned into a drunk after his wife was killed. So, here is my question: why aren't the rebel forces destroyed?"

The officer couldn't speak, but Nick could see him shake, even from the window. The Assassin sighed and let the man go. The proud man fell gracelessly to the floor, like a puppet that had his strings suddenly cut, and began gasping for air. Nick moved even closer to see the man looking up with tears in his eyes.

The Assassin scoffed. "My men and I have been working while you all have made the Emperor and his army look weak. Unlike you, we truly move in the shadows. We have people to kill, but the leader of the rebellion isn't one of them."

"He's the leader?!" the officer gasped, trying to crawl from up the floor. "He's the reason this whole rebellion has grown!"

"Is he?" The Assassin inquired. "There are other more capable leaders in the group. You'll see." The Assassin looked over the sharp talons on his gloves, clicking them together. "The building that we are standing in, what would it be without its foundations?" He looked at the man and gave him a sharp smile. "Trust me, you'll see a change soon."

"How soon?"

The Assassin looked to the window and Nick swore that the Assassin looked right at him. Nick could see a scar on the Assassin's piercing blue eyes. He didn't stay long to see if he had been seen, turning around, and running. As soon as he came back, he told them that his father wasn't the one the Assassins were after. His father relaxed, but his pride was hurt. Nick explained that they were going after the foundation and told him that it would be best to tell all commanders and advisors to be safe.

The smart ones took his words to heart, while others went out of hiding when his father did. In one week, five of his father's advisors and winning generals were killed under mysterious circumstances.

In just three months, the Night Emperor came and crushed the five-year rebellion.

Nick's mind returns to the present. No longer was he in the wood cabin or the presence of his father. He is surrounded by children instead of war-torn people. At the front isn't a man towering over him; he sees a woman with curly red hair and a smile.

As her smile returns, she moves on. "Now onto the Purple circle. They are also known as the 'Elite', not just in status, but magical power. Very few people get into this level, and many hold positions of power such as generals and advisors to the Emperor. They have a whole society of their own."

Before Leia could say anything more, Laura raised her hand.

"Yes, dear?"

"What about Black?" Laura asks.

Nick is further intrigued by the fact that the professor didn't even write it on the board. It seems to be a theme around the school. No one talks about the circle, as though it's too holy of a topic for mere mortals like them.

Miss Leia looks confused for a moment, then laughs for a good moment until she gets ahold of herself. "Sorry. Not to be rude, but not even I can get into Black. As a Purple, it is my dream to one day get into Black."

She pushes her hair from her face again and takes a seat in front of the class. "Now, the Black class is a very mysterious class. They are the 'Legendary' class. If you have further questions, I can get the Black Teacher to come and talk to you."

Some members of the class whisper that they didn't even know that there was a Black Teacher and others nod in agreement.

"I'll have to ask him ahead of time. The Black Teacher is all over the place, meeting with other teachers, handling the school, and going to the Emperor's palace weekly to inform him of student progress." Some students gasp. "Oh, yes, we tell him, and the Emperor is aware of the people in this school. Think of the Black Teacher as a headmaster or principal of the school if you will."

Laura raises her hand again.

"Yes, dear?"

"But I thought that the only Black is the Night Emperor? Who teaches the Black?"

"Good question. The Night Emperor is obviously too busy to teach the circle. So, he appoints a high-ranking Purple to teach the class. The Black Teacher must report to the Emperor's council on a weekly basis with progress on all the children," she clarifies.

"Now, what I can tell you about a person in the Black circle is that they can not only control the darkness in themselves, but also in others. For example, in the war with the Kingdom of Availa, some of our Purple generals and officers were taken captive and placed in a light room, a room where shadows can't form. The Night Emperor came to rescue them. I was one of the captives, not a general, but a high-ranking officer. They converted their hold area into a light room to stop the Night Emperor from using shadows. By using mirrors that hit the sun at the right angle, the whole room lit up. But that didn't stop him."

Leia sits up straighter and nervously rubs her hands on her thighs. "Even within the shining lights, where physical shadows were at their weakest, the Emperor was able to use the darkness from within the hearts of the men around him. I saw from my cell that the whole room was light, then with a snap, the whole place went dark."

The whole atmosphere of the room goes quiet. Nick can feel a pressure on the back of his neck again. He turns to see that Kaius's eyes are wide open and many of the students have pale faces.

"It was pitch black. I couldn't see anything, but I heard the screams of swords crashing to try and stop him. Then I heard the crumbling of walls and the screams of dying men and women, followed by silence and darkness. That day, I finally knew what it was like to be surrounded by the shadows. First, I was frightened, but then the shadows felt good, like a shield or protection hiding me away from terror. Footsteps, and the sound of chains dropping, including my own, were the first sounds I heard."

"Then," she pauses for dramatic effect. "The doors opened and the shadows receded. The sun was shining down through a split roof, and the Emperor was helping his men out from their cells. I didn't get a clear look at the Emperor because I was taken away for treatment by another general. However, I did get a glimpse of the legendary mask covering his eyes."

She giggles quietly, almost to herself. "You see, class, Black circle users are practically unstoppable."

Later that night, Nick finds himself in the cottage on the hill with Volodimir sipping his tea by the fire. He approaches Volodimir and sees a stack of paper on the small table. He notices the furrowing of his teacher's brow and the glare he's giving to the papers as though it offended him. His teacher doesn't look happy. So, he steps cautiously as the man usually acknowledges him.

"Sir?" Nick asks.

Volodimir looks up and gives a warm smile. "Nico! Let's go on a field trip tonight."

"A field trip?" he asks as Volodimir stands and opens up a closet at the side of the fireplace that he didn't even know existed.

The hidden door opens, and Volodimir throws a black cape at Nick, taking out a cape for himself. Nick puts the cape on after taking off the Black robes and watches Volodimir throw the cape on himself, tying it quickly. The cape fabric has waves and other patterns embroidered with black thread. It's a lovely cape, thick enough to keep out the cold. Yet, Nick cannot get the black clasp to close. He doesn't even hear his teacher walking towards him until his hands are swatted out of the way. Volodimir quickly fixes his cape, then steps back and smiles.

"There. However, you're missing something." His teacher reaches into the shadow of his chair and takes out two silver skull masks, one large and one small. Nick's eyes widen as he steps back, heart pumping.

"Oh, you know these masks?" his teacher asks, holding out the smaller one to him.

Nick slowly takes it, holding it in front of his face. "Shadow Assassin," he whispers to himself, remembering the man with the scar. "Are you a Shadow Assassin?"

He turns the mask over, slowly taking in its designs. It isn't just silver, there are swirls and carvings of the same runes that he saw on the testing stone back when he was tested. He brushes the runes and they glows slightly.

"Would it be any different if I was?" Nick can see the man's eyes narrow. *Never get on the bad side of an Assassin,* he reminds himself.

"It would just make me want to know even more why you want to train me." Nick answers; he prays it's a safe one.

Would he claim me by force? Miss Leia said that they take students after graduating. Nick's eyebrows rise. *But what if he's claiming me early?*

The man smiles as he can see the whirlwind of emotions cross his pupil's face. Volodimir puts the mask and hood on himself.

Nick has to stop himself from shaking as his teacher looks even more intimidating. He remembers the man with the scar and how five important rebel advisors died in a week, as well as their men.

He is so deep in his thoughts that he is shocked when Volodimir takes the mask from his hand and puts it on him. Nick can see through the eyes, but something feels strange. The voices from the shadows are louder and clearer.

"It suits you," the deeper voice of Volodimir declares. "It makes you look powerful."

More frightening. Nick can hear the shadows echo in his mind.

"Thanks, but sir, why are the shadow voices much clearer? Also, what's with the runes on the mask glowing?"

Volodimir freezes and turns to him. He hears his teacher slowly chuckle. "You surprise me every day, Nico." He whispers, even Nick could barely hear him. "The runes are meant as a form of protection and communication. It seems that the shadows really want to talk to you if they glow." He stops and sighs. "Don't tell anyone that they glow for you, not yet."

His voice is sharp, and all Nick can do is nod.

"Good. To answer your second question, the masks were created by the shadows themselves. Shadow Assassins can use the mask to hear the voices. The voices normally help them in their tasks, in finding people and understanding the area."

"But I can hear the voices without the mask."

"Yes, you can." Nick swears that he can tell that his teacher is smiling under his mask. "Now, let's go for some field study. Grab my hand."

Chapter 16
Field trip

In the narrow alley of the city, a cat runs away as a man leaps out of the shadows and catches the small lad from falling. Volodimir holds onto Nick as the world spins around the boy. First, it was darkness and loud voices, now he's in strong arms on solid ground. Nick grips onto Volodimir for dear life.

Focusing on his breathing is what keeps his mind from spinning even further, and he is thankful for the mask that covers his sweaty face. He's embarrassed for feeling sick and wants to hide in a corner.

I wonder what he'll say first. That I'm weak? Useless? A mistake?

Before he could offer up an apology, Volodimir picks him up gently and moves him over to a wood crate.

His teacher takes off both their masks and while Nick looks pale, it's Volodimir who looks worried. "I apologize, I forgot that the first time through the shadows can be… uncomfortable. Don't worry, it's normal to feel nauseated or disoriented. Just take deep breaths. When you're ready, we will leave."

Nick closes his eyes and follows Volodimir's instructions. He wants to recover quickly; he wants his teacher to not second-guess him. He breathes for what seems like ten minutes until he gives a stern nod. Volodimir gives an encouraging smile and puts the mask back on. Nick puts his on as well.

"Follow me," Volodimir beckons, before he jumps up and begins to climb the wall. Nick follows him, trying not to lose sight of him. The gloves help him grip into the cracks, but the boots are still a problem. He presses on and reminds himself that it's just like climbing a tree. He grips the edge of the roof and pulls himself up. He sees his teacher up ahead and gasps at the view in front of him. It's beautiful.

"Look at what the Emperor has built," Volodimir states.

Nick walks up to him and sees the lights of the city, tall stone structures and large pillars stretching far and wide. He wasn't used to seeing tall buildings in the south, as they normally had large basements to hide in when the weather became too hot.

Nick sighs. "There aren't a lot of light bulbs in the town I was born in. Well, Availa is still lacking in technology."

It's like a dream, he thinks. It truly does as the city is luminescent in a faint blue and pale-yellow lights.

His teacher chuckles. "Yes, before the current Emperor, this was lit by candles and gas lights. One too many fires switched everything to the electro rocks." He points into a darker section of the city. "Behind the forest and slums are mines full of electro rocks. They store lightning in their core."

Nick looks at the black patch far over the city and his eyes narrow. "At whose expense is the Empire powered?" he asks Volodimir.

His teacher doesn't turn to him, but he can feel the pressure on his neck. A short silence follows. "Everyone has to make a sacrifice."

"Even you?"

"Even me." Volodimir jumps to the next building without a word.

Nick takes one more look at the slums and follows him.

He trails his teacher, past the city's tall buildings and oddly shaped rooftops, and comes across a line of trees separating the city from the manors and estates. Each property has a flagpole flying the flag of the Empire and another that displays their family crest.

"Wow," he breathes out.

"Yes, these are the city estates of the nobles of the Empire," Volodimir chuckles

"City estates?" he repeats. "I've heard of them in Availa, where nobles had a second place in the city."

"It is the same here. These are some of the estates that belong to them. You see there, Nico?" Volodimir points to a house that has a family crest flying at half-mast. "The family crest belongs to the Visconte family. That flag position means the family is not in their residence."

Nick wrinkles his nose. "Isn't that... you know," he pauses, taking a better look at the dark estate, "dangerous?"

"It can be, for us. But don't be foolish enough to try and break into a noble's house. I said the family is away, but the place is still protected by their servants and small guards." He grabs Nick's hands. "Trust me, Nico, there are other devices the Empire has that Availa could only dream of having, such as an alarm protection and traps powered by electro rocks. Not many people can move after getting shocked by one of them. Trust me, it's quite painful."

Nick looks at the manor and can just barely make out a guard on the rooftop, partially cloaked in the shadows.

"Let us continue," he hears Volodimir whisper.

Volodimir avoids the roofs of the estates at half-mast and makes most of the trip jumping between the trees. Nick doesn't mind; he likes being in the trees.

They reach a large manor, much grander than any of the others. Taking a quick look to see that the family is indeed in the manor, Volodimir jumps onto the roof, avoiding the guards. Nick jumps, trying to be as graceful as his teacher but miscalculates his landing, making a little more noise. Nick hides as a guard looks in his direction, then returns to his post. Nick lets out a breath he didn't realize he was holding and moves towards Volodimir much more carefully.

He finds his teacher sitting on one of the many gargoyles. Most of the lights in the manor are off, except for one room, which both of them are facing. The lit window is still a long way away and Nick wonders if this is really an estate or a small palace. He hopes it's the first, as the burning and cramping in his legs increases.

Volodimir raises a finger to the skeletal teeth of his silver mask and Nick nods in understanding. His teacher then jumps from the gargoyle onto the lower ledge of the house. Nick follows him, but there are some steps that force him to slow down.

I'm not familiar with this land. It's not my home. He curses, throwing out his arms as his feet almost slide on the snow-covered roof. It isn't like the towns or forests that he knows. He doesn't feel confident, and tries to keep up with his teacher around the estate, but his teacher is going too quickly and he's afraid to be left behind. He can barely see, and he can't hear his teacher.

He can't stay silent; his panting is as clear as the steps of his feet. He focuses on the breathing exercises that the General taught him. They're working and allow him to quiet his breathing, but he is already so tired.

A prayer that sounds more like a plea enters his mind. *I need help.*

A feeling of despair rises in him as he watches his teacher disappear through another towering chimney. Nick heads in the direction that his teacher was last seen, with the light from the window guiding him. But it's not enough. He knows that if he continues like this, he will either lose track of his teacher or slide off the roof. Neither are acceptable outcomes.

Let us help you. The shadows are clear in his ears as the cold winds pass through. The voices of the shadows bring him to a sudden stop, the abrupt movement causing his feet to slip on the snow. As he slides, he quickly grabs hold of a brick and prays to all the deities that no one hears his light gasp.

Overjoyed that someone is listening to his prayers tonight, he answers the voices. *Please help.* As soon as the words leave his mind, he can feel power bloom in him, a pressure moving up his neck and into his eyes. Suddenly, he can see clearly. Nick almost loses his balance from sheer shock.

It's like daytime, only different.

He can see his teacher far ahead of him and he runs after the man, faster than before, but still carefully. A laugh almost escapes his lips at the thought of how useful this would have been during the war.

If this is what we were up against, then the war was already lost, he can't help but think.

Volodimir stops at a ledge and in a few seconds, Nick is beside him. His teacher points to the window. There, Nick can see a man in a dark green suit and with a bright blue gem on his tie. Larger hands grab his own as his teacher nods to him. Nick nods back, preparing himself for the jump.

"Stay quiet and say nothing," his teacher commands.

Nick gives a firm nod in return, as their bodies go weightless as they sink into the shadow. Nick doesn't have time to process what happens as his vision slowly goes dark, so he closes his eyes and listens. He hears various whispers, and giggles in his ears. For only a few seconds, he can only feel Volodimir's grip pulling him, until he feels warmth. The warm air is different from the cold winds of winter.

The feeling of warm air gets Nick to open his eyes. He sees them step out into a lit room, looks down to see his leg leaving the shadows, and then glances back to see that they came from behind one of the suits of armor that he saw from the outside. He would have kept looking around, if it weren't for the startled gasp of the man behind the grand desk.

The man in the dark green suit stands up quickly and starts to sweat.

"A guilty man sweats," Volodimir snarls in a deep voice, walking towards the man.

Even an innocent person would sweat and faint if they saw a Shadow Assassin, Nick thinks.

The man looks between the two of them and begins backing up to the wall. Nick sees that the wall is a map of the Empire and a part of him weeps as he sees that Availa has been added to it. He tears his eyes from the wall and looks closely at the man. The man is still fully dressed, even at this hour of night. The blue gem on him gleams beautifully in the lamplight, making Nick wonder how much such a large gem cost him. The noble's hair is blonde with a lovely silver streak at the front. He looks young, maybe the same age as Volodimir.

The man is sweating a lot now. "Please, I haven't done anything!" His back bumps into the map behind him.

"That's not what the report says. Skimming on the mines and taking a cut for yourself. Lord Nortshell, I thought that you were smarter than that."

Volodimir pulls the shadow of the desk closer to him and materializes a slender sword. There is no sheath to cover the black blade that absorbs even the brightest of light. Even from afar, Nick somehow feels that the blade is sharp. He admires it from a distance.

Lord Nortshell shakes his head, then composes himself. "I am a Lord, Shadow Assassin. My family is one of the most dedicated families to the Empire." He stands tall and firm. "I am the Right and Honourable Lord of the Chamber of Citizens. I speak for the voices of those who cannot control the shadows. I wish for an audience to speak to the Emperor to defend myself!" He glares at the two of them. Nick would be impressed if he didn't look back at Volodimir and see his teacher stiffen.

Another question enters Nick's mind as he tilts his head. *People can ask to speak to the Emperor? In Availa, not even the King's brothers could meet with him. Maybe if the King had spoken to his advisors more, the Kingdom of Availa would still be his.* He only knew of one advisor, Lord Jameson. His father and members of the rebellion liked him. However, even the King sent Jameson to prison after disagreeing with his advice. *Then again, wasn't the king's sister one of his advisors?* Nick thinks for a moment but shakes his head. *That didn't matter when he killed her.*

His thoughts go back to the scene in front of him as the noble begins to pale. Volodimir's hand grips the blade's hilt tighter.

"My dear Nigel Nortshell." His teacher's voice deepens as the room becomes darker. Nick can feel the pressure rise on his spine and he has to lean on the wall to keep from falling. "I am under the direct order of the Emperor and the High Council. I don't like wasting my time or the time of my apprentice. Now, tell me. Do you deny the charges against you?"

The nobleman is quiet, but just as he is about to answer, Volodimir snaps his finger and the man's shadow begins to talk.

If I lie to him, he'll know that I need the extra money to pay off my debts. I knew I shouldn't have gambled, my father always told me so! HE was actually going to pass the title to my half-brother. HALF-BROTHER! His mother was a whore! I am the sole heir to the proud Nortshell name. I just need to buy off the Shadow Assassin. Yes, buy him off; money always solves everything. I'll be a little more in debt, but with the mining operations in full swing, I can trim from the top for five more months and I'll break even. Perfect!

Both Nortshell and Nick look on in horror as Nortshell's shadow stops speaking.

"The shadows never lie," Volodimir declares, as the man in front of him turns white as a sheet. "Well, that solves things. I know what to tell the Emperor when he looks for a new head for the proud Nortshell family." Volodimir sounds like he's smiling under his mask, even chuckling as though it's a joke.

The man is on the floor begging. "Please, w-wait I—"

Volodimir moves faster than even Nick can see and grabs the jaw of the man, silencing him.

"Money means nothing to me," Volodimir growls quietly. "Just power, and you don't have any. The Shadow Assassins are loyal to the Night Emperor. *Only* the Night Emperor." He clarifies. He lets go of the man, who collapses on the ground. His teacher gives another small chuckle. "Have fun in prison." With a wave of his hand, the man is swallowed up by his own shadow.

The lights in the room flicker back to normal as Nick looks at his teacher in both awe and fear. That's a move that he hasn't learned in class yet. Volodimir turns to his student as Nick pushes himself off the wall.

"What did you learn today, Nico?" his teacher asks in a steady voice.

"That the Shadow Assassins are loyal to the Emperor." He gulps, seeing that his teacher wants to hear more. "That a shadow can hold truths or know secrets."

Volodimir approaches him, and Nick once again finds himself closer to the wall, saying, "that power is everything."

Volodimir stops, waiting for Nick to continue.

"That money, wealth, and all material things mean nothing when someone can overpower you."

His teacher claps his hands. "Very good." Volodimir nods. "But there is one more lesson."

Nick straightens up waiting for what else he could have missed.

"Don't lie to me."

The journey back to the cottage is a silent one, and Nick is grateful for it. As they jump from roof tops to climbing down walls, they reach what looks to be the same alley that they came from. There Volodimir stretches out his hand for Nick to take to return to the cottage, and for the first time, Nick hesitates.

When Nick is finally back in his room again, dismissed by his teacher, he can still feel the effects of jumping through the shadows. He can't help but wonder what he just experienced tonight. Clearly, he already knew his teacher was powerful, but strong enough to do all that? The Yellow class hadn't even learnt that yet.

He rubs his face as he exhales. His teacher did amazing and frightening things. To be able to do that to someone, to have that much power over them. Nick shakes his head, knowing that his cousin probably holds that power over him right now. He remembers the first lesson that the General told them, how people can just take the word of Purples without evidence.

"We're family," he whispers to himself. "Blood don't kill blood."

It was the first rule that his father told him. Nick is pretty sure that was the only reason why his father didn't kill him with his own hands. However, as much as he believed that his cousin wouldn't try to get him killed, he couldn't stop feeling that his cousin would have a sick fascination with using his powers against him. Braawen didn't even have powers that he knew of during the rebellion, but he still pushed and used him.

He sighs quietly and looks up at the ceiling. He tries not to think about Braawen with that power. He knows he can't defend himself against his cousin. Knowing that his cousin can reach that potential... for the first time, he's scared of his cousin. He's been jealous, hurt, and sometimes proud of him. But never scared.

He shakes his head and tries to think of anything happier, staring at the dark ceiling. He thinks of his run around the city and how he could see in the dark.

How did you like your power? The shadows around the room ask.

Mine?

Yes, child, this power is yours. We are able to help you access your powers. Though we wished for you to access more to be more powerful, it seems that you can only see in the dark for now. Try it.

He huffs and closes his eyes in concentration. When he opens them, he can see the room, clear as day. Everyone is asleep. Bhaltair is snoring and drool is falling on his pillow. Takara looks like she's in the middle of a dance pose. Rohana is curled into a ball with a blanket over her head. Then everything turns black.

He blinks, feeling sick again.

Work on your mind. Your powers can grow once you accept the past and the darkness in your heart. The hate, the torment, the lies, they hiss.

He huffs. *I don't hate anyone.*

Anger starts to bubble, but he finds it harder to swallow it down, as though his own body is denying him that fact. Swallowing it down used to help. It's what his mother did whenever she heard that his father was with another woman. She would take deep breaths, push down the anger, then state that she has forgiven father and move on like nothing happened.

Why isn't it working now? Nick asks himself. He sighs, rolling over. Out of nowhere, tears start to fall on his pillow. He blinks, wondering why the tears won't stop, why he can't keep his anger down.

Then it clicks. He's tired. Mentality, physically, and emotionally. He stares blankly at nothing as the tears silently roll down his face onto his pillow. He can't be like his mother who used to hold her anger down. He can't take it anymore.

The kingdom falling, his time on the ship, his training, the school, everything! He's angry at the world right now, as he clutches his hands around his blanket like a lifeline or a throat, preferably his father's. Even the scars on his back seem to claw at him. The anger boils and he turns his head into his pillow as he screams. He screams again, this time longer and harder than the one at the lake.

After a minute or two, another emotion fills him, one that he didn't think he could feel anymore. Fear. He's scared of the school. He's scared of the teachers. He fears for the lives of his friends and for his own life. He fears that he will never see his uncles again. He fears that he will let Uncle Tys down.

What if I don't get stronger? What if I do something and they kill me? What if Volodimir doesn't see any improvements and gives up on me? It wouldn't be the first time someone has, he thinks bitterly.

Instead of holding in his fear and newfound frustration, he lets it out a whimper and bites his lips hard.

He remembers the names and accusations that his father would hit him with. He remembers the nights that he would give his food to his cousin because his father said that Braawen was the next leader of the rebellion and needed to stay fit. Nick swallows down his bitterness as a feeling that is beyond hate starts to surface once again.

They're old feelings, so why do they still hurt?

He remembers the time that his father gave up on teaching him sword fighting and sent him on death missions instead.

His cousins and the rest of the rebellion children's insults ring all too clearly in his mind.

Is he really his son?

Can't be a leader, can't lift anyone's spirits. Boy looks like he can barely lift his own.

Weakling!

Just leave the fighting to us.

Then he remembers Braawen. *Give me the ideas and I will present them. They'll listen to me. Plus, this is for the good of the rebellion. No one is taking credit.*

His uncle Tybalt didn't give up on him, but now Nick can't even repay him for his kindness. His uncle is alone, looking for him, being hunted down. Nick needs to get stronger to find him, to help him! Braawen, his father, the people in his life were right: he is useless.

He throws his face into his pillow again and cries. It's been a long month. He honestly thought that he was done screaming, but if there's one thing that Nick is very good at, it's denial. He can't deny these feelings anymore.

The feeling that he was never good enough for his father.

The feeling of jealousy towards his cousin during the war.

The guilt of living when his mother took an arrow for him.

The anger whenever someone didn't give him respect.

The frustration whenever he was ignored.

The weakness when he gave his ideas to Braawen and he took all the credit.

The pain of the whole blasted royal family of Availa not caring about their people.

The disappointment when he got placed in the lowest class and has to work even harder to make it to the Orange circle.

Anger. Jealous. Disappointment. Weakness. Disrespect. Sadness.

Then there are other emotions that start bubbling out that turn his cries into screams in his pillow.

Wrath, violence, fury, outrage, betrayal… *hate*.

He's so lost in his mind that he doesn't hear that Bhaltair has stopped snoring, or see that Takara is no longer in a dance pose, and Rohana has uncurled herself. They have all already had their moment to vent their frustrations. Most of the time, Nick is there to get them water or food. They all look to his bed and decide that he needs to let out his frustration.

Volodimir sits in the cottage drinking tea and crossing off another name on the small list of nobles that have stolen from the Emperor. Everyone knows that the Emperor doesn't care if they stole from each other, but stealing from him is a death sentence. He's crossing out another name when he pauses, and hears the voices of the shadows.

The boy is acknowledging his anger… They fade away.

He takes a sip of his tea. "About time."

The next day, Nick is able to focus better during meditation.

Chapter 17
City

Rohana walks through the hall alone; she doesn't mind it. She has decided to get her hair cut by one of the barbers here. She sighs, blowing the long strands of hair out of her eye. She could wait until tomorrow when the children went into the city, but she didn't have enough coins to pay a professional hairdresser. So, she is going to one of the free hairdressers in the school. If the hairdresser does a terrible job, maybe people would look at the hair instead of her scar.

She walks into the salon with a woman with snow-white hair and green eyes. As soon as the woman looks at Rohana's face, she scowls. Even with her long bangs, her scar can still be seen. She regrets not wearing the scarf today.

"You still available to cut my hair?" Rohana asks.

She nods. "Come sit, I'll make you look good. Well, at least the hair."

Rohana just sits in the chair and lets her put a cape under her chin. "I would like it short. With long bangs."

The hairdresser looks amused. "Don't you want to show your pretty face?" she mocks.

Rohana's grip on the chair tightens as her fingers go white. "Short, please, to the chin." She doesn't play into it.

At the end, Rohana actually has to swallow the little pride she has to thank the woman. *She's rude, but she follows instructions and actually made it look nice.* She looks at herself in the mirror and gives a small smile.

"I did pretty good. You look beautiful. Now go." The hairdresser dismisses Rohana and turns to her next client.

Rohana's eyes widen at being called beautiful, and she wonders if the woman actually means it. She leaves the room and makes her way through the school to the library. She asks for some of the books that Nick told her to read, covering the basics of shadow training and meditation. At first, she thought that the boy was a know-it-all, but you can learn a lot from a person in a month.

She found out that Nick didn't sleep at night. There are nights that she can hear him leave and come in late. One time, she followed him, but he was just in the library reading. She rolled her eyes and chose not to follow him again.

As she carries the books over to a desk away from everyone else, rough hands hit the back of her shoulders, knocking the books out of her hands. She hears a cry and sees two people glaring at her.

"Argh, Yellows... such pathetic and clumsy people," the girl who clearly pushed her sneers.

"Careful." The boy in blue robes smiles dangerously. "Yellows could be contagious. We wouldn't want to be brought down to her level."

Rohana glares at them and focuses on picking up her books. The General already gave her a stern talking to earlier, she doesn't need another one. She really regrets not wearing her scarf today.

"Look at her kneeling to us, just as it should be." The girl in red gives a haughty laugh.

Then Rohana hears another set of footsteps. "Do you all have no shame? The least you can do is help the girl." She turns to see a woman who reminds her of Nick's friend Kaius, with her ebony hair in an afro. "This is a library. Take your business elsewhere, or will I have to tell your teachers?"

The two students apologize and leave. Rohana watches them retreat as the woman helps her up. Rohana recognizes the woman as the librarian. The librarian gives her a lovely smile and tells her that there is a small office for people who want peace and quiet on the second floor. Rohana finds her way there to see different rooms. Two are locked, but the third one opens to a small desk and comfortable chair. The window shows a view of the lake where people are laughing and ice skating. She takes her time in the room and enjoys it.

The next day is a day of rest, with no classes and no schedule. The children all love this day, but today is special for a specific reason. This is the day that children can go into the city to shop and just enjoy life.

The Yellows are put into their own wagons. They are each excited about the trip. Surprisingly, the war children received allowances from the Empire each week. The higher the rank, the more money you received. As they all expected, Yellow got the lowest amount. None of them spent their money on anything at the school, not even Bhaltair, who wanted a cake or two from the bakery. They all wanted to get something from the city.

When they make it into the city, all the other students are excited and run about wildly, while the children from Availa stay together. Nick can feel the anxiety in the air. He even looks over at the Purples and sees Braawen standing closely with a girl. It's as though they are expecting someone to throw something at them.

"Rebirth!" A loud cry gets the attention of the students. There in ragged priestly robes is an old man being dragged away by two soldiers. "The deities shall let us live again! Don't listen to the corrupt Temples!" His voice fades as the rest of the civilians just ignore the man.

"Is that normal?" Nick asks his friends. They shrug, but he can see the actual students from the Empire ignore the man.

"Don't pay attention to the babbling fool, Braawen," he overhears one of the Purple students tell his cousin. "They're rejects from the temple. They spread false lies about rebirth and foolishness." Nick can't hear the other words as the Purple group walk away.

"Let's go, Rohana. I know you said that you wanted to look at some clothes," Takara states, walking away with the girl in tow.

Bhaltair looks at Nick. "Want to go and get sweets?" he asks, giving a small smile.

"Sure." That simple word brings joy to his friend. They both walk off to one of the stores that Nick saw during the night.

The city is bustling. Takara had never been to a city, not even in Availa, because she was always at the farm with the chickens. She lived in a small community, a people who descended from the island of Araceli. A Kingdom far from Availa, but here, Takara sees men in bright turbans, and she passes by people who have rune tattoos on their face. Rohana thinks are from Winterborn.

The buildings are beautiful, but the people are rude, as she finds out. No one tries to move out of the way for them, and she is sure that a few people knock into them on purpose while others just glare at them.

"What's wrong with these people?" she huffs, as both her and Rohana take a seat on a bench. Rohana just shrugs.

There is a light sprinkle of snow on the ground, and the girls take the time to look around the clear roads and carriages. The city, in Takara's opinion, would have been perfect if it wasn't so cold, and she isn't talking about the weather.

"It's the fact that you have tags," another voice calls out to them.

Takara looks around until Rohana points to a girl walking towards them; she has dark green hair that is mostly covered by her stylish orange hat. The girl has on the same coat and tag on her chest, as well as an orange scarf to complete her ensemble. Takara looks at her and thanks the deities that all of them have the same black coats, but with different scarves that show their rank.

"My name is Laura, by the way," she introduces herself and offers her hand.

"Takara," she replies as she shakes Laura's hand, noticing her strong grip. "But why are you talking to us? Aren't you afraid that your Oranges won't like it?"

Laura rolls her eyes. "Does it look like I care? They annoy me. Plus, are you guys friends with Nick?"

Both girls perk up at Nick's name.

"Yes," Rohana says warily.

Laura gives a warm smile. "He's nice, and so is his friend Kaius, I hope that we can be friends. I'm trying to break away from the other Oranges. They're so pretentious, but for deities' sake, we're only one level above you."

Takara can hear Rohana chuckle.

"Well, come have a seat," Takara says as they shuffle to make room for Laura as she sits, her back straight like a perfect lady.

Laura's vibrant hooded eyes scan the area. She sighs as she takes off her orange hat, allowing her dark green hair to flow out like waves. Her tan skin shivers from the cold. She, too, is wearing a silver dragon pin on her chest like all of the other war children.

"What do you mean by tag?" Takara points to her own pin. "What do the tags have anything to do with the clear lack of behaviour of these people?"

Laura nods. "The tags are important. You see, all war children must wear it when they're out of the school. It marks them. People will know who you are until you graduate. It's so that people can keep an eye on us. Even the merchants and visitors of other nations know about Availa's defeat, and to keep an eye on us. The tag can't even be taken off." She demonstrates by trying to rip it off, with no success. "These people look down on us because we're not citizens and have no rights here, so we have to be careful."

"That doesn't give them a right to be so mean," Rohana replies.

Laura just shrugs. "They won and we lost. Many of the citizens just wanted the Night Emperor to kill us rebels. From the oldest woman to the babe." Takara gasps, but Laura just ignores her and continues. "Luckily, not everyone wanted that. However, until we prove our loyalty, they see us as 'below' them and in need of 'education.'" Laura rolls her eyes.

She stands up and dust the snow off her bum. "Come on, let's get something to eat. I also want to talk about a lighter topic. Talking about the Empire makes me want to weep."

That is something that both girls could agree on.

The two Yellows look at each other realizing that they have a small problem. "We don't have that much coin..." Takara states. Rohana nods her head.

"Did I ask if you have coin? I'm paying, come on." Laura grabs their hands and guides them to a café.

The café is a small establishment on the corner of the main street, with large windows that curve around the corner, making the place seem larger and giving the patrons a clear view of the main streets. The inside has a golden hue from the lights on its cream walls, and menus with different foods and drinks behind the counter. Mirrors behind the counter make the place seem grander and brighter, but when Rohana sees her reflection, she quickly pulls her scarf up a little higher.

Laura rings the small bell on the counter to get the server's attention. Takara can see some of the other patrons glancing in their direction, and even hears one scoff at them. However, while the two Yellows feel the pressure, Laura continues to smile and even tries to make a polite conversation with one of the gentlemen on the bar stool. He glares at her and moves away taking his drink with him, but she continues to smile as she waits to be served.

The older gentleman behind the counter smiles at them until he sees their silver tags. His genuine smile is quickly replaced by a fake one; Rohana knows a fake smile when she sees one.

The two Yellows order the cheapest dish on the menu, a chicken pie with hot cocoa. Laura orders a crêpe with ham. They take their food and make their way to one of the window seats. It's a small table away from everyone, but gives them a great view of the street. They eat, talk, and trade gossip. Not even the glares and whispers of the other patrons seem to dampen their mood until Laura tells them of the biggest rumour floating around the city.

"Apparently, there's a rumour that Tybalt Archer is in the city," she whispers.

"Impossible! He should be stuck in Availa," Takara's voice is muffled by the food in her mouth.

"Or on the run," Rohana mentions.

Laura ignores Takara's lack of table manners and shakes her head. "No. I got a letter from my father, who warned me to focus on my studies and a few other things he put in the letter to not be called a traitor." She drinks her tea slowly. "He told me to ignore the rumours of Tybalt, to remain loyal, and finish my studies with honour." She scoffs.

"Your father writes letters?" Takara asks.

"He was a scientist in the capital and worked for the King of Availa. It was only supposed to be for a short period. My mother and I were there with him. He was on the royal side first, then switched to the rebels. However, when the rebels began to lose, he switched to the Emperor's side." She shakes her head. "My mother and I left him when he joined the Empire.

Unfortunately, we returned home just in time for my province to be captured. I have no idea where my mother is. She wasn't a good woman, but she is still my mother. However, my father has a position here and sends me money. I don't like to spend it, but I give some to other kids for information."

Rohana turns to look at Laura. "You use your father's money to get information?"

The other girl puts down her cup. "Of course. You can get information three ways: friendship, sex, and money. I don't like people and don't want to be touched, but I have money."

"Why do you need information?" Takara asks.

Laura sighs but smiles. "Information of any kind can help you. I get information from people above me. I want to know who to not offend and who to keep an eye on."

"Feel like sharing that information?" Takara asks.

Laura smiles. "Kaius speaks about you and thinks that you all are good people. I need to be around more of those people. So, I hope that we can be friends. You're more fun to be around than any of the other girls I know."

They all enjoy their time together until the bell above the door rings and they see a small group of girls wearing Purple scarves enter the café.

The girl in the centre of the group is beautiful, with long chestnut hair in a braided bun and clear violet eyes. She smiles with her pearly whites and laughs at something one of the other girls says. Another girl has long pale blonde hair and blue eyes; she, too, is beautiful, however she is wearing a silver dragon pin.

"Oh, Emelie, you have to try the teas here, they're amazing and -" The leader stops mid-sentence as she looks at their table.

Rohana pulls her scarf up to her nose, covering the lower half of her face.

"I hope they don't come to us," Laura whispers. "And... here they come." She sighs as she puts on the fakest smile that anyone has ever seen. "Victoria, to what do we owe the pleasure?"

Victoria just smiles as she puts her arms on her hips. Behind her, her friends mimic her body language. Only Emelie gives a playful smile and looks relaxed. "An Orange knows my name? Good, so how about you and your *Yellows*," Victoria sneers at the 'offensive' word, "leave this lovely establishment?"

Laura sighs as she begins to get up, but stops as Takara places her hand on her arm. "This is a free place. We can sit anywhere we want."

Victoria smiles thinly at them. "You aren't free. You're wards of the state by the grace of the Empire, so leave."

Takara looks at the blonde girl. "Isn't your friend there also under the grace of the Empire?" She sees the girl blush as she quickly covers her pin.

"She's a Purple, she's special. You, on the other hand, are a Yellow, an embarrassment to our kind. So do yourselves a favour and just leave. I'm Victoria Visconte, the daughter of Ivan Visconte, one of the lords of the outer circle of the Night Court."

Takara looks unimpressed by the title. Then again, she was a farmer; she didn't care about titles or nobles, she only cared if her crops grew. She only knew two noble names, Princess Estelle, and Lord Jameson. The only two that actually cared about the poor. Nobles like the one in front of her weren't worthy of her time.

"Never heard of him or you." Takara can see Victoria flinch from that. "Now leave us. We're just trying to enjoy our meal."

Victoria sighs. "Your arrogance will be forgiven today, but I suggest you eat somewhere more your station, like the slums?" she suggests menacingly.

Takara stands up quickly, her fist clenched. "I have no problem fighting you, you rich –,"

"Oh, do be careful how you end that sentence." Victoria smiles. "Insulting me would be a slight to my father, an honourable official of the Emperor. Do you really want to insult a citizen of the state, whose tax money graciously pays for your clothes and food? Or are you ungrateful to these fair people? To the Emperor?"

That stops the chatter of all the people in the café and even the owner glares at the small table. The place goes deathly quiet.

Laura gets up and grabs the two girls beside her. "We are very grateful to all of you and the Empire." She bows slightly to Victoria and the patrons. "Goodbye." Her voice is loud and clear as she leaves more money than she intended and grabs the two Yellows. However, Emelie bumps her shoulder into Rohana, causing her to spill her cocoa on her boots.

"Clumsy you," Emelie sang as they ran out.

When they are at a far distance, Laura turns to them sharply. "What is wrong with you?" she yells.

"What do you mean what's wrong with me? She was being rude!" Takara retorts.

Laura groans. "We lost!" Her yell echoes around the busy street. Her eyes begin to water, frustrated by the arrogance of her new friends. A few people look their way, so she grabs the two and pulls them farther down the street. Once they're a good distance away, she glares at them.

"This is why you guys need to get information! She's a part of the Visconte family, one of the most powerful families, next to the Swans." She thinks that was enough information, but the two girls look clueless.

"Sit!"

The two Yellows sit on the curb of the street, not caring about the snow on the ground.

Laura groans as she walks back and forth in front of the two, rubbing her temples. She feels as though a headache could appear any moment. "Here's a quick lesson so you don't end up in an 'accident' or worse, killed! We are in a very difficult situation! The government is run by the Emperor, who is the head."

"Yeah, we know that." Rohana rolls her eyes.

Laura bites her lips in an effort to stop a few curses from leaving her lips. "Victoria is related to two powerful families, the Swans and Nortshell, the two families who run the government with the Emperor. Not only that, she is a distant relative of the Night Emperor himself. If you want to make it, ignore her for now. You will have an easier time teaching a horse to dance than her being kind to us. It's best just to move out of her way. We have no power here. I can't stress this enough." Laura sighs as Takara begins to pale slightly. "She's as close to a queen as one can get in the school."

Takara shakes not out of fear, but of anger. *If I make it out of this, I'm going to kill my Torosan. It's his fault I'm here anyways.*

"But," Laura smiles, "even queens can lose their crowns, and I have no doubt that she'll lose hers soon."

"What do you mean?" Takara asks.

Laura chuckles. "It seems that her 'loyal' father did something wrong, from what my father told me." Then she shrugs. "I guess we'll hear about it later. It's best to lay low for now."

Takara wants to ask more, until she feels Rohana's hand on hers. "Come on," Rohana pulls her up to stand. "I still want to look at some clothes."

As she gets up, she bumps into a man wearing nice clothes but his scarf lands on the ground. She quickly grabs it and apologizes expecting a scoff, yet the man gently takes the scarf back.

"Sorry, miss." The man's voice is deep and kind. She looks up at the first person who apologizes for bumping into her. She looks into his eyes; they're gorgeous. "Have a good day." He smiles and continues to walk as he ties the scarf over his nose, concealing the crescent-shaped scar under his chin.

"That was a very nice man." Takara said. Rohana nods.

"Very nice, and did you see his eyes? They were blue, like really blue. Like, *blue* blue!" Laura laughs. "And his hair! I've never seen hair like that before."

"Well this is the Empire, people from all over live here. I guess that copper hair is a regular thing, with robin's egg blue eyes," Takara says, looking at her friend's dark green hair.

"More poetic than *blue* blue," Laura replies.

"He reminds me of someone. He had a few blonde strands in it too," Rohana says, but she doesn't think of it much as she and the girls go to another store.

Nick and Bhaltair are drinking hot cocoa from a cheaper vendor on the street. They drink on the city bench while watching people. The two enjoy their drink and split a small cupcake that they pooled their money together to buy. Nick has had better cocoa from Volodimir but enjoys it all the same, and laughs at Bhaltair, who melts at the taste.

"This is a good cupcake," Bhaltair mumbles as he savours it. Nick agrees. They both go still as they see Purple students, all boys pass them by, a guard trailing behind them.

"They reek of lemons," Bhaltair squints his nose.

"What?"

"They smell of lemons, the Purple students. I can smell them from here. I hate the smell of lemons. The nobles in the Availian court used this lemon lotion thing. I think it was a cream to make them look younger or heal wounds." Bhaltair shakes his head. "Expensive stuff, but it came from the Empire, so I guess those entitled students can afford the cream."

Nick sniffs the air and realizes the lemon scent is coming from them. "They must use it to look younger. I imagine they'll do anything to look nice," he concludes.

His friend nods, then narrows his eyes. "Have you noticed that there's always a guard near them?" Bhaltair asks him.

"Yeah. I'm pretty sure it's for one individual, not them," Nick answers.

Bhaltair nods. "Yeah, got to keep a close eye on Archer. There have been rumours about something going on in the mines that got the Emperor angry. Not sure what it is, but let's keep an eye on it. Our people are in those mines." He licks the last of the icing on his fingers.

Nick sighs as he looks at the beauty of the city. It's different during the day, with more people and sounds that he tries to block out. He looks over again and sees that Braawen is laughing with the older boys; they seem to be asking him about one of the scars on his chin. Nick rolls his eyes as he tries to put his attention somewhere else. His eyes land on a man with copper hair walking down the street. He thinks that the man looks familiar, but brushes it off.

He turns back to Bhaltair, who looks at the window of a bakery from across the street.

"Do you want to go in?" Nick asks.

Bhaltair just shakes his head. "It wouldn't be the same. The dough, the yeast, the sugar... none of the bread here is the same. They even have Louest bread rolls, but not our bread." His voice drops to a whisper. "When I lost my father, I also lost my mother. She went mad after seeing my father lose his head. I had to be minded by the kitchen staff when she died of a broken heart."

"I'm sorry to hear that."

"Not your fault, it's the King's. You know, I was there on the Night of the Silenced." Bhaltair goes quiet and for some reason, it seems that the city has gotten quieter too. "I remember the kitchen staff throwing me out the window. Many of us jumped four stories to the ground. I broke my leg and the people who tried to catch me broke their arms. I was much bigger." He giggles, but it quickly dies as his eyes seem to go more distant. "I can remember the screams, Nick. I can remember the cries of the people that night. I can remember the scraping of the walls and cutting noises. The loud sounds of creatures that couldn't be seen. The darkness trying to devour us whole."

His friend turns to him. His hazel eyes look hollow and glazed. "I can't sleep without the vials; I don't think I ever will." His haunted eyes turn back to the calm laughter of the street. "When I did the test and I saw Yellow, I couldn't believe that I had the power..." He gulps. "That power, the same power that killed all those people." He shakes his head. "General Herald told me that the shadows are meant to protect us. Are they really, though?"

Nick stays quiet as Bhaltair sighs. Finally, Nick speaks. "I was told that the shadows are a tool that people can use for their own purpose."

He can hear a small chuckle from Bhaltair. "Tool. Well, the Night Emperor definitely used it well that night. If he wanted to be feared more, then he succeeded. The whole city went quiet as we all heard the screams, Nick. Then the screaming stopped. Not even his men were making a sound. Only the waves of the sea dared to make a sound."

Nick shivers, but not from the cold winds. "I only heard of that night... I couldn't imagine being there." *No wonder Bhaltair can't sleep without the vials.*

"Well, that kind of power is deity-like. I'm just happy he's the only Black." Bhaltair rubs his hands on his thighs. "It just sucks that the people here, the students here... they don't see how blessed they are."

They both watch as people walk around them. They see a little girl holding onto her mother's hands. It brings back the painful memory of the little girl who cried with her chained brother. Nick wonders what happened to those siblings. Probably nothing good, based on their luck.

"I want Availian bread. Bread from the wheat of our fields, the oil from our olive trees and the ice sugars from our mountains." Bhaltair's voice is a whisper against the winds.

"And the fruits of the forests and the wine from our vines," Nick finishes. "But we can't have that. We won't for a long time."

"Whatever do you mean?"

"I do not intend to stay at the bottom. I plan on returning home," Nick explains.

Bhaltair turns to him, confused.

"You should make plans as well. Have a goal to help you reach out of this circle, Bhaltair. Gain enough power that you can go back home and eat your bread. The goal may look simple, but it will be hard for you. But if you really want that bread, then I think it's possible."

Nick can hear Bhaltair laugh. "So, what's your goal?"

Nick looks out to the Purples as they leave the bakery; he sees Braawen laughing again. Bhaltair follows his eyes. "Purple circle? Nick, that seems more impossible than my bread. However, if you get into the circle, it would get you enough power to have no one question your word. It's a goal to aspire to."

He wants to shake his head, but doesn't.

No, not Purple. It wouldn't make me their leader.

Chapter 18

Book

Late into the night, Nick finds his way into the library of the school and goes to visit the head librarian's office. The librarian, Ms. Joy Bell is always happy to answer Nick's questions and help a fellow bookworm find what he likes. She embodies her name, as she always has a bright smile plastered on her dark face. This time her hair in an elaborate braided updo instead of an afro. He remembers Kaius telling him that he would like to get his hair braided but doesn't have enough coins to get it done. When Nick tells Ms. Joy about Kaius's problem, she readily agrees to braid his hair.

Kaius joins Nick to the library the following night and Ms. Joy jumps in delight. She neatly braids and oils Kaius's hair into cornrows in her office in the evening while she tells both of them stories and myths. Nick hasn't seen his friend look so happy in ages.

As the woman weaves her fingers through Kaius's hair and tells her tale, Nick looks on her desk to see a black book. The book draws him in, but as he approaches the book, he receives a light shadow whip on the hand. He pulls back, rubbing his stinging hand as Ms. Joy glares at him for the first time.

"Nick, do not go near that book. It's a rare edition and has to be placed back into the Black cottage in the restricted section," she states with a hint of warning in her voice.

"What is it about?" Nick asks.

"Restricted means I cannot say, darling." She pulls on Kaius's hair a little too tightly, causing the boy to wince in pain.

"Please, Ms. Joy? We won't tell," Kaius pleads through the pain, while Nick gives her his best puppy face.

They see her resolve crumble, and she sighs. "It's a book with the names of all the Black users." They both gasp. "Even if you wanted to open it, it can only be opened with the permission of a Black user. The Black Teacher has the Emperor's permission and is responsible for this book, but he needed my help to fix a page. I should really return it to him." She mumbles the last part to herself.

Nick looks again at the thin, ancient-looking book. "It doesn't look like a long read."

She giggles. "No, I'm afraid not. There aren't many people who make it into the Black circle. Now, it's just one."

"The Night Emperor," Nick whispers.

She nods as she pulls on Kaius's hair, his face showing distress. "Yes, though I do hope that another Black comes soon. It's a teachers' dream, especially Professor Arran's, to train the next Black, and have their names written in history. But the closest to becoming a Black is a Purple. From what I've heard, it seems that Braawen Archer and Emelie Snowfield may become Blacks. They seem to be soaring through the Purple spells."

Kaius gives Nick a worried look as he sees his friend's fist clench.

Of course, Braawen would be closer to a Black. Why does it have to be him? Nick doesn't roll his eyes like he wants to; instead, he puts on his fakest smile. "Good for them!"

Ms. Joy shakes her head. "Well, maybe they won't be Blacks. I've never heard of a Black who can't talk to the shadows." She shakes her head. "I'm a Blue and can talk to the shadows. If Professor Arran doesn't fix that quick, those Purples are going to have a hard time."

Kaius winces as Ms. Joy pulls tightly at the front of his hair.

"Calm down, boy, your baby hairs need to come into the braid, so stop moving." She hits his hand with the comb when he tries to touch it.

"But it hurts," he whines.

She kisses her teeth and hits his hands again. Nick tries hard not to laugh at his friend, but it's a losing battle as he sees Kaius squirm in his seat.

At tonight's lesson with Volodimir, they go over the basics of Shadow magic.

Nick smiles when he sits on his chair. "Do you think that I can master the Yellow skills before the Spring Festival?"

Volodimir sits straight in his chair. "I do believe you can. However, I don't want you to get too ahead of yourself. You still have much to learn."

Nick nods. He thinks back to the night with Ms. Joy and the book comes back to his mind. He wonders if his teacher will have a similar response as Ms. Joy. "Sir, I have a question."

"Go on." His teacher's voice is encouraging.

"I was wondering. Why aren't there more Blacks? It's just the Emperor. Were there more before him?"

Volodimir looks down, and this time he licks his lips and sighs. "Oh, Nico, you ask some serious questions." At first he thinks he's gone too far, but his teacher gives him a small smile. "There were three other Blacks before the Emperor became one. One was the Emperor's late father. The other two were old, but lived long enough to pass on their secrets. Though it's a fact that there aren't many Blacks."

His teacher pours tea into one of the cups and takes a sip from it. "There is always at least one Black wielder in the world. Sometimes, they're in the royal family or a high-ranking family of some sort. However, while the Emperor may be young, he fights in battles and has no children. The council and him need to find and educate the next Black wielder in case something ever happens to him."

"So, if the Emperor dies, will the Black techniques be lost with him?" Nick asks.

Volodimir shakes his head. "Not exactly. Historically the Black Teacher is a Black wielder. However, a high-ranking Purple can become the Black Teacher until another Black wielder can take their place. The high-ranking Purple will have access to the resources containing the Black spells, but they can't perform them."

"But the experience won't be the same." Nick states.

"No, but the student will learn. Besides, I have no doubt that when a Black wielder or wielders are found, the Emperor will teach them at his palace."

Nick giggles. "He sounds like he would be a hard teacher."

"Even harder than me?" Volodimir asks, a smile playing on his lips.

He scoffs. "Maybe not. You and the General are ruthless. I can't imagine what the Night Emperor is like."

Volodimir chuckles and sips. "If you can survive me and the General, I'm sure you will be fine."

Chapter 19
Family

The next day, Nick sits in one of the library's empty seats while the sun is still shining. Apparently, not a lot of people like the library, which works out well for him. He chooses his regular spot by one of the many desks at the windows. The windows are large enough to give natural light, and seeing the afternoon sky is breathtaking. Today he works alone at his desk, surrounded by books on improving his connection to the shadows. All the books emphasized that having a strong, clear mind allows one to merge with their inner power. One even said a clear goal and strong will can allow one to improve their abilities.

He grabs another large book on improving one's skills and becoming one with the shadows.' He reads through the first page. The book states that there are two ways to know if and when you can move into another circle. The first is by increasing one's connection to the shadow through meditation. The second is through proving one's skill by besting others.

He spends a couple more hours reading and yawns as he flips through another heavy book on the history of Shadow magic. "What bullocks," he whispers. He can't believe that people could go to the god of Shadows and receive his gift of shadows.

He turns to the next page, reading how the scholar who wrote the book theorizes that the gods and goddesses all gave their powers to different animals. However, Light and Darkness also gave their powers to people. He sighs and thinks that there should be Light magic too. He wants to look deeper into Light and Shadow magic.

Hey, shadows.

Yes, young one? they reply.

Nick licks his lips and hopes that they will allow him to get answers. *Do you know anything about the goddess of Light?*

He can hear a burst of small laughter. *Of course, we know of her.*

He snaps his head from the book. "Really?!" He yells. He hears a hush from Ms. Joy and quickly apologizes.

Really? Nick demands in his mind. *Even the god of Shadows?*

Yes, of course, they chuckle. *The shadows are always happy to spread their power. The shadows are meant for men and women. But it is up to you to use it for good or for evil.*

Before he can ask for more information, the scent of lemons surrounds him and Nicks feels a hand on his arm. "Cousin." His conversation is interrupted by the one person he doesn't want to see right now.

Nick turns to his only family member here. "Braawen." He nods politely, though it feels like it's killing him. Braawen hasn't talked to him for over a month. It's like he's been avoiding him. Nick looks from the corner of his eyes and sees that a guard is close by, watching his cousin intently.

Standing in front of him, Braawen looks better, stronger—and dare he say it—he looks even more handsome. As he looks at his cousin, a feeling of ease, knowing that his cousin is well, fades to anger. Nick remembers what his cousin did to Lorcan. It takes everything in him not to growl as Braawen wears his Purple colours proudly.

Nick even mustered the courage to speak to one of the Purples to ask about Braawen and asked if he was alright after breaking off his friendship with Lorcan. He got hit for even daring to speak to a Purple. He didn't try again after the General received a complaint that a Yellow was trying to harass a Purple. Of course, it was false, but the General would hear none of it, and Nick avoided the Purples as best he could.

"I had a feeling that I would find you here. I need your help," Braawen states with a cocky smile.

Funny, I needed your help weeks ago, Nick thinks to himself.

What do you want?" Nick moves Braawen's hand from his arm.

At least, Braawen remembers that he doesn't like flowery words and gets to the point.

Braawen ignores Nick's annoyance. "I need your help on a paper. You see, there's-."

Screw asking him why he let Lorcan go; my cousin's an ass. We haven't talked in over a month, and he comes for homework? Nick angrily thinks.

He gets up from his seat, but his cousin is fast and tries to pull him down. However, Nick is faster. He moves his shoulder in time and glares at Braawen, who looks momentarily shocked, then quickly recovers.

"It seems that both of us are improving with this school. You've even got a bit of meat on you," Braawen states.

That's an understatement, as he knows that he has muscles now.

"Aren't we family?" Braawen asks.

Nick scoffs. "Wasn't Lorcan your best friend?" he retorts.

Braawen's body tenses, and there is a hint of fire in his eyes. "You don't understand," he whispers. "I have to keep up appearances. The Purples... they all have their eyes on me. Being the child of one of the leaders of the rebellion does that." He quickly glances at the guard.

"Well, maybe if you had kept your mouth shut like I told you, none of this would have happened to you. If you were smart, you would have used your mother's maiden name," Nick whispers back, getting ready to leave.

"Please, Nick. Please, cousin." Braawen's voice is low as he begins to beg. "I need your help. Please?" He sounds so desperate, and a part of Nick relishes in it, and another part genuinely feels sorry for him. "We're the only family we have left. Uncle Tys is probably dead, from what I'm told. It's just you and me."

Nick looks at him. "You know about Uncle Tys? What else do you know?"

Braawen smiles. "All I know is that he is about to die. I can't tell you much, but what I do know is that he's here in this city, doing gods knows what." He waves his hand dismissively. "So, about that paper."

Nick rolls his eyes and turns, but his cousin jumps out of the shadows from a bookcase in front of him. He jumps and stares in shock.

"Shadow Walk. Apparently, I'm a natural at it. Didn't even get sick when I did it on my first try." He chuckles, and Nick feels a pang of jealousy. "Come on, Nick, you and me together. Your brains and my talent. Professor Arran says that I have a great chance of getting into the Black circle. Wouldn't it be great if you had someone in your corner with such influence?"

Nick steps back. He knows it would be good to have the only family that he knows safe. It's even better for him to have someone who's so powerful on his side. He always wanted to fight side-by-side with Braawen as an equal.

He takes a deep breath; if his cousin has information on his uncle, he can deny his pride a little longer. His cousin is getting information about his uncle because he's worried about him too. They're family. They can work together and find their uncle and save him. So, instead of a frown that feels real, he smiles at his cousin. "You're right. You are getting stronger. Maybe I can help you with your homework if you can help me with my shadow training? Maybe even tell me anything that you hear about uncle?"

Braawen laughs. "It's a deal. I'll try to teach you what I can, but there are some things that can't be taught."

"Don't worry, I understand." Nick keeps smiling.

In the Training Hall, he tells Kaius of his first meeting with his cousin. He doesn't know why he expected his friend to react differently when he himself could barely stand the sight of his cousin.

"You agreed to help him with his homework?" Kaius hisses as he launches a punch at Nick's face. Nick easily dodges it and flips Kaius onto his back. Kaius recovers quickly, and both boys face each other in a ready position.

"I said I'll help him. I never said he was getting a high grade." Nick smirks, and Kaius smiles in return. The General announces a break, and the two bow to each other to end their fight. "Plus, what better way to get access to Purple information?"

Kaius shakes his head. "Dude, you're already doing Yellow homework, Orange from yours truly, and even Lorcan tells you about his education in Red. I guess all you're missing is Blue."

He shakes his head as he walks over to one of the benches. "Part of me can't trust Braawen, but the other part of me just wants a piece of my family back."

"Even someone like him?"

Nick sighs. "Even him, I guess."

Braawen is in the middle of finishing a Shadow Jump from one ledge to the next. As he looks at the ledge, he looks to the next jump. It was the farthest jump for the Purple class, and no one could clear it. Unfortunately, the farthest Braawen has made is halfway. He and many of the students see it as a jump of crowning achievement. If a student could jump across, they would be seen as one of the best in the circle.

There is even a bigger jump in the Training Hall that he knows he needs to make. Rumour had it that if one made the jump, they would be closer to becoming a Black.

Braawen looks at the shorter jump and plans to achieve that goal until he jumps back, startled as someone slowly comes out of the shadows.

"Hello, handsome," Emelie purrs.

He tears his gaze from the training exercise, his eyes shining as he looks at her. Her hair cascades down her back in waves, and the lights make her pale blonde hair look silver. She walks up to him with her usual smile and shake of the hips. She makes the Purple uniform look almost royal on her, yet he could imagine what she would look like in Black.

He moves his thoughts back to the present and can't help but smile. "What do you want, Emelie? I actually have work today."

She rolls her eyes as her fingers gracefully caress his shoulders; it only makes it harder to muffle the groans that climb up his throat. "Oh please. I'm sure you're getting your 'goody smart' friend to help you." She allows her nails to softly drag on his cheeks. "Think you can get him to help me too?" she whispers.

He scoffs. "Nope." He turns around, no longer interested in the exercise that his teacher gave them.

"Does your friend know that you're just using him?" She follows him, not making a sound.

"What does it matter? He sees me as his only connection to the Kingdom of Availa." Braawen scoffs again.

Emelie brushes her light blonde hair out of her face. He looks at her and thinks that she must have been a noble or something. Her skin is flawless and soft to the touch, her icy blue eyes give her a cold but beautiful look. As she has told him before, she is a one of a kind.

Before she can ask another question, Professor Arran appears from the shadows. Silent and tall as always, the professor looks sharp and polished, from his shining shoes to his gelled-back chestnut hair. Even the silver strand at the front is gelled back. His chin is always high, and his nose almost points to the sky.

"Students," he states, hands clasped behind his back.

"Professor." They both bow.

He nods for them to stand. "It has come to my attention that you both are excelling in your powers of darkness. That is good, but not good enough. You two are gifted and special. It has been a long time that Equinox House has had students that have gone straight into the Purple circle. The first in your background."

They both smile. Being called special brings memories to Braawen's time on the battlefield. Whenever a battle or fight needed to be won, people would turn to him for hope. He would ride into battle, fighting against enemies with more training, strength, and power than him. However, he could easily see through people's strengths and weaknesses.

"I have told the Emperor your progress, and he believes that you two may have a chance of getting into the Black circle." The professor smiles. "I believe so as well." He walks to one of the windows and watches the sunshine. His eyes narrow as he looks below and sees a boy and girl in Yellow jogging.

"Yellows!" He spits. "Why the Emperor even bothers to include them is beyond me. Most of the time, they just stay in Yellow. See these children?"

Both Braawen and Emelie walk over to see two children jogging in the snow. Braawen knows only one of them and snarls. Braawen is looking at his cousin, who stops to take a breather. The dark-haired girl is running backwards, calling out to him. Then she runs over and grabs his arms, dragging him to continue, leaving their footprints in the snow.

"Remember, children," Professor Arran states. "We are above them." His voice echoes through the shadows. "Purple is the dominant colour. We hold the most powerful positions, and we have a better chance of reaching the Black than anyone else. The Yellows are the Beginner class. We are the Elite. It is the Elites that become Legendary." His professor gives a mirthless laugh. "They'll be lucky to get into Orange, the Common class. It's perfect for them."

Their professor turns to leave but stops. "Remember Braawen, your assignment is coming up. Has your uncle responded to your reply? Is he coming to the mines, and do you have everything prepared?"

"Yes, professor."

"And you don't mind going against the last of your flesh and blood?" The professor gives the young man in front of him an inquisitive look.

Braawen shrugs. "He was my least favourite uncle. Plus, the last of my family is dead anyway. They were weak, stupid, and powerless. I intend too not be as weak as them." He gives a smile, and Emelie holds his hands, smiling back.

It's what his uncle taught him anyway. *Use the people around you, keep the ones that can still be useful. The others are meant to be culled,* Markus's deep voice whispers in his ears.

Well, Braawen muses. *My uncle always wanted to go down in history. But now, instead of a hero, he will serve as a warning to all those that cross the path of the Night Emperor.* He can't help but admire the Night Emperor for that.

The professor nods as he looks at the boy's shadow. He listens to Braawen's shadow and whispers Darkest Truths. The shadows are a quiet entity. They are never loud and always speak in one voice. Everyone who could hear the shadow whisper heard the voice of a male, maybe the god of Shadows.

"Is he lying?" Arran asks the shadows.

"No, he is telling the truth," the shadow whisper back.

"Good to hear. Remember to kill any weakness. That includes anyone from your past as well. Cut your weakness out, and let the shadows in."

With that, the professor leaves. He is proud of all his students, but he has one disappointment. None of his students have heard the shadow voice. *Maybe I'll switch to meditation. I'll tell the rest of the teachers in Purple.*

Braawen looks back and sees that his cousin and his friend are long gone, and the sun has set. Emelie looks at him.

"Shall we join the rest for a lovely game?" Emelie whispers in his ears.

Braawen knows what the girl wants and will happily give it to her.

The two of them are in his bed. They all get private rooms and bathrooms, with the most comfortable bed that he has ever slept on. Though he doesn't sleep on it all the time. He can't. The first week, he slept on the floor as the bed was too soft. Being a soldier and sleeping on the ground, one doesn't get used to sleeping on a cloud.

However, Emelie worked him into his bed by breaking him in. He had the impression of being a king when he entered here. He wanted to be treated like a king when it was his time to graduate. A part of him was sad to lose Lorcan, but it had to done. Sacrifices had to be made. He was told that Red was considered the Classic circle, but it should be changed to Moderate. Braawen wouldn't survive with the Purple students if he stayed with a Moderate.

To him, Purple students are in a world of their own. They are a cult, a private group of individuals who knew they had talent and used it to get anything they could. As soon as they heard that he was put into Purple, many couldn't believe it, and others were eager to know him. He has made friends, connections, and worked hard to put down those who challenged him.

He turns and sees Emelie asleep in his arms. He carefully moves his arms out from underneath her body without waking her, not wanting his arms to fall asleep. The boy looks to the window, a beautiful stained-glass window of the moon and stars. The only light besides the moon is a single candle on his nightstand. Braawen closes his eyes and breathes deeply.

I am a survivor. I will adapt to anything and everything, he tells himself. To him, he's back in the rebellion, fighting in battles and slashing men dead to live. It was them or him.

He looks at the flames. *It's my friends or me. It's my uncle or me. It's Nick or me.* He lets out a small chuckle. He obviously knows the choice.

"It's me. I will always choose me."

Chapter 20
Fight

This morning's class is an odd one.

First off, Nick finally had a good night's sleep without the damn vials for once. He saw that everyone was still asleep, and he rolled back in bed. All was peaceful until the covers were thrown off him with such force that Nick was alert and ready to impale whoever had done that to him. He saw the General grinning ear to ear.

"I'm glad to see that you are ready to attack. It means my teachings are working!" the General yelled, alerting the rest of the group.

General Herald got them all up bright and early. He was clearly excited for this day, causing fear and anxiety for the rest of the class. As Nick and his friends enter the Training Hall, all four of them stop in their tracks. They are pairing with another class. Purple.

Nick turns around to leave, only to be stopped by the General's chest. He can hear and feel the laughter of the General as his face vibrates against his chest. His teacher's callous fingers pull Nick off him and push him and the rest of his class towards the Purple class. It seems that the whole circle is here. Nick can feel all fifteen arrogant people in one room. It's stifling and suffocating. He turns to see Takara glaring at them, and Rohana scoffs. Bhaltair is the only one who refuses to make eye contact with any of them.

"I see your small group is here and well. I hope that my class can aid in your group's learning," says a man in great scholarly robes of Black and Purple. Nick can't hide his surprise at the 'great' Professor Arran coming to this class. From what he heard, the man never did.

General Herald only grins. "You'll be surprised, professor. My students have improved greatly over these past weeks."

Professor Arran smiles frostily. "Of course, shall we test them, then? Your best against mine?"

Nick looks into the General's eyes, silently begging him not to do this to Bhaltair. The General catches his look and smiles. "Yes. I agree. Bring out your champion," he roars.

Nick looks at Bhaltair with pity. He in return, looks back at him, confused. Though, Bhaltair then sniffs towards the Purples, looking sick.

Professor Arran strokes his small pointed beard and smirks. "I choose Braawen."

Nick's body goes stiff as he sees Braawen approach them with a smug smile as he looks at Bhaltair. All around them, the Purples cheer him on. Bhaltair's eyes narrow.

General Herald clears his throat. "Then I choose Guts."

This time, all three Yellows look at Nick. He slowly turns to the General and wonders if this is some sort of sick punishment.

The shock breaks by Takara's cheers and Bhaltair and Rohana pushing him forward and encouraging him. Nick can't help but smile at the support and even sees the General give him a nod. He is representing his class. He won't fail them.

The whole Purple class looks confused, and even his cousin is startled.

"You can't be serious?" Professor Arran asks in disbelief.

Nick narrows his eyes at him.

"I'm serious. You two, in the circle, now! This is my class, and this is how I teach." With that, General Herald walks toward the circle and everyone follows him. Nick can feel the professor's annoyance but tries to act calm.

The two are in the circle and stand in their starting positions. Nick can feel the stares all over him. He can't perform well when he's watched like this. Not only that, Nick doesn't want to fight his cousin. He doesn't want to hurt his cousin.

And Braawen knows this.

"Make your opponent fall three times or throw them out of the circle. No shadow powers, no eye scratching. Fight!" his teacher roars.

Braawen is quick and aims a punch at his face. If Nick didn't have good reflexes, he would have had a broken nose. He gasps but dodges another attack. As he continues to dodge, the cheers of his team soar even against all the Purple members.

He has to use a shin block to block his cousin's kicks, but he knows his cousin's moves from the rebellion. He knows his weaknesses and blind spots. When his father turned him into Braawen's personal punching bag, he took note of every hit. There were times when he dodged him to avoid getting a hard punch or kick. He does the same now as he expertly dodges and weaves through each of Braawen's punches and kicks.

The match lasts longer than what the Purple class expected until Braawen makes a surprising move. He knows that Nick doesn't want to hurt him and knows that he likes to dodge. It is time to teach his cousin something new. He did say he would help train him.

Braawen manages to grab Nick by the neck, bringing him down and knee him in the nose. Both can hear the gasps from the Yellow and the cheers from the Purple. Nick falls, and Braawen expects him to stay down, but he gets back up, spitting out the blood pouring into his mouth. There is a roar from the Yellows as he gets back into fighting position. Nick isn't out of the circle, and he isn't staying down.

The move is a surprise to him, but Lorcan did warn him that Braawen was brutal in the Training Hall. The brutality doesn't surprise him; Braawen has survived battles. But Nick survived going into enemy bases, his father's beatings, and he survived Braawen. He isn't going down that easily.

Nick sees that his cousin intends to jab him on his right side of the head, but Nick dodges and grabs his arm, ready to flip him. His cousin is stronger and flips him instead. He lands hard and gets back up.

If he's down one more time he loses, but he doesn't care. He just wants to hit his cousin once. Bring his cousin, the man who hasn't been brought down once, to his knees.

A bloody grin stretches across his face as his cousin's eyes narrow. His cousin makes haste and punches his gut hard, but Nick uses that to his advantage and grabs hold of Braawen's arm to flip himself up. He can feel the pain in his abs, but the pain of losing without bringing his cousin down gives him strength. The anger of being his punching bag for years guides his legs as he uses them to grab Braawen's neck. The joy of knowing that he can bring his cousin down allows him to flip his opponent as he lands on his feet. Courage allows him to turn around to see his cousin lying on his back.

Braawen looks confused as his cousin lands on his feet and him on his back. The Purple class goes quiet as the Yellow's cheers get even louder. He gets up, seething, as his cousin gives a bloodied smile.

Nick knows he's going to die, but at least he was able to get the better of his cousin for once in his life.

Braawen doesn't waste time; neither does Nick. They both move quickly. He dodges and goes on the defence as Braawen punches and jabs. His arms are hurting, but he stays upright. Then he sees an opening. He's tempted to do it, but it would really hurt his cousin. Nick's arm already goes to the chin. Hitting it at his speed, he can cripple him. He knows he can break bone, thanks to Volodimir's training, and a part of him wants to do that.

"We're family," he can hear Braawen tell him in the library.

He stops when he remembers that Braawen is his only family left, and his cousin uppercuts him in the jaw. Nick goes down, and he can hear the screaming cheers of the Purple.

He couldn't do it. He couldn't hurt his cousin like that. He looks up to see Braawen's smug smile. He gulps, tasting blood and spits it on the side of the mat. He shakily gets up, his body screaming to stay down. Nick wipes his nose that's still trailing blood and nods at him. He spits more blood, and he can't breathe through his nose. "Good fight," he mumbles, but before he could say anything else, the Yellow class crashes into him, cheering.

All the Purples are bewildered.

"Why are they cheering for him? The boy lost!" Nick can hear the professor say. "Now, class, you can look at this fight and see what not to do. I hope that your pupil was able to learn from Braawen." He gives the Yellows a haughty look.

The General doesn't pay the man any mind as he moves the rest of the kids away from Nick and bestows a soft pat on the head. "Guts, you've improved tremendously. Never have I had a group of students who have improved like you sorry lots." His teacher looks down at him proudly.

"Now!" General Herald yells, gaining everyone's attention. "As the teacher and supervisor of this class." He looks at Arran, daring him to say anything. "I will explain the highlights of the fight. You can learn a lot from losing just as much as winning. First, Guts, that neck move was great. Remember, as long as you can use your body weight as an anchor as Guts here did, then you can flip anyone."

"Anyone?" Emelie asks.

"Anyone, Blondie," the General replies.

"My name is Emelie."

"I didn't ask." Nick can hear a chuckle come from Rohana as the General continues. "Now Guts, I saw that- "

But before the man can tell Nick that he saw him hesitate, Nick crumples to the ground. There are gasps around him, and he hears General Herald tell Nightshade and Ice to warm up the class while he brings Guts to the infirmary. The General brings Bhaltair as well to keep an eye on him.

Nick wakes up to white ceilings and a thin blanket on him. He sees a needle in his arm hooked up to a giant bright red and green vial. He watches as it drips slowly and looks down to see it go into his veins. His veins light up bright red, and he has half a mind to rip it off.

"Nick!" He can hear the relief in Bhaltair's voice, but everything is blurry. "You're back! It's been an hour. Not that I'm complaining, the smell of lemon was getting overwhelming. Oh, you won't believe how pissed off the General was…" Bhaltair continues, and Nick is surprised by his rant.

Nick smiles and concludes that he won't be asking for help from Braawen. Getting information on his uncle or not, he is going to find his own way.

The rest of his day is spent in the infirmary, and Nick can hear another student being brought into the room. The nurse yells at the screaming student, who looks around his age. But the other student beside him was trying to explain that they were trying a spell to make them powerful enough to move up to Red.

It is said amongst the upper years that if you didn't have enough anger, pain was a good way to gain power. Many students hurt themselves on the advice of the older kids or hurt others to lower the competition. Nick can't help but think that this way of teaching is toxic. Yet Laura told them that there were never any deaths or serious injuries before. It started happening four years ago. However, in the past year alone, under the new Black Teacher, the cases declined sharply.

Nick receives visitors in the evening. Both Lorcan and Kaius scold him, then praise him for dropping Braawen on his ass. Lorcan is very vocal about the fact that it should have happened a long time ago. The nurse comes and shoos the others out of the room, then sits Nick up so she can look over his injuries.

"Looks like someone really wanted you to get hurt." The nurse gives a questioning look. "I always thought that the General's teaching methods were a bit extreme..." She sighs. "But it does help prepare students for the outside world. You'll need to wear a nose brace for a week. The lemon balm can heal you perfectly, but that's too expensive to use. I'm sorry, but there's only so much these healing potions can do."

"It's not a problem." His voice comes out nasally. "But I am feeling a bit dizzy."

The nurse scrunches up her face as she walks over to the cabinet in her office and returns with a purple vial. "This will help with the dizziness. You have to take this after you finish eating."

A week wearing a white cast on his nose and a funny nasally voice is a small price to pay for knocking his cousin down. He will wear it with pride.

"I should just dedicate a bed for you at this point. The nose will take time to heal and I want to make sure that the rest of your body actually heals." She glares at him. "You are to stay here for the night. Do I make myself clear?"

He gulps and gives the best smile he can. "Of course." His nasally voice manages to crack the nurse's frown. She turns around and quickly leaves when a chuckle is about to break out, closing the curtains behind her. He can still hear her muffled chuckles and the clicking of her heels.

Nick falls back onto the bed, his head hitting the pillow, closing his eyes to stop them from watering. He touches his stomach under the blanket and can still feel a dull ache. Even with the medicine and painkillers, it hurts for him to take deep breaths.

Braawen, we're supposed to be family.

Chapter 21
Jump

Family. At least one family member is searching for him, caring about him, in danger because of him. As the crescent moon rises above the lake, Nick remembers that Braawen mentioned his uncle was in the city. He's been planning on going to the city to search for his uncle, but having both day and night classes always leaves him drained. Luckily, all he had today is his morning class and the night class is still hours away. He estimates the distance to the city from his memory of the wagon ride. It's a long ride and he doesn't have the strength or power to Shadow Jump such a great distance without feeling dizzy. He isn't at Volodimir's level... yet.

However, he has a small purple solution.

Nick braces himself as he slowly peels the covers off him, listening to the faint snores in the infirmary. Once he sits up, he starts to feel the dull ache in his stomach again. He slowly pulls back the curtains and looks around the room for the source of the snoring but finds the other beds empty. It's just him tonight as the other children were deemed fit to rest in their own beds.

The only source of light is from the moon. He turns to the head nurse's desk and sees that even she has left for the night. He's puzzled for a moment, as she wouldn't just leave a sick patient alone, and he slowly walks to the head nurse's office. He slowly opens the office door, revealing an empty desk but a couch occupied by a sleeping assistant nurse. Nick wonders if the head nurse knows that her assistant just sleeps all night. She looks comfortable sleeping on the couch, snoring away. It would be just terrible to wake up the poor woman just to get some painkillers. So instead, he helps himself.

He tiptoes past her, and sees that the cabinet has a keyhole. He bites his lips, then looks over to the assistant nurse again. Just as he guessed, the keys are in the pocket of the nurse. Carefully and quietly, Nick is able to take the keys, only stopping when the nurse moves to adjust her arm. Once he has the keys, he slowly tiptoes back to the cabinet and opens it. He grabs some more red vials to help with the pain, and as he's about to lock the doors, he sees the purple vials. He grabs two to help with his dizzy spells, one for the trip into the city and the other for the return trip. Locking the cabinet, he looks back at the sleeping nurse and places the keys back in her pocket. He drinks one red vial, immediately feeling the effects as his muscles begin to ache less. He momentarily thinks of the consequences of self-medicating but shrugs. He sighs as he leaves the office, knowing that he still has a class with Volodimir tonight.

Maybe Volodimir will cancel class tonight? He doubts it.

He closes the door of the office and looks down at his clothes. He is still in the infirmary clothes which are a poor choice for outside weather. He looks around the infirmary until he sees another room way in the back with piles of dirty clothes. He sees a black shirt that he puts on. Inconveniently, his yellow pants have blood stains all over, and he drops them back in the pile. He continues looking, until he sees blue training pants that are too big. He shrugs and uses his belt to make it fit and uses one of the cloaks he finds hanging at the back of the room. It's not enough to shield him from the cold, but it's enough to shield his face.

The window opens easily, and the snow is just soft enough to make the landing easier. With a deep breath and a small prayer to the deities, the little boy in blue closes his eyes and jumps out the window.

Running through the forest invigorates Nick as he follows the forest trail to the city. As Volodimir stated, the gates are always open for the children to leave. No one looks twice when a child leaves, but just in case, he hides in the shadows. He can't contain his smile as his feet tread through the snow and the winds of the north embrace him. He used to jog in the mountains; he hopes his Uncle Tys can jog with him again.

He runs past the lampposts and finds the road that leads to the city. He runs quite a bit, and makes a mental note to thank Takara for his nightly runs, because he has greatly improved. Nick grins when he sees the sea of lights ahead and still keeps to the shadows they cast when he enters the city. He stays on the rooftops and watches the people from below. Nick sighs. He can't help but feel a little jealous. They all get to live their normal lives while he can't remember the last time he's been able to enter a city normally.

He gently slaps himself on the cheeks to forget about all that. Right now, he is on a mission to find any information on his uncle. His cousin is useless, and after the beating Braawen gave him today, Nick doesn't want to try talking to him. He closes his eyes and blocks out the laughter and music that plays to the gentle snowfall. He thinks for a moment, then it clicks as he opens his eyes. Braawen is in Purple, and the higher the rank, the higher the source of information must have come from. He knows that he can't ask the General or any high-ranking person. He's still just a Yellow. A crafty Yellow, but still too low in the school. He goes for the next best option.

Hello, shadows. He pauses and waits. The shadows never take long.

Hello, friend. This is good news for him. He's a friend now. *What can we do for you?*

I need your help looking for someone. If you help me, I'll be willing to do you a favour. Not that he thinks they'll want anything, but he believes that if you're willing to do someone a favour, they'll more likely do you one in return.

How kind, they respond. *But all we ask is that you not hold back. You held back during the fight.*

He knows he shouldn't be surprised, but a part of him is. *I don't want to hurt my cousin!* he snaps.

Just try to not hold back anymore. You will enjoy the freedom and the limits that you can pass.

He sighs. He really needs to find his uncle and warn him. *Deal.*

Excellent. The shadows are loud in his ears, their voices strong and deep.

Nick waits for a response.

Go to Nortshell estate. The lord is there in his office. The shadows tell him.

He looks confused, but they've been honest with him so far. The last time he was there, Lord Nortshell was sent off to a jail cell. Volodimir was more than happy to tell him how the foolish nobleman was found guilty of all his convicted crimes and sentenced to death. He wanted to ask his teacher more about the impact Nigel Nortshell's death would have, but his teacher just laughed.

"Oh, not much. He wasn't like his father. Pity." Nick could detect the sarcasm dripping from Volodimir's voice.

As he makes his way to the Nortshell estate, not knowing why the shadows told him to go there, he expects to see the estate empty and dark with the flag down. He stops and blinks at the sight in front of him. He groans and wonders if hallucinations are a side effect of taking all those vials. It would be one reason why there in front of him is the large estate where the family flag is still up. The estate seems lively, many of the lights are on and guards stand alert at the gates.

He huffs, drinking the purple vial. "It could belong to a distant relative, or..." His mind suddenly remembers the conversation that Nortshell's shadow mentioned about another family member. His eyes widen as he smiles. "This will be fun."

Dodging the guards takes a little longer as even the smallest sound seems to make them jump. He doesn't know why they're so alert, but he ignores it for now. Calming his heart rate and focusing on the task at hand allows him to pass the rest of the guards easily. He gives thanks to both his teachers for his training and the shadows for his use of Night Vision. He would congratulate himself later. Right now, he has a mission, and the shadows told him that this man would have the answers. He makes his way over to the spot that he and his teacher stood before, looking to see the office window still lit.

He takes a deep breath and closes his eyes. *How do I get in, shadows?*

Picture the room in your mind. It is easier to Shadow Jump once you know what the room looks like.

He remembers the pale yellow room. He can see the armour and the large oak desk in the room, with the painted map of the Empire behind it. Not knowing how to Shadow Jump, he recalls what Volodimir did and reaches for the shadow of the roof. He closes his eyes and imagines the room in his mind. He takes deep breaths and opens them slowly, putting his hand on the roof, only for his hand to phase through. Frightened, he brings his hand back, touching it and making sure that all his fingers are still intact. His hand is still in working order, and a thrill replaces whatever doubts linger in his mind.

"Let's do this." He pictures the room again and jumps into the shadow of the roof. His hands reach out to warm air, and his eyes quickly adjust to the light of the room by ending his Night Vision. He grins widely as he realizes that he successfully Shadow Jumped from the ledge into Nortshell's office, but he doesn't have time to congratulate himself. This time, he comes out from the shadow of the desk, startling the new Lord Nortshell.

"Holy shit!" are the first words he hears, before he turns around.

There's a clear difference between the startled man and the last Lord Nortshell. The new lord's voice wavers, and Nick stares at the man while they both try not to panic. The man's posture isn't as confident as the old lord, with lighter hair and a sharper jaw. However, the man has the same eyes and blue jewel on the tie. The suit he wears seems to be of the highest quality, similar to some of the nobles he'd seen on the streets. He wouldn't be surprised if it is the latest fashion.

The half-brother, he concludes. The man is slowly backing up into the map, as if he's trying to merge with it. Nick looks closer at the map with the familiar sadness of Availa's inclusion in the Empire but is surprised at another edition. To the east of Availa, the two separate kingdoms of Ram and Luxor have been merged into one. He would look into that later.

The scared man in front of him grabs his attention when his hands scrabble for anything to use to defend himself, but there's nothing near him. Nick sees that at least this fellow has a normal reaction to people coming out of the shadows.

Fear.

This time, he's going to use it to his advantage.

When he takes a step forward, he notices that he doesn't feel as dizzy this time, thanking the deities that he took the purple vial. His smile is still hidden under his hood. He puts his hand up, showing that he has no weapons. He wants the new lord to fear him just enough to still get coherent information.

"I mean you no harm." His voice comes out a little nasally which disguises his voice. "I'm only here for information."

The man snarls. "Why should I give you information?"

So, the man does have a bit of backbone, Nick thinks.

He grins. "Well, if it wasn't for my master and I, you wouldn't be the new Lord Nortshell."

That's when Lord Nortshell looks at the colour of his pants. Blue, with the emblem of Equinox House. In his mind, he sees Nick as a person who would be joining the Shadow Assassins. It was well known that Blue circle students would join them.

Lord Nortshell's eyes widen. *What if this was a test? What if I laughed? What if his master heard that I disrespected his pupil? No, I must survive.* That he is determined to do.

"I do express my thanks to your master, little Shadowling." He sits back down on his chair as he starts feeling faint. The last thing he wants to do is faint in front of Shadow Assassin's apprentice. "How can I, Lord Edward Nortshell, be of service to you?"

If it wasn't for them, I'd still be hounded by my ass of a half-brother.

Nick smiles but doesn't move from his spot. "Let us both thank the Emperor for finding out the deceit of your brother."

"Half-brother," he corrects him.

"Of course. I apologize, my lord." Nick gives a small bow. "I would like to know if you have any new information on the rebel leader that still survives from the new province of Availa?" He hopes the man does, otherwise this whole journey would be a waste.

The nobleman nods, though he also frowns. "Yes, the rebel scum Tybalt Archer will be at the mines in three weeks. It's what we discussed in the council meeting."

That's sooner than I hoped, but where can he be?

"Does he have any known whereabouts in the city?"

The man scoffs. "I don't know! Probably in the slums, hiding away. He probably heard rumors about the fate of his nephews, apparently, the sons of Julius and Markus. That's why he's here. The son of Julius is at Equinox House, I think. The other is... well, no one knows. The mines? I've heard he's dead. Hopefully, the one at Equinox House can be of good use and the other is dead in the mines. It will be good for the blood of Markus to be erased from existence."

Nick grins. *So, no one knows where I am. Good.* He can use that information to keep himself safe. As long as no one knows that he is an Archer, the better.

"Yes, it would be good for the Empire if the blood of the traitorous family can be used to help the Empire. This would be ironic indeed."

"Indeed! I can tell you this for free since you did help me get all of this." The man giggles. "I was never meant to have any of this, but my stupid half-brother made a mistake and then father threatened to make me his heir. I know he did it to just put his boy in order, but look at me now!" He grins like a spoiled child.

Nick congratulates him, though the man did nothing to earn it. *He wasn't meant to rule. He never learned how. This is good, I can use this to my advantage.*

"Is there anything else I should know? We all must do our part for the Empire."

"Of course!" Edward laughs. "Just be there by sunrise on the day of rest! I was told to do my part by staying out of the way. I hear that a few Shadow Assassins will be in the area and there's going to be a great surprise."

"A surprise?" Nick hides the shock and the worry in his voice. A surprise from the Night Emperor is never a good thing. Nick's experience with surprises mainly involved bombs and attacks.

"Yes. I don't know what it is, but it's supposed to hurt Tybalt deeply." The nobleman smiles. "Can't say the man doesn't deserve it."

"In three weeks, in the morning?" Nick confirms. The nobleman nods.

Is he telling the truth? Nick asks the shadows.

Yes, the shadows hiss.

He looks at the grandfather clock in the corner and growls in displeasure. "I see. Thank you for your time, my lord. Please take care of the wonderful estate that has been given to you. I hope that I can come to you again for more information." The nobleman nods quickly, happy to be of service to the Shadow Assassins. "I also warn that it is best to keep this conversation a secret. We can't have any other nobles knowing about this plan. The Archer must be caught!" His voice is firm like Volodimir's, and he can see the man gulp. Nick internally grins at the thought that he finally has a commanding voice, but keeps his frown in place.

"O-of course," Edward stutters. "My lips are sealed, or may the gods take my head." He smiles nervously.

Seeing a nobleman, a man of power quiver before him, awakes something in Nick. He can feel a certain power bloom in his chest slowly. As he relishes in a nobleman's fear, his shadow grows and completely overcomes the man and the map behind the wall.

"Trust me," his voice echoes around the room. "The gods will be the least of your concerns." With that, he gives a small bow as he disappears into his shadow.

Edward is left alone in his room. He is both happy and nervous to be helping his Empire.

"That boy..." he mumbles to himself. "How could a boy so young bring such fear?" He looks down at his hands and sees that they're shaking. He clasps them together and looks around his office. "I fear the day when he grows up. If the students of the Equinox House are that intimidating, I understand why people fear and respect them."

Nick runs out of the shadow of the Nortshell Estate and jumps across to the other large rooftop, slowing down as his feet can't get a good grip in the snow. He makes it to the town square and looks at the large looming clock tower, gripping one of the bricks. The clock tower shows that it's almost two hours to midnight. He only has five minutes!

I'm not going to make it! He's gasping for breath as he puts his hand on his stomach. He wheezes and feels the tight and painful ache of his muscles in his core. *Damn Braawen,* he curses, grinding his teeth.

He quickly gets down on his knees and feels the cold snow cooling his sore legs. Giving his face a light slap to stay focused, he quickly takes the last of his pain vials, feeling the effects kick in. Still gulping for air as he leans on a chimney, he closes his eyes to settle his mind. The meditation techniques he learnt from the General come into play. He takes his time standing up and exhales, ignoring the sharp pain. After a minute, he feels less dizzy and the pain numbs away, but not fast enough as he takes a step and has to stop to rest. From the high rooftops, he can see the forest out in the distance. Beyond the forest, he knows, is Equinox House.

"It's still too far!" Nick curses as he grits his teeth from a new wave of pain from his nose. He looks out at the forest again and takes a deep breath for a crazy idea to form in his head.

Shadows, you told me not to hold back. How far do you think I can make it to Equinox House? Nick is fuming from the pain radiating his nose and from his centre. His arms are tired, and he's pissed that he held back on Braawen.

"Never again," he vows. "Here's hoping that this anger and pain can be used for something other than cursing!"

See for yourself, they say. *We want to see how far you can go.*

That's all he needs to hear as the smile on his face grows. This might be a stupid idea, but he's used to stupid ideas. He used them all the time during his spying days. One of his stupid ideas was to disguise himself as a soldier to sneak out of an imperial base. It worked with quick thinking, makeup, and sheer luck. He just needs that luck tonight.

Using the anger inside him, he drops into his own shadow and sees black. Seconds pass by as he feels something, sharp nails pushing him. He focuses on his destination and pictures the school. Then he pictures the lake, but his mind pushes past the lake to the forest and the little cottage in the woods. The picture is so vivid that he can smell the freshly brewed tea, and he swears that he can see his teacher sprinting towards him.

Nick realizes that he is in the cottage as his foot hits solid ground. The tea is real, and Volodimir is running towards him. Everything is in slow motion as he sees the room tilt and spins.

Then darkness.

Chapter 22
Faith

Nick feels like he's in an endless void. This is different from his jump in the shadows. For one, nothing is pushing him. Instead, he floats aimlessly for an unknown period of time. For the first time in ages, he feels light and calm, floating in complete silence until something tickles him. What feels like nothing becomes solid beneath him. Uneven, but solid. The next thing he feels is the air; it's no longer the cold air of winter but a warm breeze of summer. His eyes are still closed as he can smell daisies and listen to the chirping of birds. He brushes his hands on the ground to feel the grass. The grass leaves his hands wet, the morning dew has just come, and the air smells so clean.

"Nickolaus." The voice is unfamiliar but soft. It doesn't belong to anyone he knows, and it definitely doesn't belong to the shadows.

He slowly opens his eyes when he hears the soft call of his name again. There are trees all around him, not bare as they should be in winter. Instead, he sees green—healthy green leaves of spring. Sitting up causes a sharp pain to run through him. He gasps, holding his stomach. Sweat trails down his brow as he pushes himself up to lean against a tree. Tall trees and flowers of different colours and smells surround him.

"Spring?" he asks himself. "This is madness."

Before he can panic further, he hears a gentle voice. "Nickolaus." He hears his name again.

He looks up to see a woman with flawless, sun-kissed skin and lilies in her earthy black hair. The earth itself covers the woman with grass and vines. Precious stones of all colours, shapes, and sizes trail down the bottom of her green gown. It is a gown fit for a queen, even though the woman walks with no shoes. Flowers erupt from the ground as she walks towards him, leaving a trail of wheat, daisies, and other flowers that Nick doesn't recognize. She stops as she gets close to him, towering over the boy, who cranes his neck to look up. Her eyes are closed, but she knows where he is and smiles down at him.

The woman opens her hand and reaches for him. He looks at her hand, and after a moment, he takes it. Her hand is bigger than his, more than twice the size. Instead of fear, he feels like he knows this woman. He stands up slowly, wincing slightly at the pain.

"Forgive me for being rude, but…who are you?"

The woman giggles, not the slightest bit offended. "Normally, a man bows to give reverence to a goddess." Her smile allows the ground from around her feet to bloom flowers from the earth.

The first creator! His eyes go wide, and he drops to his knees. "Apologies." He gasps, forgetting the pain. He hears her laugh, and she grabs his hand. The goddess before him picks him up like he's a pebble.

"You seem to require assistance. What do you need?" she asks.

At first, Nick can't form words. He is still in awe that a goddess is in front of him. However, after seeing his surroundings, the flowers, and feeling his pain, he concludes that this is not a dream, he believes her. He licks his lips, recalling the book he read in the library that the gods can only be called on in someone's greatest time of need.

"I am... dead?" Nick asks, honestly afraid of the answer.

"Not yet," she muses.

Oh no. He doesn't say that out loud. "Then, my goddess, I would like to not die, please," he asks, hoping that it won't be too much of a problem.

She smiles, putting him down. She gently takes his arms in her hands, and green vines transfer from her to him.

"May you be blessed with healing and strength, dear boy, for your kind heart. When you awaken, you will feel better." Her voice makes him feel warm and safe, surrounded, but protected.

He smiles, feeling no pain in his body, he bows to the goddess again. "Thank you so much. I don't really deserve it, but I am grateful all the same."

He can hear her laugh, and he looks around to see that the flowers are blooming all around them, blooms of oranges, purples, reds, and blues.

"Ask your question," she commands.

"What?" Nick raises his head, startled.

She smiles. "I know what you wish to ask. Please ask, and I shall answer."

He licks his lips and asks, "Can you help me find my uncle?"

"There is another question that you can ask, but the answer is no. Your uncle prayed for my protection, and I fear that I can tell no one his whereabouts, not even you." Nick's heart sinks at the news. "However, I don't know why he even asked me that. He's been doing such a good job hiding from the Shadow Assassins without my help." She looks him over and her smile widens. "Well, I see how good you are at hiding; I shouldn't be surprised that your master is better."

He looks confused. "My uncle is better than me, but not enough to hide from the Shadow Assassins. I know that my family and my country worshipped you. You have blessed our lands and allowed our people to survive the winter months. You answered my uncle's prayers, so why not the others? Why did so many people have to die? Why-?"

He is hushed as she places her finger on his lips. For the first time, there is no smile on her face and no laughter from her lips. "I fear that it was all meant to be. Not even I can go against fate." The flowers around them close their petals, and even the birds are silent. "It grieved me greatly to see the suffering of my people. But I am the goddess of the Earth. I can only deal with the land. In the end, it was the choices of the people that decided the fate of themselves."

"What do you mean?"

"You will know soon enough. I begged the Fates to change what had been written and to allow my people to be spared. They allowed three chances, but they were in vain. All of this could have been avoided if a man had swallowed his pride. But ask another question."

Nick doesn't know what to ask, but then it hits him. "Why is there no Earth magic?" *Can I one day learn it?*

A smile returns to her face, though it is small. "You are not the first to ask that. Many men and women have been asking that question, but once there was a time that it was not asked. You see, I gave the powers of the Earth to everyone. There was a time when humans could plant anything and it would grow in abundance. They could move mountains with a wave of their hands."

He gasps as he imagines that power, looking down at his own small hands. It must have been amazing. When he looks back up at the goddess, she is no longer smiling.

"But humans began to show their greed, and turned on the land and my creations. So, I stripped them of their powers and gave it to the beast of the fields and forest to defend themselves. However, I allowed the humans to have the knowledge of how to grow their own food. That is all."

He wants to say something but cannot find the words as she picks him up and begins to grow. As she grows, her hands expand, and Nick grips onto her fingers for dear life as they go higher into the sky. The goddess of Earth becomes the size of a mountain when she stops above the clouds. As she lowers her hands, Nick stays in the clouds. He would have screamed if the clouds didn't feel so solid.

"Good luck, Son of Archer," the goddess whispers as she disappears into the clouds.

It is just him in the sky and the cool winds on his cheeks. Before he could ask the goddess what is going to happen, the winds begin to blow harder, pushing him onto his rear end. The clouds move and twist and turn as he desperately tries to hold on to anything. He is at the mercy of the winds until the clouds start to form a face of a man. He slowly opens his eyes to see that the cloud he's sitting on is in the shape of a hand.

The cloud-shaped face smiles but his eyes are closed.

"Son of Archer," the winds bellow from his mouth. The winds would have blown him away if it weren't for the hand holding him, but they are so strong that Nick bows lower to stay on the cloud hand.

"There is no need to bow," the winds chuckle. "I shall make this quick. I am the god of Air; the winds obey my every command. Every breath you take is a gift from me."

Once the winds die down, Nick slowly rises, trying to balance himself. "Thank you, second creator," his voice shakes as he tries to stay balanced. "Thank you, god of Air, for giving me breath. Thank you for allowing me to breathe. I hope that you keep me breathing." He can hear the god chuckle again, which almost pushes him back down. "I also thank you for the breath of my friends and the family that I have left! All I can do is hope that you will allow them to keep breathing!" he yells.

The god of Air laughs. "Always thinking of others, son of Archer, I shall allow you to breathe again." He blows directly at him, and Nick can feel fresh air enter his lungs.

"Thank you."

"Son of Archer, I know what you wish to ask. The power of the Air belongs to the birds and the creatures of flight. When I saw what man had done with Earth and Fire, I decided to never give my powers to them."

The clouds form a frown where his smile once was. "There is also the matter of your family. Both your uncles Tybalt and Malcolm still breathe, but be warned." He moves closer to him. "There will be one whose breath will be taken away."

"But," Nick can't say anything else as he is silenced by the god of Air.

"It's time for you to wake up. I hope you meet the others on better occasions." Before Nick can ask anything else, the god blows a cold breeze in his face, then darkness surrounds him once again.

This time he can hear the familiar voices. They beckon to him, calling him, but he can't make out the words. Then comes light. He blinks, slowly opening his eyes but shutting them quickly as a splitting headache hits him. After the headache subsides, he can feel that he is neither on grass nor clouds, though the mattress he's on closely resembles the clouds. Next come the feelings of warmth and something heavy on his body. He slowly opens his eyes to see wood beams with different dried herbs and spices, and candles make the shadows dance all around the room. Slowly turning his head to the side, he sees a simple wooden black door. He sits up, groaning from the headache that slowly leaves him again.

Where am I exactly? he asks himself. He struggles to get out of the bed; he's lying down on the most luxurious mattress he's ever been on and covered by a thick wool blanket. Once he manages to sit up, the first thing he notices is the size. The bed is large and spacious, the bedding of exquisite quality. His fingers trail smoothly across the simple oak bed frame. It reminds him of his parents' bed. He pushes those memories away and gets up.

A sigh escapes him as he gets a better look at the room. His cape is folded nicely on a large dark green armchair near a small fireplace. He thinks this must be Volodimir's cottage, as everything is still made out of rich wood, not stone and steel like the school. The room is simply furnished with a bed, closet, and an armchair. *Whoever sleeps here doesn't have many belongings*, he thinks. The only thing that seems to stand out is a purple flower in a vase. He looks at it in confusion, as it's winter and flowers should be dead. Yet, it looks healthy and beautiful.

What a beautiful colour, he thinks. *The flowers seem so familiar…*

Don't give up on… A woman's familiar voice fades in his mind leaving a ringing in his ears. It's like a dream, a voice that isn't his mother's or any woman he knows. Nevertheless, he feels that he does. The flower must be from one of the greenhouses he hasn't seen yet.

He looks down and notices that he's still in his blue pants and a black turtleneck with the emblem of the school on his chest.

"My dream…" he whispers in the empty room. His uncle is safe. Both of his uncles are safe. Now that he thinks about it, he should have asked for more information on his Uncle Malcolm.

He groans as he rakes his fingers through his hair. His hair has grown quite a bit, healthier and longer than before. *I need a haircut.*

He doesn't see anything else in the room, so he steps out of bed and walks toward the black door, opening it to see a wide hallway. He creeps along the wooden floorboards, trying to not make too much noise. He walks across the hall and sees three small steps leading down to a larger room. In fact, he realizes without a doubt that this is the place where he meets Volodimir every night. He steps in quietly, peeking his head through the door, expecting to see his teacher there but all he sees is an empty chair and a dead fire. He ventures in more to see that the area is brighter than he expected during the day. With only two windows, he didn't expect the room to get much light.

"You're up?" a voice startles him.

He jumps back and sees a tired Volodimir holding a tray in his hands. He looks at the man he calls his teacher. The man who wears nothing but suits and scholarly robes during his lessons now wears a black short-sleeved shirt and loose black pants tucked into leather boots, his dark hair hanging loose around his head. Nick hasn't noticed how muscular Volodimir's arms are until now. His teacher wasn't big like the General, but the man looks like he is built to fight.

No wonder his punches hurt, Nick thinks. This is the most casual he's ever seen the man.

"Yes, I just woke up," Nick answers.

"Good, I went into the room and saw that you weren't there. Come, let's eat in the kitchen." Volodimir turns without saying another word and makes his way towards the kitchen, going down the same hallway and opening a door with five steps leading down.

Nick follows behind, still confused by his teacher and now at the size of this cabin. At first glance, Nick thought that the cabin was small; clearly, he was wrong. They enter a kitchen that has large windows letting in natural light. The place looks too clean, like it's been barely used, or maybe Volodimir is just that immaculate.

His teacher places the tray on the small round table that has a cup of steaming tea. The tray has a bowl of soup, and he motions for Nick to take his seat across from him. The boy does so with caution and looks at the soup. It looks more like a hearty stew, full of meat and potatoes.

"Thank you for the food." Just as he's about to put the spoon in his mouth, he stops. "And... thank you for the bed." He gives a smile, and Volodimir sits across from him and smiles back, taking a sip from his cup of tea.

The two sit in comfortable silence as one eats and the other drinks. As the clock ticks, Volodimir looks down at his cup. He is thinking of something; Nick can tell at this point. Whenever his teacher thinks of something, he never looks at anyone, but his eyes sometimes dart around or stare intensely at something.

"Nico," Volodimir's voice breaks the silence.

"Yes, sir?" Nick places the food down and looks at his professor.

His teacher had his hand on his cup, but his dark red eyes were piercing Nick's blue. "Nico, how far did you shadow travel? And remember, don't lie."

Nick could have sworn that Volodimir's eyes glowed, but he must have imagined it since he still feels lightheaded. He bites his lips, worried that his teacher will be upset.

"I was in the city, but I lost track of time. I know you like me to be on time, so I asked the shadows how far I could go. They told me that they wanted to see how far I could go as well." He licks his lips and looks down at the bowl. "At first, I just thought of the school, then I saw the cottage.

Then I imagined the smells and you running towards me. I didn't realize that they were real. I just blacked out."

He looks up and sees that his teacher's hands are clasped together under his nose. Volodimir seems to be pondering all that he tells him, and Nick can swear that he sees a small smile.

"Nico... who taught you how to shadow travel?" Volodimir asks.

He glances at him, then back at his hands. "You did."

His teacher gives a confused look. "When?"

"When you first Shadow Jumped, I remembered what you did. I also read some books on the topic and wanted to see if I could do it."

A low chuckle fills the room. "Well, that is very good. I am happy that you can Shadow Jump. Though, I would be even happier if you knew your limits." Then his teacher's face changes. "What you did was extremely dangerous. You were at death's door, and if I hadn't been there to save your life, you would have died." He trails off at the end of his sentence, and Nick can feel the pressure not only on his back but grabbing hold of his neck.

He looks down and tries not to shake. He nods his head and asks for forgiveness, but instead, he can hear his teacher scoff.

"Well, at least you won't do anything like that again. I would hate for someone with so much potential to just die from over travelling. Such an underwhelming death." Volodimir cocks a smile, and Nick feels the pressure leave his body.

He is proud of you, he can hear the shadows speak loud and clear. *You have exceeded our expectations. See what happens when you don't hold back.*

Yes, I could die, Nick retorts scathingly.

A minor setback. He wants to roll his eyes at their response. If they put him through more life-threatening scenarios, he's going to stop listening to them.

"Having a lovely conversation with the shadows?"

Nick's head snaps back up to Volodimir, who is smiling. He rubs the back of his neck, embarrassed at getting caught. "Sorry. It's probably bad table manners."

Volodimir chuckles. "Never apologize for that. I am glad that you and the shadows are speaking together. It is your gift."

"Gift? I thought you said that others can listen to the shadows?"

His teacher takes a sip of his tea and his smile widens. "You're right, to a degree. Everyone with practice can hear the shadows. It takes years of training. But the gift is that you can hear them clearly and so quickly. Few can just hear one voice of the shadows, and only in a whisper if they practice for years. Tell me, boy, what do the shadows sound like to you?"

"I can hear them clearly. Sometimes they're loud; other times they like to speak calmly. They also give me advice. It's not just one voice. It's many voices that come together to tell me things," Nick replies.

Volodimir even looks more pleased. "That is the description I was hoping for, Nico. Not many people can listen to the shadows like you and I can. You see, anyone can listen to the shadows with practice, but sometimes people like to confuse power and darkness with arrogance. Once a person becomes too arrogant, they are the only thing stopping themselves from listening to the shadows. They see themselves as above people, and most importantly, they hear what they want to hear. When someone does that, there is no room for the shadows to give advice on how they can improve."

His teacher straightens up in his seat, clenching his cup. "Nico, I have been told that none of the Purple students can hear the shadows. I have also seen it myself. Whenever I walk around the school and visit their classes, I can hear the shadows cry out to them, but they hear nothing. It isn't the shadows, it's their mentality."

Volodimir's mood changes quickly as he cocks his head to the side and smiles again. "Tell me, Nico, what allowed you to jump so far? Was it anger at the loss of your fight with Braawen?"

Nick is surprised that his teacher heard about that.

"Oh, come now, boy," he drawls. "Word made its way around the school that the once unbendable Braawen did, in fact, bend and fall on his arse."

Nick giggles at the description but stops as disappointment hits him. "But I lost..." he whispers, sadness seeping through his wounds.

"Yes, but what did you learn?"

His voice cracks. "I—I should have made the punch." He looks up to see that Volodimir is looking intently at him, waiting for him to continue speaking. "I could have gotten him down. I was aiming for his chin."

"Like I taught you."

"Like you taught me. I could have... no, I couldn't have broken his bone, now that I think about it." Volodimir looks confused at that statement, but he continues. "I could have left a nasty bruise on it, but..." He looks down at his hands and clenches it, biting down on his lips. "I hesitated. I didn't want to hurt him."

If Nick was looking up, he would notice Volodimir's shadow creeping up to his own.

"Why?" Volodimir's voice seems so distant.

He bites his lips hard. "We were comrades," he growls, as he can feel the anger and frustration rise. "We were supposed to have each other's back. But I was stupid and a fool!" He spits, closing his eyes shut.

We were family, he thought.

Volodimir gets up from his seat and grabs his clenching hands, holding them gently. He whispers, but to Nick, it is so clear. "Remember this feeling." This time, Nick can feel the shadows all around him. "Remember the anger and the pain, and never let him take advantage of you again."

He opens his eyes just in time for the shadows to retreat into their proper places. He can see his teacher's eyes gazing into his own. He doesn't know why, but he throws himself at his teacher and hugs him.

Volodimir, to Nick's surprise, hugs him back.

"I promise not to hold back," Nick whispers into his shoulders.

"Good." Volodimir pats Nick on the back. "Because we will begin a new set of training for you."

The sun begins to rise as Volodimir sees Nick off, watching as his apprentice walks onto the path and disappears into the trees. Volodimir sighs as he takes a moment to admire the sunrise. It's a wonderful sunrise, and the sun looks beautiful on the trees. The branches are heavy with snow, yet the sunrise tints them a beautiful colour. Maybe if he has time, he'll paint this moment.

The boy won't hold back again. He's tasted power. He will like it more and more. The shadows' voices ring clearly in his ears.

I know. The boy has so much potential. He just needs more confidence; he could have broken that boy's bone. I know how hard he punches. He just needs... a push. Volodimir smiles at the thought. The boy is beginning to grow on him now. He wants to see what Nico could do. He just knows that the boy has talent.

Though, I would like for Braawen and Emelie to also grow, he tells the shadows. He closes his eyes and sighs. *Shadows, be truthful to me. Can Braawen and Emelie handle it?*

The shadows remain quiet for a moment. *No.*

He rubs the back of his neck, exhaling deeply to calm his rising anger. He was hoping that they would be the next Blacks, with how well those two were progressing. Still, Volodimir has to be honest with himself. He really wants Nico to succeed in his training and move beyond Yellow and Orange. He likes that Nick looks for things, his thirst for knowledge, his willingness to learn something new, and Volodimir even enjoys their conversations. General Herald has also told him that the boy got along with everyone outside of his class as well. Yes, he wants his student to succeed in his goals, but he also wants him for something else.

He'll be strong enough for it and take all that you taught him to heart, the shadows confirm his thoughts, making Volodimir smiles.

"Ugh, finally a worthy candidate!" He throws his hands up with a chuckle and turns back towards the cottage. He can hear the shadows laugh as he walks back into the cottage and shuts the door.

Chapter 23
Council

The day goes by quickly, and the General announces that each of them is doing well. However, at feasting time, Nick can tell that the General has something on his mind. There is no yelling, grumbling, or threatening. The man seems lost in his own thoughts, as if he is debating something.

"Children," the General calls out, getting everyone to stop. "I'll be away tomorrow, but do not fear. Miss Leia will take care of you."

"Is everything alright?" Bhaltair asks.

The General nods. "Yes, I just have a job to do. Plus, I get to see my Elena." With that, the General leaves, giving a nod to Leia. The four students are left at the table, wondering what would require the General to leave so quickly.

"Do you think we can sneak in desserts?" Bhaltair whispers with a grin. Nick rolls his eyes as Leia comes over to stop Bhaltair from cheating on his diet.

Later in the evening when most students are asleep, a group of students continue their studies in the Yellow dormitory, including Kaius and Lorcan.

Nick and his friends created this group to help each other in their studies and fights. Lorcan's insights are more than helpful for fights. Nick remembers Lorcan's last spar with Bhaltair. Poor Lorcan was confused when Bhaltair kept repeating 'Get that bread, get that bread.' He had to tell Lorcan that it was a phrase that helped Bhaltair concentrate on his goals. Lorcan shrugged, as long as it wasn't a curse, he didn't care. So far, each person has seen improvements in their fighting and studies.

Tonight, the fireplace burns brightly, and the new lamps that the General's wife sent them brighten their room. The lamps are gifts from the kind old lady whom Nick hasn't seen yet. The cellar is still filled with spiders, humid air, and painful mattresses; however, the lights at least make it less dark. The students work in a comfortable silence until the door suddenly opens dramatically, Laura enters, gliding as she makes her way around the group. She gives everyone a cookie from her bag and almost floats to her seat.

They all look to Kaius for answers but he just shrugs. "She's been like this all evening."

Laura sits down and smiles at everyone as she takes out her homework. They wait to see if she'll bring up the reason for her good mood, but after ten minutes of just smiling, Rohana can't take it any longer.

"Why are you so happy? Did Daddy die?"

Everyone looks appalled, but Laura continues to smile.

"No, he's still alive, but he told me something a while ago and it turns out that the rumours are true. The queen has lost her head." She grins, clapping to herself. "Thank you, deities, for answering my prayers." She looks upwards at the ceiling.

Nick wonders if the deities actually did answer her prayers. After what he's been through, he definitely can't deny that they could.

They all look to her for more information. She sighs. "Girls, remember what I told you about Victoria Visconte?" They nod. "Do you all know her?" she asks the rest of them.

"She's the most popular girl in the school," Nick answers. "The girls told us about her, and I saw the way Braawen looked at her. I wouldn't be surprised if he's slept with her."

"He did," Laura confirms. Nick just rolls his eyes in response.

"Then why are you happy?" Lorcan asks.

She sighs. "She's the queen of the Purple circle students, but my father told me how there was a huge but quiet reshuffling amongst the nobles. Apparently, a few of them were stealing profits in the mines from the Night Emperor."

Nick remembers his meeting with Lord Nortshell.

"It became a huge deal, starting with Lord Nortshell's execution. Many of the nobles who were guilty tried to destroy evidence, while others gathered evidence to prove their innocence."

"Okay, first of all, who would be dumb enough to steal from the friggin' Night Emperor; and secondly, an execution?" Kaius asks. "He executed a noble?"

Laura nods. "The Night Emperor cares a great deal if you steal from him, especially if it's by the nobles. It's such a big deal that nobles from the Chambers, Inner and Outer Courts, were charged, which is why there's been a shuffling of the courts."

Nick raises his hands as though he's back in class. "

"Yes, Mr. Westmore?" Laura teases.

He smiles. "Who are the nobles being charged? I heard that Lord Nortshell was charged a while ago. Can you explain the Chambers and the difference between the Inner and Outer Courts?"

"Of course." She takes out a blank sheet of paper and begins to draw a chart. "Excellent questions, Nickolaus, though I'm quite surprised that you've actually heard of the dear old Lord Nigel Nortshell, so I'll begin with that. Lord Nigel Nortshell comes from a very old and ancient noble family of the Empire. Their dedication and loyalty to the Royal family have allowed them to always be one of the Chamber of Citizens' leaders along with the Blackwood family. He's one of the four members of the inner circle as well. That's why it's a huge deal that the current head was executed. People thought he was basically untouchable."

Everyone looks at each other with a mix of shock and surprise on their faces.

"The Emperor has a lot of power, doesn't he?" Rohana asks.

Laura nods. "Yes, but even he can't go around executing nobles. He also needs the majority of inner council members' approval. However, he can arrest a noble without approval. He did gain the approval of three out of the four members of the inner circle——Lady Swan, Grand General Oxfords, and Lady Blackwood."

"I'm guessing that dear old Nigel Nortshell didn't have a say?" Kaius remarks sarcastically.

"He didn't even know. Actually, he was useless from the start, and preferred spending his wealth than attending his meetings. Lady Blackwood had most of the responsibility." Laura sighs again. "Well, hopefully, the new one does better."

"Useless nobles, no different from Availa," Nick states. "Only Lord Jameson was useful, and what did they do?"

"Arrested him when he spoke out against the King. He died during the Night of the Silenced. The jail was completely wiped out," Bhaltair states. "He would have been a good leader."

Everyone nods at that. "What about the other nobles?"

Laura takes out her notes and passes them around. Written in black ink are the family trees of some of the school's noble families. Nick reminds himself to ask Laura how she got that information. She points to the Visconte Family, so everyone can see the lines connecting them to the Nortshells and Swans. There is even a distant line to the royal family. All the boys look surprised at the news.

"Well, no wonder Victoria thought herself a queen," Bhaltair mumbles.

"Yes, and even they weren't safe from the Emperor's wrath. Ivan Visconte, Victoria's father, and head of the family was convicted yesterday of stealing from the Night Emperor and the citizens' royal funds. He also embezzled from the mines and tax resources, so he's under trial and may be executed. But because of his influence, he may just be locked up. At the moment, Miss Victoria is under a lot of stress and has been sent home. I don't believe her or her brothers will be chosen as the next head of the family."

Takara shakes her head.

"The disgrace," Rohana chuckles.

However, Nick doesn't know how to feel about it. Yes, Victoria may have been rude from what the girls told him, but should she really be accountable for her father's crimes? *How am I any different?* he ponders.

"So, two heads of office were caught doing a serious crime. What happens next?" he asks.

"That leads to your second question, the Inner and Outer Courts." Laura rolls her eyes at another mention of her father. "From what my father tells me, luckily it was just the Visconte and Nortshell, with only a few minor nobles. In total, six families and a dozen other merchants and businessmen were involved."

"That's not a lot compared to all our messed up nobles back home," Takara points out. "We only had what? One good noble, and Lord Jameson ended up dead."

"Yes, but the Night Emperor wants none of that. Let me explain the basic system." Laura draws a triangle with four different levels. "I'm going to explain how the Imperial Court or the Night Court, as they like to call themselves work. On the top is the Emperor, he has the last say on everything. The four people below are the Inner Council, the people who give the Emperor the laws that need to be approved. Two belong to the Chamber of Shadows and two for the Chamber of Citizens."

"So, Lord Nortshell had a lot of power, if he had the ears of the Emperor," Nick whispers.

"But why are two from the Chamber of Shadows and two from the Chamber of Citizens?" Lorcan shakes his head.

Laura smiles. "In the Empire, the Chamber of Shadows are for Shadow Wielders and the Chamber of Citizens are for non-Shadow Wielders. Both shadow and non-shadow wielders are to be represented in court. The ruling Emperor and Empress must remain neutral and help both sides. Normally, both sides have no problem working beside each other. But if the two sides can't agree, the crown will decide," she explains.

"But I'm rambling. So, back to the Inner Council or 'the Council' as some call them; they also act as advisors to the crown. Currently the head advisor is Lady Swan. Below them is the Outer Council. Think of them as the assistants and second in command for the Inner Council. They are representatives from different powerful families. The lower tier are the Courtiers, where nobles and people of great influence can gather and debate certain laws and ask favours in the Night Court."

"Inner and Outer," Nick repeats. "But I'm guessing that even being in the outer circle makes you powerful."

She nods. "Very powerful. The Shuffle of the Chambers means that representatives can make a case to fill in the empty seats. So far, Nortshell's position has been replaced with his half-brother, Edward. Visconte's position is still undecided. They might choose a different family if they don't choose quickly."

"Who's they?" Lorcan asks.

"Their family, the other Viscontes," she replies, "once the family chooses a representative, the Chamber must deem them fit. Then they make a case to the Emperor, who decides if they stay or not. There have been rumours that the other noble houses in the Chamber of Citizens won't vote for the Visconte. Apparently, they were all corrupt."

"Sounds like a mess." Nick shrugs.

"Yes, it does." She takes a sip of water. "And the Night Emperor is wiping them clean."

"But what does this have to do with us?" Lorcan asks.

Laura blinks in surprise at the question. "W-well, everything!" She scoffs. "I mean, it's the Council that decides whether we continue to even live. We are wards of the state. We are under the mercy of the Night Emperor and his Council. If the Council votes to stop us from ever leaving, the Night Emperor can approve it, and there goes our chance of going home. Right now, we don't know how Edward Nortshell views us. He could be a deciding vote on our lives. Every vote counts. We were one vote away from all of us getting executed."

"Excuse me?" Nick cries.

"We were what now?" Kaius' eyes go wide with fear.

Laura nods. "Swan and Blackwood voted for us to be executed. Nortshell and Oxfords voted for us to live. The Night Emperor made the deciding vote to spare our lives. However, if either Nortshell or Oxfords had said yes to the execution, there's a high chance that the Night Emperor would have allowed it. No one knows how the new Nortshell votes yet." She shakes her head.

"Deities, I thought that this couldn't get any worse." Lorcan slides further down into his chair.

They all stay quiet for a while until Takara speaks up. "Well, I shall pray to the deities for mercy's sake. However, I know I speak for myself, but I'm happy that the Queen of Equinox House is no more." She chuckles, trying to lighten the mood. Rohana cheers at that.

Nick shakes his head. "The Queen is still here," he states, getting everyone's attention.

"What do you mean?" Bhaltair asks.

"There will always be someone after her, always. No one leaves a powerful seat empty."

Laura claps, looking happy as can be. "Nick, a man after my own heart!" She grins. "He's right, there's always someone to take another's place. Remember, 'The Queen is dead' is always followed by 'Long live the Queen'."

"And who could be the next Queen?" Kaius asks.

In one of the Purple rooms, a young woman looks at her vanity. She already has one girl from Victoria's little group. Now, she just needs the others. She tells herself that she can get them by the end of the week.

Emelie smiles devilishly at her reflection. "Long live the Queen," she whispers.

Chapter 24
Training

After Nick's experience with his surprise Shadow Jump into the cottage, Volodimir plans their next scheduled training to focus on Shadow Wielding.

Finally! He's so happy to hear that his teacher will start to train him on different shadow spells and techniques. He eagerly leaves to meet his teacher already outside the cottage.

"Nico, my boy. Today, we will need to go somewhere different."

He stops in front of his teacher. "Oh?"

Instead of giving a response, his teacher smiles.

"Fail," his teacher tells him for the fifth time.

It is a clear cold night, and the city lanterns still shine, even with only a few people out so late at night. Nick moans as he rolls off a pile of garbage, his chest rising and falling with rapid breaths. Gagging twice from the awful smell gives him the small burst of strength he needs to sit up. He looks up the four-story building to see Volodimir on the roof one second, then beside him the next. He gracelessly yanks Nick out of the bin, and Shadow Jumps them both back to the top of the roof.

Nick tries to see straight as his teacher dusts some of the garbage off him. "Can't we try another method?" Nick whines. He doesn't mean to but falling off a four-story building five times will do that to anyone.

"Nonsense." Volodimir rakes his fingers through Nick's hair to get the last bit of spoiled food out of it. "All you have to do is jump from one end to the other."

Nick looks from one end of the roof to the other. "I don't think it's working."

His teacher flicks him on the head. "I want that negativity out of your mind. You can do it, and you will! You made it from the city to my cottage. You damn well will make it on the other side," he commands. "It's not even that far." His teacher points to the ledge.

He's right, of course. It's just a little out of jumping distance. Nick sighs and shakes his body. He doesn't like the way that Volodimir is eyeing him. It makes him nervous. He doesn't have to crane his neck anymore to look at the man; he's grown and isn't as short as he was before. Nick even has real muscles now. Nevertheless, the added muscles only seem to mean more added aches and pains—unfortunately, the scars on his back pulse in anger.

Nick gulps. "I don't perform well when people watch me."

His teacher stares unimpressed at his response.

Nick turns his attention to the roof again. *I can do this,* he repeats to himself. He takes a deep breath and runs off the roof. He spreads his arms out, thinking of the other end... until he feels gravity pulling him down. With a cry, he falls into the bin again.

"Fail," Volodimir states again as though it's nothing.

Nick doesn't like that, doesn't like thinking that his teacher sees him as nothing.

Fail. Failure. Worthless. He can hear those words nagging him. He shakes his head and feels a strong hand pull him out, then feels the gravel on the roof. He's a little dizzy, but he wants to believe that it isn't from the jump.

"Come now, boy," Volodimir drawls with a cutting grin. "I'm sure that this isn't the extent of your powers."

Nick just shakes his head as his teacher pushes him closer to the edge of the roof. "This isn't the extent. I know it isn't."

He sees Volodimir watching him. "What do you do when you normally fall?" His teacher asks. "I'm sure you're a good climber, but even professionals fall."

"Do you fall?"

"No, I'm an elite," Volodimir says, and Nick rolls his eyes. His teacher's eyes only narrow and he demands, "Now, what do you do when you fall?"

"I look for a ledge, something to grab. If I'm really prepared, I have a rope or a hook to catch on to something." Nick looks over the ledge.

"What if you don't have your tools? What do you do when you know that you're falling?"

Nick shrugs. "Do what I've been doing, preparing for the fall." He gets flicked again; he's sure that his forehead is bruised.

"That's your problem, you're preparing to fail. I need you to prepare to succeed. Just as you see the ground and plan for a less painful way to land, I need you to prepare a way to softly land on the roof." His teacher gives a thin smile and motions to the roof again.

Nick looks past the flagpole at the ground then at the roof ahead and nods.

Volodimir draws in a long breath. "Alright. Let's try a different method." His teacher pushes him off with no warning.

Nick lets out a short gasp and sees himself falling faster. *I need a rope, a hook! Anything!* His mind focuses on anything but falling, and then he feels something come out of his hand. He grabs it for dear life as he stops midair.

He gasps again, looking down, seeing that he is halfway down. He looks back up to a slightly confused teacher. "I didn't fall all the way!" Nick smiles, pointing with his free hand at the shadow that wraps around his hand to the flagpole above.

His teacher looks at him and gives a small smile. "I'm proud of you, Nico, but I asked for a jump, not a whip."

Before he could say anything, his teacher's shadow slash cuts his whip.

"You as-!" He doesn't get a chance to finish his sentence as he crashes to the ground, but Volodimir knows what he wanted to say.

Volodimir just dusts his own jacket. *The boy was going to insult me, how rude. I'll have to teach him respect and etiquette. My teacher was a monster, but I didn't insult him. Never. Not once. It's all about respect.* Volodimir remembers when his own teacher threw him in a cage with a tiger and told him to train it. All he is doing is dropping his student from a four-story building. There's even padding below so his apprentice can't break any bones.

"Fail," he states as he grabs his student and takes him to the roof again. "But pass for saving yourself."

It takes another three tries for Nick to finally reach the other side. He dances and jumps back to Volodimir, holding up his hand. "High five."

Volodimir scoffs. "We aren't children."

This doesn't seem to discourage Nick. "Come on, I just fell ten times. You must be happy." He still has his hand up. His teacher sighs as he high-fives him, glad that no one is watching this.

At the cottage, Volodimir patches him up and gives him three vials.

Nick looks at them curiously. "I don't want to become dependent on these. Dying from an addiction to health vials isn't how I want to go."

He can hear his teacher chuckle beside him as he finishes bandaging his arm. "Trust me, Nico, they put a lot of research into making these so they would not be addictive."

"What about the black vial you gave me on the first night? That was a powerful healing vial."

Volodimir stops wrapping his arm. Nick can feel the man stiffen and swears that he's smiling. "Oh... you remember that?"

"Yeah, it's kind of hard not to. I still have the bottle if you want it back?"

"No, Nico, you can keep the bottle. That healing vial is very expensive, more like an experiment."

"You used me as a test subject?" Nick widens his eyes in disbelief. "I feel insulted!"

His teacher scoffs, ignoring his distress. "It's safe, I use it and I'm fine." He chuckles. "Come now, Nico, I want to show you another place." Volodimir gets up from his spot.

Nick drinks his three vials. He hates the bitter taste, but he can feel soreness fading away. The two of them walk to a door where the cloaks are kept. Volodimir pushes past the cloaks to reveal a grey stone wall. Nick peeks his head into the closet and sees that the markings on the grey stone look very familiar.

"Those markings... those are the same ones that were on the circle test stone."

Volodimir nods. "They also mean so much more."

Nick gasps as Volodimir's hand gets closer to the markings. Black veins slowly spread from his teacher's hand to his elbow, turning his hand and arm black. His nails grow long and sharp like claws. The markings on the stone glow from white to yellow as he touches it. The stones shake, and Nick can hear the scraping of stone on stone as the door slides open.

There is nothing but darkness on the other side.

"Where are the lights?" He asks.

Volodimir chuckles. "Shadow Wielders don't need lights. Now, come Nico, your real training begins."

Nick uses Night Vision, but has to concentrate hard. He can see the hall continue to go downwards. It is a steep slope, and just when he thinks his head is about to pop from the stress of using the shadow technique, he sees another door. It's painted in gold and looks fresh. The door smells of rich lumber, the trees of his homeland, and is covered in intricately carved designs. Volodimir places his hands on the door, which opens easily. Nick looks at Volodimir, who motions for Nick to follow him. Nick walks in, and the pain in his head slowly fades away as he stares at the grandeur of the room.

The stone walls are black, but the golden carvings on the walls resemble living beings with golden veins. The weapons on the walls seem old but sturdy, and remind him of the weapons in the training hall. Gold drapes cover the edges of the walls. A large golden banner hangs proudly in the centre of it all. He looks down to see polished white and black marble floors inlaid with a huge circle in the centre of the room.

"What is this place?" His voice echoes, and he is startled as his teacher's hand rests on his shoulders.

"The fifth floor of the school has a Shadow Room where students can train in the ways of the shadows. It's the most coveted space, well, second to this cottage." He motions to the room. "However, this is the real Shadow Room, where a person can completely be one with the darkness around them. Some lights can be used to create shadows, but that will be at the third level. The first level is to get you completely in tune with the dark. There are no lights, as you can see. There never has been."

Nick looks around, and inhales sharply as he shuts his eyes. He opens them to see nothing, but darkness, and he fears that he's gone blind from using Night Vision for so long.

"Oh, my head..." He rubs his temples. "I think I've gone blind," he whispers.

Volodimir's laughter rings around the room, and he can feel his teacher's hand grip his shoulder. Nick can feel something quickly move from his shoulders to his eyes as he blinks to see the room once more.

"This will be the only time that I will help you with Night Vision. Keep your focus on it as we train. By the end of the week, I want Night Vision to become second nature to you," he commands.

All Nick can do is nod.

"I want an answer."

"Yes, sir."

"This is only one of six underground levels of the cottage. As you can tell, the cottage was placed on the hill for a reason. It was built in the darkest area of the forest, alone and away from distractions. These exclusive rooms will sharpen your skills to become one with the shadows. This place will be to our knowledge alone."

Nick nods; he knows a warning when he hears one.

His teacher smiles and continues. "Each level will increase the difficulty of our training. I want you to make it to the fifth level before the Spring festival."

"Five out of six?" Nick grins. "That sounds like a challenge."

Volodimir grins back. "Five should be easy enough, though I wouldn't be surprised if you ended up in the sixth."

Chapter 25
Goals

A new day dawns after last night's snow. The snow is slightly above their ankles as Nick jogs along the rim of the forest. He remembers the lessons from two nights ago, in the Shadow Room; he can't wait to train in. Takara is beside him, beside him, smiling throughout most of their jog as she talks about her private dance lessons with Mr. Apolus.

"He says that I'm doing better. Though he can't believe a simple commoner like myself can dance so well." She huffs as they slowly stop among the trees.

Nick loves his jogs with Takara. It gives him the perfect excuse to run in the forest, but also to think.

"I guess that's him complimenting you?" Nick suggests, taking deeper breaths.

She shrugs and exhales slowly watching her warm breath against the cold. "A rude teacher, but a teacher that will help me in my goals."

Nick watches her as she stares into the distance of the forest. "What are your goals?" he asks.

"I need to do well during the Spring Festival. We need to impress everyone if we want any chance in the Empire," she explains.

"Oh," Nick states quietly. "Well, I'm sure we'll do well in the circle test."

Takara rolls her eyes. "Nick, not everything is about the shadows. We won't be students here forever. We're going to become citizens of the Empire, and as citizens, the Empire is no longer responsible for our well-being. Instead of asking: 'What can the Empire do for us?' it will be: 'What can we do for the Empire?'. There will be nobles, politicians, merchants, and a whole lot of influential people at that festival." She waves her hands as she explains, "We need to make a good impression; one while we eat, and the other while we dance."

She shakes her body, loosening her stiff muscles. "So, I'm going to impress a family, and hopefully, they'll adopt me. If not, the Shadow Assassins are my last resort."

Nick's whole body goes stiff, and he swears that even winds stop. "You want to join the Shadow Assassins?"

She sighs tiredly, closing her eyes. "I want to go back." Her voice breaks. "I miss the farm, the chickens… I miss my parents." She opens them and turns to Nick, her eyes glossing over. "When me and my family were captured, we were taken to another prison, where they kept people whose family members joined the rebellion. Some were let go. Others, well… others like me and my family were not." She licks her lips as though trying to get the words out of her drying mouth. "We were beaten black and blue, but they didn't always use methods that left marks. They used a wet cloth that became a cold whip. It felt colder than the snow right now." She huffs. "It left marks that healed quickly but hurt all the same. I got hit plenty of times."

Nick doesn't know what to say. He never knew what happened to most of the people of his kingdom, especially those who weren't part of the rebellion. Hearing this just makes him angrier, but it also makes him feel guilty. *If only my father didn't start this rebellion. Maybe I could have done something?*

"After that experience and being separated from my family, I vowed that I would get stronger to protect my family. I am willing to use any resource to find them, even at the Empire's expense. That is why we need to impress these people even before the test happens. As much as I hate to admit it, I need to get into a Noble family. They'll have the money and resources to find my parents. Or at least…"

Nick sees the way her body begins to shake. He walks over to her, holding her gently as her eyes start to water. She gives him a look of understanding and takes a deep breath, nodding as he slowly lets her go.

"Well, ask me anything. I'll definitely help you."

It's the least I can do. My father's rebellion is the reason why you're here. The thoughts and feelings of guilt rush inside him.

She gives a small smile and hugs him. The hug surprises him, but he hugs her back. It's a nice hug. He hasn't had a hug from a girl since before his mother died. He forgot that hugs could be this soft.

When she lets go, he's reluctant but lets go.

"I can't believe that two-left-feet Nick is helping me with my dance," she giggles.

Nick likes her giggles. *Is it getting hot?* he asks himself as he feels heat creep up in his face.

"W-well," he stammers, "I'll try not to step on your feet." He looks down at his feet, willing them to cooperate for once.

"Well…" Takara's voice seems so smooth. "You do go on jogs with me, and I feel *oh so safe* when you're with me."

He looks up to see her dark brown eyes so close to his face. He backs up quickly, almost stumbling. She giggles more, causing his heart to race.

"And I do enjoy the educational trivia on trees." She looks around and points to an evergreen. "See, that one's a maple tree."

Nick smiles, "You're right."

She smiles back at him, then frowns. "Are you lying? Don't lie to me." She playfully hits his arm, this time he chuckles. "How can I learn if you don't correct me?"

Nick stops chuckling and raises his hands in surrender. "Alright. It's an evergreen. I won't lie to you." He keeps smiling at her, unable to stop.

Takara smiles back, feeling a heat go on her cheeks. She turns from his smile and looks ahead. "Good, let's continue. Bet I can beat you to the school!" she yells and runs off with Nick following behind her.

Chapter 26
Secrets

As they enter the school and walk towards the feasting room for mid-meal, they see students of all ages running from the room.

"Is it the chicken?" Nick jokes with a cunning smile. Takara rolls her eyes and gives him a playful shove towards the room.

"It's probably another fight," a voice says over their shoulders. They both jump to see Lorcan beside them.

"Stop doing that!" Nick snaps. "Wear louder shoes or something. I may be young, but my heart can't take any more surprises." Lorcan just chuckles as they pass the other students, entering the room with caution.

The first thing they see are flipped tables, with broken dishes and shards of glass covering the floors. Hiding under the Yellow table which seems to have the least damage, is Bhaltair. The three of them crawl to meet him.

Bhaltair turns to them with a nervous smile. "I just got here, but I think two girls are fighting... and it's not pretty." The boy shakes his head.

"Drama. I bet it's about a boy," Takara scoffs.

"Or a girl," Lorcan smiles.

She rolls her eyes but then nods.

Nick sighs, ignoring the pang of hunger in his stomach. "Great, we get a meal *and* a show today."

He slowly pokes his head out from under the table and sees two girls flailing with each other on the floor, away from the broken glass. The bottom one is grabbing the hair of the other while the one on top is choking her. He squints his eyes to see the girl on top blow strands of her hair out of her face. Nick's eyes widen as he sees the angry scar on her face.

He bolts up. "Rohana, stop!" His voice rings throughout the room. Ignoring Takara's worried voices and the yelling of Bhaltair, he grabs Rohana and rips her off the girl whose face is turning blue. The unknown girl is gasping, but Nick knows he's seen her somewhere before.

The words die in his mouth when the girl quickly kicks both of them to the floor. The girl glares at them with icy blue eyes, then a mad grin comes over her face, and she moves her hand towards the tables. Nick watches as the table's shadow bends to her will and turns into a weapon. The madwoman's shadow begins to slash at them quickly, but Nick and Rohana work faster. He sees the attack coming towards him in slow motion as he can feel Rohana's weight shift. He remembers what the General told them;

nothing can stop a Shadow Slash. They both dodge the slash, diving in opposite directions. Nick rolls on the floor to one side while Rohana flips over to the other side. Both look at the ground briefly to see the split stone that could have been them.

He doesn't dwell on that thought for long as he realizes he now has an enemy in front of him. He knows that he can't get hit by a Shadow Slash, but at the same time, he finds it fascinating. Nick and Rohana move around distracting the madwoman while she turns the shadow into a whip. They continue their dance as Bhaltair comes from behind, gripping their attacker and lifting her up in the air. He can hear the girl commanding Bhaltair to drop her. Nevertheless, Bhaltair's grip is strong, not letting go even when she turns the Shadow Whip into a knife and stabs him, leaving the knife embedded in his thigh.

As Bhaltair falls, bringing the woman with him, Rohana roars in anger holding a chair, ready to hit their attacker. Nick jumps in the air and tackles her before she could land a hit.

"Let me go!" Rohana cries as Nick holds her tight. He doesn't let go until he sees Lorcan running in with another teacher, a small brown-haired woman with a Purple stole.

"Emelie! What on Asteria is going on here?!" The teacher commands Bhaltair to let Emelie go, as the knife disappears, returning to the table's shadow. The teacher runs to Bhaltair's side, using her stole to bandage his thigh to slow the blood seeping from his wound.

Emelie fixes her hair but looks out of breath and shoots a heated glare at Rohana. Nicks sees her glare and notices that Emelie looks very similar to Rohana, except for the scar on her face and longer hair.

The glare disappears as quickly as it came, and Emelie turns to the teacher with a sad expression on her face. "Mrs. Avion, a Yellow student attacked me! I was only giving her pointers on how to improve herself in the shadows, but as you can see, she didn't take it very well."

"Did those pointers require you to stab a student?" The teacher looks at her in disbelief. Then she looks at the floor, and her eyes widen. "Emelie! What have I told you about using Shadow Slash? We do not do that here or against any students! Someone could have been killed! You could have been hurt."

Before Emile can retort, another teacher comes in, pushing away students that were crowding around the doorway. "Mrs. Avion!" The teacher looks at the professor, and her whole body stiffens.

"What have I told you about criticizing one of our promising students?" Professor Arran stops in front of the woman with a stony expression on his face.

Bhaltair looks at the teacher who shrinks into herself. Even Rohana, Takara, and Nick look in surprise at the change in the teacher's body language.

"I -I apologize, professor, but Emelie psychically assaulted a student and could have killed a student or hurt herself. Young man," Mrs. Avion turns to Lorcan, "please take this student to the infirmary." Lorcan nods and looks at Takara who nods and helps Lorcan take Bhaltair to the infirmary.

Nick stands next to Rohana as she glares at Emelie, who gives her a sly smile in return. Something doesn't feel right. There's a sickening feeling in the air that arrived as soon as Professor Arran entered the room. He has a feeling that this is not going to end well for the Yellows.

"Mrs. Avion, it seems that I will have to have a talk with you again on your unfair critique." Professor Arran shakes his head.

"Unfair? She almost killed us!" Rohana yells. Nick must hold her back again.

The professor looks at them disdainfully. As he walks towards them, Nick can feel a pressure on his back. Nick steps in front of Rohana, but she pushes him, and they stand side by side.

"Young lady," Professor Arran snarls. "If I heard correctly from my student, she was only trying to help you. I teach all my students to help those that are beneath them. Isn't that right, Ms. Snowfield?"

Emelie smiles. "Of course, professor. I was just trying to help and give some tips on what she could do to improve. But she must have taken what I said out of context. Though, I believe that hitting me first was a bit of an overreaction."

The professor turns to both of them and glares. "Then there should be a punishment for you, Miss... Who are you?"

"Rohana. Just Rohana." She glares back, not backing down.

"And you, boy. Yes, I remember you." The professor looks at him and Nick's eyes narrow. "What was your name again?"

He stands tall. "Nickolaus Westmore."

"Rohana and Mr. Westmore. You both will be punished for attacking a Purple student who was clearly defenceless." The Professor waves his hand dismissively.

"Defenceless?!" Rohana roars.

"Emelie almost killed us!" Nick yells.

"Not only that, Nick was the one who pulled me off of that tramp anyway. He has nothing to do with this!" Rohana snaps.

The professor merely chuckles as he walks away. It should have ended there, but then Nick feels it; the pressure is back again in full force. However, when he looks around the room, he can see that he's not the only one who feels it this time. Rohana looks towards the door, her eyes open

176

wide. Emelie and even both of the teachers stop to look towards where the overwhelming presence is coming from.

The students crowding around the doorway have gone completely silent. The temperature drops as light footsteps on the stone floors slowly approach them. The students part ways, and some even give a little bow as a man wearing all black and a scholars' robe with the school's emblem enters the room.

"Black," a few dares to whisper.

But Nick thinks must have heard wrong because all he sees is Volodimir walking into the room with full confidence and authority. However, unlike the smiling and welcoming Volodimir he knows, he only sees a face as hard as stone and eyes as sharp as cut rubies. The man looks like a teacher of this school from top to bottom.

Volodimir stops just short of Mrs. Avion, a displeased expression on his face. He then looks at Emelie, who stiffens in fright and looks down at her feet. His eyes then travel across the floor to Nick and Rohana. He doesn't even bother to look at the professor.

Volodimir narrows his eyes and finally speaks. "I believe we had a rule about using Shadow Slash outside of the Shadow Room?" He turns to Mrs. Avion, who looks like she's been slapped.

She looks down, frightened. "Y-yes, sir. There is a rule."

He nods to her. "I would like to speak with you in twenty minutes. Meet me at the Black cottage." Her mouth is open but nothing comes out. She nods and leaves with haste after quickly bowing to Volodimir.

Volodimir turns to Emelie, who's still looking at her feet. "Young lady." His commanding voice gets her to look up slowly, her body shaking. "As great as it is to see that you've mastered the Shadow Slash, I'm afraid that we have rules that must be followed. You also will be punished."

Emelie wants to say something, but the glare that he sends her keeps her mouth shut.

"Professor Volodimir, I think that you are mistreating her. She is one of the students that I told you about." Professor Arran comments, walking closer to Volodimir. "Plus, it was these mongrels who started it first. That girl attacked her after Emelie gave her pointers on improving herself. The boy is also a troublemaker." He gives a glare at the two Yellows, then quickly smiles at the man in front of him.

Volodimir doesn't smile back, and Nick can feel even more pressure flowing down his spine. His teacher looks at him and Nick furiously shakes his head, biting his lips. There is no way on this plane of existence that he would let Emelie go unpunished. Volodimir looks back at the professor.

"Then I will let General Herald know. The General will deal with them. That will be all." Then Volodimir turns but stops and looks at the floor to see blood. "Whose blood is this?" he asks, shifting to them.

"My friend, Bhaltair. Emelie stabbed him with a knife when he held her after she almost sliced us in two with her Shadow Slash," Nick explains.

Volodimir cocks an eyebrow and turns to the professor. "Professor Arran, I hope you give her a suitable punishment. Or I'll give her a Black punishment."

There are gasps from some of the students at the doorway as they whisper, 'Black punishment'. Even Professor Arran's eyes widen slightly at the degree of punishment, however, the man clenches his teeth and gives Volodimir a sharp nod.

Volodimir gives one final glare to Emelie, who trembles and gives a respectable bow. He leaves and the students part as he passes them. Many look on as the man walks away, calm as ever, as though he didn't just frighten everyone in the room. Professor Arran grabs Emelie's arm and angrily pushes past the students.

The wave of pressure leaves with the two men, and all that's left are the two exhausted students in the room.

"Let's go. We've got to check on Bhaltair and pray that the General doesn't give us a hard lesson." Nick takes his friend's hand and pulls her towards the door. For once, Rohana doesn't move her hands. Instead, she holds his hands tighter.

Bhaltair is on a bed eating a pudding in the infirmary. The nurse had pity on the boy and gave Bhaltair five puddings, placing them on the nightstand. Takara happily helped herself to some as well, smiling at the sweet dessert. Lorcan just looks at the two of them strangely.

"This pudding is divine!" Takara comments as she finishes the whole container, reaching for another.

Lorcan gives a strange look. "It's just the regular pudding that we get at lunch."

Both of them stop eating and look at Lorcan. "You get pudding at lunch?" Bhaltair asks, eyes wide in amazement.

"Wait... don't you guys get desserts?" Lorcan asks. They shake their heads and Lorcan puts his hand over his mouth to stop the gasps from escaping. *What the hell kind of training are they going through?* he wonders in disbelief. He is so happy he isn't in Yellow.

Just then, Nick and Rohana burst into the door, following the smell of pudding mixed with the sterile smell of the infirmary. Before Nick can wonder where the smell is coming from, the nurse quickly walks up to him, but he tells her he isn't the one hurt.

"Hmpf, that's a first," she mutters, walking back to her desk. She ignores the children as they crowd around Bhaltair at the far end of the room.

"So, what'd I miss?" Bhaltair asks.

Rohana looks at Nick, then she says, "We had a talk with Professor Arran. He wanted us to be punished for attacking a 'poor and defenceless' student." She rolls her eyes.

"The markings on the floor and the hole in my leg say otherwise." Bhaltair points to his now-bandaged leg.

Rohana looks at the wound, guilt is written on her face. "I'm sorry, Bhaltair. I would never have guessed she would do that."

He smiles at Rohana. "Don't apologize. It wasn't you who turned a table into a weapon. I hope that she's at least getting punished."

Rohana's expression turns into a smile. "Oh yes, she will definitely be getting punished, or else the Black Teacher will give her a Black punishment. He said so himself." She chuckles.

All three of them gasp.

"You met the Black Teacher?!" Bhaltair screams.

"Damn, I missed that!" Lorcan chastises himself.

"Was he good-looking?" Takara winks.

"Tall with black hair and dark eyes," Rohana answers.

"Oh, just my type of man!" Takara swoons, then bursts into giggles.

Rohana can only laugh, while Nick looks on in confusion.

"What do you mean?"

They all stop to look at the young boy in front of them. They wait for a few seconds to see if he's joking, but the oblivious expression on his face tells them no.

"Come on, Nick, you're the smartest out of us. The guy was wearing a black stole, which means he's the Black Teacher. You could tell that there's something special about him. Even Professor Arran was on edge," Rohana explains.

Nick just looks down at his feet as his face pales. *Volodimir... he's the Black Teacher.* He grabs his head and groans out loud in frustration. *I'm such an idiot!* He wants to yell.

"Nick, are you alright?" Lorcan asks in concern.

He shakes his head, and both hands cover the lower half of his face, his eyes wide.

Bhaltair's sudden chuckles join Nick's groans. "He's probably just noticing that he's stupid for not recognizing the Black Teacher."

Nick nods, getting the rest of them to laugh as well. *Well, he got half of it right. I've also spent time with the most dangerous person in the school.*

Lorcan gives Nick a playful slap on the back, making him wince from his scars. "Don't worry about it. I don't think that any of us are going to meet with him soon. I hear that he's very busy."

I'm seeing him tonight. Nick groans even louder, wondering how he's going to face him.

"What does he even do? He doesn't have any students, right?" Takara asks.

"Yeah, but remember what Ms. Leia said? That the Black Teacher has a responsibility to the entire school. I believe he's the head of the school," Lorcan says with a shrug.

"Oh, he's more than that." They all turn to see the nurse walk up beside them. "The Black Teacher is a chosen individual." She takes out a piece of candy and pops it in her mouth; and everyone can hear it crunch between her teeth. She gives a feral grin. "Though, Professor Arran has been vying for that position for years."

"Then who is the Black Teacher, and why did the Night Emperor choose him?" Nick asks, rubbing his sweaty palms on his legs.

The nurse shrugs. "I don't know, but my Blue circle butt is telling me not to underestimate the man. I can sense his power, and I don't want to be the one to upset him." She then turns back to her desk.

Nick knows that the man is dangerous. His looks could kill. Nick was going to have a talk with him tonight. *Maybe I should reconsider the whole teacher and apprentice situation.*

Lorcan grins, "I want to meet this man."

Rohana shakes her head. "No, you don't. His dark eyes were tearing into my soul, finding my weaknesses. Plus, that tramp is getting punished, but so are me and Nick. Sorry, Nick," she apologizes, turning to him.

Nick is surprised by the apology. He was half expecting her to snap at him for even butting in. Then she turns to Bhaltair. "I'm sorry that you got hurt too. But that girl!" She screams in frustration.

Nick looks at her, really looks at her. Her pale blonde hair and her blue eyes shimmer like ice, just like…

"What?" Rohana snaps at him.

Nick didn't even realize that he was staring at her. He bites his lips and looks at his other three friends, but they all shrug. "I have to ask you something." Rohana just looks at him silently. "Are you and Emelie related?"

Takara gasps at the question as Rohana's eyes narrow, before the girl looks away.

Nick puts up his hands defensively. "I mean… it's just that... that you two look alike. I mean, you have the same glare." She snaps her head back towards him and glares. He points at her. "See, that's the glare. Except hers is more heated and yours is icier, if that makes sense?" He gives a sheepish look.

She sighs and tiredly rubs her hand over her face before turning to them. "That's because that tramp is my half-sister."

Takara and Bhaltair drop their pudding.

Rohana sighs and pushes her hair, revealing more of her face. Nick notices that she is still pretty even with the scar on her face, but she would be considered beautiful without it. As beautiful as Emelie. She gives them a small smile.

"We're half-sisters. Born of the same mother, but with different fathers. My mother..." she sighs. "My mother was a maid in the King's court."

"Oh no..." Bhaltair whispers, a remorseful look on his face.

Rohana nods her head and looks down at her feet. "The King took an interest in my mother, though my mother said that she had none in him. You see, she was just about to get married, but the King didn't care. She just wanted it to be over," she whispers.

Everyone knew what that meant, and for the tenth millionth time, Nick is happy that the King is dead. He just wished he had been there to see him die. This isn't the first time that he had heard of a story like that. Many women were willing to go into the King's bed, but many more were unwilling. Apparently, the man had a thirst for women and didn't want to be tied down to one person.

Well... there was one person, some said, but that had to be only a rumour.

"She was fired when she was found to be with child. Nine months later, she had Emelie," Rohana whispers, gripping the edges of her chair as the group gasps.

"There's still a member of the royal family of Availa left?" Takara whispers in horror.

"Yeah. Two years later, my father and mother had me. My father was a simple soldier and raised Emelie as his own." Rohana hiccups. "Emelie wasn't always so... cruel. She was kind... a-and a loving sister." She bites her lips to stop her tears. "Then one day, the King came to our home and acknowledged her heritage. After that, she refused to be kind to my father, the man who raised her even after our mother died years before. She left to live a life of luxury with the rest of the King's children." Rohana grips the edges of her chair harder, her knuckles turning white from exertion.

"But when the rebellion started, my father brought her back into our home to keep her safe. It had been years since I had last heard of or even seen my sister. I was so excited, so happy." Her shoulders sag. "So naïve."

She sighs and leans her back head looking up at the wide ceilings. "Emelie couldn't believe that we looked alike. She had been told by the King that she was one of a kind, that her mother was the most beautiful woman in the kingdom, and since her mother passed, she was now the most beautiful." Rohana scoffs, looking at the group around her. They each have different looks of anger and pity on their faces. "Well, my father had to explain to her that he was happy that both of his daughters took after their mother. She told him that he wasn't her father, but her caretaker."

She shakes her head. "I saw my father's heart break that day. But he continued to protect her, even when we left our home and went into hiding from the Night Emperor's soldiers." She sighs. "One night when my father went hunting, my sister called me over to a river. She looked at the river, and so did I. We both looked so similar, standing beside each other, like twins. I smiled, but Emelie did not."

Rohana touches her scar, feeling the slight thickness and tightness around the skin that had healed many moons ago. She doesn't need a mirror to remind her of how large and angry it looks. "I didn't see the knife that she had. She threw me on the ground and screamed 'I'm one of a kind!' as she carved the scar into my face. She told me that if I told my father that she had done it, she would slit my throat. I told him it was a soldier who attacked us." Her hands slowly leave her face and make their way back to the chair.

"Then the rebels lost the rebellion, and my family and I were trying to escape. Somehow, the Night Emperor caught wind that one of the royal illegitimate children had escaped the great massacre. My father fought with the soldiers and fell. When he fell, I collapsed on my knees and cried. Then out of nowhere, Emelie ran to my father and cried out, 'Father, don't go,' for the first time since she was taken away. It made my father happy, but I was enraged. I wanted to hit her, smack her. She only said it to save her skin. But then, my father looked at me and I made my way over to him. He said, 'Take care of each other, my daughters.'"

Her eyes tear up, but she brushes them away quickly before they can fall. Her voice goes down to a whisper again. "My father saved that tramp's life again and again. When he died, the soldiers grabbed us and carried us away. I honoured my father's request as the two of us were questioned together." She sighs, even Nick could hear the regret in her voice. "I told them she was my older sister, and that our mother was a dairymaid and our father a soldier. Emelie became Emile Snowfield that day, but as soon as we got to Equinox House, she abandoned me."

The group is silent at her tale, the air around them tense and heavy. The knowledge that their friend must deal with her tormentor every day and see her succeed brings understanding to Nick, while everyone else is angry and sickened by Emelie's behaviour. If Emelie comes anywhere near here, they all would hurt her or worse, consequences be damned.

Accidents happen all the time here, Nick muses. He has to stop himself from smiling; it would be a very awkward time to do so. *No, Nick, this isn't you!* he snaps at himself. *You don't enjoy another person's pain!* Except, he believes that deep down, he could make an exception for Emelie and Braawen.

"Well," Bhaltair's voice breaks the silence. Instead of the wobbly or quiet voice they're all used to, the voice that breaks through his lips is commanding, laced tightly with anger. "I hated her before because she was an arrogant little prick at the fight between Nick and Braawy. But now, I hate her even more."

Lorcan narrows his eyes but looks around first, seeing the nurse busily preparing a new batch of potions. "We should tell the General."

"What?" Rohana asks.

"Tell the General, your teacher," he clarifies, receiving a glare from Rohana. "Tell him that a royal member of Availa is still alive and well."

Rohana shakes her head. "She'll deny it and probably say I'm the lost princess. They'll believe her over me. I'm a Yellow, and she's a rising Purple star on her way to becoming Black. Just look at what happened to Nick and me today. If it wasn't for the Black Teacher, then the witch would have gotten off."

"Then we'll need to get her to confess," Nick whispers.

"How?" Rohana snaps. "She'll never do it. I know that she's probably manipulating a lot of people." She sighs.

He looks around. *Use their skills to your advantage*, he hears the shadows whisper. He looks around the group of people around him. They all had skills both before and during the rebellion. They were learning new skills now, skills that needed to be moulded and polished.

"The world is a scary place out there Nickolaus." He can hear his father's cold and raucous voice. *"When you are surrounded by beasts, become the monster."*

He always believed in slaying monsters. He doesn't want to be a monster. His mother always told him that *'beasts can be tamed, but monsters must be slain'*. No, he won't become a monster, but he isn't going to be devoured by beasts.

"Guys," he states. "We have to do better. We have to get better." He turns to Rohana. "Rohana, remember what the General said? If we can't beat them at Shadow magic, beat them in hand-to-hand combat. We both survived a fight with her today, even if it was small. Work on your fighting."

He turns to Takara. "Takara, you're really good at dancing around people. I see you dancing around your opponents in class and when you want to get somewhere. Work on what the General told you, too."

He turns to Bhaltair and smacks the new pudding cup out of his hand. "You're going to gain so much muscle and become so strong that even the General won't want to take you on. We'll be starting weapons training tomorrow. I have a feeling that the General is going to give you something heavy, so be prepared." Bhaltair nods as the fire in him begins to burn.

"Lorcan, you are crazy good at reading people's body language. How good are you at Shadow magic?"

Lorcan shrugs. "Average, especially when it comes to Shadow Walk."

"Then you're gonna be the best. You have to be the best. Show them and yourself what you can do. You can already sneak up on people, now use it to your advantage as a warrior."

Lorcan nods and gives him a smile. "What are you planning, fish bones?"

Nick straightens his back from his seat. "We're going to outperform the Purple class." Their eyes go wide. It's a wild idea, but wild ideas can bring unimaginable results. "Come on, Rohana, you admit that no one will believe you if you stay in Yellow. Even if we can't get your sister—"

"Half," she interrupts.

"My apologies. Even if we can't get your half-sister to admit she's the princess, we still need to get stronger. Don't you want the power to protect yourself? Right now, she's in the second highest class, and the highest here in the school. We need to be on her level if we want to bring her down." He turns as he hears Takara chuckle.

"It's a crazy idea, but I'm tired of people looking down on us because we're in Yellow," Takara admits. "We're going to be the best Yellow class ever and rub it in everyone's faces." She gives a firm nod and then a sly smile at Nick, who nods back in response.

Bhaltair nods. "Even the General is going to be surprised."

Rohana snickers and turns to Nick. "And what are you going to improve on?" Everyone looks at him, waiting to hear his response.

"I'm not holding back anymore. I'm giving 110% and more. I'm not letting them show any disrespect to me."

He can hear the mocking voices of the students here. He's tired of them, and even more tired of being frustrated by them. They've taken up too much space in his thoughts. He's not giving them any more room to grow.

His lips start to tilt upward as he can see the surprised faces of those who mocked him. A small smile emerges as he can finally see himself and his friends feeling safe. "I am the son of Markus. A son of the Archer family," he whispers. "I'm from a proud family of warriors on both sides. It's time that I act like it."

Despite the negative feelings that his name brings, there's also something in Nick that surprises him. Like a light, something in him leaps for joy. Maybe the child in him that always wanted to make the Archer name proud is finally coming to light. *Funny, I thought my father put an end to that.*

He looks up to see varying degrees of surprise on his friends' faces. Lorcan nods his head, patting him on the back. "About time, Archer."

"You're his son?!" Bhaltair whispers.

"Yes, didn't you get that when I said that Braawen and I were cousins?"

Bhaltair, Rohana, and Takara shake their heads. "You do not look like Markus. You were so skinny, I thought that you were a distant relative." Takara admits, a slight blush on her cheeks.

Rohana looks amused by all this. "It's a good thing you don't look alike. I'm sure they would kill you."

That thought entered his mind plenty of times, and it isn't the first time that he is thankful for his mother.

The group is silent as a sense of calm and determination surrounds them.

Suddenly, the infirmary door bursts open, startling the group. The doors are so loud that even the nurse runs from her office and tsks when she sees who has just run in.

Kaius runs in sweating, a worried expression on his face. "Guys, you won't believe what I found out!"

Chapter 27
Blood

The Yellow cellar is dark and damp at best. However, each of the students has tried to brighten the room and make it their own. Takara made a makeshift wind chime from scrap metal in the weapon shop. How she managed to take metal that people saw as useless and turn it into something amazing was beyond all their understanding. As it hangs near the open window near the fireplace, its tinkling sound creates a calming atmosphere. Nick listens to the chimes as he practices his breathing exercises, but nothing seems to be working. He is numb as he sits down on his bed, trying and failing to process the information that Kaius just told him.

As the group was in the feast hall, Kaius walked away from the room's crashing sounds. He'd had enough experience on the battlefield and knew to move away from danger to stay alive. As he walked deeper into the hallway to escape the sounds, a figure caught his attention. He ducked behind a pillar, then slowly poked his head around. Out of the corner of his eye, he saw Braawen whispering with a woman. The woman looked familiar. She had grey hair, black eyes, and wore a black military uniform. There on her neck was a large purple jewel gleaming in the light. Kaius watched from a corner and found out that they were talking about Tybalt from the movements of their lips. He could only make out a few sentences but what he found was damning enough.

"Nick, Braawen is a part of whatever plan they have for your uncle. I'm not sure, but I could only find out that Braawen contacted your uncle and told him to come to the mines. He's been sending him messages while working with some of the teachers here. He even told your uncle that you were in the mines," Kaius told him in the infirmary.

Braawen never told him that he actually contacted their uncle. Nick had to walk out of the room to compose himself. He was sure that he would have thrown something, and no one needed to get hurt.

He sighs as he opens his eyes, listening to the soft chimes on his bed. But the anger he feels takes over again and he bites down hard on his lips. *I need to speak to Volodimir first about him being the Black Teacher. Afterwards, I can talk to Braawen about his contact with uncle. Gods know it's easier to talk to Volodimir than Braawen.*

Luckily, their dinner is brought to their rooms since the feast hall is being repaired. After eating, Rohana takes a shower while the rest of his friends do their homework. Not wanting to sit down and do nothing, he gets up from his bed and tells his friends that he's going for a walk. Takara asks if he wants to jog, but he declines. He draws his new curtains around his bed. Laura was kind enough to make each of them a set to give them a bit of privacy from their open room concept.

He changes quickly into his slightly oversized winter coat with the Black uniform under it. He sneaks past his friends and leaves the cellar shutting the door behind him. Nick looks around to see that no one is around him and he jumps into his own shadow. Shadow Jumping in front of the cottage doesn't seem like a hard journey. At first, he was winded but now jumping to the cottage is beginning to feel like second nature. He walks up the stairs and knocks using the door handle. Hearing the reply from Volodimir, he opens the door and feels the heat embrace him. The scent of tea and cookies is now an enjoyable smell for him. The company isn't bad either, as Volodimir smiles and motions him to sit. He notices that Volodimir looks more pale and tired than usual.

Nick sits across from him and grabs a cookie, as Volodimir puts down his cup. "I have a feeling that you have a lot of questions tonight. Please ask them."

Nick finishes his cookie, licking the crumbs from his lips. "I didn't know that you were the Black Teacher." He didn't mean for it to come out so bluntly, but he is too tired and just wants answers.

Volodimir cocks an eyebrow and smirks. "I didn't think it was important."

Nick rolls his eyes. "You are literally the most powerful person in the school, and you don't think that it's important?" He scoffs. "Please. Are there any other secrets that you have or things that you aren't telling me?" He crosses his arms.

Volodimir crosses his leg, and Nick can feel the tingle on his neck as the room darkens. *Maybe I went too far on that one.*

His teacher chuckles. "Nico, I shall tell you more things in time, but all I need is for you to trust me. I believe that you also have secrets that you don't want me to know as well." He gives a small smile.

Nick begins to sweat. *Does he know who my father is?* That's the last thing that he wants. He sees what it did to Braawen. His cousin is watched all the time.

Instead of panicking, he grins. "You're right. Your teachings haven't screwed me over. So, thank you. I know you're very busy, and I'm sure that you've made time for me." Nick nods his head and carefully takes another cookie, breaking the one cookie rule. Somehow, the cookie doesn't taste as sweet.

Volodimir puts down his cup. "Come, Nico, let's go on another field trip. This time, we're going shopping." Nick looks puzzled as his teacher gracefully gets up from his seat.

· ☽ ·

He's now in a luxury clothing store, the one in the city's main square. All he can do is stand straight, trying not to touch anything he can't afford, which is everything around him. He wishes he could float off the floor since the floors are made of rich marble. As his eyes roam around he's assaulted by the bright cream coloured walls with golden trim on the edges and lamps set into the wall. The lamps give a golden glow that seems to make the clothes look even richer.

I've been in Equinox House for too long. Everything is too bright for me. He sighs as he looks over to his teacher, who is speaking to one of the ladies in a lovely pink and black silk uniform. Actually, there are a lot of colours here that burn into his retinas.

So, Nick quickly looks anywhere but the walls and his eyes land on a coat. The coat looks nice, with silver and black patterns. He doesn't realize that he is staring at it until Volodimir asks one of the ladies in pink to take it down for him.

"Would you like the coat?" Volodimir asks, startling him.

"What?" Nick looks shocked. "I already have a coat."

"No," Volodimir replies, "you have a school's coat, and right now, you're wearing a coat that I lent you from the cabin. You need a coat, and I think that this coat will look lovely on you." His teacher smiles as he asks for the coat.

Nick can only say thank you. He hasn't had a new coat in years and smiles as he tries on the coat. It fits him perfectly, and as he walks over to one of the mirrors, he feels normal. The coat sparks a small glimmer of hope in his weary soul. Though reality has a habit of smothering that glimmer. So, he takes it off, putting back on the borrowed coat that Volodimir gave him. Even when his eyes linger on the coat, he still kindly hands it back to one of the ladies in pink, telling them to put it back. He doesn't need it. He doesn't even know when he'll get the chance to wear it.

"Nico, come over here." Volodimir waves his hands towards a selection of expensive clothes. Volodimir looks like a regular citizen in his coat and fur hat. Nick shoves his hands deep into his coat pockets as he walks over.

He tilts his head, trying to understand why his teacher is doing this. He gives a pleading look to his teacher, who ignores him. "Why do I need these clothes? I have clothes," Nick grumbles.

His teacher gives a small smile as he looks over the choices in front of them. "My boy, as I said, the only clothes you have are the ones that the school provides you. You need to think about clothes for the Spring Festival."

"Spring Festival?"

"Yes, Nico," Volodimir tsks. "Remember, you all have until the end of Winter to move up a circle. We're halfway there. At the end of Wintertime, we have a Spring celebration. Students and teachers are invited to the Palace for a grand banquet and dancing. It will be a feast of the likes that I am sure you have never seen. It will not only be Equinox House of Andromeda, but all the other Shadow schools in the Empire will be present. The next day, all the students get together and complete the circle test. Once the students complete the circle and successfully move up, the head teachers will hand you a new stole befitting your colour. The celebrations will be a week-long venture." His teacher sounds excited.

Volodimir looks at the darker coloured suits of purple and blue. However, both of their eyes land on a black suit. Volodimir catches his gaze and smiles.

"Only the Night Emperor gives a black stole to the student that passes into the Black circle. It rarely happens, but there was a time when there were more Black circle wielders. Now, there is just the Emperor, and he is eager for another Black." He points to the black outfits, and the lady in pink silk picks them up.

"I know that you can make it to the Black circle," Volodimir states.

Volodimir looks down to see the surprise in Nick's eyes. "You... you think that I can make it?" Nick whispers.

His teacher points to another vest that ties the look together. "I wouldn't be making time for you if I didn't."

Nick waits outside as Volodimir pays for the clothes, enjoying the snowfall and chatting citizens. When his teacher exits the store, he carries more bags than expected. Volodimir hands over one of the larger bags for Nick to hold without saying a word. Which only creates suspicion, yet, he takes it from his grinning teacher. Instead of anxiety, a small smile graces his lips.

There in the bag is the coat.

The next place shouldn't have been a surprise, and yet, it still is. They eat at a restaurant, a costly one that Nick hears only nobles can get into. The restaurant features the best cuisine, second only to the imperial palace. A war orphan and a school teacher dine together in a private room with a view that overlooks the city.

The room itself is something that Nick can only imagine the nobles in Availa were used to. He sits nervously beside Volodimir, wondering if they can afford it; in contrast, his teacher sits, perfectly relaxed.

"Calm yourself, Nico." His teacher smirks at the flabbergasted look on the boy's face. "This is a dinner, not a torture session. Though, I did do that yesterday."

Nick looks at him, a hint of fear entering his expression.

"What?" Volodimir chuckles as he takes a sip of his glass. "I have other duties than being the Black Teacher." He smiles again, telling him to relax.

"I've never been in a place like this before. It seems very grand." Nick shrinks deeper in his comfortable chair.

"Get used to it." Volodimir takes a sip from his wine. "I see that your future will have you dealing with people in higher office. Get acquainted with the finer things in life."

"Even working under the Emperor?" Nick chuckles. He means it as a joke of course, however, working under the Emperor would get him closer to becoming their new leader.

Volodimir's eyes flash red. "Why not? I think you would do well in the Emperor's service." He takes another sip from his glass, looking at him. "Now, Nico." He puts the glass down and gets up from his seat. "Sit up straight, and I'll coach you on what and how to eat."

Nick looks dumbfounded as his teacher continues to smile. "Are you teaching me... table manners?"

Volodimir chuckles. "Why not? I like the food, and I was getting hungry. I hate the school's food. Plus, I've seen you eat. You're no longer in the rebellion. No one will steal your food."

He wants to say something to defend himself, but keeps quiet. His teacher has a point. *Who would want a leader who makes them lose their appetite?* He remembers how his cousin adopted better table manners than his friends, adapting quickly to Purple culture. This time, Nick decides to take a page from his cousin. He nods his head and promises to take everything Volodimir teaches him to heart.

He's hammered and coached by Volodimir on everything from his posture to which fork and spoon to use. His elbows were hit off the table, and Volodimir threatened to pull his teeth out if he chewed with his mouth open one more time. All in all, Volodimir deems his manners are atrocious. In Nick's defence, rebellions don't have the budget to cover table manners. They barely had enough to eat.

After eating their main course, which Nick couldn't finish, he builds up his confidence. "Volodimir, I have something important to ask you," he says, putting down his fork. Volodimir looks up and nods for him to continue.

Here goes nothing. "What would we do if we found out that a member of the Availian royal family… was still alive?"

Nick can see his teacher's eyes darken. "What do you mean?" Volodimir's voice is on the edge of ice.

He gulps. "There is a student who knew one of the many bastards of the old King, and one is still alive and well in Equinox House."

Again, Volodimir nods for him to continue.

"It's Emelie Snowfield." Nick immediately feels a wave of pressure go down his spine.

His teacher sits up even straighter, and he can feel the pressure go from his back down to his knees. It is a good thing that he's sitting down. They stay quiet for a few minutes, and he can see his teacher's eyes wavering as if battling himself.

Finally, his teacher exhales through his nose and turns to him. "That is interesting," Volodimir drawls. Nick believes this is what it must feel like to face a dragon. His teacher's eyes are sharp on him, and Nick has to use all his willpower to not cower. "You will need evidence on that accusation. The person who told you must be willing to speak up, and Emelie will have to confess. You must remember, Nico, the girl is doing well, from what I've seen. The Night Emperor hopes that she can go into Black one day."

"What does it matter if she's in Purple?!" Nick snaps. "She's a terrible human being and only thinks about herself! She's dangerous! She almost killed me today!"

Volodimir looks unimpressed by his outburst. "Nico, you must think clearly. You have to prove that she will be dangerous to the Empire. Neither the Emperor nor the people in power will care if she's dangerous. They want someone to be useful for the Empire. If she is dangerous for the Empire, she will be eliminated. Just like if Braawen turns out to be rebellious..." Volodimir pauses, "or even you."

Nick's whole body freezes up. His flame of anger is snuffed out by an icy cold shock of fear spreading across his entire body. "M-me?" he stutters. *Do they know?*

"Even you, Nico. If you or the rest of the rebellion children try anything to destroy the Empire or get revenge, then we will have no choice but to cut you down before you grow."

Nick feels the blood draining from his face; the steady pace of his breathing is the only thing that's keeping him from passing out. "Would you kill me?" he whispers, trying not to sound hurt.

"No," Volodimir shakes his head, to Nick's relief. "That will be Herald's job. I would watch." His relief quickly disappears. "However, I hope that day will never come. You are an intelligent boy, with so much more potential in the Empire than you ever did or will have back in the Kingdom of Availa. That is why I believe you will do great things. I believe that Braawen would do something foolish before you ever do." He takes a sip from his glass. "That boy seems to not care about his family."

Nick suppresses the urge to roll his eyes.

"We asked him about his cousin, the son of Markus Archer. He said the boy didn't have a speck of talent and was probably dead."

He feels a little happy that Braawen didn't rat him out, but then again, Braawen could have done it just for himself. *Why take all the attention off him?*

"What would the Emperor do if the son of Markus was still alive?" He steadies his breathing and hopes that Volodimir can't hear how loudly his heart is beating. He takes a drink from his glass, which seems to help.

Volodimir looks out the window, watching the snow fall. "If he was like his cousin and had potential, I'd let him live. But if he had no potential, then the Emperor would see death as his only option."

Thank you, Lady Adele, for wearing a magical outfit. Nick lets go of a breath he didn't know he was holding.

His teacher turns back to him smiling. "I know that you and Braawen were comrades, but have you seen Markus's son?"

"No." He shakes his head. He looks Volodimir in the eye as the one word comes out so easily. The lie comes tasting like honey, yet deep down inside, he feels sick. He feels like he denies a part of himself, however, there's dread in his stomach. He was lying to his teacher. To himself.

Volodimir looks at him, then to his glass, where he takes a sip of wine. "Pity. Oh well. In any case, I will keep an eye on Emelie Snowfield for now. If what you say is true, then the friend that told you will be rewarded."

Nick looks confused. "I never said it was a friend."

Volodimir just smiles as he drinks his wine.

The rest of the dinner goes much better, except for the consistent sighs and looks of disappointment that his teacher gives him as he eats. As

Volodimir pays for the food, Nick changes into his new coat, and has to admit that he does love it. He leaves the restroom and waits out in the waiting area, patting his full stomach. The food is richer than the food that he is used to. He can't imagine the food back at Equinox House being this rich. Then again, he eats the plainest food at the Yellow table. He remembers all the times he would look over to see what the Purple table was eating. *They would probably be more accustomed to food like this,* he thinks.

Laughter from one of the private dinning rooms next to him draws his attention back to reality. Nick slowly turns around, his eyes shine bright with the light coming from a door that stands ajar. His body moves closer to the noise, listening to chatter of voices, the footsteps fade and the creaking of the seats.

Looking through the slight cracks of the door, two men sit at a small table; one man wears a purple suit while the other wears a grey suit. However, a small smile forms on Nick's lips, as his table's view was much better than theirs. His eyes goes over their table, which bore rich foods and delicacies that would have made his stomach rumble uncontrollably an hour ago. One of the men wears a ring with a ruby as big as an eye. The other is breaking what looked like to be his third lobster. They eat in the fashion that Volodimir was drilling him in tonight. After seeing their food and apparel, Nick concludes that they're Nobles. His back turns from them until he hears them talk about the new Lord Nortshell.

"My friend, the new lord is a fool and a mere puppet to the Night Emperor," one of them say.

"It's a pity, my friend. The Nortshell family was one of the most prominent founders of this Empire." Nick leans in closer behind the door to hear them better and looks through the crack to see who is speaking.

"Yes, *was* is the correct past tense, dear friend. If the old Lord Gerald Nortshell had listened to me, none of this would have happened." He can hear the noble tsk as he puts a forkful of lobster in his mouth.

"And what, pray tell, did you tell old Gerry?" Nick can hear him munching on something crunchy as he wipes his ruby ring.

"Well, that he should have done a blood transfer."

Nick narrows his eyes, confused.

"Blood transfer? You mean you wanted him to adopt?" The ruby ring noble asks.

He can hear the other noble tsk again, wiping the lobster from his lips. "Adopt and then transfer his blood to the child. There——another son." The man says as though it would solve all the late noble's problems.

"Yes, it might have been better. But the man already had such failures for sons. I don't think he had the heart to be disappointed a third time."

He hears the lobster eating noble laugh as he takes a sip of his wine. "Ah, true. Poor fellow, I guess his family legacy shall end." The two laugh and toast to the dead noble, drinking their merry way.

Nick moves away from the door and moves back, feeling sick. Of course, nobles would feel that way. *But is having a puppet noble good for the rest of the realm?* His thoughts end as he bumps into Volodimir.

"My apologies." He turns, looking at an amused teacher.

Volodimir looks in the direction of the laughing nobles and narrows his eyes. He then turns to Nick and smiles. "Hear anything interesting?" His eyes gleam mischievously.

"I don't know," Nick responds honestly.

"Come now, let's go on a walk." Volodimir gently guides him through the door, and the cold winds claw at his face.

Nick always stayed in the shadows, away from everyone whenever he came into the city. Even in Availa, he mostly stayed in the shadows when he went into towns. His memories of him walking with his parents are few and far between. The little time he did walk with them, people would look at him with pity for his skinny figure. Yet, as Volodimir and Nick walk tonight, no one looks at him with pity. They smile or nod hello. Nick feels like an actual human being.

As they continue to walk, he absorbs the bright atmosphere around him, enjoying the lights and the sounds. They even stop by a jewellery store. The store is packed with precious gems and metals that have Nick's eyes boggling.

"This piece is a special." The old shopkeeper appears out of nowhere. "It came right from the castle in Availa. They say it belonged to a very beautiful duchess with eyes as green as emeralds and hair as gold as wheat." He holds up a hairpin of dark purple gems.

Nick has to stop himself from staring at it. His teacher buys it and has it sent to the Grand Palace. Nick has to tune out the price of the piece.

I'm pretty sure that hairpin is the school's entire budget for the Red circle students. Maybe even Blue, he can't help but think.

They return back outside and continue their walk deeper into the heart of the city. As they walk, Nick watches his teacher. Volodimir walks with the air of a noble, his head held high and back always straight. He, too, straightens his back and pulls his shoulder down. He hesitates, but he looks straight ahead and puts a small smile on his face.

No one knows who I am. I can try to be a noble as well. He tries to have confidence, even if it's just this once. As those words enter his mind, he can't help but grin.

As they walk, the snow falls gently around them and the sounds of children laughing draw his attention. Even late at night, many parents are still walking with their laughing children. One father even carries his sleeping child on his shoulders. Nick's fantasies begin to dim as reality sets in. He bites his lower lips. He has no memories of the time his family was happy. There was always fighting, betrayals, and empty marriage beds.

He lowers his head, and his mood begins to sour at the thought of his family. Looking at the laughing children with their parents only dampens his mood. As they pass a particular family, he gasps. A son about his age was walking with his father, laughing and talking. He looks away. He's never had a relationship like that with his father. Now, he never could.

"Nico," Volodimir's voice is smooth, pulling him away from the memories of his family. "What's wrong?"

He shakes his head. "Nothing, I'm just enjoying the lights and the sounds. It's… it's all very nice." He doesn't sound too convincing.

His teacher sighs and brings him to one of the many benches along the street. The snow has already been dusted off, and they both take a seat. Nick stares out into the streets, sinking himself deeper into the new coat that Volodimir bought him. The collar's fur tickles his nose, and he looks down at the black and silver designs that go to his knees. They remind him of the coats that he saw when he first came here.

He closes his eyes and listens to the street music, and the people walking by him. He used to play a game called Pretend as a child. He would pretend that his father loved him, that his mother wasn't always fighting, and that he could stand by Braawen's side.

Maybe I can pretend to be a normal citizen of the Empire going shopping with my fat- His eyes snap open, not daring to finish that thought.

"Your father wasn't very good, was he?" Nick slowly turns his head to his teacher, whose red eyes seem to show understanding and sadness.

He looks back on the street and sees more fathers holding their children's hands. He remembers when he tried to hold his father's hand once; Markus smacked it away.

He shakes his head. "No," he whispers.

Volodimir rolls his neck, giving a satisfying crack that startles Nick at first. "Fathers are supposed to protect and guide their children. That's what they sign up for when they mate."

His eyes widen and his cheeks go red, but his teacher continues. "Here in this Empire, we have more adoptions now. Many men choose to be fathers, and mothers want kids but don't want to submit themselves to the whole pregnancy period. I don't blame them. Sounds horrid."

Nick turns to him. "I heard the nobles talking about the adoption."

Volodimir gives a hum. "Yes, blood transferring is very different from a normal adoption. You see, blood is important in the Empire. It can get you access to places that normal people can't get into. But, a name is also a powerful weapon. If you don't have the blood, you have to have a great name."

He nods. "Well, I guess all I have is a name. Well—not yet, Westmore doesn't really have any power here."

"Not quite." Volodimir smiles. "The names Swan, Oxford, and even Nortshell, can get you almost everywhere in the Empire. However, Nox would be the most powerful name; so is the blood."

"The imperial family? They adopt too?"

Volodimir chuckles. "Yes, a few good emperors have come from blood transfers. It doesn't make the royal family any different. Their blood still belongs to the first ruler, and can still open doors and places that regular people can only dream of accessing."

Nick just nods. Archer was once seen as a name of hope to the rebellion. Now, that name is nothing but seen as traitors all over the realm.

"Tell me about the conversation you overheard."

He tells him about the Nortshell situation, and Volodimir laughs. "Maybe, they're right, Nico. Blood transferring is a bio-engineering revolution. You see, with the right ingredients and time, a person can take another person and make them their child not by birth, but by blood."

Nick looks confused. "By blood?"

"Precisely. Let's take the late Nortshell situation, for example. Since the two sons were such failures, the lord could have taken another child, drained the child of their blood, and replaced it with his. The child would have the blood of the late Nortshell and become his third son.

"In the past, it was called a blood ritual, where nobles who feared dying out would choose a child and replace their blood with their own. Now, only the blood transfer can be done once."

"So, you can have only one donor?"

"Not quite. Let's say the late Lord Nortshell's wife wanted the child to have her blood. During the ritual, she and her husband would both give their blood at the same time to the child."

Nick nods. "So, that child could have been the new head of house Nortshell?"

Volodimir nods his head. "No one would bat an eye, for his child will also have the blood of the late Nortshell. Once the blood transfer is done, none of the old blood remains, and the new blood changes your colour and your body structure. You can even inherit your donor's traits. Some side effects I've seen are people's hair, skin, or eyes turning the colour of their donor or new parent. Like I said, inheriting their parents' traits."

Nick can only imagine the possibilities. "Really? Does it work? People can do that?"

"Yes, it works, but it can only be done once. Once your body changes, it has become accustomed to the change and will not change back."

"That's so amazing. So, nobles do it?" Nick says, but his mind is still trying to wrap his head around everything.

"Yes, nobles. For example, if I give you my blood, whatever blood your father and mother gave you will be gone. I would have to drain you of all your blood and replace it with mine. It would take three days and is very dangerous if not done properly. Many have died by going to illegal doctors. Though, there is a hint of magic to it. Old magic that we're not even sure of." Volodimir looks at Nick and smiles.

"Old magic... I read in a book that there was magic that goes past the elements. However, the General told us that there is just Shadow magic."

Volodimir chuckles. "No, Nico. There are ancient magics that we're not so sure about. Our ancestors were able to do terrible and great things. One theory is that this could be blood magic. Blood magic was spoken about more in the southern region of the Empire. That's also where blood transfers began. I believe they still do it in magical circles, but the use of science makes it go faster." He sees that he still has his student's attention and continues.

"I saw a transfer happen once. It was fascinating. The child I saw took on the adoptive parents' blood and his features began to change in just a couple weeks. His blonde hair turned brown, and his eyes changed to match his new mother's, almost as though he was a naturally-born child of theirs."

Nick looks at him curiously.

"What are you thinking, Nico?"

He shrugs. "I'm wondering if I would get your eye colour or keep mine."

A small chuckle escapes Volodimir's lips. "Boy, my eyes are a strong family trait. I have no doubt that your blue will be gone."

Nick can only shake his head with a smile. "I don't know. The blue in my family is strong."

Chapter 28
Pain

Volodimir transports them back to the cottage and places Nick's new clothes in the bedroom. Nick also gives him his new coat as he changes back into his school's coat. He's told that the General has a surprise for everyone in the Yellow circle during the Spring Festival. Instead of the joyful surprise that Volodimir is expecting, Nick becomes very nervous and pale. His teacher laughs at his reaction and guarantees that it will cause him and his friends no harm. He only sees Nick reassured when he mentions that the gifts are also from Elena.

Before Nick leaves, he asks him a question. "Volodimir, forgive me for asking this." He takes a breath and speaks. "But why did the Emperor choose you to teach?"

Volodimir just gives a small smile. "The truth?" He asks. Nick nods. "Because I'm the only one who can."

He doesn't quite understand, but asks another question. "You're powerful, and you seem important. So, why are you willing to teach a Yellow?"

His teacher's eyes look startled for a moment; the only sounds are the crackling of the fireplace. He thinks he's asked a silly question until his teacher's lips curve up into another smile.

"Because," Volodimir says, "my first teacher was my father. He was the first to see potential in a little Orange."

Nick can't hide his surprise fast enough from his teacher. "Orange?" he repeats. He narrows his eyes, looking over at his teacher.

His teacher looks puzzled at first. "Well, of course." Then he chuckles, realizing why his student can't picture him as an Orange. "I didn't just get to where I am on day one. I had to grow, evolve." Volodimir looks down at his hands, then back at his student. His smirk slowly disappears as memories of his past come to light. "Much of the growth was painful, but necessary." He sighs.

"Did he teach until you reached Purple?" Nick asks.

Volodimir shakes his head. "No. I had another teacher. I didn't even realize when I reached Purple. I just remembered the fighting and training. But, back to your question. It was only my teachers that had faith in me. When my second teacher died, she told me to always believe that a person can achieve their goals with proper guidance. I also promised her that I would never turn away a person with great potential, no matter their background."

Volodimir places a hand on his shoulder. "Nico, it is our job not only as teachers, but as experienced Shadow Wielders, to ensure that the younger generation is encouraged to get stronger and more confident in their abilities. I, personally, believe that anyone can do well no matter what circle they're in." The man smiles. "So Nico, I see you becoming the best Yellow in existence or moving up at least two levels."

"Two levels?" Nick smiles back.

"I said at least. By the end, I expect you to be Purple or Black."

Nick's confidence seems to grow, and so does the light feeling in his chest. Not many people believed in him growing up. The ones who did are either dead, missing, or being hunted down.

He brings his thoughts back into the present and wonders about another question. "I apologize, Volodimir, but I need to ask another question." His teacher lifts one eyebrow but nods for him to continue. "Can you show me why the Emperor picked you? Like, can you show me a trick that everyone finds really hard to do?"

Volodimir bursts into laughter. "You mean after all this time, you don't see why I came here?" Nick smiles and shakes his head. Though he knows that the man in front of him is powerful, he feels that he is different from everyone here. The only one he can imagine coming close to his level is the General.

Volodimir snaps his fingers and steps back. Out of his shadow comes a second Volodimir. "A Shadow Clone." The two Volodimirs say in unison.

Nick runs around them and sees no difference. They both smile at his antics as the boy rapidly asks several questions, not giving time for him to answer. He only stops when Volodimir puts his hands up.

"Shadow Clones are hard to do because the person must remain focused on their clone," Volodimir states.

"But I can leave my clone alone," The clone sounds just like his teacher. "I know what I have to do."

Volodimir waves his hand, and the clone disappears. "My clones can move around the area, and tell me what they see and hear. It's like I'm in more than one place at once. It's very helpful on missions, especially when I need to be here and the Palace at the same time. In fact, one of my clones is at the palace speaking to Lady Adele on the students' progress right now."

"What?" Nick gasps.

"Do not worry, I'm the real Volodimir. My clone is talking to Lady Adele. Oh, speaking of Adele, I hope she loves her birthday gift. It's never a good idea to forget the birthday of the second-in-command of the Night Emperor."

"Sh-she's second in command?" Nick asks.

Volodimir nods. "Why, yes. I believe you met her at the testing of children, correct?" He grins. "I do remember her telling me about a Yellow with a *seed* of talent."

Nick groans, regretting opening his mouth every day.

"Go to bed, Nico. You've had a long day. I have to go to the palace for a week, and it will need all of my attention. Meeting with both the Inner and Outer Council will do that. They want to know the progress of the war students here, and I cannot miss it."

Nick looks up. "So, you'll meet all the members and even the Night Emperor?" He nods. "So, I get a week of sleep, then?" He smirks, causing Volodimir to frown. "Do you even sleep?" he teases.

This time, Volodimir groans. "Good night, Nico," he states firmly as he pushes him out the door.

Nick laughs as he runs through the forest toward the school. He Shadow Jumps to the hallway and quickly changes when he sneaks into the room. His friends are asleep, and guilt hits him. He wishes that he could have grabbed some food from the restaurant for them. He slips into his bed and feels one of the springs pinching the scars on his back. Used to the feeling, he closes his eyes, not bothering to take the blue vial, allowing his body to naturally sleep.

Darkness is the first thing that Nick notices when he comes to. Then, comes the pain and the cracking of his own voice. His voice is small, though it doesn't diminish the pain that he's feeling. As he opens his eyes, he can see a candle's soft light illuminating the small cot that he lays on. His eyes wander around the room and he quickly comes to the realization that he's not in his room. There are no toys, no maps, no tiny hourglasses, no blanket made by his mother on the bed. The room is plain, and the window above his head lets in a cold breeze. This is not his home. The familiar smell of strawberries is not present either. Instead, the smell of medical herbs lingers in the room and on his body. He tries to sit up, but winces as he looks at his arm. It has been bandaged up, with a thicker roll on his wrist.

"No," He whispers, his eyes tear up as he remembers his most recent memories return. His home burning, the soldiers, and his mother lying next to him, unmoving.

Before he can let out a scream that threatens to erupt, he hears the soft whispers behind closed doors.

"You could have waited!" a man's voice snaps.

The other louder voice is deeper, one filled with dread and disappointments. He knows that voice well. "Why?! She's my wife! I decide how to bury her," his father snaps back.

"But she's my sister!" a younger third voice yells.

"Quiet, Malcolm, Nicky is sleeping!" It's the voice of his uncle. The last he remembers, Uncle Tybalt was calling for help as he held on to his wrist. "And Markus, your son deserves to be at his mother's funeral!"

Mother. It wasn't a dream. Nick's eyes begin to swell, but he bites on the small blanket that he has. He can't have them hearing him cry.

"Markus, please, at least let me take my sister's bones. She needs to be placed with her ancestors. She died a warrior's death. Please allow her the honour of being buried there," he hears Malcolm plead through the door.

"I said no!" his father yells.

"Markus!" Tybalt snaps. "Please let us continue this conversation elsewhere."

"Why?" his father snaps. "He's going to die anyway!"

"Markus!" both his uncles snap.

"What? It would have been better if he had died. But no, my wife just had to take the arrow for him. She should have taken the arrow for me, at least! Isn't that what she promised me? To give her life to me?"

Instead of tears, bile threatens to erupt from him. He feels sick hearing that his father wanted him dead. *Was it really my fault?*

He can hear Malcolm scoff. "Like you told her that you would stay true and stray to no other women?"

There's silence until he heard shuffles and yelling from the door. Frightened, he slowly pulls the covers over his head, ignoring the pain on his wrist. The next thing he hears is a door slamming shut. He hears footsteps outside, and looks out the window. There, he sees his Uncle Malcolm looking back at him one last time from the window before disappearing into the winds.

He doesn't turn when he hears the door behind him open. He isn't expecting his father, so he feels safe to keep his back turned.

"He's not turning back." His voice quivers under the sound of the door softly closing. "I-is he leaving too?" He slowly turns to his uncle, who looks worn. Tybalt has bandages around his arm and a fresh bruise on his cheeks. "Is… is it my fault?" He begins to sob.

His uncle is quick to wrap his arms around him. "No, no, Nicky. You are not at fault."

"Bu-but papa-"

"Is an idiot who is grieving." Tybalt rubs his back. "You are not at fault, and your mother would have thought the same."

Nick cries as wet tears and snot stains his uncle's shirt. He apologizes quickly and tries to dry his eyes. *Men don't cry!* he can hear his father's voice hit him.

Before he could properly remove himself from his uncle, Tybalt gently pulls him back to his chest. "It's okay to cry." Tybalt's voice is soothing, and his hands warm him as he rubs his back. Nick cries for the death of his mother for what seems like ages. Tybalt only hugs him more, protecting him from the world.

When Nick can control his breathing, he looks up to see the beautiful blue eyes of his uncle. There's no doubt in those eyes, no lies or hate. They're real and full of truth. The truth that little Nick at the time didn't realize that he needed.

"Now, I need you to sleep and I need you to heal up, okay? I need you to rest. Can you do that for me?" his uncle asks; to Nick's ears, it sounds like pleading.

He nods with reddened eyes, and his uncle hums him a tune as he falls back asleep.

Later, he wakes up to his father looking at him. He frightens Nick as he looks at him with cold blue eyes. His father's face is stony, and his blonde hair is tousled. He doesn't even know if his father is breathing.

"Papa?" he whispers, his throat still sore from crying.

It takes a minute, but his father moves. Blue eyes glare at his own.

"It should have been you." His father's voice isn't full of its usual boom and anger. It is quiet but not soft, and pierces right through to Nick's soul. He prefers the loud anger.

"I—I didn't…"

"It was your fault." His father sounds so sure. There's no room for argument.

"But Uncle Tys said…"

"Your uncle knows nothing!" Markus snaps, causing Nick to wince in pain when he moves his arm away from his father.

"If you weren't there, she would have lived! If you weren't so weak and useless with a sword, you could have defended yourself! If you weren't bothering her to train you on how to use a spear, she would have trained more and lived! Why are you so weak?! Why did you hurt her in the end? If you weren't born, she would still be alive!" Markus stops as he feels his blood boil. He looks at his crying son, which only fuels the burning fire that rages in him.

"Stop crying! You're not the one who had to bury the love of their life!" He slaps the boy hard across the face. Nick tries to reach for something as he falls out of the cot, but hits his wrist instead, causing it to bleed. "There, now you have something to cry about! If I see or hear that you cried about your mother again, I will, personally, be the one to put you next to her!" his father yells, storming out of the room.

Nick stays curled on the floor as he grabs his wrist to stop the blood. His father's words ring in his head a lot. *I hurt mommy, I'm the reason why she's gone.*

I want to be with mommy. The little boy cries silent tears as the pain in his head becomes too much. His grip loosens on his wrist, and as the blood leaks out, he closes his eyes for what feels like the last time.

However, he opens his eyes to see himself in another room. His wrist is bandaged again, but instead of his father, it's Uncle Tybalt crying, his hands covering his face. Uncle Julius is also on his knees praying. Nick can hear him sob as his Uncle Tybalt prays to the deities to let his nephew live.

"Please, not my Nicky, not my little Nicky."

Nick wakes up in the cellar with tears in his eyes.

'Blood don't kill blood,' but he knows his father damaged him more than the King's soldiers ever could.

Chapter 29
Time

Before the attack that Nick and Rohana faced, another person had an interesting day.

As the sun rises, Volodimir sits at his table. He has already drunk his third cup of tea, yet is still utterly exhausted. *I'm either using my powers too much, or Arran is poisoning me.* He looks at his teacup and shrugs as he continues to drink.

He's finished his reports for the Emperor's council and has a list written of potential students that will most likely move up into a new circle. The first name he writes is Nickolaus Westmore.

He rubs his eyes, knowing that it will be a long day. His day begins when he receives a surprise visit from a blue-eyed 'friend' called Abram. The man is still in his Shadow Assassin gear, and his tall frame makes his appearance more menacing. Abram prefers to meet with people unannounced, which scares most people but annoys Volodimir. They sit at the small round table with two teacups and a kettle in the kitchen. The man smiles as Volodimir groans, rubbing his temples.

"Wow." Abram's eyebrows rise. "You have changed, Volodi." The unapproved nickname causes Volodimir's eyes to flash a deathly red. Abram grins, his sharp canines more pronounced. "There's the pain in the ass I know and love." His friend gives a raspy chuckle.

"Why aren't you dead yet?" Volodimir mumbles as he drinks from his cup of tea.

His friend tsks. "That's not very nice. Admit it, you would be disappointed if I died. Who would you talk to?" Abram rests his boots on the table, leaving pieces of dirt too close to the kettle.

An irate growl escapes the back of Volodimir's throat as he takes another sip of tea. He debates whether or not he should kill him, because Abram isn't the only person he can talk to now.

"You really have changed. You seem… calmer." Abram's voice sounds whimsical. "No Shadow Whip or slashing my feet off the table?" He takes his feet off the table and leans in closer to Volodimir. "Are you really my friend?" He asks with an inquisitive look.

"Abram, do you want a matching scar on your other eye? Or do you want to lose that eye altogether?" At that comment, Abram sits back down on his chair, distancing himself from Volodimir. "Why are you here?"

Abram looks a little too comfortable in that chair for his liking, which means that he isn't leaving anytime soon. "I missed you."

"Liar!" Volodimir snaps, then chuckles as Abram lets out a burst of laughter.

Abram looks at him and smiles. "You haven't chuckled or laughed in a long time, my friend."

Volodimir's chuckles slow down as he gives Abram a small smile. "I haven't, have I?"

"Nope." Abram lets the 'p' pop. "But it's good to hear you chuckle. I wanted to check up on you. I know that the war in Availa was tough, and I know you hated being here before you left for the war."

Volodimir remembers his time here before the war very well. "It's better now." That would be the best way to phrase it. "I hated it here. At least the General made it more exciting."

Abram nods. "That's good. I also wanted to let you know that I'm thinking of claiming a student. I'm ready for an apprentice."

Volodimir puts down his cup. He wasn't expecting his friend to claim a student. From what he remembered in training with him, Abram swore to never take on any apprentices. "Really? They must have impressed you then. May I know who you're thinking of claiming?" He picks up his cup, ready to take another sip.

"I've only been here a couple days, but I see potential in him. He has such a zeal to improve himself and those around him. You know him. I see him jogging and his improvements in the Yellow circle. He's smart in the shadows and in his education, and I see him climbing all over the school to get to you. He even tried to climb the Black tower." Abram chuckles. "I will enjoy training Nickolaus Westmore."

"You will not!" Volodimir bursts out angrily, slamming his cup on the table and startling his friend. "Nico is *my* apprentice. Find another." He didn't mean for his tone to be defensive; it even surprises him.

Abram has never heard such a tone from his friend before, but smiles wickedly. "Alright. I'm surprised, though. I thought you hated teaching," he states as he takes a sip from his own cup.

Volodimir ignores the man and realizes that he needs to finish his duties here quickly. He takes out a letter from his pocket and places it on the table. He got a letter from the council summoning him to the palace. He shows it to Abram, who laughs and throws the letter on the floor.

"They're enjoying this," Abram states as he leaves Volodimir's cottage, flashing his trademark beastly grin.

There in front of Volodimir is an empty seat and a dirty cup. *The least he could do is put the cup in the sink.* He finishes his fourth cup of tea and places it in the sink. He decides to quickly clean his kitchen, leaving it spotless. Once complete, he goes back to his room and puts on his robes. As he puts the finishing touches on his hair, he waters the only flower alive in his room. He takes a long whiff of its perfume and closes his eyes, smiling; he swears that he hears laughter, but he blocks it out and Shadow Portals to school.

His day is simple. He has three interviews, a meeting with the medical staff, and his daily rounds. Today, his round will be Purple and Blue.

Volodimir walks into the Shadow Room on the fifth floor. He will be seeing the Purple class first. Standing to the side, holding onto his cane, is the man who will cause him the most headaches, Professor Arran. The man who could be poisoning him gives him a small smile and taps his cane on the floor, gaining his students' attention. Volodimir never understood the cane. The man can walk perfectly without it.

"Students, today we have the Black teacher here to watch our training. Do your best and more." They bow to him and Volodimir nods in return.

Volodimir watches from the sidelines as the students are placed in different groups. The two teachers stand beside each other in silence for which Volodimir is grateful. He watches the students move and fight. Some are doing drills, while others are practising Shadow techniques.

"Volodimir." There goes the end of that silence. He nods at the mention of his name. "I would like you to watch Braawen and Emelie." Arran walks away, not waiting for him to respond. Volodimir doesn't even hide his eye roll.

As they walk further down the room, he looks around. There are fifteen students in the Shadow Room, all focused on their tasks. He sees that the room is well maintained. The walls are a dark purple, and the room are fitted with the newest electro lights. The lights allow the shadows of different objects and people to be cast in different directions. He notices that some lights are not turned on.

Arran catches him looking at one of the unlit lights. "Ah, yes. I made some changes to the room myself. Some lights are turned off, while others are turned on. This allows the room to change the angle of the shadows. Since we have no windows in here, I made it so that the students would have to take into account where the shadows were." He giggles. "One student didn't and ended up crashing into an object after Shadow Jumping."

Volodimir compliments him as Arran did something he can agree on for once. Arran sees this as a way to glorify himself, which Volodimir tunes out, and instead, he listens to other voices around the room. He listens to the children, their exhausted breaths and the rapid beating of their hearts.

However, the voices that he hears loudest are the shadows. They cry out to the students, trying to tell them what they are doing is wrong.

One student falls on his backside, and he can hear the shadows giving him tips on making a safer jump. However, the student gets up and tries the same trick again... with the same results.

As Volodimir and Arran approach the two star pupils, they can see Braawen making a Shadow Object Clone of a vase. The vase is almost perfect, and Emelie touches it. It stays solid for a few moments but disappears in a puff of black smoke, returning to the original object's shadow. They both turn to Volodimir and bow.

Volodimir nods to them. "That is a good attempt at creating a Shadow Object. I have no doubt that you will succeed soon."

Braawen smiles broadly, arrogance in his eyes.

He's used to praise, Volodimir thinks. He can't help but think of a boy with similar eyes who refuses to see himself as great.

"How far have the two of you progressed in the Purple shadow techniques?" he asks.

They smile proudly. "As you saw, Black Teacher, I can do the Shadow Objects," Braawen states, remembering that the Black Teacher can only be called by their title. He demonstrates by materializing a silver knife with a black handle from his shadow. "I can also summon a sixth level Shadow Weapon."

"I can also summon a Shadow Weapon," Emelie adds.

"Shadow Objects and Weapons, that is all very impressive. I will let the Emperor know of your achievements." He turns to Professor Arran, who smiles, but then he turns to see the look that Volodimir is giving him. The man hasn't smiled once.

"Have any of them heard the voices of the shadows?" Volodimir asks.

Arran frowns and looks at his cane. "No, but they are still progressing well without them."

That response doesn't please Volodimir, and he turns back to the students. "Can anyone hear the shadows?"

The silence is palpable as he notices that everyone has stopped to look at them.

"Well?" Volodimir asks again, his voice ringing across the room.

Silence and shame greet Volodimir.

"Professor Arran, do you know what it means when a person, especially one in the Purple circle, can't hear the shadows?" he asks.

The professor nods, but Volodimir continues anyway.

"They can't reach their full potential. They can't complete the steps necessary for their training. How can they use Darkest Truths? A spell that can allow the shadows to tell a person when someone is lying to them. What about Black Out? The technique one uses their shadows and the shadows around them to turn an entire room black, or blind their enemies." He walks closer to Arran, who tenses up as his hands tightly grip onto his cane. "How about Shadow Beast? They'll never be able to summon one, let alone tame one."

Arran is barely holding in his temper, but Volodimir doesn't care. "I could hear the shadows when I was in Blue. I even spoke with the other Purple users who graduated here years ago. They are shocked that none of your students can hear the shadows."

"I could," a small voice state. It's a girl with curly red hair who was doing her drills. They all turn to her. "I—I was able to hear them when I was in Blue, but then they stopped. I don't know why."

He looks at her and scans the room. Some nod in agreement, while others look uncomfortable with the situation.

"The shadows just aren't speaking to them." Arran explains, shrugging his shoulders.

Volodimir's eyes widen for a split second before a chuckle escapes his lips. "We both know that's a lie."

He walks out through the front door, leaving the class.

He spends the next hour with the Blue class, and the atmosphere is different. They are all practising meditation, and Volodimir is glad, for he needed this time. The shadows around him are happily whispering with three of the students. He smiles as he hears a girl giggle from her conversation with the shadows.

They are humble and they listen. Some more than others, but they listen, the shadows tell him. Volodimir just nods and continues to meditate with the class.

His meeting in his school office with the nurses and the other faculty members is going well. That is, until one of the guards runs into his meeting with the head librarian.

The guard bows. "Black Teacher, there seems to be a Shadow fight in the feasting room!"

Volodimir sighs. "We will continue this conversation later, Ms. Joy. It has just occurred to me that I am needed elsewhere." The woman bows and disappears in her shadow.

He doesn't even bother to Shadow Jump as he makes his way over there. With each step bringing him closer to the noise, the shadows speak to him with urgency.

It seems that our boy is there as well.

Volodimir raises an eyebrow. *Is that so? Was he the one who started the fight? I would be very disappointed in him. I did not teach him to do that.*

He can hear them chuckle in every crevice of his mind. *No, he is trying to help a friend.*

"Of course he is," he mumbles. He waits in the background, cloaking his presence around the students. He stays that way until he hears Professor Arran's voice. Irritation flows through him, and he releases a small portion of his presence. The students immediately see him and gasp, staring at him as they part for him.

As he walks down the hallway, what he sees makes his blood boil. He deals with it quickly and gives a fair warning to Ms. Snowfield and Professor Arran. If they don't deal with her, he will. He would normally let the teachers in their circle deal with the punishments. However, when he heard that Nico was almost hurt, or worse he wanted to give her a Black punishment right there and then.

The girl should thank the shadows; they were able to calm him down before he unleashed a true Shadow Slash at her. He makes his way over to the Black cottage, as he has another interview to do.

In the cottage, Mrs. Avion looks pale and afraid. Volodimir ignores her as he fixes up some lavender peppermint tea. He looks at her when he's finished.

"Now, Mrs. Avion, how long have you been a teacher at this school?" he asks. It's a simple question, yet she looks petrified to even answer that.

"I—I've been here for five years, Black Teacher."

"That's quite some time." He takes his cup and pushes her cup towards her. He sips and enjoys the sweet taste of the tea, smiling at her.

She slowly takes a sip and gives a small smile.

"I'm not here to reprimand you in any way. I just have a few questions. As you can see, I am quite new here but in my short time, I have reasons to be concerned."

She lowers her cup to its saucer. "Concerned?" Her lips tremble.

"Yes," he states, red eyes staring into her own. She quickly looks away from them. "You're a Purple?"

"Yes," she mumbles, looking perplexed.

"Well, I remember my Purple teacher being far more confident. You're a Purple, so look me in the eye when I speak to you," he commands harshly. She looks at him, though he can see fear in her eyes. "I've been requested by the Emperor's Council to come to the school because there have been some rumours about the Purples. The recent Purple graduates have all had the same problem; one that never used to occur."

"A-and that would be?" she whispers.

"Speak louder. I want to hear some confidence in your voice," he commands.

"And that would be?" she repeats, this time with some strength to her voice.

He tilts his head. "None of them can speak to the shadows." He can see her eyes widen. "At first, we thought that it was just one strange occurrence but after the next graduate class, it became a problem. The last Black teacher was old, though in the beginning, he was strong of mind and will. So, the Emperor allowed him to continue to teach as he looked for another replacement. However, the Council was shocked that in one year, the man had seemed to age so much. For years, the Purples have been lacking. The school has been doing poorly."

He lets the word 'poorly' sink in as he can see her flinch.

"But do you know what really pissed off the Night Emperor?" He glares at the woman as she shakes a little.

"No sir."

"He got a letter from a teacher confirming the rumours that none of the Purples could hear the shadows. That the children and teachers were being treated terribly." He crosses his legs and clasps his hands together. "Now, the Emperor had left the Black teacher and the five heads to run the school accordingly. The Night Emperor is a very busy man." He grins.

She nods. "Yes, he is."

"So, the Emperor was surprised to hear how the school was being run. I was even more surprised when I was chosen to become the new Black teacher. It definitely wasn't what I was thinking of doing this year. I had just come back from the war with Availa, hoping I could leave early, but *no*." He draws out the last word. "I have to stay till the Spring Festival. It was a choice that was made by the Council and agreed upon by the Emperor. It seemed to be a unanimous decision." He chuckles.

"But that's amazing!" she gasps. "I heard that it can take all year for the Council to nominate people. However, isn't it the Emperor who chooses the teacher in the end?"

"Yes, and I was chosen. Can't say no to all those people, can you now?"

She shakes her head.

"I have some questions that I would like us to keep a secret. I have been observing the Purple classes and teachers, especially with how they interact with other students and their fellow teachers. I see a few students that need some sense knocked into them. Humbling them will be a good start."

She giggles, but quickly bites her lips to stop the rest. "Sorry, please continue, Black Teacher."

"It's alright to laugh. However, I see that Professor Arran has a tight hold on you."

She gulps.

"Your behaviour changed when he entered the hall. All of your behaviours change when he's around. Like he is the parent and you all are the children." He leans in his seat, the room getting darker. "Please tell me, what has the good Professor Arran been up to these past five years?"

After the meeting is finished, he has a headache the size of a mountain. He gave Mrs. Avion a black vial that healed her of all the wounds she had from her weekly 'training' with Arran.

He drinks his third cup of tea as he remembers how in three years, Arran planted his seeds. The first year, the Black teacher followed Arran; he got his claws into him. Mrs. Avion couldn't go to the Black teacher as he agreed with Arran's methods. In the last three years, there had been two Black Teachers. Now, it was Volodimir's turn.

"Professor Arran. How will you destroy a teacher this time?" he says to himself. "Will you poison me like Alesander?" He giggles. He takes a sip from his drink, wishing it was alcohol until he hears a knock at the door.

So late? He looks out the window and sees pitch black. *I've had a long day, and I'm too tired to train. We're doing something fun.* "Come in."

Their dinner is fun, and he enjoys teaching the boy some table manners. The deities know his apprentice needs them. He will have to speak to the General to put table manners on their agenda. He will not have them eating terribly during the feast.

The talk about Nick's father gives him a new perspective on the boy. It seemed that the child lacked any emotion for his father, besides the negative ones. Volodimir didn't think that he would use himself as an example for the blood transfer but when he looks at Nick, he can see it. He can see the boy with hair black as night and shining crimson eyes.

He locks the door to the cottage, with papers and packed suitcases beside him. He's excited to leave. He has a stressful week ahead, but at the same time… it's a break, of sorts. A sigh escapes his lips as he creates a Shadow Portal and enters, disappearing from the trees.

Shadow Portals are different from Shadow Jumps. Portals could allow one to travel a great distance. He wonders if he should tell his apprentice that he didn't Shadow Jump the night he collapsed in the cabin. Anywhere that requires over 100 knots of travel is a portal. Not many people could do portals. Many had tried and failed. His apprentice succeeded, but almost died from using too much of his powers. He's just happy the boy hasn't tried anything that reckless since.

He passes through the portal, leaving the cold winter air for the warmth of a dark red and black hallway. He sighs and relaxes as his feet touch the rich red carpet from the Kingdom of Ram, something he hasn't done in a while. Then, he remembers why he's here, and a dark and ancient pressure penetrates him.

"You!" The sounds of clicking heels and a fierce voice grab his attention. A woman glides down the stairs, head held high with her signature purple jewel around her neck.

He turns around with a wide smile. "Lady Swan, how good to see you again too. Happy birthday, by the way." He holds out a box of chocolates.

Her frown still in place, she takes it, eyeing it warily. "How thoughtful of you... You do know I'm trying to lose weight, right?"

"It's sugar-free."

"What the hell does that even mean? Is it even still chocolate?" She throws the chocolate in the nearest bin. "You better have another present."

He chuckles. "Of course, my lady." He gives a mock bow.

Her black eyes glare at him but soften as she looks at his pale complexion. "How is the mission going?" she asks concernedly, brushing her long grey hair out of her one eye.

"I shall have everything set and prepared for the Council by morning." With a snap of his fingers, his belongings are transported to his room via shadow.

"You look tired. The Council can wait for another day."

He shakes his head. "I know you all would like to know the newest report on the school. It's quite fascinating." He smiles.

She rolls her eyes. "You take your teacher position seriously. I'm surprised."

He scoffs. "It's hard to say 'no' when everyone tells me 'yes'. I remember you begging at one point." He grins.

She scoffs. "I don't remember that. I just remember giving valid points on why you should go."

Volodimir hums, not believing a single word. "Plus, you all should be happy that none of you are doing this. Teaching is stressful, and I don't enjoy it. Give me my office job back."

Well, I don't mind one student, he thinks, but he would never say that out loud.

She chuckles softly. "Nonsense, this will teach you patience."

He nods. "Thank you, but I have patience. However, I'm concerned about the Outer Council. How has the Shuffle of the Council been going? All the teachers are talking about it."

He knows that it's a hard subject for her. One of her distant relatives, a Visconte, just lost a lot of respect. In his opinion, the Viscontes were getting too powerful and needed to be knocked down a few pegs. He knows the Council will talk about that, as well as the school and the war children. It will be a long week.

"It's coming along. Ivan Visconte is no longer head and will be in jail for ten years. Nigel Nortshell was executed, and his brother Edward, is now firmly in place as the head of the Chambers of Citizens." She sighs. "He's a tool."

Volodimir grins. "I know."

He disappears, leaving a worried Lady Swan.

He teleports to his temporary office and heads over to his overflowing desk. He hasn't had the time to clean it yet. Adele states that it's a mess, while he states it's organized chaos. Though even he has to admit that this time, the papers are a complete mess, as there's no room to even place the new set of reports. He sighs and begins to organize them.

Two hours later, a knock draws his attention as he finishes separating another pile. "Come in," he commands.

There, in front of him is an older gentleman. He wears his butler uniform proudly and has an embroidered royal black dragon on his upper right chest. He carries a tray with a cup and kettle. Volodimir can even smell the rich tea from his seat.

"Thank you, Mr. Collins."

The man just smiles as he makes his way to Volodimir's tidier desk. The older gentleman looks over the desk and sees the piles that have accumulated during his time away. "Now sir, may I ask why you are still up and about? You should be resting."

Volodimir takes his eyes off his papers and smiles at the man. "Shouldn't you be too, old friend? Getting sleep is good for your ancient bones."

Collins laughs quietly before his attention is caught by one of the papers that Volodimir's holding. "Sir, I don't mean to pry on personal matters but... are those adoption papers?" Collins asks in confusion.

Volodimir looks in his hands and smiles. "Yes, they are. I'm thinking of adopting."

Collins's eyes widen. "Is it the boy that you always talk about?"

He rolls his eyes. "I don't always talk about the boy." He pushes the paper back into a messy pile.

He can hear the old man chuckle, causing a vein of annoyance to grow in him. The man is lucky that he is the Head Butler for the Grand Palace; killing him would cause too many problems. The man is well-liked and serves anyone that needs help. Of course, the Night Emperor comes first. Still, Volodimir has seen the man serving nobles, helping servants and even playing with children. He wouldn't be surprised if Collins is the most beloved man in the Palace. He decides to stomach whatever comments the man makes tonight. He doesn't want to get on anyone's bad side.

"The boy... His name is Nico, correct?" Collins asks and Volodimir nods. "It seems that your relationship goes beyond that of an apprentice and teacher. Dare I say, you seem to act more like a father to the boy."

Volodimir head snaps up to the butler and glares. *No, I will not take whatever comment tonight,* he thinks to himself.

"I have crossed a line, and I do apologize. I have been too bold, it seems." The old man actually bows.

Volodimir continues to glare at him. "Yes, you have indeed." He sighs. "I don't think we're at that stage yet." Taking a sip of his tea, a thought comes to mind. "Collins, did you get the book I requested?"

Collins nods. "I was able to speak to the Imperial Librarian. She will have the book ready for you. But may I ask why you need the book on ancient shadows? Haven't you already read it?"

Volodimir chuckles. "Of course, every high official reads it. It's not for me."

"Oh?"

"Yes, it's for Nico. Do you think he'll like it? He always talks to me about all the books he's read in the library. Even the librarian asked my permission to let him read the advanced books."

Collins smiles. "You gave her permission."

"Naturally. The boy has a thirst for knowledge. I want to encourage him in his reading. Can you also get some books on etiquette? The boy has terrible manners! I know that you do classes for other noble children, and I'd appreciate your help. I think only you can help him."

"I would be happy to help," the butler says with a small smile.

"And I'd like a book on nature for me. The boy has a peculiar understanding of trees. I want to be able to know what he's talking about as well. Whenever we train in the woods or go for a walk, the boy names trees like a little girl naming her latest dolls. He's very excited about trees. Did you know that…"

For the rest of the night, Volodimir talks to the head butler about the wonders of nature and Nick's terrible adventures of finding out which mushrooms are poisonous.

Collins doesn't mind; he stays until he is summoned for his royal duties. It's been a long time since he's seen the man speak so fondly of someone. He can't wait till the Spring Festival when he can meet the child in person.

Chapter 30
Empire

Nick made a fine speech yesterday on improving oneself, but if his friends doesn't do anything to change themselves, that's all it would be. A great speech, nothing more. However, it didn't just mean training and fighting. Nope. He also meant in their scholarly classes.

Ms. Leia seems extra happy today as she teaches class. This class is special as it consists of twenty-five students who are required to meet once a week. All twenty-five are children from Availa in the Yellow, Orange, and Red classes. There are no Blue children, and it seems that Braawen and Emelie receive their own private lessons. Leia doesn't mind. She continues teaching the History of the Empire.

"Now, students." She pushes her flaming hair back. "Last week, we left off at the Nine Kingdoms. Can anyone tell me what the Nine Kingdoms were called?"

Nick raises his hand, and she points to him. "Andromendor, Availa, Kur, Araceli, Winterborn, Ram, Luxor, Louest, and Anthurium."

She smiles. "Correct. These kingdoms are each powerful and have different skills and resources used to help the realm. Now, the focus of this class will be on the Empire. As you all know, the kingdom of Availa is the most recent addition to the Empire."

Nick wants to roll his eyes. They make it sound like his country was a recent purchase.

"In the beginning, there was just a small kingdom by the name of Andromeda. During that era, women were treated as nothing to men. They could not hold positions of power and had to remain home. The throne never went to a woman anywhere, not even in the cold clans of the North. However, that all changed when the first Queen took the throne of Andromeda. She was Queen Olivia Nox the first. She was known as a great beauty, but her mind was her real weapon. She was able to keep her crown from other noblemen who wanted to be the new King. To solve that, she married a distant cousin, became pregnant, and gave birth to a son. Her husband died soon after from the sweating sickness."

Rohana raises her hand. "Did he actually die of illness?" The rest of the class begins to clamour; they want to know too.

The teacher just giggles. "Who knows?" She smiles. "But after having a son, her line was secure, and the Royal house of Nox could continue. Her late husband's family wanted the boy to take on his father's name, Solaria, but she made it clear that Andromeda had always been ruled by a Nox and shall always be ruled by her family. She dealt with domestic issues and made friends with important nobles," she grins.

"Then came the outer kingdoms near her that saw her rule as an opportunity to take control of the region. They thought that being ruled by a woman made our kingdom weak. However, what the Queen lacked in muscle, she made up in mind. She was a great tactician who later won many battles and expanded her lands through war and trade. However, the Empire remembers her for an even greater thing. She was the one who brought Shadow magic into the world."

The class goes silent as their attention is piqued. Nick no longer makes fun of any story of people meeting with deities. Heck, he's met two.

"All the deities were more pronounced in that era, and all the countries worshipped a god or goddess. However, no one asked the god of Shadows or goddess of Light for help as they were neutral, unlike the elemental gods who took sides. The god of Shadow was willing to help anyone who asked. So, the Queen asked the god of Shadows for help, and he gave his power to a select few. She became the first Shadow Wielder. By the end of her rule, she took over the neighbouring five kingdoms. She changed the name of Andromeda to the Andromendor Empire, which means 'great being'. Now Andromeda is the name of our capital city, which is why we are Equinox House of Andromeda." Leia pauses for effect.

"Many people did not go to the god of Shadows. They saw the power of shadows as evil and vile, while the Empress saw it as a tool. She used the shadows to defend her kingdom and attack her enemies. She became the first Shadow Wielder, but her son became the first Black." She smiles again.

"The first Emperor, Alastair Nox, expanded the Empire once again when the kingdom of Kur refused to open their doors to trade. So, he and his men used the shadows to conquer them. During the battle, the Emperor released a power so mighty that it decimated the enemy. He became the first Black when he summoned a Shadow Dragon, and he has not been the last to do so.

"The Empire, after taking over Kur, was stopped from taking over any other by the other larger kingdoms. They rightfully feared our powers. The Emperor made a vow to the god of Shadows himself that he and his descendants would only expand if they were attacked first. That vow is still held to this day."

Ms. Leia fixes her hair and sits on a stool at the front of the class. "The Emperor Alastair Nox made many of the social rules that still apply today. In fact, he and his Council created the circles to rank shadow users. Later on, his descendants added the Kingdom of Anthurium to the Empire after Anthurium assassinated our fourth Emperor. The fourth Emperor was known as the Light Emperor, as he had no Shadow magic. Some believed that he wasn't a child of the ruling Emperor and was actually the child of the Empress and a servant. His brother, Emperor Azrael Nox, who looked exactly like his father and had shadow powers, created the Shadow Assassins and conquered their lands.

"Oh!" She jumps from her seat. "I can't believe I forgot! People doubted the Light Emperor's parentage because it is said that all members of the Nox family will have shadow powers, as the god of Shadows promised that to the first Empress."

Ms. Leia sits on her seat again and calms down. "Back to Emperor Azrael. He encouraged anyone in the kingdom to have a shadow-blessed name, a name that the shadows can call you by. He led by example by changing his name to Emperor Azrael Nicholai Lazlo Nox. His son, Alastair Volodimir Ragnar Nox, also known as Alastair II, made it so that anyone could have a shadow name. The shadow name is a name bestowed on people devoted to the god of Shadows to have a blessed life. Later on, it just became common for people to have a shadow-blessed name. The first name is the name that people wish for you to become. The second is the shadow-blessed name. The third name is something that only those of noble blood can have, the name of character. The last name belongs to the family," she explains.

"Names are just as important as blood. Here in Andromendor, names must have great meaning. We'll look at the name of the current ruler, Emperor Ragnar Volodimir Vallen Nox. What are the first names for again? Just call it out."

"The name that people wish for you to become," Lorcan says.

"Ragnar, the warrior from the deities and a protector. The second name?"

"Shadow-blessed name," Nick says.

"Volodimir means ruling the world. It's an extremely popular name. Two in my family are named after the Emperor, and our own Black Teacher is named after him. The next name is ...?"

"Noble name," Kaius answers.

"Good! Vallen, glorious ruler. These three are powerful names for our current ruler." She stands up again, writing the name of the current ruler on the board. "Now, class, the current ruler of the Empire is Ragnar Volodimir Vallen Nox. He is the son of the late Emperor Allerick and Empress Isabella. They both died in a tragic accident when he was young. They were taking a tour of the Empire, and their vessel sank to the bottom of the sea. There were no survivors. Prince Ragnar became Emperor Ragnar at the age of ten."

Wow. Nick can't help but think. *So young.*

"The Emperor wasn't of age to rule until his sixteenth birthday, but back then, the Council wanted to seize more power and moved the ruling age to eighteen. The boy was pushed and pulled in every direction. His family wanted to control him and treated him more like a servant than an Emperor. As they wore the crown jewels, the young Emperor wore servants' clothes. They would mock him in public and forced him to wear a mask to cover his eyes, something that he still does to this day. Many believe that they blinded him, or he has a scar that he wishes to hide. He doesn't like portraits and has only sat for one so far. Any time he's in public, he wears a mask and black armour. In fact, the black armour is very important, and brings fear to his enemies when he enters the battlefield. In fact, I remember…"

She stops and realises that she's getting off course. "However, back to his childhood, his family let him live in one of the smaller palaces as they moved into the Grand Palace. His life was threatened many times by his uncles while the court just watched. The Empire seemed to have a weak Emperor, and that wasn't good, as many of the smaller regions wanted independence." She jumps up from her seat again, excited about this part of the story.

"The Emperor came to the council at the age of sixteen and asked to be sent to the front lines to quell a revolt in one of the provinces. They allowed him to go, and let's just say, he exceeded everyone's expectations. At the age of sixteen, he led a small garrison and told them to wait and watch. He used his shadow powers and crushed his enemies by summoning the great Black Dragon. He came back a hero, and the capital cheered at his arrival." She looks around to see the children's eyes widen.

"He completed the circle test in front of the court, and when it reached Black, he demanded his seat and took power from the Council back to the Emperor. He 'banished' the family members that abused him and publicly executed nine of his uncles that tried to kill him, personally taking each of their heads. He did not use the imperial Shadow Weapons to kill them, as he deemed them unworthy of such an honour. He used their own weapons against them, one by one. I, honestly, believe he killed the 'banished' ones as well in private. Through this, he secured his place on the throne. He had the council members executed for treason and reshuffled the members completely, all before his seventeenth birthday."

The class begins to whisper to each other.

"Nick, I don't want to go against him," Bhaltair whispers to him. "If you want to, you know 'lead', won't you have to go through him?"

He groans. "Hopefully not."

Maybe we can become friends, or he can die of old age. I'm patient.

Takara raises her hand. "Ms. Leia, why doesn't the Emperor have an Empress?" The class turns their attention back to her.

Ms. Leia seems caught off guard with the question as she blinks and smiles. "The Emperor was supposed to marry. In fact, he was supposed to marry Princess Estelle of Availa." The students gasp as she continues. "Yes, they were to marry so they could increase trade and build a great friendship. The treaty was signed with the aid of Lady Swan and Lord Jameson, one of the Availan King's councilmen. The Emperor fell in love with Estelle, and I was told that your people loved her as well."

There were many nods to that. Nick didn't know much about her, but the few things he heard about her were good.

"However, the princess never came, and your King went mad and attacked our ports going against our treaty. It wasn't until the Emperor came that it was revealed that the King, in one of his many fits of rage, killed his sister and tried to cover it up. The Emperor unleashed his fury, and well... I'm sure you all know the Night of the Silenced."

The clock tower chimes and Ms. Leia jumps from her desk again. She puts out her hands, stopping the students from leaving. "Before you leave, I want you all to know that when you graduate, you each must choose a shadow-blessed name. I advise you to choose wisely."

Chapter 31
Steel

Today is weapons day, and the General has brought in some of his men to train them. Each of the Yellow students has a weapon, and just like Nick thought, the General gives Bhaltair a war hammer. The poor lad stands in a corner smashing bricks and practising swinging under the glare of the General himself.

Takara is given a fan that has knives hidden inside it. She spins and dances without pulling out any of the knives. Her teacher, a woman from Araceli, explains to her how to be graceful and deadly at the same time.

Rohana is practising archery on one side under the watch of one of the General's assistants. The man is an archer who recently became a sharpshooter. He says that after archery, she can switch to a new weapon, guns. Rohana had never seen a gun before. She made a comment about the guns blowing up, she did not want a smaller version of a cannon in her face. However, the man just laughed and commented on the outdated weapons that the Kingdom of Availa had. The Emperor's new guns are more advanced, though they only hold one bullet at a time. The sharpshooter mentions, that it was pity that guns were just approved when the war ended.

Nick, on the other hand, was tempted to use the sword. He thinks that if he gets an actual teacher, then he could wield it. But before he came to the sword, he saw the one weapon that he's been dying to use, and his father wasn't here to stop him.

"Again!" his teacher yells.

Nick thrusts his spear forward again and pulls back. "Try again, *bràthair beag.*" The man smiles. Nick smiles too, but tries and fails to not make it look genuine. This assistant surprised him at first because he knows who this man is.

"*Thank you, uncle,*" he whispers in his mother's language.

Nick doesn't care that his uncle is working for the Empire or the history of how his uncle came to work under the General. He only cares that his mother's brother is still alive and is finally teaching him his mother's family weapon.

"Told that damn man the spear was right for you!" his uncle whispers.

As a child, Nick was always fascinated with watching his mother train. However, his mother was forbidden by his father to even let him pick up the spear. His father's younger brother, Tybalt, tried to explain to his father that Nick couldn't fight with a sword and that he could be talented with a spear like his mother. That enraged his father so much that he chucked his cup at his brother's face, leaving a crescent scar on the man's chin.

"The boy is an Archer! He will fight with a sword!" Marcus swore.

Though Nick always believed that his family should specialize in archery, he wants to laugh. The spear comes naturally to him, and his Uncle Máel Coluim, or Malcolm in the common tongue, isn't going easy on him.

Nick is finally able to take a break, sweat dripping from his brow. He wipes the sweat away and takes a good look at his uncle. The man seems to have aged, even though he is only twenty. His black hair is peppered with strands of grey, and his hooded grey eyes have aged as well. Nick is sure his uncle has seen death and destruction. However, at least his uncle's people were smart enough to surrender.

At least, they had a chance to surrender, Nick thinks to himself.

At the end of the lesson, Malcolm takes the spear and smiles. "I'll be in the Noxus Hotel, room 405. I'm free on the fourth day of the week," he whispers.

Nick smiles sadly as his uncle leaves with the other instructors and the General.

At that moment, it is just the Yellow class together in the training room, talking about how they loved their weapons. As they speak, Nick looks down at his shadow and thinks.

Shadows? he calls them.

Yes, friend? Their voice is soothing to hear, and Nick wonders why they're in such a good mood.

I know that I have to keep the secret of Volodimir being my teacher, but can I teach my friends some Shadow magic? It's not just me who needs to be stronger. I need all of us to be stronger. We need to protect ourselves and each other.

He waits for their response. *Of course, you can teach them. Spreading the knowledge of the shadows is always welcome.*

Nick smiles at their approval and coughs, getting everyone's attention. "Guys, I said that we need to get stronger, right?"

They all nod. "Of course. We can't beat them with magic, but the least we can do is try to defend ourselves," Takara states.

Nick smiles. "Then, why not learn some Shadow magic?"

They all look at him in surprise.

"But.... the General said later," Bhaltair stutters.

He nods. "It is later. Almost two months later. Now, I saw how to do Shadow Walk from a book. Just watch." He steps into his own shadow and pops out beside Bhaltair, startling them all.

"Wow." Rohana whispers.

Takara jumps and claps excitedly. "Nick, you did it!"

He blushes from the praise. "Shadow Walk is a basic skill we have to learn. But remember, the first few times will leave you dizzy." They nod, the girls excited and Bhaltair nervous. "Let's get learning." Nick grins.

Nick spends the next hour teaching them how to Shadow Walk. Takara picks it up easily and walks through the shadow of a piece of equipment, but Nick has to help her when the poor girl passes out as she comes out. Rohana is next to Shadow Walk and chooses to exit behind the shield racks. However, she ignores the shadow's angle and walks straight into the shields, knocking them down.

"Always know the angle of the shadows and be aware of your surroundings. I read that people come out slowly just in case there's something in front of the shadows." Nick explains. Rohana nods and lays down, waiting for the dizziness to pass from her Shadow Walk.

Bhaltair is last. It's a challenge, as he is scared to go into the shadows but Nick encourages him.

"Nothing is going to attack you. Trust me, Rohana and Takara came out fine." Nick whispers to him.

Bhaltair is shaking but he takes deep breaths to calm himself down. He knows that he has to survive for his parents and the kitchen staff who risked their lives for him.

In the end, they are all able to travel a short distance through the room.

They help Bhaltair get out of the door's shadow. Bhaltair catches something that flies at his face, even as dizziness hits him. He opens his hand to see a piece of chalk. They all look at where the object came from and see the General looking gruff.

Oh no... we upset the General. Nick curses himself.

"G-General. H-hey." Bhaltair kneels down unsteadily.

The General approaches them, silent and deadly.

Nick can see that he's angry but before he can say anything, Bhaltair begins to speak. "We apologize for going behind your back sir, but... we're tired." The General stops as Bhaltair tries to get up, with the help of the others.

"We're tired of the other colours looking down on us," Takara says next.

Rohana grips onto Bhaltair. "We want to be stronger. We want people to know that the Yellow class isn't one to mess with."

"And we wanted to surpass even your expectations," Nick adds.

"We just want to make ourselves and you proud," Takara blushes, almost whispering.

There is silence as they wait for the General to speak. The General's face goes through waves of emotions; anger, surprise, and then… he begins to laugh. It's a laugh that thunder could not rival as he holds his chest.

"Proud? I'm already proud of you all, especially with how much you've improved in less than two months!" He wipes his mouth. "I'm just angry that I didn't see all of you do your first jump, but that's alright. I'm sure they were shitty." He turns to Nick with a grin. "Guts, you've been doing some research, haven't you?"

Nick shakes his head.

Rohana is the one who speaks. "We couldn't have done it without —."

"Each other," Nick interrupts Rohana, "We couldn't have done it without each other." He turns to them, smiling. They all nod and turn to the General, who just laughs again.

"You lot have already made me proud. Now, you can just make me prouder!" He laughs. "Plus, Bull, you caught the chalk. Now, you all know what that means."

Bhaltair smiles.

"Starting now, we will begin Shadow wielding training." The General gives them a feral grin, causing the back of Nick's neck to tingle.

"There are two things that all Yellows must master: the Shadow Walk and the Shadow Jump. Shadow Walk can also be perfect for dodging and moving away from people in a fight. An advanced method is when black coils envelop your body, protecting you as you walk. The coils act as a shield as you jump faster. We call that Shadow Glimpse. Shadow Jump allows a person to be transported a distance of no more than 100 knots."

"By the end of the day, you will master walking past me and jumping 100 knots. The hall here is 250 knots, so there's still plenty of room for you to hit a wall," the General jokes, rubbing his hands together. "Now we can get serious."

Chapter 32
Pride

During feast time, Nick watches his cousin, and sees his cousin get up and walk away from the Purple table, leaving the hall. A guard follows him.

Some habits just never change.

Nick quickly drinks the grey liquid in front of him and turns to the General. "May I use the washroom?"

The General, who is eyeing the girls to make sure they eat everything, stops and nods. "Do not throw up any of the smoothies. I'll know," he warns.

Nick nods and makes his way over to the communal washroom. The guard is standing outside, looking bored. Nick goes in when the guard only briefly glances at him. Inside he sees Braawen is just finishing up and meets him at the sink washing his hands.

"Guess old habits are hard to break." His voice startles Braawen, who looks genuinely surprised to see him, glancing around to see where he came from. "The door, in case you're wondering," Nick answers his cousin's question.

"I didn't hear the door. Then again, you were always good at hiding, not fighting." Braawen smiles. "I'm sure you're not here to mock me for still following the washroom times. Your father beat those times into me. Sad to say that I can't take a piss until it's morning or feasting time."

Nick smiles thinly. "I guess my father has left a lasting shadow over us all." Braawen begins to frown at that. "But I'm here for one thing and one thing only." His steps echo across the marble floors of the bathroom as he moves closer to Braawen. No one needs to hear their conversation.

Shadows, are there people that can hear us? Nick asks them.

No, my boy, they reply. *How about you create a sound barrier? Just in case the guard hears you. Spread your shadow out thinly and create a dome so no one can hear you.*

Nick does as he is told, focusing on his shadow. His shadow is behind him, but he can feel a part of him spread around the area.

Very good, the shadows tell him.

Feeling more secure, he refocuses on his cousin. "Braawen, I've spoken to a few people and they tell me that you know more than you're telling me."

If Braawen is hiding something, he doesn't show it.

"I just need to know where in the city our uncle told you he was staying. I don't care about your deal with whomever, and if I do meet uncle, I'll leave."

There is a flash of happiness in his cousin's eyes. A slow chuckle escapes Braawen's lips. "You'll actually leave, Nick?"

"Do you want to come along?" Nick asks.

Braawen shakes his head. "You and I came from nothing, but now I'm treated like a king here. I'm finally being treated to my station." His cousin smirks at him. "We both are."

Nick holds back a growl, refusing to take the bait. "You didn't come from nothing," he says firmly. "You came from two loving parents who tried to protect you. I also didn't come from nothing. My father managed to bring a group of people together who helped bring others hope."

That is as much of a compliment that he will ever give to his father.

"Your father failed."

"He did, but at least he didn't sit down and do nothing. Even your father tried to do something. And I also came from my mother, a warrior and protector."

"She died," Braawen remarks, the grin falling off his face.

Yes, I know, and it's my fault. Nick pushes that thought back down. "Died protecting someone she loved. We came from people who were trying to make a better world for us. The least we can do is try to save one of them." Nick inhales slowly, feeling his muscles relax. He needs the information that Braawen has on their uncle and refuses to show his annoyance. "Where is he hiding?"

Braawen smirks again, giving his most charming grin. "Last time I checked, he was in the slums. But be careful, Nick, the slums are a large place. Not even the Shadow Assassins can find him."

Nick scoffs. "Why does the Emperor want Tybalt? He's just one man! Surely you can try to convince them to let the man go?"

His cousin gives a mirthless laugh. "One man can give people hope. People at home know that he is alive and are waiting to raise arms with him as their new leader. As if!" Braawen scoffs. "The Emperor wants to crush that ember before it becomes a raging fire."

"And you, dear Braawen. Is that why there are guards following you around when another Purple isn't in sight?" Nick asks.

His cousin's smile falters. "I'm just a boy trying to not pay for my father's mistakes."

"We both are."

The two boys stare at each other, the weight of Markus's shadow looming over them. Braawen moves first, walking past him. "Good luck,

Nick. The slums are not kind to people like us. Those who are touched by the shadows are feared."

"Even Yellows?" Nick asks.

His cousin opens the door to see a guard still outside waiting. "Even Yellows," he says over his shoulder.

· ☽ ·

After his encounter with Braawen, Nick makes his way to the Orange quarters but is stopped by one of them. "I'm just here to ask Laura a question."

"She's in the library." The student glares at him, shutting the doors.

He walks to the library, and there, next to the fireplace, is Laura. She's sitting in one of the tall armchairs sipping a cup of tea. The green-haired girl looks simultaneously elegant and dangerous, with the fire behind her casting a large shadow across her face. Her skin seems to glow with the light of the flames.

She smiles when she sees him. "Nick, so good of you to join me on one of my tea nights."

Nick happily smiles back, knowing that Kaius made an amazing friend in Orange. "Sorry, Laura, but I'm here to hear a rumour." He always wondered how she was able to have so many connections so quickly.

She grins as she puts her teacup down. "What would you like to hear? There have been many tales I have heard, but what's the payment?"

"Aren't we friends?" he asks, grinning.

"True. I can give you one for free tonight, but I'll have to ask for payment for the really good stuff."

Nick nods in understanding. "Any rumours of Tybalt Archer?"

Laura's eyes widen, and she gives a low whistle. "Now, *that* one needs a payment. If anyone hears us talking about that, we could lose our heads." She whistles in a playful tone, though Nick can hear a slight shiver in her voice.

"Secret for a secret," he replies.

"Done," She agrees without skipping a beat.

Nick thinks of a secret, not one of his own. "I know that a lot of girls have been trying to get Braawen's affection. You could get more customers if you have the right information." He smiles as her eyes look on with interest. "Braawen prefers girls with red hair or green eyes." She looks at Nick skeptically. "I've fought with him for five years. I've seen the girls he kissed."

"Anyone to vouch for that?" she asks, raising an eyebrow. She could get a lot of coins from those noble girls.

"Lorcan. He was Braawen's best friend."

Laura leans back in her chair. "True, their breakup made for lovely gossip." She motions for Nick to take a seat next to her, and slides her chair up closer to him. "Tybalt is rumoured to have been at the mines recently. He's looking for the rest of his family, and then he wishes to leave for good. That's all I can tell you."

There's more, he knows it. He looks around, making sure they're alone, but just in case, he spreads out his shadow to soundproof them. "Braawen likes the scent of roses and strawberries. Also, one of his weaknesses is his left knee because he took an arrow to it."

"He's looking for Markus's son in the mines," she continues. "My father tells me that the Emperor has ordered for the traitor to be killed on the spot. If you go to the slums, you'll find more information. You should venture there when we go into the city once a month. When you leave, find the women near the White Lady fountain, because they hear everything. Also, why didn't you use Braawen's weakness on him?" Laura asks, tilting her head.

"I'm not that cruel."

"Or that smart," she scoffs. "Here's some advice for free. Use your brain more and heart less."

"Are you heartless?" Nick asks.

Laura's body stiffens. "I said use your heart *less*, and I'm not heartless." Her tone changed and he realizes that he's hit a nerve. "I'm not my father, if that's what you're thinking. I don't betray friends. I just don't let my feelings take control." She takes a sip from her tea to calm her nerves. "I see where that has landed him. He has a good job, but no wife, no real relationship with his daughter, and friends who don't trust him. I don't want a life like that, but I use my mind. Like I said, free advice: Braawen hates you." She sighs. "I wouldn't be surprised if he prays for your death. Kai told me that he was cruel to both of you. I see that nothing has changed." She takes another sip of tea, green eyes not leaving his blue.

He huffs. She isn't the first person to speak about Braawen wanting him dead. However, he can't see Braawen killing him. Blood don't kill blood. *He'll most likely break my back, so I could be useless – Wait! That's even worse!*

He shakes his head, leaving his thoughts. Before he leaves, he has to ask. "Are there any rumours about me?"

She puts down her cup. "Only that you're weak and won't make it to the Spring Festival. There's a poll going on in the school for all circles to participate in, except Yellow. Students place bets on where you'll all end up.

You're the lowest, and the majority of students believe you'll die. Mind you, the bets are placed at the beginning and can't be changed." She crosses her legs and sits up straighter. "Not advice, just common sense: have someone powerful to help you outside of Equinox House, in case you don't make it after the Spring Festival."

He raises an eyebrow at that. "Did you bet?" he asks.

She doesn't answer, but her smile is large.

He nods. "Keep your secrets." He leaves the library and begins planning his night, but can't get the poll out of his mind.

Good, I prefer it when people underestimate me, he thinks with a smile.

Chapter 33
Slums

Nick runs towards the city that night. He can't wait until the next time he goes with the school. This time, he wears the dark cloak from the infirmary but keeps the black pants and boots. However, he stops before entering the city. He's being followed. He can tell. He can hear that the person has stopped and is waiting for him. He runs over to the person and surprises them by grabbing them by their coat and throwing them on the ground. Nick peers at another boy in dark clothes.

"Kaius?" Nick asks in disbelief. "What the hell are you doing here?" He looks down to see that his friend wearing filthy red pants. "And, where did you get those?"

Kaius gets up from the ground and dusts the snow off him. "I got these from Lorcan. Though, apparently, he had a filthy training day. The rest, I nicked from the infirmary."

Nick closes his eyes and takes a deep breath. "Go back, Kai, this is dangerous."

His friend stiffens at first, but with shaking legs, Kaius walks past him. "Let's go already." Kaius stops the shaking in his voice. "You're not the only one who can sneak into places. Or have you forgotten that I also had to sneak around to get materials from the junkyard?"

Nick watches as his friend pulls down his sleeve, hiding his wrist, and makes his way towards the city. He just huffs, not even bothering to fight with him. *Eyes on the ground would be good*, he tells himself. He runs after his friend and walks alongside Kaius.

The night goes better with two, once the other knows what to do. Kaius isn't the best at sneaking around, but they have done missions together when collecting materials for their bombs and weapons. Kaius is rusty, and Nick has to pull him out of a few close calls.

"So, Braawen told you to look in the slums, and Laura confirmed it? I would trust Laura more," Kaius says.

Nick nods, sticking to his right. "But Braawen, didn't tell me where. Apparently, even the Shadow Assassins can't find him. The goddess of Earth had mercy on my uncle and gave him a blessing. Luckily, Laura told me to go to the fountain and ask the women there."

He can hear his friend scoff. "Where was the goddess when we needed her?" Kaius asks bitterly.

Remembering what the goddess said, Nick sighs. "She can only help with growing and protecting the land."

"But she protects your uncle?" Kaius asks.

Nick turns to face him. "From the shadows. Remember, it was my uncle who taught us how to hide. If anyone can hide, it's him." He taps his friend, and they move over to the slums.

The slums are different from the rest of the city. They are separated by a small forested park and three bridges. They cross under a bridge using the icy river, where Kaius slides and Nick slowly walks and falls.

The smooth, paved stone throughout the city slowly transforms to the country's dirt-covered path that reminds Nick and Kaius of home. The changes from the city to the slums are incredible. While the city's light is powered by electron rocks, the slums are still filled with gas lamps, and half of them are completely dark while the rest are just dim. The lamps that light the walkway are giving the area a sickly yellow hue. The beggars on the street—as well as a rotten stench– have increased. The slums are dark, while the city is full of life and light. Unlike the city bustling with people, the slums are sparse. Every grimy building they pass has its doors and windows firmly locked to keep outsiders away.

"Let's keep walking." Nick pulls Kaius closer to him.

After a while, Nick climbs up one of the buildings to get a good look at the slums. However, the buildings are not sturdy. Brick walls crumble at his touch and he has to grab the rusted pipes to pull himself up. He almost falls when one of the tiles on the roof gives way, smashing to pieces on the ground. He dangles on the ledge and looks down, seeing Kaius's worried face in the darkness. Thankfully, Nick manages to swing his arm up and grab a sturdier tile. With a grunt, he slowly pulls himself up, thanking Rohana for her workouts. Once on the roof, he gazes at the crooked buildings around him. The slums are dark, a perfect place for the shadows to grow and hide. He looks and sees the mines in the distance. Closer to them is a well in what looks to be the centre of the slums.

He jumps off the roof and lands next to Kaius on what's left of the cobblestone path. "We need to stick to the shadows, but I think I saw a fountain. Maybe we can use that as a focal point."

Kaius nods stiffly, not wanting to breathe in the rancid air.

As they make their way through an alleyway, they cross over one too many bodies; Nick and Kaius don't know if they're alive or not. As they walk, Kaius wonders if he will pass out from the smell. Luckily, they exit the alleyway to an area which looks to be the main square, with a fountain standing in the middle. The stones are dirty and uneven, but the fountain itself is tall. At the top is a statue of a woman whose face is worn down from the years of neglect. The statue still has flakes of white among the filth that covers it. If Nick is being honest with himself, the whole place looks neglected, as do the people.

"Look at this place, it's terrible," Kaius whispers.

Nick turns to face his friend. "Yup, but there's nothing we can do right now."

His friend grabs his hand. "Don't you care, Nick? People are suffering. *Our* people are suffering," Kaius states solemnly.

Nick muffles a laugh while Kaius looks hurt. "I'm not cruel. I haven't forgotten about them. But if we get caught, we will probably be one of the bodies on the street. So stay focused." With that warning, he makes his way to the fountain.

Standing near the fountain are a few women in shabby torn clothes, their hair in knots and tangles. They stand near a lamppost, smiling and laughing. There are some men in a corner looking at them. One of them walks up to a woman and gives her a bronze coin; she takes his hand and walks them both to an alleyway.

Kaius pulls on Nick's hand. "Maybe we should go somewhere else..."

Before Nick could snap at him, a dirty hand suddenly grabs his own. Both boys jump at the ragged appearance of an old man wearing tattered priest's clothes. Even in the shadows, Nick can clearly see the wide green eyes of the man. Both boys stand still as the old man looks into their souls.

"Rebirth!" The man cries out in a shaky voice.

"What?" Nick asks, wincing at the man's tight grip.

Kaius frowns. "Hey, man, let go of my friend. We have no money and no problems with you."

The man snaps his attention to Kaius, but then turns back to Nick. "Rebirth! After death! Second life! Second chance! I saw it! The deities will allow us to live again, I know it!" The man's voice gets louder. Nick turns to where the other ladies and gentlemen are, and he sees the men shaking their heads and leaving, while the women quickly glare in their direction, then turn around and ignore them.

Nick places a gentle hand on the clearly delirious man and pulls his hands out of his grip. "Thank you for letting us know." The man smiles and nods as he leaves, walking deeper into the alleyway.

"Those crackpots..." Kaius shakes his head. "No wonder the Temples denounce them. Spreading heresy of 'second life' after death. Everyone knows we go to our ancestors." He sighs and pulls on Nick's arm. "Let's go back. If that wasn't a sign from the deities to leave, then I don't know what is!"

Nick shakes Kaius off and whispers in his right ear. "No, we stay. We came for information, and we will get it! Women like them know everything here." He makes his way to the fountain with his squeamish friend beside him.

One of the women catches his gaze. She has wild blonde hair and wears a loose green dress that had seen better days. She smiles through her yellow teeth and bright red lips. "Oh, look at these two handsome gentlemen! What can I do for you tonight?" Her voice slurs, getting the other three women's attention. "I'm happy that crazy rejected priest didn't scare you away. I guess you boys are made of stronger stuff." She winks at him.

Nick just gives a polite smile; he may not like the profession they are in, but it makes them money. He can't judge them. Right now, he's sure that the Empire is turning him into a living weapon.

"Do ye wish to become a man tonigh'?" A red-haired woman with a heavy accent looks them over and smiles at Kaius, who squirms even more.

"No, but we do have questions." Nick takes a few bronze coins from his pocket. He had found these coins on the floor in the infirmary and kept them, believing that they would come in handy one day. If these coins don't please these women, he has a very special treat for them.

The redhead holds her hand out, but Nick puts the coins back into his pocket. "Not very trustin', are ye?" She raises one eyebrow.

He tightens his cape around him. "Have you seen any new people around here?"

One of the other girls with tanned skin and dark brown curls laughs. "Boy, this is the slums! A couple months ago, we had a whole shipload of war prisoners carted here for the mines." Her voice goes cold. "Those people, they took some of our jobs in the mines. Ungrateful wretches. If I were the Emperor, I would've just killed the lot of them." The other ladies nod their heads in agreement.

Kaius looks at Nick with worry. "Well, then, have there been whispers of someone important here? Or can you just tell us where the people from Availa are?" Nick asks.

The blonde lady narrows her eyes. "Why do you want to know? If you want names, you'll get none. They may be annoying Availa people, but they're slum people now. Slum people protect our own." Her sweet voice turns sinister.

Nick's getting a headache from the conversation's twists and turns, but he smiles brightly. "I don't want anyone here to get hurt. I just have a message to give to one of them."

"Then who'd ye like?" The redhead purrs.

"A man in his late thirties. Blonde hair and blue eyes. He has a crescent-shaped scar under his chin," Nick answers.

"Like a robin's egg," Kaius pipes up. "Or a dark-skinned man with a tattoo of a sun on his wrist." Nick knows he shouldn't be surprised that Kaius is looking for his father. They don't even know if Kaius's father got on the ship. The man wasn't with them when they were captured.

The women look like they're thinking. Finally, the last woman who wears heavy blush and looks aged far beyond her years begins to speak. "If ye'll go closer to the mines, then maybe. But…" She drawls, flashing a yellowing smile. "My memory 'tis a little fuzzy." She puts out her hand.

Nick puts two coins in her hand and she quickly places them between her breasts. They are big enough to hold a knife, but he can also see that there is a bruise peeking out from beneath her clothes.

She whispers to him, "Go towards the mines. That's where most of them are."

He can see that her blue eyes look sincere. He takes out a vial and gives it to her. She gingerly accepts it, looking at Nick in confusion.

"It's a healing potion. I know that men are cruel. So are other women."

"This ain't poison?" the blonde one asks.

He takes a knife from his pocket and cuts his hand. He takes an extra vial from Kaius and drinks it, then shows the women that his wound is healed. They look at the vial and smile at Nick. However, their smiles suddenly turn to frowns. He wonders why until he looks at where they're looking. There, under his cloak embroidered onto his black turtleneck, is the Equinox House emblem.

Realization and fear overcome all their faces. Even Kaius looks confused at the change in their demeanour. "Don't hurt us." Tears stream down their faces as they whimper, pressing closer together and backing into an alley.

"Dark magicians," the dark hair one whispers, just loud enough for them to hear. "They'll probably kill us. We ain't worthy to be near no dark magicians."

Nick has never had anyone look at him like this before, no one except Lord Nortshell. "W-we're not going to kill you." He said.

Kaius takes a step forward, but Nick pulls him back as he sees them flinch. "We—" Kaius's voice is cut when one of the women screams, and they all run, dropping the vial.

Nick covers himself with his cape as he feels the pressure on the back of his neck. A shadow creeps up in front of the two boys, and Kaius grabs Nick's hand, shaking. They slowly turn around.

There, taller and broader than the two boys combined, stands a man with a silver skull mask.

"S-Shadow Assassin," his friend stutters.

Nick's breathing is all over the place. The tall man just tilts his head as he watches them pale. They stay like this for a minute until the man finally speaks through his silver mask.

"What are two little boys doing all the way out here?" His voice is deep, but Nick has heard this voice before.

Nick gulps. "Just nobodies." The assassin quickly moves his hands across Nick's face, and he feels a sharp pain on his cheeks. Unable to move his head, he moves his eyes to see that Kaius is in the same predicament as the man's deadly sharp claws are holding his chin, piercing his skin.

"Try another answer. You only have one more try," the man warns them.

Nick looks back at Kaius, who is breathing slower, almost like he's about to pass out. "We're students from Equinox House," Nick quickly explains as the claws dig deeper into his skin.

Kaius nods and shows the dirty emblem of the school on his red uniform. "We're looking for family, that's all," Kaius gasps.

Nick hopes he takes it. "We just want to know if our family is here as well."

Shadows, help us, please, he pleads.

The Shadow Assassin moves his hand from Kaius and puts them both on Nick. The mask is so close that Nick can feel his breath, and through the shadowed eyes of the mask, he swears that he can see blue.

"How strange that a Yellow can hear the shadows. Very strange indeed." The Shadow Assassin lets him go, and Kaius grabs Nick's arms.

Nick gasps. "How do you know that I'm in Yellow?"

The Shadow Assassin takes his mask off to reveal a man with a scar across his eye. *The man from the base.* Nick remembers him, making a mental note that this man is beyond dangerous.

"You look like the boy from the base." That recognition surprises Nick. "But that boy was a skinny thing. You have some muscle on you. I could be wrong, but my gut tells me that you'll make an excellent Shadow Assassin. Or a politician from your half-truths." The man gives a smile, so different from the glare that he gave one of the the Empire's generals so long ago now.

Nick finds his words after steadying his breath somewhat. "Thank you, but I'm just a student as you said."

The Shadow Assassin scoffs. "You'll do well, Nickolaus." Nick's eyes widen as the Shadow Assassin turns to Kaius. "Kaius will do well in the sciences. We could always use an inspiring inventor like you."

Kaius grips Nick's arm tighter.

"Remember, boys, the Emperor knows what you children do in school. We just make sure that his information is kept up-to-date." The

Assassin puts on his mask again and lets out a menacing chuckle. "Go back to the school, boys. Can't wait to claim you when you graduate."

All the lanterns flicker out. When the flames return, the two scared boys huddle together in the square, alone.

"Let's go back," Kaius quickly mutters. He doesn't even wait for a response before he grabs Nick's arm and starts heading back to the school.

Chapter 34
Heads

As the boys head back, a figure stands perfectly on the shattered roof of a building, ready to collapse at any moment. The man takes off his own silver mask and watches as the boys run from a distance. He narrows his eyes as the Shadow Assassin appears before him.

The Shadow Assassin with the scar on his eyes beneath his mask, walks up to him and gives him a pat on the back. "Hello, Jacques. How is the school treating you? Miss your old position?" The man's beastly grin is audible in his voice and Jacques groans in response

"Abram, we've been friends for years, but we need to be professional now." Jacques moves his shoulders away from his friend's hand. As the Shadow Assassin removes his mask revealing a beastly grin.

He and Abram have been friends since the day they were claimed by the Shadow Assassins. The two of them fought together, with each other and for each other. He will never admit it, but Abram is like the brother he never had. Yet, when Jacques was given an opportunity to teach at Equinox House and look for potential Shadow Assassins, he took it, leaving behind a friend. Even with their change in positions, the two still keep in touch.

Unfortunately, he's been away from his friend for so long that he forgot that Abram could be... clingy.

"Alright, *Sir*," Abram mocks, still standing close to him. "How is my friend Volodimir treating you?"

Jacques's eyes widen slightly. He forgot that Abram and Volodimir were friends. Abram was kind enough to give him a heads up that the Council was sending his friend to help with Arran and the Purple situation. Abram warned him ahead of time that Volodimir wasn't an easy person to get along with and wasn't pleased to be selected because he hated teaching. Even with the warning, Jacques was excited to meet the man of whom Abram spoke so highly about. Abram spoke highly of no one. Jacques had always heard the stories of Abram's adventures with Volodimir throughout the years, and wished that he could have been with them on their missions.

However, when he finally met Volodimir face-to-face, Jacques wanted to murder his friend. Abram forgot to mention quite a few very important details, one being that Volodimir is *ruthless*.

"I still haven't forgiven you about Volodimir. You didn't give me a good warning."

Jacques can hear the man chuckle. "I did give you a warning. It's not my fault you couldn't use your skills to better prepare yourself." Abram just continues to laugh.

"You're an ass," Jacques mumbles.

"Come now." Abram playfully shoves his shoulders. "The school needs him."

"You could have been the Black Teacher, too."

"Hell no!" Abram shakes his head. "I don't have the patience to deal with incompetence."

"Then why are you all so incompetent?" a voice growls behind them, startling the two men.

Jacques turns sharply, wondering who could sneak up on him. He is about to attack until he sees cold, black eyes.

"Black Teacher!" Jacques drops down to his knees, not daring to raise his head. Sweat beads down his forehead to his nose, and he can feel the man's presence suffocating him under all that pressure. He doesn't know how to react, and he's patiently waiting for the man to speak first.

He can even see Abram losing his playful nature.

In the silence of the night, they finally hear the man sigh as he looks in the direction of the two boys.

Volodimir heard Jacques's conversation with his friend; he'll have to talk with Abram to find out what his apprentice is up to.

My little Nico even brought a friend. It seems I'll have to speak to Nico as well, he turns his attention to his fellow teacher and gets a headache.

"Rise, Jacques and Abram. We still have a traitor to find. The Council isn't pleased with the Shadow Assassins," he pauses. "And neither is the Emperor."

Jacques slowly raises his head. "I have the Shadow Assassins looking through the slums and even in the main city. I have also contacted the other regional heads to see if he's in their provinces as well."

"We all have been looking, but not even the shadows are giving us clues," Abram answers with a shrug.

"Neither the Council nor the Emperor want excuses, which is why I'm here tonight." Volodimir glares at Jacques, who, even in all his years of bringing fear to people, begins to stutter.

"T-then we must find him quickly. With your help, I have no doubt we will."

"Old friend." Abram grins, receiving Volodimir's glare in return. "May I suggest that Tybalt could be under a deity's blessings? I would not rule it out. Pity he's not a Shadow Assassin."

Volodimir just scoffs. "I hate to admit it, but you're right. It's a shame that he's not a Shadow Assassin. However, if he's under the blessing of the gods, most likely Earth, then we'll have to smoke him out." He gazes out to the city and then to the direction of the school, wondering why Nick can't stay put.

He sighs and turns to Jacques. "Being a teacher is hard."

All Jacques can do is smile, while Abram's grin widens.

· ◐ ·

Leia is working late work tonight and smiles as she skips along the empty halls. All that accompanies her is her humming, as she walks to her office to prepare for her special class for the children of Availa, but halts when she sees Arran in the hallway. She doesn't like the man, but Leia knows that he's above her in rank in the Purple circle, and she must show respect. She holds in a sigh when she sees him walking towards her.

Please, make this quick, she prays to the deities; any god would do.

"Leia, how nice to see you." Arran smiles, though it does not reach his eyes.

"Arran, I would love to speak with you," that's a lie, "but I have to go prepare for my class. Maybe another time, over tea, perhaps?"

Gods, please say no, she begs.

He smirks. "Not alcohol?" he remarks.

Her heart stops, then beats quickly as her face turns as red as her hair. "I'm sober," she grits out. She's happy for the empty hall so no one can hear their conversation. People already think she is unstable due to her constant moving.

Arran mockingly chuckles before glaring at her. "Sober? For what, a month? Well, congratulations," he mocks. "Be careful not to damage anything like the last time. Was it not your fault that the Training Hall had to be repaired because you lost control of your powers, and almost endangered your students?"

They can both hear the tapping of her heels. "I was grieving the loss of my sister." Her voice crumbles as her eyes blur with tears.

"Yes, the tragedy of Port Kitchener." Arran shrugs, unimpressed. "What would have happened if I didn't step in to cover your mistakes? Heal all those children you hurt under the nurse's nose and lie on the report that the training hall required an upgrade? It did cost us quite the pretty coin to fix your mess. You would have lost your job, your teacher's license would have been revoked, and you would be out in the streets if it wasn't for me. It's a good thing Alesander was too sick to complete his Black Teacher duties. I stepped in to help a fellow Purple." He walks up to her, his shadow taking over hers. "Remember the Shadow Promise you swore to me," he whispers, "You owe me that."

She looks down but swallows what little courage she has to look up again. "I didn't say anything to make the Council send for Volodimir, though I wish I had the courage. I will hold my Shadow Promise to you. I will not say anything to Volodimir, but I don't have to. I've already advised you that what you're doing to your students is damaging."

"Oh, and what am I doing?" he challenges.

She narrows her eyes. "You think you're so smart, hiding the cuts you put on those children. The only reason you haven't been called out is that everyone fears you. But Volodimir doesn't."

She smiles when she sees Arran's eyes dart to the shadows, almost expecting Volodimir to appear. She finds that hilarious, since the man will be coming back soon. "The smell of lemon is powerful on your students. You can't keep denying the nurse. She knows you're using the lemon balms but can't get the students to confess. But don't worry, Arran, I won't say anything. You made me swear to the shadows. But your actions speak louder than words."

With that, she walks past Arran, proud that she could say all those words, but ashamed that she made a promise to him in the first place.

Early the next morning, Catherine sits with Jacques, teacups spread on the table in front of them, with the sun rising behind them. They are both in her office, which is decorated in red and black. Jacques bundled up because Catherine, in her old age, says that she gets too hot so she always keeps a window cracked open allowing a cold breeze to enter. He doesn't mind too much. He enjoys the sound of her wind chimes hanging around the room, making beautiful music with every breeze. He prefers the smells of tea to the waste of the slums.

Yet, today they do not talk about old war stories. Catherine talks to Jacques about Lorcan, wanting to know if there's more that he can do for him.

"I fear that I will be retiring soon. I can't keep up with Lorcan's training." She sighs, as though it hurts to admit that she's getting weaker. "Can I ask you to help him when I'm gone?" she asks.

At first, Jacques is surprised by the request, but smiles warmly. "I will happily train him if he wants me to."

That answer satisfies her, but then she sighs again. "I fear another Purple student will leave."

Jacques shakes his head. "Those children need help."

She nods. "And that's why you sent the letter. Don't deny it. I know you did." She smiles sadly. They both sit in silence. Only the wind chimes in her room dare sing a song.

"Why didn't you?" Jacques asks, breaking the silence. "Arran has no dirt on you, like the others. You also don't fear him. The only reason it took me so long was the lack of evidence. So, why did you let his cruelty reign?"

Catherine seems to age in front of him. "I'm old, Jacques. I've been in this school for over forty years. The rule of this school, 'that each circle must focus on their own,' is too ingrained in me. I— I can't use that as an excuse, but I focused too much on my students. I was blinded and did not wish to see the suffering of the children." She shakes her head. "This may be my last year, for I do not deserve to be the Head of the Red Circle."

Jacques gets up from his seat and kneels in front of her, grasping her hands. Her hands are smaller than his, with a few wrinkles and callouses from years of wielding a sword.

"Then stand up with me," he whispers, looking her in the eyes. "Do this one last act of kindness to those kids."

A small smile graces her lips again. "Yes, if Arran acts up, I will stand. I don't care what the other Purples outside of the school will think. Arran has a good reputation in the Purple society. Too good." She lets out a breath and nods. "I'm tired, Jacs," she whispers.

He grips her hands gently. "I know."

Chapter 35

Past

When they return from their little trip, the two boys go their separate ways and Nick lays in his bed. The thought of a Shadow Assassin tracking his every move terrifies him.

Shadows, have they been following me all the time? He prays that they haven't.

No, they reply. *Only recently. But do not fear, their eyes will be on other people. When your teacher returns, it will be safer for you to venture out once more.*

He sighs and turns over to see that the rest of his friends are sleeping soundly.

That night, he dreams of his mother sitting next to an unknown woman who seemed familiar. He can only recall her black and golden dress, and lilac eyes almost pleading to him not to give up. Though, he can't remember if it was to not give up on someone else or himself. His own mother didn't make sense either. When the stranger lift, his mother comforted him, causing him to once again beg for forgiveness for her death. The only word he remembers her saying is 'not.'

He wakes up feeling lighter than usual, though frustrated at not understanding his dream. This isn't the first time that he's dreamt of them. This would be the third that he can remember, but he feels as though he's dreamt of them many times before. He also wonders about the woman who tells him to not give up on him and who he's supposed to help.

The night before may have been frightening, but the day makes up for it. The training with the General is hard, but Nick loves it. He isn't as sore as he was when he first started, which is a sign of growth. He even needed to get another uniform. He finally grew out of the smaller clothes, and the nurse commented that he was beginning to look like a young adult. He could fight against the General longer and keep up with Takara when they jog together.

But I need to grow stronger, he thinks to himself.

After classes finish for the day, Nick grabs Kaius and both look for Lorcan. Surprisingly, Lorcan is in the library reading. Nick makes his way over to his friend and is happy to see Lorcan smiling back. Two months ago, if someone told him that Lorcan smiled at him, Nick would ask if it was because Lorcan was beating him up. However, as Nick takes his seat and

Kaius too, he can see Lorcan's muscles relax. Nick wonders if Lorcan is always on edge.

"I know each of us has been improving in the school and shadows, but I have a question. Hopefully after this, we can share ideas to help us improve. In Yellow, we focus on physically building ourselves before we go onto Shadow Training. But what do you all focus on?" Nick asks.

"We focus on the theories of Shadow magic and its laws," Kaius says. "However, my teacher tells us that to get stronger, we need to remember to strengthen our bodies and minds."

"Yes, I hear the mind is essential to the development of Shadow Training," Lorcan agrees. "It is something that my teacher repeats."

Nick nods. "Then, do you guys have any input on mind and mediation growth? Any teachers?"

Lorcan and Kaius look at each other and begin to think. After a while, it's Lorcan who speaks. "Well, there is one teacher who I heard is very keen on mediation, the Head of the Blue Circle, Jacques. The professor focuses on mediation and encourages all of his students to focus on it as well. There are even rumours that all Blue students can hear the shadows."

"I think that's true! So far, all the Blue students that I've seen were talking to their shadows," Kaius adds.

Now, that is impressive. Nick ponders.

"Then, let's go to the Blue head teacher," he suggests.

"Nick, the Blue Head teacher is very busy. Not only that, he's not even *our* circle teacher!" Kaius exclaims.

"I'm sure that he'll allow fellow students to ask a few questions about meditation." Nick smiles at them.

Evening comes as everyone eats at feasting time, but three students wait at the door to the Head of Blue's office. Nick is never been in a waiting room like this, it's colourful and welcoming. He can only imagine what the office looks like. The General's office is in the Training Hall. It isn't welcoming, to say the least, when weapons of death are proudly hanging on the walls, especially the General's war hammer.

Now that he thinks about it, he guesses that he has been in Volodimir's office, if the cottage counts as an office. His teacher's office is always warm and smells of tea. The Blue Head's waiting room was also homey in a way, reminding him of the tales that his mother used to tell him of Ram and Luxor's desert lands. There are elegant, patterned carpets, and the scent of herbs and spices are in the air from the candles along the walls, calming his mind and nerves. He looks at his friends to see how they're doing. Kaius isn't a nervous wreck and Lorcan looks comfortable. For once, Lorcan isn't looking over his shoulders every two seconds.

He would have remained comfy until a young bronze-skinned man with bangs covering one of his eyes opens one of the double doors and steps in. All three of them are quickly jolted back to reality, and fear creeps in. However, the Head of Blue just gives them a friendly smile.

"Come in, boys." The man motions for all to enter, and he holds the door as they do.

Nick enters first and sees that the office is brightly lit, with large windows and dark blue walls that remind him of looking across the waves of the sea.

The three boys find chairs in front of the large desk full of papers and large books. The Head of Blue motions for them to sit down. Kaius is the first, followed by Lorcan, and lastly, Nick. The large window behind the teacher reminds him of his time in the testing area before he was sent to this school. Instead of grey skies, the sky is actually a beautiful orange hue mixing with purple to the blue night sky. Nick's eyes drift from the sky back to the man smiling in front of him.

He is genuinely happy to see you three, the shadows whisper to him.

"Now, how can I help you, young gentlemen?" Jacques asks politely.

The three boys look at each other, and surprisingly, Lorcan is the first to speak. "We were wondering if you had any advice on meditation. We know that the mind is just as important as the body, but we all are lacking in the strengthening of our minds," he states politely.

The teacher nods his head. "I can assist you in that. There are exercises that we can do, places that I can tell you about to help you mediate. The Library has a small meditation room. However, might I suggest the Temple? It's a quiet and lovely place to speak to the deities and clear your mind. I can guide you through clearing your mind. Though, some of you will have more problems than others."

He turns to Nick and gives him a bigger smile. *I already know you can hear the shadows,* he hears Jacques voice echo clearly in his mind as though he is speaking to him in a cave.

Nick's eyes widen. "H-how?" he asks out loud.

"Shadow Communication, a lovely little skill to have when you're on a mission," Jacques responds out loud. "But you have a good grasp on the shadows. Shall I say, you and the shadows are well acquainted? However, remember the promise you gave them. Remember to keep it." His voice turns serious, causing the other two boys to look at Nick. "Shadows are not forgiving in nature," he warns.

Nick nods. He had a feeling that they weren't.

244

Do not worry. We like you… maybe one day, we will love you, the shadows purr in his ears. Nick blushes as Jacques raises his eyebrows.

"Here's one piece of advice to you all. You all need to find what's holding you back."

"Holding us back?" Lorcan asks.

"Yes. You each have a debilitating blockage that's stopping you from reaching your potential. For example, I remember each of you in your test. Lorcan looked around like the world was about to attack him, Kaius was about to pass out, and Nick looked nervous and already feared failure."

They are silent for a moment.

"You… remember us?" Nick asks incredulously.

Jacques chuckles. "Of course! I remember you all. I remember everyone. It was my duty to give a detailed report to the Emperor. The Night Emperor wanted to know everyone, who made the cut and who didn't. He also wanted to know where the ones who didn't were sent. The last thing he wants are children trying to ruin his Empire."

Nick looks over at his friends, and he sees Kaius about to ask more questions, but shuts himself down.

"Ask, my boy." Nick almost thinks that it's Volodimir talking to him until he sees from the corner of his eyes that it's Jacques.

Kaius looks at Jacques with wide eyes. A bead of sweat falls down his brow, and he bites his lips, looking down. Kaius opens his mouth time and time again, but no words come out.

Remember, boy, keep your head down and don't ask questions if you want to live, Kaius remembers his father saying. He thinks of his older brother questioning his orders and getting killed; his mother asking a simple question to one of the nobles and getting killed; his father obeying orders to go on suicidal missions.

"It's hard for you, isn't it?" Jacques whispers. Kaius nods. "And it's hard for you to not feel like someone isn't hunting you down." He turns to Lorcan, whose eyes narrow. Jacques signs and leans on his chair. "I know about the laws of the Kingdom of Availa. How not everyone is equal, especially based on where you're born within the kingdom."

Nick shuffles uncomfortably in his seat. Luckily, his father was born in the Capital region of the Kingdom.

"I was born in the Nial region of the Kingdom, the very south of the capital," Kaius answers.

"The region that produces most of the food and textiles. Though, it is also a place where technology is growing," Jacques comments.

Kaius nods. "My family, my people, are the farthest from the capital but everyone is marked as soon as they are born." He shows Jacques his wrist with a tattoo of the sun. Nick remembers the way Kaius described receiving it. Uncomfortable, tagged, and hot.

"We were not allowed to question those closest to the capital or those of higher authorities. Many of my family members were killed for that. My mother died because she asked a question. She died trying to create an invention to help my people who worked late into the night," Kaius gulps. "Many of my people wanted to help the rebels since they were promised that everyone would be treated equally, no matter where they were born. Tattoos were seen as the lowest class."

Jacques sits up straighter. "Let me see if I understand this correctly. No matter where you go in your kingdom, those living furthest from the who were marked by a tattoo, were looked down upon?"

Both Kaius and Lorcan nod their heads. "The Capital province was the first region of the Kingdom and the original border. As they expanded, we were told that the lesser regions served the capital," Kaius states. "They call themselves a Kingdom, but they acted like an Empire. Whenever they took over a smaller province, they treated its people as secondary citizens."

"Nickolaus, did you experience such things?" Jacques turns to him.

Nick shakes his head, adjusting himself in his seat as his back scars prick against the seat. "No, not really. I was born in the Capital province. I was able to be born there because my father was. However, not everyone can be born in the Capital. You need to prove that your family had been born there for centuries. The Capital crowed about its culture, technology, and arts, but most of their resources came from the other regions." Nick can't hide the sadness in his voice, because his mother's people are seen as barbaric, while the Kingdom took their forest and iron.

"So they saw those born in the capital as the 'true' people of Availa?" Jacques says.

All three of them nod.

Nick rubs his sweaty hands on his thighs. "Later on, my family moved out of the province and further north into the Kipal mountains. My mother was from the Kipal mountains, near the borders with Winterborn. Kipal spear warriors were loved in times of war, as the kingdom used them for fighting. But after the war, they were feared and seen as an unnecessary group of wild secondary citizens. When there were no wars, the Capital commanded them to work in the mines or cut down forests. The most dangerous jobs were given to us. I remember as a child that the other children and I had to look in the forest to see what trees needed to be cut down. If we weren't careful, we could fall off the mountain or get attacked by wild animals."

Nick sighs, remembering the bitter cold nights. "It's the only job we were allowed to do. We may have experienced hardship, but what Kaius and

246

Lorcan experienced was worse. They were born further from the capital than I was. While my people could carry weapons into the mines, his people couldn't even ask a question about their safety."

There is shocked silence from Jacques, and Nick could have sworn that he sees disgust in the man's eyes. After a few moments of silence, Jacques speaks with a calm voice. "Your lives didn't matter?"

"No, our lives didn't." Lorcan's voice cracks. "And tattoos do not symbolize a lower class. In my clan, they mean courage."

This time, Jacques turns to Lorcan. "I can tell by your eyes that you are of the Plains."

"The Ursa family." Lorcan beams with pride.

"I heard that you were a mighty family in the plains. But I hear that when children reach the age of maturity, they get tattoos on their face. Are you not of age?" Jacques asks.

Lorcan tightly holds onto his chair handle, as the room seems to get colder. Nick doesn't know much about Lorcan's past, but he knows that is a subject not to cross.

"I was of age," he growls, anger and pain written on his face. Nick and Kaius move slightly away in shock. Lorcan is always in control of his emotion and never gives into outbursts.

However, Jacques wasn't moved by the boy's anger. "Then why weren't you marked?"

"War. War killed my teacher. Revolt killed my family who had the knowledge of tattooing. Conquering and chains destroyed any chance of me earning my marks." Lorcan sneers, then takes a deep breath to calm himself.

"Tattoos are meant as a blessing and honour in my culture. They also serve as a reminder of where we come from and all that we've been through. My grandfather... I remember." His voice seems far away. "I remember that every inch of his body had tattoos. Many outsiders thought of him as a deviant, while my people saw him as a hero, a warrior, a teacher, and a worthy leader. My father also had tattoos that covered his face and shoulders. My mother had them too. I was set to have my first tattoo, but the rebellion broke out, and then the Empire attacked. Now, my parents and people are gone."

Jacques looks at him. "I see that the Empire has done you a great disservice."

Lorcan scoffs.

"No shit," Nick hears Kaius mumble.

"However, in order for you all to grow and develop your powers, one must look into the past and take control of your anger and fears," Jacques continues.

Jacques looks at Lorcan directly in the eye. "Focus on the shadows. The shadows can find truths. If you look deeper within yourself, you may find the answers to your clan's ritual markings. There have been times when people found the secrets of their ancestors through the shadows. There is an exhibit in the Imperial Capital museum here in our fair city. I'm sure that there are artifacts of your people there. Go there and look to one of the shadows of the artifacts. It's a difficult skill to master. But with a clear and focused mind, I'm sure you can do it." Lorcan nods, still tense.

"Kaius, I want you to look into your past. I want you to remember every moment that someone questioned your abilities and shut you down for wanting to know more. Then, I want you to remember each and every single emotion that comes to you. I want you to do better. I want you to ask more questions. I want you to smile when you get an answer. I want you to have a drive to know the truth," Jacques states, turning to face the boy.

Kaius looks down at his feet. "W-why?" he stutters. He starts taking deep breaths; he almost looks like he's about to pass out and Nick is genuinely worried about him.

"Why what?" Jacques asks. He gives him an encouraging smile.

Kaius licks his lips. "Why were you at the testing? Why were the General and that Swan lady at the test? Why wasn't Professor Arran or even the Black teacher there? Are they not the heads of the school? Those were the original questions I wanted to ask."

Nick turns to Jacques to hear his answer. *I didn't think of that,* he realizes

"You're the first to ask that question," Jacques chuckles. "Not all of us are just teachers. As a matter of fact, many of us were in other professions before teaching. One prime example is the General: he refuses to be called professor or teacher, but he teaches. The reason the General was at the testing is simple. He's a military man. He wanted to see who would make the cut, but he also wanted to know who might threaten or aid the Empire in the future."

"But how can he know just by seeing us once?" Lorcan asks.

"Ahh, but you can," the teacher corrects. "You can learn a lot about a person by their first impression of you, especially when one is backed into a corner." His smile is more feral. "The General has a talent for seeing people's potential, even when others may see them as a lost cause. That's why he oversees Yellow. Even I would have disbanded the Yellow class, but the Emperor believes that everyone can move up a level or two. He hasn't been wrong yet."

"The Emperor?" Nick asks.

"They both haven't been wrong in their decisions yet." Jacques smirks playfully at Nick. *So, don't disappoint the General,* he can hear the man whisper. Nick prefers the shadows speaking.

"As for Lady Adele, she is the Emperor's second-in-command. The woman is strict, but she gets results. As for me, well... let's just say that my skills were needed. Plus, my other duties are," he chuckles, "dare I say, much more important than Arran's." His voice is like honey.

"But not the Black Teacher?" Nick asks.

Jacques's eyes flash for a moment, but all three boys pick up on it. "No." Jacques leans back into his chair. "He was busy," Jacques chuckles, and leaves it at that.

As the three boys walk out of Jacques's office, the teacher puts his hand on Nick's shoulder, holding him back. He tells the other two boys to wait in the hallway; it's just him and the man alone.

"Are you friends with them?" Jacques asks.

It wasn't a question that he expected. "Yes," Nick almost whispers.

The man's eyes narrow. "Close?" Nick nods. "Apparently, not close enough to see they're hurting." It's like a slap in the face to Nick. Before he could talk, Jacques raises his hand to silence him. "I'm not judging you, because I know that you went through your own hell as well. You, too, need to move on from feeling inferior and guilty to continue on your path. But your friends, especially Kaius, have been hurting long before this rebellion even began."

Nick wants to say that he's been there for his friends, but as he opens his mouth, nothing comes out. He stops and thinks.

"I try to help them get stronger."

Jacques chuckles. "Yes, in the shadows and fighting. It's as though you're training them for war. Yet, there is more to life than fighting. Have any of you had regular talks or conversations? Do you ever talk about your past?"

What Jacques says next startles him. "Do you just listen to them?"

Nick blinks, wondering if there was a time that he just listened to one of Kaius's rants. Now that he thinks about it, he hasn't, not once.

"It seems that this is the first time that Lorcan has brought up such feelings. Even your friend Kaius is still too afraid to ask questions," Jacques remarks. "Though, it's not all your fault."

They both stand silent for a moment. Nick remembers when he first met Kaius, the boy was too afraid to talk. He thought that Kai had finally gotten past his 'too afraid to talk, too afraid to ask questions' stage. But now that Nick thinks about it, Kaius isn't afraid to question him, just others, his years of just following orders still ingrained in him.

"Take this advice, Nickolaus. A good leader knows the weaknesses and strengths of his allies. However, a great leader also knows when their members are hurting and helps them help themselves. Recognize when your friends are hurting." Jacques opens the door and smiles sadly at Nick.

"I hear that you are a good person and a good friend. I hope that you will remain that way, even after achieving your potential." Jacques looks him in the eyes before dismissing him.

Nick takes his leave and enters the hallway. There are already a few Blue students walking past the teacher's door without a care in the world. He sees his friends are leaning against the wall across from the office, waiting for him. Now that he looks at them, really *looks* at them, he can see how Lorcan is still aware of his surroundings and the nakedness of his skin. He mentally conjures up an image of one of Lorcan's tribesmen. The man had tattoos from his face all the way down to his arm. Lorcan has none. The boy has scars, a few still remain on his arm, but he has no tattoos to mark his courage and honour during the war.

Nick turns to Kaius and sees how his friend continues to pull on his sleeves. He thought it was a nervous habit at first, but instead, Nick realizes it was to hide his tattoo, hide the mark that was given to him at birth. The sun on Kaius's wrist doesn't remind him of where he came from, but to whom he belonged. Nick remembers some of the people who Kaius came with from the southern regions. He didn't understand why everyone from the rebels stayed away from them at first or why the southern men and women sometimes got served last at meals. But each of them had a tattoo on their wrist or neck.

If Nick could go back in time, he would call his father and his men hypocrites. Their whole promise of equality was just smoke and mirrors. How could they achieve equal rights in the kingdom when they weren't equal even in the rebellion?

No wonder his mother's people, the Clansmen of the Mountain left, he thought. They weren't treated any better either. People were too afraid to even talk to them properly, and they were always sent into the thickest of battles. They weren't seen as humans, just products of war.

"I'm sorry," Nick apologizes as he focuses on the two boys who need him. At least, he hopes they do, because he quickly realizes that he needs them more.

They both look confused. "I'm sorry that I was so stuck up on my own problems that I didn't realize that you all were hurting too. And I mean, even before and during the whole war."

"Nick, there's nothing to apologize for... I mean, you were kind to me. At least, I can speak for myself," Kaius says.

"No, you were good to me too," Lorcan interrupts.

"Still," Nick's voice is low, "I could have done more."

They all look at each other and smile. Seeing Lorcan smile is still new to him, but Nick's happy that he is smiling.

"Help us make changes that can help everyone. Make it a law to not tattoo someone unwillingly," Kaius states.

"Put it into law that people, no matter where they live, are considered equal," Lorcan adds. "We believe that you can become the next leader."

Kaius puts his long arms on Nick's shoulder. "Leader." Kaius smiles.

· ◐ ·

Later in the evening, Nick listens. He doesn't talk or make any fancy speeches tonight. He listens to how his kingdom treated their people, how people outside the Capital province were treated as second-class citizens. Something that the Empire is still doing now.

Nick and Kaius are in the labs, Mr. Teslan is in the next room grading assignments and making sure that the boys are safe. Kaius asked the teacher if he could use the lab with his supervision; the poor boy was sweating and almost gasping for air by the end of it, but he did it. Nick was right behind him to catch him if he passed out. Nick found out that it was Laura who had asked on Kaius's behalf about going to the labs during the mornings. Now, Kaius could ask permission for the night on his own.

The teacher could see that the poor boy was nervous, but allowed him in when he finished asking. Nick stays by his right side the whole night, always facing him.

His friend is working on a box with wires and an electro stone. Nick looks over the diagram next to Kaius and deduces that when Kaius adds the lens, it should be able to light up.

"I wonder how the people in the Capital Province feel about being second-class citizens now," Kaius laughs mirthlessly. His voice draws Nick's eyes away from the diagram. "I doubt they like to be treated that way. I bet you they hate having soldiers watch over their every move, that their resources that they worked so hard for are going to another person without so much as a thank you."

Nick passes him the screwdriver and watches Kaius work. He can see that his friend's hands are shaking. They used to be so steady. He remembers a time when the boy was the fastest at putting things together and taking them apart. Now, Kaius is more cautious. Even though Nick is happy that his friend isn't trying to blow himself up anymore, there's something missing. Kaius normally lights up in a lab and takes risks for his inventions, even if they end up blowing up in his face. However, the explosion damaged more than just his body.

"Arrgh!" Kaius drops the screwdriver in frustration and places his hands on his head. "I'm trying to recreate my mother's experiment. I think that it could be useful for us. But…" he sighs. "Her works were burned under suspicion that they were a weapon. I guess she had terrible timing as the Rebellion was fully underway at the time. She told me that this box could be used as a portable light to help my people find their way home at night after working in the fields."

Kaius pauses as his lips form a snarl. "They killed her. A handful of people ran, including my father and me. We came to Markus Archer to help, yet, we were treated no differently." Kaius then looks at Nick. "But you, Nick, you were the only one to eat with us, to talk to us and learn from us."

Nick just smiles.

"I hope that the people who look down on us experience what we went through and more. I hope the Empire gives them hell." Kaius's eyes grow dark. "Because that's all I ever received from them."

Later that night, Nick Shadow Jumps into the Imperial Capital Museum with Lorcan. They wander around until they find the exhibit of their fallen kingdom. He sits and watches Lorcan look at one of the tools on display for a few minutes.

"They marked it wrong," Lorcan points out. "They marked that tool wrong. They think it's to torture our enemies." He scoffs. "We don't torture. We just kill. You don't feel joy in killing, it's just a means to survive and protect. Those who felt joy were considered unstable and were watched and counselled by our elders."

Lorcan shakes his head, but it's not the only thing that shakes. "That's a tool to mark one's skin for tattooing," his voice quivers. "I had one like it in my house. When a person gets their first tattoos, the whole clan comes together, and we sing and pray over the man or woman to be blessed. We celebrated under the stars as an elder marked and encouraged us."

Nick looks at the tool. It looks like it could hurt, and he can see why people would assume that it was used to cause pain. However, a tool that is insignificant to him means the world to Lorcan. Nick looks more at the glass than the tool and sees a single tear run down Lorcan's face in its reflection. Nick pats him on the shoulder and walks away, giving him some privacy.

Lorcan stands in front of the case for what feels like hours. He can feel tears streaming down his face, and instead of stopping them, he lets them fall. He doesn't know whether he's the last of his clan, and he doesn't have the knowledge to pass on his traditions. He doesn't know how to tattoo... and no one can do it for him.

Chapter 36
Warrior

Lorcan grew up following a strict Warrior code that defined his culture and his people. They were fighters; they won battles and fought till the last man or woman was standing. He can still remember his grandfather and aspires to be like the tattooed man. His grandfather was the most fearsome warrior of their people. He only stopped fighting once he became an elder. His grandfather stayed behind with their people when Lorcan and the rest of the warriors joined the rebellion. They didn't like the King and they feared the Empire. They felt as though they had no choice but to join the rebels. The rebel leaders promised them freedom and rights. That reminded them of their ancestors before being conquered by Availa, so they fought. When Lorcan left with hopes held high, his grandfather gave him one last word of advice; however, to this day he can't remember it.

Tonight, he heads over to the library to find out what exactly happened to his people. He heard nothing in his time in prison and on the ship. He heard bits and pieces of the fate of his people from the students. The sources were untrustworthy because firstly, they hated him, and secondly, they thought his people are savages and bloodthirsty warriors who ate babies and were a threat to the Empire. He rolled his eyes at that one. Their men were brave warriors, and their women were great elders and leaders. Lastly, the third reason: their opinion meant nothing to him.

Nick always told him to look for more than one source. The museum didn't give him much information, so he heads over to the fireplace, waiting patiently as another Orange stands ahead of him. When the student leaves, quickly averting their eyes from him, he spots a pair of green eyes. Laura sits on her chair by the fire and offers him a seat next to her. However, even from afar, the girl appears to have the face of grave news. Well, he did ask her a favour three days ago. He just wasn't expecting information soon.

"Welcome to Tea Night, Lorcan," she sighs and pours a cup of tea for herself and him. "Fortunately for you, my father dealt with the accounts with the Western and Eastern Plains while in the Empire's service in Availa. The bad news is that I think the little friendship we have may be broken. Please don't hurt the messenger."

He sits straighter in his seat, bracing himself. "Tell me what you know, and I'll be the judge of that."

He can see her shift around to get as comfortable as she can. Her hands are sweaty, her eyes avert from his gaze, and he can hear her trying to control her breathing. She's nervous, scared even.

"I've already accepted the fact that I'm the last of my people. The Eastern Plains burnt, and I'm the only one here."

"You're not the only one," she replies quickly.

Silence surrounds them as Lorcan tries to process what he hears. He believes that if the room was quieter, he could hear her rapid heartbeats.

"Excuse me?" He blinks. "What did you say?"

She slowly raises her green eyes to look at him while rubbing her hands together. "You aren't the only one. The Eastern Plains may have been destroyed, but a few of your people still remain."

Before Lorcan can smile, she continues. "While many did die, what they did was horrible." She shakes her head.

"I agree, the Empire—"

"I wasn't talking about the Empire," she states gravely.

Lorcan glares at her. "The Empire attacked my people. They killed many of my people. I'm surprised to even hear that there are still some of us left!" His voice raises with each word.

"Calm down," she hisses. "Or do you want the whole world to know what we're talking about?"

"How can I calm down when you're telling me that my people are at fault for our land being destroyed!" he hisses back at her, his eyes blazing.

Laura glares at him, unwilling to back down. "Look here, Lorcan," she warns. "If you can't handle the truth, I'll give you a pretty rumour so you can sleep easy tonight. But if you want the truth—that I had to beg and plead with my father to get by the way, you're welcome—then you will shut up and stop glaring at me!"

Lorcan chews on his lips as he slowly sinks deeper into his seat, taking deep breaths to calm himself. He closes his eyes for a moment, then opens them to see Laura sip her tea, calming herself as well. He nods for her to continue.

She puts her tea down and sighs. "When you and the men left to fight in the rebellion, three years later, soldiers of the Empire came and fought against the Western and Eastern Plains. They were a mighty force together, but even with their might, most of their warriors had gone to fight in the front lines." She takes another sip of her tea and cradles the cup in her hands. "The Western Plains surrendered when the Empire proposed a treaty. If they all surrendered and vowed to no longer aid in the rebellion, then they were free to live in peace under the Empire. The Western Plains encouraged the Eastern Plains, but they were stubborn about the Warrior code and insulted their brethren. However, it wasn't until an elder from the Eastern Plains agreed with the Empire's treaty that there was peace in the Plains.

"Who was the elder who surrendered?" he asks.

"The Great warrior elder, Red Hawk."

Lorcan's head snaps up and he almost leaps out of his seat. "My grandfather!" Even Laura looks surprised at the news while he shakes his head. "No, I don't believe it. My grandfather was a warrior through and through. The wisest of them all! There's a reason he's called Red Hawk. He would fight to the very end to protect his land!" He wants to get up and leave, but he can't. He doesn't know why but the way that Laura is looking at him puts him on edge. She looks at him, not with pity or surprise, but something else; he can't put an emotion to it.

She finally answers him softly. "But he was protecting his land and people." They sit in silence for a moment, listening to the sounds of the few people in the library so close to closing time. Most were in the upper levels, staying away from the fireplace when Laura conducted Tea Night.

"Lorcan," she continues, "your grandfather tried to stop further bloodshed. He apparently said, and I quote, 'I want a home and family to greet the men when they come home.' Lorcan, your grandfather knew what he was up against, that neither he nor his people would win. So, the leaders of the Eastern and Western Plains signed a peace treaty to allow them freedom once the Empire won."

Lorcan sits back in his seat. "There were still a few months left in the rebellion," Lorcan whispers. "They already thought of us as a lost cause." He looks down and closes his eyes, trying not to feel the sting of betrayal. He feels a warm, gentle hand enveloping his. When he opens his eyes, he sees Laura is kneeling beside his chair with a gentle smile on her face.

"I believe that they were doing what they could to save the people that they loved. However, from what I've seen in you, I believe that deep down, they were still hoping for you all to win." She gets up and sits back in her seat, the smile falling from her face.

"There's more to it, isn't there?" He waits patiently for the final blow.

"The reason why the Eastern Plains are gone is because they went back on their word and attacked the Empire's smaller and weaker garrison that stayed behind to give out medical aid."

He stops breathing and shakes his head, eyes blazing again. "That's against the code. We don't attack allies or people we treaty with. Especially the healers. That is deceitful and dishonourable. You don't kill a man when his back is turned to you. My people would never stoop so low!" he sneers.

"Lorcan!" she hisses. They both calm down as a few students look their way.

"What? We're having a conversation here!" he snaps, and the other students scurry away. He turns to her and nods for her to continue.

"Well, many of the younger warriors who believed in 'fighting till the last man' decided to end the little garrison that was left. Your grandfather was horrified, but what was done was done. The Western Plains refused any involvement, and he heard that the Emperor was sending more men to burn the Eastern Plains."

She sighs with a heavy heart. "Your grandfather was able to gather some of the men, women, and children who disagreed with what the majority did and left for the Western Plains. Your grandfather remained and fought with the other men and women who refused to give up their lands to foreigners." She doesn't want to continue, but finds the strength.

"They say your grandfather fought like a warrior, that even the reporting general respected his end. The general wrote that 'He died protecting his people. He took three arrows in the back, protecting children who were running away. He got up and fought until a sword in the chest brought him to his knees.'" Tears stream down Lorcan's face as Laura gulps and continues.

"Those that ran to the Western Plains became one with the people there. They had to take their oaths and their culture, and those of the Western Plains fought to keep them safe. They argued that they were their people now and not of the Eastern Plains. After that, they renewed their oaths to the Empire."

At the end of her report, she can't even bring herself to take a sip of tea for her dry lips. She tries to think of any way to comfort Lorcan, but all that comes out is an apology.

Lorcan nods, pulling himself together, his gaze unfocused. "Thank you for getting this information to me quickly. It's late. You deserve to rest. For this secret, I'll let you know that Braawen is still afraid of spiders and loves the scent of roses."

She smiles. "Any other information?"

He returns his smile with a small one of his own. "Don't underestimate Nick."

· ◗ ·

Lorcan is in the Training Hall again with Ms. Catherine; he prefers fighting over talking. When the war children were first sent to speak to their counsel, Ms. Catherine found that Lorcan wasn't a talker but a fighter. They fight weekly, allowing Lorcan a safe way to release his anger. However, tonight, Lorcan's anger distracts him.

"What's wrong?" Ms. Catherine asks after knocking him over for the second time. "You seem distracted. I left you two openings, and you didn't take advantage of either of them." She sits on the ledge of the raised platform and pats the empty spot next to her.

Lorcan sighs and sits beside her, wiping the sweat from his brow. They stay silent for a moment until he's ready to speak. "I just found out what happened to my people." She nods for him to continue, and he tells her the story.

"I see. Tell me about your warrior code," she asks.

"Fight to protect our land and people. Fight till the last man standing. Fight and never give up what the goddess of Earth has blessed us with. Have the courage to face your fears. Never leave a brother or sister behind. Never abuse your power on the weak and those that you treat with," he ends, staring across the training hall.

"The Western Plains broke some of those codes... And look, they're still alive, while my family broke those codes and died." There are tears in his eyes. "It's not fair!" he cries.

Lorcan can hear his teacher sigh as she rubs his back. Normally, a person would lose a hand for that, but this feels comforting. They wait for what feels like hours, but the old woman is patient and sighs when his cries slow down to sniffles. "I know that you are angry, and you have every right to be. We, of the Empire, have changed your life to the point that you believe that you have no home to go back to."

"Because I don't," he interrupts.

She gently hushes him. "Now, now, didn't you say that the Western Plains were your brethren? They may be different, but clearly not so different to fight together."

"Until they surrendered."

Ms. Catherine sighs, shaking her head. "Let's look at what your people did. Their first code is 'Fight to protect our land and people.' You say they did not protect their land and people. However, when the fight was looking grim, the Western Plains swallowed their pride. In doing so, they saved their people and their land. From what I heard, they're living their lives the way they want to." Her voice sounds so soft.

"Now, you also stated another code was 'Fight till the last man standing.' Well, I believe that you forget your own history."

Lorcan glares at the old woman, who just smiles back in response. "What did you say?" he seethes.

"Lorcan, your people were conquered by the Availian Kingdom centuries ago. They were the ones who split your people into two different plains. In order for you to exist, that means that one or more of your ancestors surrendered to the Kingdom to continue to live. That's what the Western Plains did. That's what your grandfather was trying to do. They were trying to live," she explains.

"'Fight and never give up what the goddess of Earth has blessed us with.' The Empire wasn't asking you to give up your land. They just wanted your loyalty. The Western Plains still have their land," she points out.

"'Have the courage to face your fears.' The Western Plains fought alongside your people. And if we look at, 'Never leave a brother or sister behind,' they welcomed the people of the Eastern Plains that came for shelter and fought against the imperial soldiers to keep them safe."

She then sighs as she repeats the last one. "Lastly, 'Never abuse your power on the weak and those that you treaty with.' Well, the Western Plains didn't attack the weaker garrison. There's a reason why your grandfather was angry. It seems very cowardly to attack people who were giving you aid."

Lorcan's expression turns even more sour, but Ms. Catherine continues. "So, in conclusion, it isn't fair that this happened to you. However, what happened to those foolish people is fair. You break your word, you get hit. It appears to me that they forgot an important message about the warrior code," she sighs again.

"My people have a similar code to yours. Now, when I was a leader of a small garrison to protect my home, I stood by the whole 'till the last man' nonsense. We were up against a mightier force. I could have escaped with my army and lost a bit of land. But my men and I decided to fight. We fought and we won. 5,987 men and women were lost on the enemy side. I only lost 3,890 of my soldiers and my position."

"But you lost fewer men. How could you lose your position?" Lorcan asks in confusion.

She chuckles ruefully. "I had 4,029 with me in the beginning. Does that sound like much of a victory while only keeping 900 knots of land?"

"Oh..."

"Yes. If I had left to get more reinforcements, I could have lost fewer lives. I forgot the other part of the warrior code. I forgot to protect the people. It's in the first code. The code is not meant for attack alone. It's meant to protect."

Lorcan remembers when he and Braawen were in prison, fighting with the guards. He was willing to put innocent lives in danger, calling it a 'warrior's death'. But he wouldn't have had a warrior's death, nor would the little children. Did the warriors that fought against the imperial healers believe they were following the warrior code?

No, they didn't think of what consequences their actions would bring and who would pay the price. They just died. The people who refused to attack the soldiers and had nothing to do with the attack are the ones who paid the price. The people who rushed to the Western Plains and watched their homes burn paid for it. They knew that they couldn't be buried with their family in the Eastern Plains because of what the rebels who attacked the Emperor's soldiers did.

Lorcan wonders about the warriors who broke the code, wonders how they felt as their homes burnt, as little children were killed around them. Did they believe that they were going to be rewarded with a warrior's death?

His grandfather died a 'warrior's death' protecting his people from the mistakes of the younger generation. He knew his grandfather would have felt responsible for what happened. All he wanted was for a place for them to return home to.

As Lorcan sits quietly, he finally recalls a memory of the last words of advice his grandfather gave him.

"Remember, fighting till the last man will get you nowhere when there's no one to protect your home, so you better return. I will make sure that you and your father have a home to come back to."

Lorcan throws himself on his teacher and weeps. She comforts him, reminding him of his grandmother, a woman he hasn't thought of in years. Ms. Catherine stays late into the night, hushing and comforting him, and makes sure that he makes it to his room.

Chapter 37
Truths

Early in the morning, Kaius and Laura make their way to the labs. Mr. Teslan sits in his office, drinking coffee and grumpily tells them not to disturb him. Mornings are perfect for Kaius. No one wants to wake up early. His shadow lessons won't start for another two hours. The labs are right above the greenhouse overlooking the back of the school, facing the lake, giving a beautiful view.

"Kaius?" He feels a tap on his left shoulder and turns to see Laura perched on a stool pouring a green liquid into a flask on the burner in front of her. "Why are you looking in the forest again?"

He smiles. "Just admiring the view. I remember a time that Nick and I would wake up early and watch the sun rise. It was the only time that we had peace. I wonder if he can still wake up early after the brutal training the General puts him through?"

He walks past his project that is now scattered on the desk, to her station, and turns the burner off from under the now-bubbling green liquid. Laura is quiet for a moment, but then she smiles. "You're really close to him, aren't you?" She moves closer to him, their arms almost brushing against each other.

Kaius can feel heat rise in his cheeks. "Yeah. He always talked to my fellow scientists. He sat with us, ate with us and always encouraged us to ask questions."

"But those are basic things to do, aren't they? Sorry, you have to remember, I'm from the Availa Capital," Laura remarks.

"No. We're second-class citizens." He smiles sadly, as realization hits her. He moves back to his project, screwing in a screw.

"I'm sorry for my ignorance," she says with a blush. "But, at least the rebels fought for equality, right?"

Kaius purses his lips, then chuckles, all while he continues working. "Yeah, you would think that. That's what we all thought too. But when we joined the rebellion, we were ostracized; they only saw us for our strength and minds. You see, my people, the ones with the sun tattoos, worked on technology. So, we would build weapons and bombs for the rebellion."

"Like the one you're making now?" she asks as she points to the box in his hands.

He lifts up the small box and turns it over. "No, this was something that my mother was working on before the King's soldiers killed her for treason. They, too, thought that it was a weapon."

He looks over the box and stares at the stone he recently placed in the centre with wires. He walks over to one of the scrap boxes in the labs and rummages through until he sees what he's looking for. He walks back with a lens and starts to screw it on, continuing his story. "When my mother asked a royal scientist question about electro stones, she was killed. They believed that she was making a weapon." He shakes his head. "She just asked a simple question: 'Can electro stones become power sources?'" Laura places her hand over his as he finishes screwing in the lens and says, "her research, her life's work… they burnt it all that night. I can only remember bits and pieces."

"It's okay," she whispers. He frowns and turns a bit, allowing her to be on his right side. "I'm sure you have the brains to rebuild what your mother lost." Her voice is clearer now, but not by much.

Laura continues talking as he rubs his left earlobe. *I need to stop doing it. No matter how hard I rub, the nurse and doctor made it quite clear that I wasn't going to hear from my left ear again. I need to stop hiding it.*

"Laura, I'm sorry for interrupting, but can you speak on my right side from now on?" She looks confused. He points to his left ear. "When the Empire attacked our base, an explosion knocked Nick and me, along with another person. That man took most of the blast, but I got a ruptured ear."

Laura blushes and stammers, quickly waving her hands. "Oh-oh deities, I—I-I'm so sorry! I'll make a note of that! Why didn't you tell me!" she cries.

He laughs. "It's not good to have your weaknesses out in the open. You're the first person I've told," he admits.

She looks at him quietly. "You trust me? The gossip queen?" she asks, flabbergasted.

"Yes. So, don't go blabbing," he teases.

"I won't." She walks closer to him grinning. "I trust you too. But… if you have hearing problems, why doesn't Nick?"

He sighs as he takes out a stool from under the table and sits, watching the green liquid cool down. "I was always near explosions. My father was an explosives expert. He normally blew up mines, but converted his expertise to bombs in the war. I was his assistant and went on many adventures with him. When we weren't creating bombs, we tried to invent things that still exploded in our faces." He chuckles. "I guess my mother was the real inventor. I always had earplugs in to protect me because my hearing wasn't great to begin with. But on the day of the explosion, the man's arms hit my ear on impact and knocked one out."

"The left one."

He points to it and nods. "I went to the nurse to let her know about it. But the injury had been left for too long. She cursed the soldiers, because the Emperor ordered that all children were to have medical attention. Plus, they say my right one might go deaf as well."

Laura sighs. "Thank you for telling me, and no, I will not tell it to anyone else." She shakes her head then gives him a comforting smile.

He lets out a breath he didn't realize that he was holding. Even the tension in his shoulders were beginning to loosen up. *Talking about these things and having people listen really does help.* He knows that not everything is healed, but he can feel the pent-up frustration slowly leave him.

Kaius and Laura sit silently for a few moments, then Kaius claps his hands. "Now, let's try this box and see if it will light up." He grins excitedly.

"But what about the green liquid?" she asks.

"Just put that to the side. It's not done. Hopefully, it will help clean things easier."

She looks confused for a moment, then frowns. "You're making soap? You're making me make soap?" She crosses her arms.

He leans in closer to her. "Does soap normally have acid in it?" he whispers.

She slowly uncrosses her arms. "It's to clean and get rid of nasty vermin." He giggles.

They gaze at the innocent-looking box as Kaius flicks the switch.

Mr. Teslan runs into the room after seeing a bright light flash through his doors and hears the two students on the ground screaming as they cover their eyes.

"What in the blazes is going on here?!" he yells, helping the two students up from off the floor. They blink and seem beyond dazed.

"Experiment gone wrong," Kaius whispers as Laura slumps over.

Mr. Teslan sighs as he effortlessly picks up Laura and guides Kaius to his office. There he puts aside his work and takes care of his two reckless students. After two hours, including a move to the infirmary, they are finally able to see properly again and because of that incident, Mr. Teslan gifts them each a pair of light-protecting goggles for any future experiments.

Chapter 38
Treaty

At night, Kaius and Nick decide to sneak out again that evening. However, this time, Lorcan is tagging along. Lorcan isn't used to sneaking around the Empire at night, but the boy could hide his presence while walking through a crowd. Tonight, they would be walking among people, wealthy people. Before they leave for the evening, Lorcan reaches into the backpack strapped behind him and pulls out outfits for each boy; they are different from the ones they usually wear.

Kaius unfolds his outfit and coat. "Lorcan, where did you get these?"

"Lost and found. Now put them on," Lorcan replies.

"These are nice clothes." Kaius feels the soft fabric, so different from his own.

"I know. These students are so spoiled, they don't even look for their lost clothes. While we stay in, these fools can go to the market at the school or outside." Lorcan throws a coat at Nick. "See? That coat still has a price tag on it."

Nick turns the coat over, mentally comparing this coat to the one that Volodimir got him. That one was warmer, but his new clothes are locked up in the cottage. "Why do they have so many clothes? All we wear are uniforms most of the time," he asks brushing his hands against the high-quality fur on the coat; wolf fur, from Winterborn he thinks.

"Like I said, they can leave the school. We can't. The number of times I've seen Red students visit their parents and go shopping. You know what else the students don't look for?" Lorcan takes a few coins from his pockets. "They also don't look for loose change."

Under cover of darkness, the boys head towards the city. Kaius looks at everything in awe, while Lorcan eyes everyone with suspicion. Lorcan's glare is so lethal that people cross to the other side to avoid him. Even a man wearing fine priestly robes crosses to the other side.

"Lorcan," Nick whispers. "Tone it down. If you manage to scare a priest, you know that you're glaring too hard." Kaius chuckles as Lorcan sighs.

Nick would have joined in on the chuckles except they stop in front of the Noxus Hotel, the richest hotel in the capital. The three boys stand outside the towering, brightly lit building, watching nobles walking in and out from the grand entrance. The three of them look the part. He can see Lorcan glance around, and Kaius begins to shake. He remembers what Volodimir told him about nobles and confidence.

"Come on guys, no one knows who we are, remember? So, put on a smile and act as if you belong here. Tell yourselves that until you can believe it." He smiles encouragingly at them.

Kaius glares at him. "Easy for you to say. There isn't enough time in the world to make me pretend that I belong here."

"I don't even like it here," Lorcan grumbles.

"You just got here!" Nick exclaims tiredly. "I regret bringing you guys. Maybe I should have asked Laura." At that, both boys glare at him but put on a grim smile. Nick sighs and hopes that this will work out.

As they enter, an older man opens the door for them. Nick nods while the two boys thank him. Nick keeps moving and grabs them when they stop to look at the towering ceiling painted in rich designs.

"Close your mouths," he hisses at them. "We belong here."

The two nod and look on as he makes his way to the front desk. Kaius is amazed at how, in a split second, the nervous boy he knows becomes a confident man. He watches as his strides are firm and tall. Nick reminds him of some of the teachers that walk around the school. If he didn't know his friend, he would believe that he belonged here.

Nick approaches the front desk and tells one of the front desk workers that he's here to see Malcolm Huntsbane, room 405. The woman smiles and the two boys hold in their surprise as they're led to the upper floors.

Kaius listens as the woman and Nick talk, and Kaius is surprised that his friend has an imperial tint to his accent.

"Enjoy your stay." The woman bows.

Nick and his friends smile. "Thank you and may the god of Shadows bless you." Nick says with an imperial accent. The woman smiles even more and leaves.

"Nick, you're walking in here like you belong here!" Kaius comments once they're in front of his uncle's room alone.

"As long as they believe that, that's what counts." He knocks on that door, and they hear a key turning the lock.

There in front of them is a man, only a few years older than them, with long black hair and silver eyes. "*Bràthair beag!*" He hugs Nick and drags him inside with the other two following him and closing the door.

Nick looks around the room and realizes that it's a suite. The hotel feels luxurious with black and silver motifs all over the walls; the suite screams wealth and importance. Malcolm pulls him over and throws him on the couch.

"Come, you two." Malcolm points to his friends. "I'm happy to see that you all are safe. Well, as safe as one can be. But what can I do to help you all in this difficult time?" He takes a seat across from them, gesturing for them to take a seat on the couch.

Nick gathers his thoughts together, but before he can ask a question, Lorcan beats him to it. "You're Nick's mother's brother, correct?" he asks.

"You look so young," Kaius can't help but comment.

His uncle nods. "My name is *Máel Coluim*, but everyone calls me Malcolm, in the Asteriala tongue. Yes, I'm five years older than Nicky or *Neacel* as we like to call him in the mountains. I was an unexpected arrival for my parents. My sister was the most surprised; she also helped raise me. But who are you two?"

They look at Nick, who introduces them. "These are my friends, Kaius and Lorcan. They were a part of the rebellion. Kaius has been with me throughout the entire rebellion, while Lorcan has been with us throughout the whole capture. We're the same age. Well, I'm still fifteen."

"Turning sixteen soon," Kaius adds with a smile.

Malcolm nods. "I'm sorry, *Neacel*. I'm sorry for you all. No child should have to face what you all went through. And now you're left dealing with these entitled pricks." He shakes his head. "I have a feeling that you're all here after hearing the rumours of Tybalt?"

The boys snap their heads up, their attention on Malcolm. "Rumours?" Nick asks, surprised that Malcolm has heard of it as well.

He nods. "Yes. I went to the mines to train some of the guards there. Trust me, I did not feel comfortable training the men who continue to enslave those people. However, I heard the whispers from some of the people of Availa. They're hopeful. They believe that Tybalt will come to save them."

"They believe that one man will save them?" Kaius asks.

Malcolm sighs again. "Aye. They talk about his skills in battle and fighting in the wars. The man could always find his way in any nook and cranny. The reason that he can't be found is because of his skill as a spy. Some believe that he already infiltrated the guards in the mines," he sighs. "Because of those rumours, the guards are rotated and tested regularly."

Malcolm rubs his hands along his tired face. "Now, the General is on all our asses to find Tybalt as well. The Emperor doesn't want there to be a rebellion happening in his own city. Luckily, the General put me in charge of teaching you to give me a break from the mines."

266

As happy as Nick is to see that Malcolm is alive and well, it still doesn't explain how he got here. "Malcolm, how did you get here? How are you involved with the General?" Nick asks.

His uncle seems to age in front of them all. He gazes out at the city from his window. In the distance is the grand palace on a small hill, shining brightly. He turns back to his nephew.

"I wanted to take you with me. I fought with your father. But you have to remember, I was only your age when she died. Your father threw me out with only my spear on my back. I couldn't even take my sister's bones with me. I looked back and saw you. You were looking out the window."

"I remember that. I wondered where you were going. And why didn't you take me..." Nick looks down at his hands.

Malcolm sighs. "I wanted to take you. But your father was screaming that you were an Archer and that you were still useful. I saw you and vowed that I would return. I ran back to my people and told them what happened. Running back to the mountains, that's a two-week journey one way. So in a little over a month, we came back with a small army, but you and your father were already gone. However, my sister's bones were buried there. We took them with us and placed them in the grave of warriors. We decided to not fight alongside your father when your mother died."

Nick chews on his lips for a moment, then sighs. "It's what she would have wanted."

"No, she would have wanted to live and make sure that you were safe." Malcolm corrects him. "I'm sure that all of your parents wished that you weren't in this place. However, as for how I came here, General Herald came and attacked us. He saw that I was a good fighter, and it was either join him or die. I decided to live and change my name from Westmore to Huntsbane. I didn't know if they knew the name Westmore; I didn't want to take the chance. I was just a translator at first because no one would speak the mother tongue for them until the Emperor came and took over. I started small and worked my way up."

He sighs. "I'm not overly proud of my decision. However, it saved not only my life but the lives of my men. Many of them are still home, living a good life. We made a deal with the Emperor, and we have been happy ever since. We're no longer second-class citizens. We are all full citizens of the Empire." Malcolm smiles softly.

"The Emperor didn't cut a deal with us," Lorcan snaps bitterly.

Malcolm narrows his eyes. "With your people, or with the rebellion?"

"With the rebellion," they answer in unison.

He opens his mouth, then closes it. "Are you sure about that?"

They nod in response.

Malcolm's eyes narrow. "You might not believe me, but speak to the General or someone that was there. I heard that the Emperor did make a truce with Markus, but he refused. Him and his damn pride. It would have stopped the rebellion much sooner, and your father would have been the governor. A crappy governor." He shrugs. "I would have preferred Lord Jameson, but he was out of the picture. However, the governor would have been from Availa, instead of from the Empire."

Kaius and Lorcan quickly turn around to face Nick. Nick feels anger boiling in him. "No," he growls angrily, shaking his head. "We were all told that there was no deal." His voice is tight and sounds foreign to him, reminding him of how Volodimir speaks when he's holding in his anger.

All of this could have been avoided if a man had swallowed his pride. He remembers the words of the goddess of Earth.

His uncle shakes his head. "Ask the General, he was there."

Nick does one better. *Did the Night Emperor try to make a truce with my father?* he asks the shadows.

He can hear them chuckle. *No.* Nick calms down a little at that, trusting the shadows. *The Emperor gave Markus **three** truces.*

Malcolm and the two boys jump out of their seats as the room suddenly goes dark and they hear a huge cracking sound near the window. His uncle gasps as long, angry cracks appear all over the glass. He turns to Nick, who wears a murderous expression on his face.

"Please keep us informed of the mines and people," Nick says before quickly beckoning Kaius and Lorcan to join him as he stalks out of the room.

Chapter 39
Purple

As the rebellious group of boys discovers the truth about their former leader, another person finds the courage to talk about the truth... and faces the consequences.

All nine Purple teachers sit together at a table in the Purple teacher's lounge, a room that is used only for meetings. Some teachers don't want to be present but when Arran summoned you, you came.

Elizabeth Avion lets her mind wander when Arran begins to preach about his accomplishments. Arran is great at reminding them of those, but there are other issues that no one likes to bring up; it brought out a sensitive side from the man.

No one is stupid here. Elizabeth may be the youngest out of the group of individuals, but she knows why Volodimir was here—another topic that Arran hated having to talk about. *Why would the Council and the Emperor himself appoint an unknown man in our school?* she wonders to herself. Elizabeth doesn't dare get her hopes up that a Black Teacher will be helpful.

"Ms. Avion!" Arran's proud voice cracks through her thoughts. She winces as a whip-like pain strikes her head.

"Yes, sir?" Elizabeth keeps her voice low and steady, both looking and sounding weak. Any show of strength in front of him is a challenge.

His piercing eyes claw into hers. "Were you listening to what I said?"

She quickly looks away. "No, sir."

He chuckles and lets his shadow dance around the room. Some teachers give her a disgruntled look, while others pity her. She doesn't want their pity. "And what, pray tell, is more important than my funds to the school?"

Elizabeth drags up what little bit of courage she has to cross the forbidden line. "The shadow voices, sir. Once again, I was questioned by one of the students on why they haven't heard the shadows."

The room tenses as Arran's eyes narrow. "Which student?"

She remembers Brutus. The boy is physically robust and could intimidate grown men. However, when he asked her, he looked desperate to hear the voices and was too afraid to ask anyone else for fear that his identity would be discovered.

"Just a concerned student." She won't betray what little trust she has gained from her students. She remembers the last time she brought it up.

· ☾ ·

That memorable night in the Training Hall, Arran dealt with the Purple teachers one by one. Elizabeth ended her training with Arran by dropping off the platform. She fell hard on the ground and bit her lips to silence the cries that tried to escape.

"Now, Ms. Avion," Arran smirked as he landed gently on the ground. "Next time a student asks you why they can't hear the shadows, what will you say?"

She looked at him, eyes watering but defiant.

He doesn't look impressed. "May I remind you, what happened to the last Purple teacher who stood up against me? I heard she still can't get a teaching job. It's a pity that they found out about her husband's illegal gambling addiction. I'm sure you don't want my friend, Lord Nortshell, to hear about your brother's flight from the war? Hmm?" Arran's smirk widened.

Elizabeth paled, remembering her brother packing his belongings and leaving in the middle of the night. She had covered him in darkness, allowing him to slip away.

"The reason why the students don't hear the shadows..." She swallowed hard. "...is that they limit their own potential. If fear isn't enough to draw power, use pain." She hated saying that.

"Good," Arran whispered, yet his voice could be heard clearly in the silence. "Now, I know that some of you question my methods, but they prepare each student for a hard life outside these walls." A few teachers nodded, and Elizabeth couldn't believe that some of these people believed this lie. "Now, fix yourselves up. Tomorrow is a new day. Remember: cut the past, cut the weakness."

Only five teachers remained in the Training Hall, after the rest of the teachers left with Arran. The remaining five disagreed with Arran's methods. However, Arran had blackmailed all of them into silence.

"When did we fall this low?" one of the teachers' voices cracked at the weight of her words.

"The day he beat me in the Training Hall in front of my students..." the eldest Purple teacher whispered. They all nod, each knowing where it started for them. He had been the first one that stood up to Arran, but had been soundly defeated by Arran three times in front of his students and teachers. The man's pride and spirit had been crushed by the third fight.

"The day he paid off my debts," one of the new teachers sighed. It was the lowest moment of his life when Arran 'helped' him by paying off his debts; he had taken on more loans than he could afford to continue his lavish Purple lifestyle. Paying off his debts also bought his silence.

One of the teachers looked expectantly to Elizabeth next, but she only said, "He has dirt on all of us." If people found out that her brother had run away from his conscription and she had covered his trail, she could be thrown into prison for treason.

"No!" one of them snapped. "It started the day the Black Teacher did nothing! Wilhelm was useless and encouraged Arran's entire 'pain is the way!' rhetoric. Then, when we *finally* had an excellent Black Teacher two years ago, Alesander goes off and retires!"

"Susan, you saw the condition Alesander was in before he left. He couldn't run the school anymore. Arran was—"

"Come on! You know that wasn't a natural sickness. I wouldn't be surprised if Arran poisoned him. We all know he has the resources." She scoffed, shaking her head.

Elizabeth sighed. There was no way to prove that theory. Arran had friends in high places. Lord Nortshell, for one, who was one of the most influential people in the Empire, third to the Emperor. There were rumours that Arran knew a few Shadow Assassins as well. Not only that, Arran was viewed highly in Purple society. Attacking him and losing would make them outcasts in the Purple circle, a fate worse than death for many.

"Well, our current Black Teacher seems good. The number of students getting injured has decreased," the eldest one spoke with confidence in his voice.

"Volodimir?" Elizabeth whispered, almost afraid to say his name. "We need a Black, not another Purple. I've heard nothing about him, and knowing Arran, he's already planning that man's downfall."

The old man shook his head. "Arran can't do anything to him. He's not stupid. Volodimir was sent by the Council himself. That means the Council is getting involved."

"Good," the young man said. "Arran made a mistake when he beat that student. What was her name?" He tapped his chin thoughtfully and smiled when it came to him. "Yes, Chloe. Chloe isn't like the other students. She's from the Fedorov family, an old family. They must have complained to the Council before the new Lord Nortshell could stop them."

"Interesting theory. Lord Nigel Nortshell isn't as quick as his predecessor when it comes to hiding things." The old man smiled as well.

"Maybe there's finally a crack in Arran's armour?" Elizabeth hoped.

Now, she's back in the meeting, seeing Arran's eyes narrow. "You are right. I will let the student know that they should focus more on the shadows." She sees that Arran approves of her answer. She smiles. *Yes, soon Arran will fall.* She only hopes she'll be there to witness it.

Chapter 40
Water

As the week draws to a close, Nick is thrilled about going back to his lessons with Volodimir. While he missed practicing Shadow magic, he is glad for the chance to focus on his friends. Each of them is hurting, including himself, but they are choosing to help one another.

Lorcan is telling the rest of the group more about his past. Nick is very interested in Lorcan's people's history and asks as many questions as possible; Bhaltair asks about their food; Kaius wants to know about their irrigation systems. Lorcan grows calmer by the second as he speaks.

"Braawen never asked me about my culture. Just about the war," Lorcan whispers. "I wonder if he saw me as just a warrior, a soldier... never a friend."

"Maybe he did once," Nick whispers softly. "There was a time he even liked *me*. But war changes people, and on most occasions, it's not for the better."

After their talk with Jacques, each of them grows. All of them quickly improve their meditation skills. Nick remembers that Takara is the best at meditating and asks if, during their group meetings, she could give them all pointers. Takara smiles and tells them what her father taught her on meditating comfortably.

Throughout the week, each of them mediates. They focus on their minds during the day and talk about their vulnerabilities at night. The group seems to grow closer as each member expresses their pain and anger. Bhaltair expresses his fear of the 'Night of the Silenced'; Rohana shares her anger at her half-sister; Takara confesses her worry for her family; Laura admits that she's worried about her parents. They listen to each other to help relieve some of their burdens. All of them are determined to grow. Even Lorcan tells the group that his teacher has praised him on his improvement and Kaius nods in agreement.

During practice on the last day of the week, both Takara and Rohana scream in fear. As the boys turn to them with questioning expressions on their faces, Takara and Rohana stammer that they can hear voices, whispers, surrounding them. Nick throws his hands in the air and excitedly tells them that they're hearing the shadows. Bhaltair gasps, exclaiming that he's been hearing them for a week now, but thought that he was going mad.

Shadows, Nick asks. *Why are they able to hear you now?*

The Shadows laugh. *We've always been talking to them. But now, their ears are open. They are not fearful of us, or too proud. They are willing to learn.*

When they tell the General, the man congratulates them and states that they will have desserts on their dinner table in celebration. Nick assumes that they will each get one pudding cup, but no, the General makes sure that the whole table is laden with enough sweets to catch the entire school's attention at dinner. Bhaltair eats dessert in moderation, and so do the others in a show of support. The General boasts that his students had earned the right to eat desserts because, after all, every single one of them could hear the shadows.

That news was met with gasps from students, staff, and teachers alike. Some students are jealous, while others are amazed; the Purple table looks at them in fury. The Yellow table is too busy eating the dessert to care about the shift in the hall.

After his meal, Nick walks to his room. Tonight, he is going out one more time before Volodimir returns. He puts on the black uniform, which is getting a little tight in some areas. No one outside the school has seen it in years. There's a high possibility that other people won't recognize it, so he feels confident about wearing it while journeying to the city. After the talks with Malcolm, he decided to tell the rest of his friends about his journey into the city. When he showed the black uniform to his friends. They were amazed and asked if he could get them their own. He declines because taking another one is too risky. He looks himself over and covers the school emblem with coal. Then he puts on his hood and goes hunting.

Nick is treated to a stunning view while sitting on a rooftop overlooking the city. He believes that it should be safe for everyone to come. This time is different; he has all of his friends involved looking for his uncle, Tybalt. They are all heading towards the slums near the mines, each of them taking a different route.

They meet at the fountain in the slums, separating to cover more ground. Each of them uses the shadows to talk to one another, and the shadows graciously act as messengers for them. Nick thanks the shadows more these days, feeling more comfortable travelling through and talking to them. He doesn't know why, but he knows the shadows approve of his use of power. They're becoming a part of him. Yet, deep down, he can feel that there is also something there that the shadows feel, something that is trying to reach out to him and come out

He has kept his promise so far. He doesn't limit himself and puts everything into his training and studies; he is determined to be the best. By doing so, Nick finds that he's improving in everything.

The mind can really cripple a person. His mind and insecurities were like chains suffocating his body, dragging him deeper into the cold abyss of his thoughts. It takes Nick a while, but the chains are slowly breaking, rusting and crumbling at his touch. He likes the power that he's wielding now, likes that he's improving, and enjoys the things he can do with his power.

Nick looks from the rooftops and sees a family hiding in a corner. From the looks of it, they are trying to leave the slums. However, one of them makes a sound and they all freeze.

Why are they hiding? he asks the shadows.

They are from your country. If they get caught escaping the mines, death awaits them, the shadows reply.

He growls as he knows that the guards will see the family. With a stretch of his hand, he moves the shadows to engulf them in darkness. The guards walk past them, oblivious to the family hidden mere feet away. Nick keeps them hidden until the guards leave. When the coast is clear, he releases the shadows cloaking the family and they run deeper into the night.

May the god of Shadows grant them safety through the night and the goddess of Light in the day, he prays for them, hoping they'll be safe.

Nick knows he needs to move on. There is much to do and so little time as his feet leap off one of the tattered roofs and land on the uneven cobblestones below. He carefully walks in the shadows around the sleeping and even dead bodies littering the street. The deeper towards the mines he goes, the more disease and death he finds.

Kaius is right. They need help. No one should live like this. He thinks back to the times that he had to hide in alleyways, eating rats and bugs to survive. He wants to help them, but the more he looks around, the more he doesn't know where to start.

Water. Clean, fresh water, he thinks as he stands next to another, smaller well. He doesn't need to look inside to know that the water isn't clean; the stench coming up from the well confirms it.

Shadows, my friends. He can feel that they are happy he calls them friends. *I need your help again. I can't find my uncle.*

Our friend, it seems that the goddess's favour is wavering, giving us only a glimpse. We have tried to track him, but your uncle moves swiftly. Go to the frozen river. He's heading there.

This time, Nick climbs onto the roof, gripping the pipes tightly to climb. He jumps up to see a large river on his right that heads towards the mines.

He can see a few children playing and having fun on the river. However, what they're doing is dangerous given the season. The winter months are almost gone and the ice that once gave the lakes its serene aura, now cracks with the approaching spring. He watches the children play, shabbily clothed in too-thin garments but joyous.

He catches a sudden movement in the corner of his eyes. He slowly turns his body, seeing a man standing a few feet away, watching as well. A man whose once-golden hair is now dirty, his once clean-shaven face now covered with a sparse beard. When the man turns to him, Nick sees his eyes, blue like a robin's egg. Even from a distance, he can see the scar under his chin peeking through the beard. He quickly alerts the shadows to tell his friends.

"Tybalt?" Nick cries, gazing upon his uncle. The man snaps his head towards him, wide-eyed and, to Nick's surprise, begins running in the opposite direction.

"Wait!" he cries. *Why is he running?* "Uncle, it's me!" he yells. He realizes why his uncle is running away from him when he feels his hood flop on his head. He unties the knot and pulls down the hood, his hair blocking his eyes for a second.

"You're not my family!" his uncle yells, not looking back.

"Look back, uncle. It's me, Nick!"

"My Nicky doesn't sound like that."

Damn puberty! He curses his deeper voice.

"Uncle Tys!" Nick is the only one who calls him that.

Tybalt stops ahead, turning around in disbelief. There, standing a few feet away from him is Nick. He can see his nephew now, even from afar. Before he can run towards Nick, they both hear a crack and a shriek. Both men quickly turn their attention to the lake and see that two children have fallen through the ice. Nick looks back to see his uncle watching him. He makes a split-second decision and darts to the lake. His uncle watches and then runs off to the streets when more people appear, following the sound of screaming children.

Nick slides across the ice, then dives into the hole without a second thought. The water begins to freeze his body; he can feel the pins and needles all over. He pushes through the pain, even though he has to shut his lips tightly to stop an involuntary gasp. He knows that the children aren't near the hole, so he follows the current and uses Night Vision to help him find them. He finds one child and grabs her. The little girl grabs him back, which comforts him for a bit. He puts his hand on the ice and uses his strength to break through, leaving him with a sore hand.

He feels other hands grabbing him and people breaking the ice, giving him momentary relief. He passes the child to an older man at the river's edge, and even though one of the men is trying to get him out, Nick slaps him away and wipes the water from his face.

"One more," he gasps through chattering teeth.

He dives back in, hearing people call out to him. He sees that this child is deeper in the river, and she looks like she could be asleep, she's so small. Nick grabs her, but as he swims, his muscles start to ache, his eyes going dark. His clothes are heavy, she's heavy. Not knowing if they'll make it, he pushes her towards the hole and sees someone grab her as he starts to sink.

So cold. He remembers falling into one of the lakes in autumn. He thought that was cold, but this is worse. He can't feel any of his limbs and the world slowly goes black.

Shadows… he calls softly.

"Wrong," he hears a sing-song voice say.

His eyes open widely to see a man with gills and scales swimming in front of him. Well, the top half of him is a man, but the lower half is a fish. The man-fish looks about the size of the ship he took to get to the empire. The man blows a large air bubble which encases both of them.

Nick takes a haggard breath and starts coughing up water, throwing up all the good desserts he had with dinner. His limbs are shaking uncontrollably, and he collapses onto the floor of the bubble, taking shallow breaths.

The man swims over to him and places a hand on his cheek. "You risked your life for two foolish children. You chose them instead of your uncle." Nick wishes he could talk, but he's too busy trying to breathe. "Do not fear. It is not your time to die. As the god of Water, I will make sure that you live until the dark one comes to your rescue."

Nick wants to ask what he means, but the god of Water starts to fade away and the water surrounds him again. He wonders if it was all a dream as the cold invades him. His eyelids begin to close until the pressure on the back of his neck shoots out, and the sound of breaking ice wakes him. With heavy eyes, the only thing he can see is darkness, then red glowing eyes. He feels a tight tug and his saviour pulls him, swimming towards the surface. Nick's senses are dull, but he can still hear the strong cracking of ice. His rescuer effortlessly breaks a new hole and pulls them both up.

People are slowly walking over to them, careful to not crack the ice even further, watching as Nick violently throws himself to his side and throws up water. After clearing his burning lungs, he is pulled on his back. In mere moments, he feels warm hands on his cheeks, turning his head from side to side.

Red eyes bore intensely into blue. "Nico, stay with me!" There's panic in a voice that is usually so steady and confident. Nick barely feels a slap to his face. Nick can hear the man calling his name, pleading with him to stay awake, but the world goes black anyway.

· ◐ ·

Nick feels warmth, then warmth turns to heat.

Hot... Too hot! he wants to yell. Instead, he snaps open his eyes to the fire surrounding him. He jumps up with a startled yell. *Oh shit!* he curses. *How did I end up in the Halls of the Wicked?* He didn't believe he was that wicked in his life; he's had dark thoughts but never acted out on them.

He quickly drops to his knees and prays. "Dear deities, please forgive this humble sinner. I'm sorry I didn't believe that you could speak to people. I'm sorry I didn't go to your temples! I'm sorry if I was that much of a prick. Please also forgive my friends, and Braawen because he's even more of a prick than me!"

He hears a loud peal of laughter snapping him out of his prayer. *Damn, even the demons are laughing at me!* His head snaps up to see a woman wearing a dress of lava and fire, her eyes closed. Her hair is a radiant fire, and her skin is red.

"You truly do have a good heart," the goddess speaks, hot air passes through him. At this point, he's not even fazed that there is a goddess in front of him. "What a reaction you had! It's the funniest I've ever seen. For that, I shall warm up nicely so you can recover quickly." She opens her glowing eyes and winks.

The fourth creator. He recognises the goddess. *A goddess winked at me.* No one would believe him. He can barely believe it himself.

"T-thank you, oh goddess of Fire. I don't know how to repay you!" he stammers.

The goddess laughs, causing another wave of heat to surround him. "Think nothing of it. You saved two children's lives. Though, I also came to warn you. Beware of Braawen. While you spare a prayer for him, I know what he whispers in the flames when no one is watching."

"What does Braawen want with me?" he asks, though the thought that his cousin wants him to harm doesn't surprise him.

The goddess chuckles. "He wants to see you and your uncle's demise. Be careful, Nickolaus. Your cousin is one for dramatics and wants to see you fail in front of an audience. So, be careful of crowds until you put him in his place." Her voice holds a strong warning.

Nick shakes his head. "I can't kill family, my own blood."

The goddess laughs. "You'd be surprised at how many people say that until they have no choice. Men like your cousin shouldn't prosper, and I would hate to see a young man such as yourself die by his hands."

"He really wants me dead?" Nick's voice wavers.

The goddess smiles. "He will always choose himself."

Nick sits down on the hot ground, feeling chilled despite the heat surrounding him. He takes haggard breaths in an effort to calm himself. He looks at the goddess and gives a sly smile. "I guess I can't ask for fire powers to just burn him?"

The goddess chuckles, but not happily "My boy, I would, but I made a vow to never give humans my powers. Not after humans used my gift of fire to destroy forests and people's lives. Fire was meant to give life, not destroy it! I chose to pass on my powers to light the sun, so its warmth can be used to give life like it is supposed to do!" she is yelling by the end, all fire and smoke.

This goddess has quite the temper, Nick thinks.

The goddess takes a deep breath. "But I am not a cruel goddess and allowed people to be able to use fire with the aid of tools. However," she warns with a smile, "fire will never be fully under their control. Why do you think fires cause a lot of damage when a human isn't careful?

"Besides, I can't be like the god of Water who gave his gift to the creatures of the sea. There are so few animals to which I can give fire to. Firedrakes, salamanders, and dragons are the only ones who have my gift."

"Dragons?!" Nick lights up. "They exist?"

"Yes, though rare. You people make it a sport to hunt them, then get angry when they burn down a village after they've been provoked."

"Sorry," he winces. "But—aren't there Shadow Dragons as well?"

The fires and heat immediately flare up. "DO NOT SPEAK OF THOSE ABOMINATIONS!" she yells. "The damn god of Shadows took my creations, MINE, and twisted them into monsters of darkness and death!"

Nick gets on his knees and begs for forgiveness.

She calms herself and the fires die down as Nick slowly lifts up his head. The red flames are now blue, causing an eerie glow to surround them both.

"Besides, the god of Shadows, only the Night Emperor can control the Shadow Dragons. Be wary of the Night Emperor. Remember, as much darkness you allow in, make sure to allow just as much light. Do not let the darkness take you, Nickolaus." Her voice fades, and a bright light hits his eyes.

Nick jolts awake, startling Volodimir who is sitting next to him reading a book. He looks around and realizes that he's back in Volodimir's cottage, in his bed.

His teacher puts his book down and places a gentle hand on his chest, whispering comforting words that he cannot make out at the moment. Volodimir's voice relaxes him and Nick feels a wave of calm surrounding him. He turns his head and sees that the candles are lit and it's still dark outside the window.

"H—" He begins to cough, unable to finish his sentence. His teacher gets up and grabs a glass of warm water.

Air slowly enters his lungs as his head slowly stops spinning. He can feel his teacher's hand on his back soothing him as he takes deep breaths. Nick looks down to see that he is wearing a simple black tunic, baggy and much too big for him. He remembers that Volodimir once wore this shirt when Nick was at the cottage with him.

"I did not change you." His teacher's voice brings him out of his mind. "It was your friends; Bhaltair, Lorcan, and Kaius. They and the girls are waiting in the living room. I have not told them of our connection, and I am thankful that you have kept this a secret."

Nick nods. "Can I see them?" he asks.

"Soon," Volodimir replies. "But I want to know something. Why were you and your friends outside the gates and in the slums? Remember, do not lie to me," he warns.

Nick knows there is no point in lying. He's sure that the Shadow Assassins probably told Volodimir something. He's the Black teacher of this school after all, and in charge of all the students.

"The traitor, Tybalt. We heard that he was here. We wanted to speak to him. Ask him if any of our other family members escaped or are alive," Nick says, gasping between his words.

It isn't a lie. Kaius does want to ask his uncle that.

Volodimir's eyes narrow. "And would you let him go?" His voice is dangerously threatening. Nick can feel a tremble from his spine to his knees. He wants to pass out, so he rests his back on the headboard to help him stay upright.

"Y-yes," he whispers.

Volodimir's eyes flash a dangerous red.

"But also no," Nick states quickly.

His teacher's eyes still glow. "No?" he asks menacingly.

It is the truth. If Nick could hold on to his uncle, he wouldn't let go. He would hold his uncle tight, never letting him out of his sight. He would tell him about Braawen, and they could both leave and take his friends too.

But he knows that they would be caught and executed. That's why he wants this power. He needs to keep the few people he trusts safe.

"I can't lie to you," he whispers. "You said no lies, and I won't lie. I only ask that you do not punish my friends. They're innocent."

The glow fades from Volodimir's eyes. There are times that Nick wants to ask why his teacher's eyes do that.

Volodimir grabs his hand tightly.

"My boy," Volodimir chuckles. "Nico..." Soft red eyes meet blue. "I know that you and your friends want to know more about your families. However, that man is dangerous and the Empire will have better records than a lone, wanted criminal." Volodimir's eases up on his hand, almost comforting now. "Let them go, Nico. It's time to embrace the future and let go of the past."

Nick nods slowly, as Volodimir tilts his head and looks into his eyes again. "What's wrong, Nico? You have something else on your mind."

Nick's eyes narrow in confusion until he sees the small candle flame behind them. "I had a strange dream," Nick whispers. Volodimir moves closer to hear him. "Braawen plans to harm me, but that can't be right... can it?" He can feel a small pit begin to form in his stomach.

Volodimir gives a small smile. "You seem unsure." Volodimir can see hesitation in his student's eyes. "Braawen does seem to have a grudge against you, yet he refuses to explain why."

Nick just shakes his head. "Can he really be planning something? I haven't done anything to him." There is a hint of hesitation in his voice.

His teacher nods in understanding at the dilemma going through Nick's mind. "Nico, a man does not build weapons when he believes he is safe. Nor does one plan the demise of a friend."

The pit in Nick's stomach seems to grow.

"Right now, you need rest." Volodimir gets up and takes the candle with him. As he closes the door, he turns around and gives the boy one last smile. "In the future, please try to swim in the summer. Ice cold water is something I wouldn't recommend."

Nick's head snaps up. "How did you find me?" he asks.

"The shadows told me." With that, Volodimir shuts the door.

Nick is left with the room's shadows, the only source of light coming from the moon. He lets out a breath he didn't know he was holding. His arms continue to shake as he breathes a slow and steady intake of air. He's frightened. He was so close to meeting and warning his uncle, but at the same time, possibly ending his own life. He doesn't want another close encounter with death. He sighs as he looks at the flowers in the room, his eyes slowly closing.

He dreams of a woman with the same eye colour as the flowers he was looking at. She is patting his head and singing songs that make him feel joyful. *Don't give up,* she whispers.

"But... I'm not," he answers in his sleep.

Don't give up on Val-

"Who?" he mumbles.

The woman shakes her head as though she's running out of time. *Please protect. Protect Rohana.*

Nick nods his head, wondering why he needs to protect Rohana. He is protecting her anyway. Also, she's his friend and more than capable of protecting herself.

The woman with the beautiful eyes and long, flowing hair kisses his head in thanks. As she fades, his mother's voice calls from behind him. However, he turns to see a stone under two large pillars of ice, surrounded by white lilies. Tears start to fall on his pillow as the only thing he can remember from her in the morning is 'fault'.

As Volodimir walks into the living room, he sees the children stand up straight. He tells them that Nick will be back in the morning after questioning. He also tells them that he informed their respective head teachers of them running around the city. He can see Lorcan and Kaius flinch, and the Yellows groan.

He sends them away, then moves closer to the fireplace. He stares at the fire, still vexed by his apprentice's actions. Though the boy was admittedly closer to finding the traitor than even the Shadow Assassins, much to their confusion. It's almost as though the man can hide even from the shadows. Like someone is protecting him.

I can't believe Abram was right. Volodimir leans on his chair, letting out a breath of frustration. Even when he asked the shadows about the traitor's whereabouts, they told him it was not up to him.

Why the boy? Why Nico? Volodimir cries to the shadows.

The boy and his friends have a connection to the man called Tybalt. Tybalt is the key to unlocking a new Black, they reply.

Volodimir sighs and puts down his cup. *Yes, everyone would love a new Black to appear. That's why everyone's putting their hopes on Braawen.*

The shadows laugh.

Volodimir rolls his eyes. *Why are you laughing? Isn't he the one? The boy is in Purple, and the traitor is his living uncle. Surely, Braawen will become a Black when he betrays his uncle, his only blood?*

The shadows continue to laugh, and even Volodimir remembers that they are an entity on their own. However, he is nothing but patient and waits.

The shadows finally respond, *We know that you put more faith in our friend than that boy*. Well, Volodimir couldn't deny that. *Negative emotions can bring anyone to the Black circle. Anger, betrayal, envy. And one cannot forget sadness*. The shadows whisper in his ears. *Loss and sadness; losing someone can be the greatest push of all*.

Chapter 41
Gift

It would have been a day like any other day, but right now, Nick is in the middle of a little problem. He did the impossible and found his uncle before anyone else could. However, his uncle didn't recognize him right away. Honestly, he can't believe his uncle fled the scene as he saved those girls. Well, he hopes that the floating angel is still alive; she was so small. Although, all of that isn't the problem at hand. The problem is that after his little stunt, he is in a warm and comfortable bed, the best bed that he has ever slept in his entire life...

...with Volodimir right by his side, glaring at him.

Today's tea is an herbal concoction that Nick doesn't know the name of. He sweetens it with honey and quietly takes a sip, trying not to make eye contact with his angry teacher. Volodimir is having none of it, and after having a quiet moment, opens his mouth.

"Nico," he sighs. "Why is it that when I leave you, something always happens?" His tone isn't too serious, so Nick looks up. That turns out to be a bad idea; his teacher is still glaring at him.

Nick takes another sip of tea to gather his thoughts. "Sometimes bad things just follow me." he replies, knowing it's a bullshit answer.

Even his teacher rolls his eyes, which on any other day, Nick would find hilarious.

"You must take better care of yourself," Volodimir says, sighing again. "I can't be there all the time, and you do worry me."

Nick looks up. He doesn't know whether or not to be surprised. Honestly, dare he say it, the man acts more of a father to him than his own ever was. This worries him, since Volodimir is supposed to be on the enemy's side, and he shouldn't actually like the man.

Nick cups the tea in his hands and sighs. "I'm sorry. It's just... I couldn't let those children die if I knew that I could help them. Plus, I felt sorry for them." Volodimir gives him a confused look. "I mean, the children, all the people in the slums..." He shakes his head. "Those people need food, clean water, and so much more."

Volodimir smiles. "And what do you think the Emperor should do to help those who do not help themselves?"

Blue eyes become sharp as steel. "How can people try when they're too busy just trying to feed themselves?! Some people try, but others physically or mentally can't!"

Volodimir's smile drops. "And the others that can but choose to do nothing?"

"We shouldn't group entire people based on what a few people do. The people that would like to do something about the situation shouldn't be punished! I was in a situation like that, and if I wasn't at this school, then no one would know my hidden potential."

Nick glares at Volodimir, remembering how the last King of his homeland would starve his people and call them lazy, then act surprised that there were riots and the people refused to come to his aid. Volodimir stares back at him, apparently unmoved.

"For example, what happens to all the food here that doesn't get eaten?" Nick demands. "We can't possibly be eating all the food?"

"I believe that it is thrown away," Volodimir replies.

"Then that could be one thing that can be done." His voice slowly goes from steel to velvet. "We can give the food that hasn't been eaten to the slums. Trust me, if I could get food from a warm table, even scraps? I would praise all the deities to bless the Night Emperor. There were days that I was tempted to join the Emperor's army after seeing the food they got."

He actually knew a few men and women who did.

"As for dirty water, is there any way to clean it?" he asks.

Volodimir scoffs. "Why? They will just make it dirty again in no time."

So, there is a way. Nick thinks. "Then, at least they know you cleaned it. If it becomes dirty again, then clean it again, and figure out a more permanent solution." He shrugs. "Plus, I believe that the Kur region has indoor sewage that separates waste from their drinking water. Are there any engineers that the Night Emperor can bring in? This is supposed to be Andromeda, the capital of the Andromendor Empire, the glorious city with innovation and freedom, yet the people at its doorsteps die from preventable diseases."

Volodimir remains silent for a moment, and Nick wonders if he went too far until Volodimir chuckles. "I understand what you mean. I will have to see if this can be brought up in the next Council meeting. As the Black Teacher, I can guarantee the food, but not the water."

Nick sighs and lays back in the bed. "Why is the Night Emperor trying to rule the world instead of looking closer to home? From what I've read, history isn't kind to rulers who stretch themselves too thin."

Red eyes gaze softly at him. "Our Emperor, only conquers those who refuse to trade peacefully and attack him. We swore an oath to the god of Shadows that we would never attack another kingdom unless provoked, or we would lose our Shadow magic. For example, your old King was a fool and destroyed our trade agreement. The men around him didn't stop him.

The only one who tried was Lord Jameson from what I heard. Poor fool, or the only wise person in the room, was thrown into prison. The King then provoked us when his soldiers attacked one of our ports, stating that we were supplying the rebels with weapons from Port Kitchener, our closest port to Availa. Many people were wounded and some died from the attack."

Nick is dumbstruck for a moment, trying to understand the blatant stupidity of the King. "That's madness. We've never received any aid from the Empire, or from any other nations because they were too busy with their own messes. My King was an idiot."

"Yes, very much. Trust me, many of us were shocked. I was in my office when I found out. That's when I knew that we were going to war." Volodimir sighs. "Your King believed that we wouldn't help the rebels based on the trade agreement that we had. To summarize, there were three main points that the Empire had to follow; the first was that the Emperor would marry; the second was that the Empire could not aid the rebellion in any way, shape, or form; and lastly, the Empire could not attack the Kingdom of Availa. The fool didn't read that it would be void if any port, city, or region of the Empire were attacked. All the man cared, or saw was that the Empire could not attack the Kingdom."

Blue eyes could only narrow in confusion. "Why would the Empire not attack the Kingdom? It seems too good to be true."

"Easy answer—the King of Availa was allowing his sister to marry the Night Emperor. It was a quiet affair. The Princess was to come to the Empire a month after signing the agreement. She was eager to leave her brother. However, Princess Estelle never came."

"Princess Estelle..." Nick remembers that name. "I heard that she was a kind and lovely lady. She was intelligent and great at calming her brother's temper. Even those in the rebellion wanted her to be queen, and many asked for her aid." He laughs. "I even heard that she begged her brother to help us, though it did nothing in the end. There was even a rumour that the King lusted after his own sister, but I think that was just slander from the rebellion."

"Yes." Volodimir's voice sounds far away. "It was a pity that she died, for she might have been a good Empress. She was able to make a god feel human, but now she's gone. It's in the past." He shakes his head and looks at Nick. "Now, Nico, this is the present. But I do like your idea of giving untouched food to the slums. It wouldn't hurt us." He smiles, and Nick feels that he's done something good for once.

Nick stays with his friends during the day, but returns to Volodimir at night to continue their studies in the cottage. Volodimir stated that he's going to be punished for his actions and to prepare for a fight.

He's now on the fourth stage in the underground levels. The room is similar to the first three, with blue pillars holding up the room. However, he can't seem to understand why it feels darker and pushes his Night Vision even further to see his teacher's training rod almost hit his head. He dodges and continues to spar with him. Volodimir has given him three weapons of which to practice; a sparring rod, a knife, and a spear to practice with. For each weapon, he has to know its shape and how it feels without looking at it.

"Shadow Weapons," his teacher states. "Each weapon has a grade carved somewhere on the weapon. The darker the weapon, the more powerful it will be with the shadows. You can channel your powers and let your weapons phase through anything to reach its target." He picks up the knife that looks like a normal kitchen knife, except for the thin black line on the blade. He points to the small number one engraved on the handle. "Weapon grades go from one to ten. Each circle can have control over the weapons, starting from Red. Red is one to five, Blue is six to eight, and Purple is nine. Only Blacks can wield ten. There are only two weapons that are graded ten—the Emperor's sword and the Night Spear."

Nick remembers hearing about the sword, the one that defeated his father, so that the Emperor could drag him here to be executed. Some stated that the sword was large and had a wide blade that was pure black, while others heard from a friend of a friend that ran from the final battle, that the sword was a two-handed weapon that could summon black flames. After his talk with the goddess of Fire, Nick doubts that.

"Are you listening, Nico?" His teacher's voice pulls him back to reality.

"No." Nick shakes his head. He can hear Volodimir's exhausted sigh and watches him pinch the bridge of his nose.

"Both weapons," Volodimir continues, "are national treasures with a rich history. I believe that they are still kept in the royal vaults. The Emperor can summon the sword whenever he needs it. Maybe with your spear skills, should they improve, you'll become the third wielder of the Night Spear."

Nick tucks a lock of hair behind his ear. "Who were the other two?" he asks as he spins the shadow knife in his hand.

"The past wielders were both Emperors—Emperor Alastair and the late Emperor Allerick. Both were great warriors and Emperors," Volodimir answers.

Nick stops spinning the knife around and feels some of his power funnel through it. "It feels nice and light."

His teacher nods. "Good. Even grade 1 weapons are coveted amongst the circles. Weapons graded six and above are rarer, but we have a few at the schools." Volodimir throws him a training rod covered with black and dark blue swirls.

Nick catches it and can feel more of his power funnelling into the weapon, and the rod glows black. He turns it around to see the number 6 engraved on it.

Volodimir ends the sparring session and they bow to each other. Volodimir takes the rod and places it on the weapons stand as Nick catches his breath. His teacher is pushing him harder, and he can feel every ache in his muscles. He feels muscles where he only felt bone once. It feels good; it feels even better knowing that he can hold Night Vision without discomfort or dizziness.

"Shall we continue with the knife throwing? I'm doing much better," Nick asks.

Volodimir nods. "Maybe later. However, there is something that I would like to give to you." His teacher walks over to the edge of the room, to one of the small tables, which has a black box sitting on it. He picks it up and walks back over to Nick, handing the box to him.

Nick can feel his teacher's eyes on him as he opens it. He gasps as he sees five long and three short black knives lying on a red velvet cushion. He looks at Volodimir, who has a large smile on his face.

"I... wow," Nick stutters as he takes one of the short knives out.

He can feel the immense pull on his power as though the knife's hungry for more. He looks at one of the training dummies and the circular target behind it. He wants to aim for the centre in the circle, so he throws it and channels his powers to phase through the dummy and pierce the target's centre.

"Yes!" he cheers and walks over to see that the dummy is unharmed, but the knife is behind it, stuck in the centre of the target. "I don't know how to thank you; I mean, can I have this?"

Volodimir chuckles. "You've been working so hard. You deserve them. I have a feeling that you will know when to use them," he calmly states, placing his hand on Nick's shoulder.

Nick smiles, embarrassed by the praise. "I'll keep them safe and use them well." He can't put them under the bed, but his small desk drawers already have a million books and papers. Adding a small box under all that should be fine.

"I know you will."

They finish for the night and head back upstairs to the cottage. As Volodimir makes some tea, Nick looks at the knives again, swearing under his breath, almost dropping the box.

The blade is practically black with the number nine engraved on each one.

Chapter 42
Tool

"Bye Nickolaus!" Wendy waves to him as she and her friends leave the library.

It's a quiet afternoon in the library, and Nick waves to the small study group he created. He looks at one girl, Wendy, an Orange who was also from Availa, and remembers her shyly asking Nick to help her with an essay. He happily helped Wendy, and she brought more friends later on. He's happy that he could help some Availian students. He wants to see them succeed, and hopefully, they can rank highly enough to return home, if they want to.

"Hey, Nickolaus, good luck on the test." Brandon, a Blue student, waves as he goes to his friends to study, and Nick waves back.

Brandon came to him late one night to ask Nick for help finding the right books for his homework, and later on helped him with his paper. To say that Nick was surprised was an understatement. However, helping some of the students from the Empire also helps his reputation.

As more people leave, Nick goes to the shelves and picks out a number of books to read. He's reading his third book on Shadow Weapons, searching for information on the knives. There are many things he needs to learn about the knives that Volodimir had gifted him and he wants to master them as soon as possible. The knives are in his desk, hidden under his notes, safe and sound. Yet, there are times that he feels an ache, almost as though he feels incomplete without the knives near him. Nick hopes that one of the books in the library will have information on that.

Can a person bond with a Shadow Weapon? he wonders to himself. He would have continued to read about shadow weapons, but the clock chimed. It's late and he still has other work to do.

"Well, that's enough for today," he whispers as he closes yet another book that doesn't answer his question.

He takes out his notebook from his art history class and begins to write his essay. Even though this is a school dedicated to Shadow training, it's still a school. Volodimir has made it quite clear to him that if he skips any of his classes or fails a single assignment, their nightly classes will be over. A second warning has never been uttered, as Nick makes sure to stay top in his classes. In fact, the boy is top amongst those in his age group when it comes to his regular studies. As he finishes the first paragraph of his essay, a shadow covers his paper.

"Hello, Nick," a soft voice whispers in his ears.

It takes everything in him not to shudder. He turns to see familiar ice-blue eyes in a not-so-familiar person. "It's Nickolaus to you. However, hello, Emelie." Nick decides to stay courteous. He's in the presence of a Purple, surrounded by other students who will probably be on her side if anything happens. He has worked too hard building a good reputation among all the students and does not plan on losing it to this girl who could destroy it in one second.

The girl uses the shadows to drag a chair up next to him. She sits beside him like a proper lady, far too close to his liking. He can smell cherry perfume on her mingled with a hint of cologne.

Emelie begins to speak with a purr in her voice. "I heard that you're the smartest student in our age, and I must say that is quite impressive for being a—"

"Yellow, I know," he interrupts, trying to end the conversation as quickly as possible.

She softly chuckles. Nick can imagine that any boy would go crazy for it, and he's ashamed to realize a small part of him does. Despite his reaction, he remembers the warnings Rohana has given him; her half-sister is a viper.

"No, silly. I was going to say your background. Braawen told me that he, Lorcan, Kaius, and you never had a formal education." She flutters her eyelashes at him. "You work so hard, and I was wondering if you could help me."

Kaius is the smartest science student, and Lorcan is the best at art, so Nick hopes she needs help in one of those subjects. "Help you in what way? You seem pretty capable."

He starts to put away his things, but her hand darts out to tightly grip his. He turns to see her pout. She looks cute and innocent.

"But, Nick, I need your help. I was hoping that you could write a paper for me," Emelie says, almost whining.

"It's Nickolaus, and why in all good Asteria would I do that?" He tries to pull his hand away, but her grip is tight.

Emelie smiles. "Because I could help you with some Shadow Training," she whispers in his ears. She even gives him a soft kiss that makes his cheeks burn.

He gulps, getting a grip on himself.

"I heard that if you don't move up a circle, you and the other Yellows will get kicked out. I can help you. You might even go up two circles with my training."

Nick couldn't hold in his chuckle. He bites his lips and takes a deep breath to stop himself from full-out laughing in her face. One, it would be rude, and two, as he looks at her, he can see a gleam in her eyes, almost like a wolf catching its prey.

"I have to kindly decline. There are other people much higher in the circles who can help you, even the older Purples. I'm sure they'll help you with the regular curriculum. Please excuse me." He tries to walk away, but her grip is still on his hand.

He looks back at Emelie glaring murderously at him. "Come on, Nick, don't you want to have a friend in Purple."

He glares back at her. "It's *Nickolaus*, and you're not used to people telling you 'no', are you?" He can see her eyes widen in surprise. "My answer is no, so please ask someone else." He yanks his arm out of her grip, and she lands on the floor, hitting the chair.

The chair falls over, and Emelie's yelp draws people's attention. Nick looks at her, wondering how she was on the floor. He didn't even pull his arm that hard. Then he sees it—the fake tears pooling around her eyes.

"Nick, why did you push me? I was just asking for help!" she whimpers, and just like that, the students that didn't hear the conversation but heard her fall run to her defence.

Three boys from different colours help her up as two other girls from Blue chastise him.

"You didn't have to push her so hard, Nick!" Brandon exclaims.

This shocks Nick. He sighs. "Brandon, I didn't —" He tries to say, but more people come to Emelie's defence as she continues to cry and hold onto an elbow that he's certain hit nothing. As the group of five starts drawing more attention, Nick does the only thing he can do.

"Listen, I didn't do anything!" He tries to explain, but no one listens to him.

"Then why is she on the floor?!" an older Orange student yells.

Nick shrugs. "She must have tripped."

The students scoff. "Emelie is a talented fighter. She wouldn't trip."

Many come to her defence. Tired of trying to explain himself, Nick walks away. As he leaves, he can hear comments being made about him, and he walks out as Ms. Joy tells everyone to remain silent.

Feast time consists of hearing snide comments behind his back as he drinks four cups of the awful grey stuff. He can feel the eyes of most of the kids in the school boring into him. He looks up to see the Purple table glaring at him and Braawen putting a comforting arm around Emelie. Nick continues his meal in silence.

After dinner, he dodges many of the vengeful pranks that students try to pull on him. However, he misses one, and cold-water sloshes onto him from a hanging pail. He is completely soaked, and can hear laughter down the hall. He's fuming but carries on to his room.

"Nick," Rohana softly calls to him from her bed as he enters the Yellow rooms. "I heard that you pushed Emelie in the library when she was trying to help you with your homework. I know that's not true. Are you okay?" There's genuine worry in her voice.

The others stop getting ready for bed as well, turning to face Nick.

Nick nods. "She asked me to write her paper. When I said no, she threw herself on the chairs to make it look like I pushed her." He sighs. "Don't worry, I'm used to people saying terrible things about me. I'm sure it will pass."

Bhaltair, Rohana, and Takara look at each other, worried.

The next day he's attacked in the hallway. He finds out that Emelie has a group of boys who follow her every word. Nick arrives at science class with a black eye. Whenever he tries to work in the library, everyone glares at him, and many students knock his books out of his hands. That stops quickly when Ms. Joy puts an end to it. Only Wendy tries to speak to him, but she gets pulled away by her friends.

"Don't stay near to him, Wendy." One of the Oranges, another student from Availa, pulls her away. "Didn't you hear what he did to Emelie?"

"But Nick wouldn't —" Nick can't hear the rest of Wendy's words as the girls leave the library.

Later on, Laura comes running into the library to sit by him. "I've heard some awful things about you," she states, shaking her head.

Nick closes his notebook and sighs. "I didn't push her."

She waves her hands dismissively. "I know that. I'm saying that there are other things they say about you. Many, I was able to quiet down. Others, I refuse to repeat. I think that you should keep your guard up," Laura warns him quietly.

Emelie sits in her room alone, recounting the events of what Nick did to her and how he threw insult after insult. She grins as she looks at her reflection. It will only be a matter of time before the little Yellow will give in. She knows that Nick is an intelligent boy, even smarter than some of the Purples here, so she needs him to get good grades. She had to be the best in the Shadow Training and the regular classes for finals. She sighs. Really, she could have chosen anyone, but seeing him defend her half-sister made her want *him*. Why should her sister have the best tool in the school? Braawen always said that he used Nick's intelligence in the rebellion to make himself look like a genius. She just wants to use him too.

She grins when she remembers how people came to her aid with just her words against his. She remembers the attention she received, the girls and boys who stood in front of her and fought to keep her out of harm's reach.

She chuckles. *I already have enough power that a single word can change the truth. If I say that I'm not the daughter of the last King, who will deny me?*

She doesn't feel threatened by Rohana knowing the truth, because even if her dear sister tells someone, no one will believe her. There's no evidence; Rohana already told the guards that Emelie is her father's daughter. The man certainly acted like she was, so to her, it isn't truly lying. There's no way that she will ever admit to it. All she needs is to continue getting in her teachers' good graces, making friends with students whose parents have high positions in court, and making it into Black. Maybe the Emperor would be so impressed that he'd make her his successor.

She can only dream, but right now, she has to make sure that if she can't get a grip on Nick, then no one can.

"Best get rid of the tool before it strikes you," she says and hums to herself.

Over the next week, Nick has to run from five potential fights, three attempts at food poisoning that stopped when the General got involved, and three of his notebooks being burnt to a crisp. Because of the increasing attacks, at least one of his friends stayed by his side.

Kaius offered to give his friend mini smoke bombs, and Nick quickly told Kaius no. Firstly, they didn't have the materials, though Kaius did point out he could 'borrow' materials from the scraps in metal class. Secondly, the teachers would definitely think it's a treasonous plot, and Nick does not want any of his friends dying. So, Lorcan, Takara, and Rohana advised him to carry hidden weapons. He denied those as well.

So, instead of using bombs or hidden weapons that can get him into more trouble, Nick denies every rumour that he knows Emelie is spreading, and that Braawen is encouraging.

Volodimir says nothing on the matter, and a small part of Nick is upset by it. However, the other half is grateful for his teacher's silence.

On the fifth day, three students in Purple ambush Takara and him with snowballs during their jog in the forest. One snowball has a rock in it, and hits Takara in the head. She has to be brought to the nurse's office, when the bleeding on her head continues. The attacks are now spreading to those who defended him, and Nick is furious.

After Takara tells him that he can leave her with the nurse, Bhaltair goes with Nick to the library to study. Both are looked at with scorn when they enter the library.

Nick looks over and sees that even though Bhaltair is shaking, he stays next to his friend.

"Thank you," Nick whispers to Bhaltair.

The boy smiles. "You would do it for me, and don't worry, Lorcan said he's coming later. He will definitely scare people away."

Both boys huddle in a corner of the library near the windows, studying for an upcoming math quiz. Bhaltair leaves for a short time to get them snacks. However, in that short time, Nick hears multiple footsteps approaching. He sighs and looks up to see the whole Purple class standing in front of him, glares on all of their faces. He puts down his quill and picks up his books, getting ready to leave, but Brutus, a Purple student, roughly pushes him back into his seat. His back slams against the chair, causing his scars to flare up in pain.

"You hurt one of us, you mess with all of us," the larger boy growls.

Nick grimaces as he sees students gathering around them.

Ms. Joy stands up as she sees the students gathering in an area that she told Nick to sit in, but stops when a strong hand pulls her down.

"For the last time..." Nick sounds tired, "I didn't hit, push, curse, slap, or scream at her."

The rumours were getting out of control, he thinks to himself.

"It's not just about me, Nick." Emelie smiles. "There were other things brought to light that concern all of us students."

The rest of the Purples nod in agreement. He looks to see Braawen smiling at his humiliation, arms crossed.

Nick gets up slowly from his seat and keeps his face neutral. "May I know what the other rumours are?"

"Don't play innocent," one of the Blue students sneers. The girl looks like a noble with her soft brown hair and jewels adorning her neck. She glares at him, even though he's never spoken to her before. "You must have heard of the big three?"

Nick shakes his head.

"Nick." This time it's Braawen who speaks up. "Maybe you should stop using artificial means to improve yourself. It's unfair to the rest of the students like us who train and study hard." The other students nod in unison at his cousin's words.

Nick swallows down a growl. "Unless you mean the health vials that we all take, then no, I don't take any artificial drugs or artificial means, whatever the hell those are. I train hard and study hard, just like all of you. I look healthier from eating well. Since I've arrived here, Equinox House has allowed me to get the nutrients needed to grow, something that the rebellion sorely lacked. I have no problem doing a drug test since you're all *so* concerned about me," Nick spits out sarcastically.

Though a part of him is dying from praising this school, he knows he has to. Showing that he's a grateful student may just save him, or at least make him look good. As he looks around, he sees that some of the students look unsure, while others seem almost pleased that a war child finally accepted how gracious they and Equinox House were for allowing him in their presence. Nick wants to hurl.

"Then, why do you go into the forest at night? Is that where you eat strange things, and curse students and teachers?" another girl asks, appearing more curious than horrified as she adjusts her glasses.

Nicks sighs inwardly. He wants to know where the little Blue girl heard this. He'd never done anything to curse anyone. Maybe his father and the Night Emperor in his head, but never an actual spell. One, it's ridiculous; two, it's messy; three, he's already dealing with enough magic as is.

Nick puts on a neutral expression, composing himself. "I go there to relax and meditate. You can ask Lorcan or even Braawen. He knows that I spent most of my time in the forest gathering food. Food that helped him survive." He glares at his cousin, who has the decency to blush. "Also, have any of you ever taken a walk in the forest? It's lovely. It relaxes me and helps me clear my mind. Haven't you also seen me going on walks or jogs in the forest with Takara? I know a few of you have," he narrows his eyes to the three Purple students who attacked him and Takara in the morning. They don't look regretful at all.

Some nod at the memory of seeing him and Takara run, and one even says that she saw him walking in the forest and he pointed out that the mushroom she was about to pick was poisonous.

Emelie glares. "Then what about you cheating in class?" she yells. "You cheated in your fight with Braawen! Not only that, how is it that someone with no prior education can get such high marks?"

The rest of the students seem to ponder this as Nick's anger reaches a boiling point. He can see the looks she and Braawen are giving him. They want him to react, to attack. He wouldn't give them that satisfaction.

"I study." Nick's voice is low, yet it reverberates through the library as people quiet down. "I come here almost every night to study." He can see that a few students give a small nod. "I ask for help from fellow students." He glances at Brandon, who has the decency to look bashful. "I asked Brandon for help, and he helped me. I grew faster because of the other students here, who took the time to give me good advice. So, I do help students who ask me. I don't just do their homework for them."

The glare she gives reminds him so much of Rohana.

Nevertheless, he continues. "I will admit that I love my books and studying, but the teachers here also deserve the credit. Equinox House has the best teachers and greatest minds here. They were able to push a child with no prior education to receive some of the highest marks. Not only that, the resources at Equinox House allowed me to succeed. So, no, I cannot say that it was just me, when the students and the teachers here have helped me grow."

Some students actually brighten up at that statement, knowing that someone depended on them. Even Brandon seems proud to hear that he was able to help one of the smartest students.

"You still cheated in our fight," Braawen adds.

"I lost that fight."

Braawen scoffs. "I didn't say you were good at it."

Nick really tries not to roll his eyes. "I didn't cheat when fighting with you. You've improved, and so have I. You, of all people, should be amazed at what the teachers can do. I was a skeleton when I came here and look at me now." He gestures to himself. "I have the muscle to hold my bones." He stares at Braawen, blue eyes to blue eyes, not looking away. "You're not the only one improving here. I believe that everyone here improves."

He then stares at Emelie. "And, Emelie, I remember getting a warning from the teachers that cheating isn't allowed and all the teachers here can sense when a person is cheating. Neither the General nor Professor Arran said that I cheated. Neither have any of the other teachers. I work hard here. I will say this only once—I did not attack Emelie, and I deny all of these rumours, *especially* cheating. Now stop hurting me and my friends who are only defending me."

"Then you're lying," Emelie snaps.

This time Nick rolls his eyes as he turns his back to her, his face colliding with a muscular chest. He moves back, hearing the gasps of other students. As his eyes travel up the black stole and robes, he sees red eyes.

"Where did you come from?" Nick asks, forgetting that they weren't in the cabin.

Volodimir gives him a frown and a swift slap on the head.

"My apologies, Black Teacher." Nick bows.

Every student gasps. Many haven't even seen the Black Teacher in person, except for a short class visit. Everyone stood in anticipation, waiting for the teacher to speak. Yet, instead of addressing all the students, he turns his attention to only one.

"Ms. Snowfield says that you've been cheating, Mr. Westmore. Do you deny it?" Volodimir asks, straight to the point.

"Yes sir. I've never cheated," Nick answers with every fibre of his being.

Volodimir nods. "Mr. Westmore tells the truth. Not only that, I have been monitoring the Yellow class from the shadows and have seen the growth in each of you. In fact, I would be surprised and very disappointed if you all didn't go up at least two levels."

The rest of the students gasp while Nicks gulps as Volodimir turns his red eyes to the students behind him.

"So, Ms. Snowfield and Mr. Archer, are you saying that we, the teachers of Equinox House, who have years of experience in the shadows, and have been hand-picked through a rigorous process, are incompetent at our duties to not notice a single Yellow student cheating?" Volodimir asks quietly.

The silence is deafening as both students pale and the other Purples distance themselves from them.

Emelie begins to stammer. "N-no, Black Teacher... w-we would never—"

Volodimir puts his hand up, stopping her from talking. "Ms. Snowfield and Mr. Archer, you not only insult me but the General and your very own teacher, Professor Arran, who also presided over the match." He glares at both of them and the two remain silent, almost as though they are forced to do so.

"Ms. Joy," Volodimir calls.

The librarian appears out of the desk's shadow and gives him a graceful bow. "Yes, Black Teacher."

"Has Mr. Westmore been studying and helping students here regularly?" Volodimir asks.

"Yes, Black Teacher." She nods and gives a soft smile towards Nick.

"And what about Ms. Snowfield? Did he push her?"

Ms. Joy shakes her head. "No, Black Teacher. From what I remember, Ms. Snowfield asked Westmore to write a paper for her, but he denied her request. She grabbed him, and he pulled his arm out of her grip. The force of the pull would have pulled her forwards, not back. I believe that Snowfield must have 'tripped' by accident. She is such a highly regarded student; I wouldn't dare believe that she could do something so vile on purpose and demand for a student to do her paper."

Emelie flusters at the librarian's sarcastic comment.

There are more whispers, but before Emelie can say anything, Volodimir puts up his hand up. "This has lasted far too long. I want this whole situation to end. If I hear one more thing on this matter, everyone in the room will receive a Black punishment."

The silence is palpable; a dropped quill could be heard from the second floor as everyone pales. Nick doesn't know what a Black punishment is, but he knows Volodimir.

"You all may go and focus on your own progress." With that, Volodimir slips into the desk's shadow and disappears.

"Well," Ms. Joy yells for the first time. "The situation has been dealt with. You heard the Black Teacher, return to your own work. Now, go."

As everyone disperses, Nick can see both Braawen and Emelie glare at him.

Great, now I have to deal with them.

He thanks Ms. Joy and leaves with Bhaltair's books from the library, with his head held high. As he walks, Lorcan suddenly appears by his side, ruffling his hair.

Nick looks over at Lorcan and sees the huge smile on his face. "Where were you?"

Lorcan ignores his questions and puts him in a headlock, ruffling his hair some more. "You held yourself up well, and even got Braawen and Emelie in trouble. Now, all you need to do is ace your test and call it a day!"

Nick gives Lorcan a playful push. "I just didn't give in to their drama."

But then Lorcan looks at him seriously. "I have a question, though. I saw the Black Teacher from afar, and I've never seen red eyes."

Nick's head snaps to him, confused by what Lorcan said until he repeats the sentence in his head. "You can see them too?"

Lorcan nods. He looks around, quickly pulling him into a windowed corner. "I remember everyone saying that the man has dark or black eyes. Even Rohana says that his eyes are dark, but to me, they're not and I know that my eyes are still working."

Nick always found that strange, he'd never seen red eyes before. *Shadows, why does Volodimir have red eyes?* he asks them.

Why are your eyes blue and Lorcan's eyes are amber? Family, boy, they reply, and they say nothing else.

Nick nods. "I think it would be best to keep this quiet for now," he whispers to Lorcan.

"But Nick... isn't it strange that we see red eyes and everyone else sees black? I mean, in my family, we say that we are blessed by the deities to see things, the truth in people that no one else can see. At first, I thought that it was a myth, but..." He shakes his head and signs. "My father had the gift. He always told me that he didn't like Braawen, that he was using me. I told him that he was lying and just didn't like him because he didn't like Markus."

Lorcan leans on the window and lets out a slow breath, continuing, "I remember him saying that I was blinded by my own sight, that I wouldn't let the truth be revealed. He told me that once I was ready to see and accept the truth in people, I would be able to see everything more clearly."

"That sounds like an amazing ability. Definitely one you didn't have at the time," Nick says, and stops as he sees Lorcan glare at him. "I mean, you were friends with him and hated me."

"In my defence, I didn't know you very well and you were gone a lot. Where did you go, Nick?"

Nick recalls all his missions to collect information for the rebellion. He starved for them, hid for days on end, learned town and enemy layouts in days to sneak into their territories. He remembers the nights of him trapped and alone. Those nights, he was desperate enough to pray to the god of Shadows to cover him in the night. No one knew what he did. No one knew that their surprise attacks were successful because he gave them the Imperial army base's layout and plans.

No one would ever know the story of how he warned his father about the Shadow Assassin, and how his father thought he knew better and got his best soldiers killed. Because of that incident, his father whipped him to the point that he couldn't stand, and he had to stay with the women and children.

Nick pulls himself out of his memories and looks at Lorcan, who waits for an answer. Nick swallows, but it does nothing for his dry throat. The scars on his back claw against the fabric of his clothes. "I was gathering intelligence," he states simply. "It doesn't matter. I just hope that you can see the truth in people now?"

Lorcan nods. "After Braawen left me, let's just say that my eyes opened after that."

Nick nods. "Well, we do have our meeting tomorrow. I hope you're ready to hand in your assignment?" He smirks as his friend groans.

They both go their separate ways. As Nick leaves, Lorcan looks back and his eyes glow as he sees a sad and deeply scarred child. He wonders how many scars his friend received without telling anyone. No one was as skinny as Nick in the rebellion; Lorcan thought the boy was just sick at the time. No one was as quiet as him. No one flinched whenever Markus entered a room except Nick. Lorcan already knew that Markus and Nick didn't have a good relationship, from what Braawen told him. However, he can now see why he didn't cry for his father's death.

When he helped change Nick's clothes back at the Black cottage, he and the other boys swore not to say anything. The horrible thing was, Lorcan knew that the old scars on his back were only the surface of the hurt and pain that the rebellion, war, and his father caused. Dare Lorcan say, that even he caused.

As Nick walks away, Lorcan wishes that Markus Archer had received a harsher punishment.

Chapter 43
Whisper

Braawen stands alone in his room. He breathes heavily and winces as he removes the cap from the healing vial he clutches in his hand. Downing it in one gulp, he feels the effects quickly, but it's not enough. He has to use lemon balm, a healing vial mixed with lemon-scented lotion.

He wonders how Emelie is doing—the poor girl almost didn't make it to her room. Well, he did warn her to leave Nick alone.

Braawen has never seen Professor Arran so angry. He remembers him yelling at him and Emelie, saying how badly they had embarrassed the Purple circle. The beatings Braawen received tonight were the worst he's ever gotten. Not even Markus beat him that badly.

His breath hitches as he places a hand on his ribs, and he thinks one must be broken. However, he was warned by the other students never to go to the nurse. One student did and the Professor found out. They never told him what happened to that student, but he can only guess with the beating he got tonight. So, he'll deal with it. He can use this pain to make himself stronger.

He stumbles to the bathroom and turns on the light. He looks to see his lips are purple from the bruise but no longer cut. The Professor usually doesn't aim for faces, but he must have been blinded by rage.

Braawen picks up a small tin from his counter, which holds the lemon balm. It was the first thing he and Emelie received when he entered the Purple circle. He was warned not to use too much, and it was to be used only on facial injuries. He puts a small amount of the balm on his fingertips and gently pats it onto his lips and cheeks, smiling when the bruises begin to fade. He also doesn't mind the lemon scent, but it always lingers for days.

Braawen sighs at his reflection. Maybe he can take tomorrow off. The Professor might allow that. He remembers one of the older Purples, Astor, the student who the Professor once put all his focus on becoming a Black. Well... that was until Braawen showed up. Astor didn't leave his room for three days after a fight. Astor used all his vials and lemon balm too quickly and had to heal on his own. On the fourth day, the boy left the school and never came back.

"I'm not weak like him," Braawen spits at his reflection. His blue eyes look back at him. For a second, he doesn't even recognize himself. *Dad would never let this happen.* He flinches and quickly turns his head from his reflection. He bites his lip, making it bleed again. He doesn't care.

He takes deep breaths, trying to stop the tears. "Don't think like that," he tells himself, his voice cracking. "Don't go down that road. Focus on the present." He slowly looks back at his reflection. He sees his eyes, red-rimmed and wet. "Become a Black, mourn later. Make this pain your power," he whispers over and over again.

Maybe one day, he'll believe it.

Late at night, when most of the school is asleep, one teacher is still up. Arran locks his office and draws his curtains closed, not letting even the moon or stars see his secrets. The only light source is a candle on his desk. He walks across his office, decorated in purple and black, running his hand along some of the awards and trophies mounted on the wall to commemorate his achievements. Yet, as soon as he got into Equinox House, he knew he could be so much more than these old things. He knows he could be the Black Teacher if the Night Emperor would only allow it.

Maybe if I produce a Black, I could become head of this school?

He shakes his head and strides over to the other side of his office, where a built-in cabinet is hidden from sight. He pulls out an expensive bottle of wine from the very back of the cabinet, next to a grey vial holding clear liquid. The clear liquid helped get rid of Alesander. He hopes the wine gets rid of the headache. The wine was supposed to be opened when he became the Black Teacher, but he sees that reality happening less and less.

He brings a knife from his shadow and pricks his finger. Once the blade fades back into the shadows, he presses his bloody finger to the end of the cabinet. There a red mark appears with the symbol of his family. His blood opens a hidden door inside the cabinet. A small door that only reveals a small compartment with a book. He takes out the book and closes the hidden door. He makes his way over to his desk and lights another candle, causing the furniture's shadows to dance around the room.

Arran did not have a good day. Braawen and Emelie, his two prime students, got into trouble because of a Yellow. A useless Yellow! When he heard what had happened, he tried to speak with Volodimir, but the man was too busy to talk to him. By the deities, he hates that man. He will have to deal with those two. They have to focus on their own growth instead of trying to get a useless Yellow in trouble. If they don't prioritize themselves, no one will take them seriously.

He shakes his head and puts that problem behind him for now. He opens the book and passes the pages with everyone's secrets that he uses against them. Oh yes, his little black book holds their shame… and his own. He looks at his journal and reads the progress of his powers—or lack of progress. He turns to the beginning of the book and sees that when he entered Purple, he could control and summon an entire pack of shadow wolves. Now, when he turns to the latest page, he sees that he can only summon three at a time.

Arran opens the bottle with his teeth, not caring about the pain. With a pop, he gulps the whole thing down. He slams the bottle on the desk, narrowing his eyes.

Shadows? he calls to them. He remembers when they sounded so clear; now they are so quiet. *Shadows? Have you forsaken me? Did you not promise that you would not take away our gifts? Please, speak to me.*

After emptying another bottle of wine, Arran feels dizzy and sick. "Ohhhh..." he moans. "I'm not so young anymore." He knows he'll feel even worse in the morning.

You don't listen clearly, a voice speaks.

Even when Arran is clearly drunk, he immediately recognizes the voice. *Shadows?* he calls to them with a small smile.

Do not fear, the voice responds. *The shadows do not take away gifts. The god of Shadows made an oath that once a gift is given, it can never be taken away. We will speak to you.*

Arran smiles, happy that he isn't as useless as his students.

But you refuse to listen.

Arran's smile fades as he abruptly stands up. He has to brace himself as he grips the desks. *I listen,* he almost hisses, but he stops when he hears the shadows laugh.

You hear what you want to hear. You do not listen to us. The voice gets quieter. *You're stubborn, and you aren't...* The voice disappears completely, much to Arran's relief.

Arran sits down slowly and places his head on his ears. "I'm not stubborn. I listen to the shadows. I love the shadows!" he cries to no one.

No one answers at first, not even the shadows.

After a moment, the shadows whisper, *You stunt your own growth and the growth of others. If you do not listen, you will never access your full powers.*

By then, it's too late. Arran passes out, dreaming about the day one of his students will become the newest Black. If his students fail, then he will succeed.

Chapter 44
Soldier

As the night ends, a new day dawns and Nick returns to reality as his dreams leave him. He had another nightmare about his father, but this time, it was strange. A woman with black hair and lilac eyes shielded him from his father's wrath. Nick has never met the woman before, but the dream ended with both of them in a garden. He laid on her lap as she sang to him, calming his mind. The last thing he remembers is her whispers through the leaves. 'Be the light in the night, don't give up.' The dream gives him a renewed sense of hope.

The day's lessons go smoothly, and he and the General have a lovely spar that actually gets them both sweating at the end.

"You've done well, Guts," the General acknowledges. Nick nods, overjoyed to hear that he's improved. "Maybe you'll be able to beat me when I'm too old to walk."

After morning lessons, he goes to his art lessons. He's not very good at art, but he likes to watch Lorcan paint. He never knew Lorcan could paint, and Lorcan admits that he didn't know he could either.

"Stop watching me. It's weird," Lorcan whispers.

Nick only moves his seat closer to him. "But your painting is turning out lovely so far. Is that a hawk?"

Lorcan doesn't answer, he just continues to paint the hawk flying free in the air above the Plains. Nick knows that one day, that'll be Lorcan.

The rest of the day goes by quickly and at the end of his night lesson, Volodimir is impressed with his progress. Before he leaves, Volodimir warns him to not hold back. He hasn't been holding back, but shrugs as he leaves. Nick quietly Shadow Jumps into his room after his lesson.

As he puts away his uniform, he hears a slight rustling behind the curtains of his bed. He pulls the curtains back, using Night Vision to see the moving forms of Takara and Rohana moving restlessly in their own beds. He carefully sneaks over to Takara, who's closer, and gently taps her on the shoulder.

"Takara," he whispers. Though, he believes she probably can't hear with her bed creaking under her and Bhaltair's snores. He taps again, a little harder, which startles her.

The two stare at each other until Nick remembers why he disturbed her. "Takara, are you alright?"

The girl just nods. "Yeah, yeah." She doesn't sound convincing as he hears a slight moan of pain in her voice.

However, before she can say anything else, Rohana jumps from her bed, quietly running towards the door. The slamming door makes a sound that rivals Bhaltair's snores. Nick and Takara look to the empty bed and back at the door in shock at how fast Rohana moved. Yet, before they could even go after her, Takara looks under her covers and jumps out.

Nick is left alone in the room until he looks at Takara's mattress. His eyes widen at the sight.

Rushing water echoes between the halls of the cellar, along with Rohana's colourful cursing. "Why the hell did it come early?" Rohana cusses. She lets the water run as she hears the quiet chuckles of her next-door shower mate. "Shut it, Takara!" she snaps.

Takara continues to chuckle through the pain, holding her own stomach. "Well, at least I can go through this hell with someone."

"Damn it!" Rohana kicks the edge of the shower wall. Her first few days are always painful. "We have our weapons test in the morning." She huffs in frustration. *How the hell can I shoot a bow when my whole core is trying to separate itself from me?*

Takara falls silent at the reminder of tomorrow's activity. "I guess we'll just have to soldier through. We did it last month, and it's never stopped us before." Takara's voice seems to waver.

"Really wish we had separate rooms now," Rohana grumbles, and Takara nods in agreement.

They stay silent as they both have different, yet similar dilemmas. As the two succumb to their fate, they enjoy the warm showers for as long as they last, before having to crawl out again. They feel the cold embrace of the cellar, and Rohana hesitates to leap back in. However, Takara hands her a towel. They dry themselves without uttering a word, knowing that this would be an awkward conversation for Nick.

However, when the two girls enter their room, they are surprised to see an empty room, with Nick and Bhaltair nowhere to be seen. Takara heads to her bed, but stops suddenly as she sees that both her and Rohana's beds have been neatly remade with fresh linens. Before they could wonder where the two boys went, the door opens and Nick and Bhaltair walk in with full arms.

Takara blinks away tears as she sees what's in their hands. Bhaltair looks dishevelled, yet still proper in his nightwear as he carries a small tray laden with muffins and cookies. Beside him, Nick carries a few handfuls of colourful vials.

"I got some sweets from the kitchen," Bhaltair says with a grin. "Devour them. We can't have the General knowing that I got these." There's a hint of fear in his voice. Takara smiles as Rohana happily grabs a handful of different muffins and cookies and gives half to her.

"These, I got from the infirmary. Don't ask how I got them. Take this to help with pain." Nick points to one. "The purple for dizziness, and the orange... Well, the orange is for blood loss." He gives them a sheepish smile.

Rohana laughs. "Nick, that's not how the trial works. We won't need the orange, but thank you for the other vials." She laughs, wiping a tear from her eye as Nick's cheeks burn crimson.

"I love you guys," Takara declares as she runs over and hugs both boys, kissing them on the cheek.

They wake up to an angry General, suspiciously asking why he could smell sweets in the air. The boys prepare all sorts of excuses, but Rohana just rolls her eyes.

"Sir, Takara and I are going through our trial of womanhood," she states so bluntly that Takara blushes a new shade of crimson. Even Nick and Bhaltair's eyes widen in surprise. The only one who doesn't seem fazed is the General. The two girls wait for their punishment.

"Alright then, ladies," he finally sighs after a few moments of silence. "Good luck during your trial. Since you won't be at your peak performance, we can reschedule your test to a later date."

The two girls look shocked. Her mother always told Takara that the trial was natural and doesn't excuse her from working in the field. Rohana only had a father, but all the older ladies she grew up with told her that it was a wonderful period of blooming. Both girls found out that it was all bull.

"Oh...uhm...thank you, but I would rather do it today," Takara stammers.

"So will I. I just need the red vials. I did the test last month. I can do it again," Rohana smiles.

"But sir, can we still have treats? It does help with the cramps," Takara begs sheepishly.

The General nods. "Alright, everyone will do their test. As for the treats, maybe. However, I guess it's time to educate you on your changing bodies," he grins.

All of them gasp.

"Please, no," Nick whispers.

"What? You all should have gotten this education years ago. It's a natural course that everyone goes through. Miss Leia, I believe already talked to her class about it. So, I'll ask her to help the girls if you have any questions or need anything during this time. Boys, you'll be with me right after feasting time."

The two girls nod their heads in relief. While the boys look at each other, wondering what the General would teach them.

Nick stands beside Malcolm in the training room, spear in hand, waiting for his test to start after Bhaltair finishes his. He turns his attention from Bhaltair's fight with the General, and watches Takara and Rohana go through their drills, warming up for their tests. He sees that each weapon assistant is attentive to them. Although there are times when the two girls would take a short break, they aren't letting what would naturally happen to them each month stop them. His attention is brought back to the rest of the group when the doors to the training room slam open.

Everyone stops moving when they see the Purple class enter, surrounded by their cloud of arrogance and a scent of lemons. Nick sees Malcolm stiffen in his peripheral vision when Braawen strides in. His cousin looks even more arrogant and proud with Emelie, the cold-hearted shrew, beside him. He guesses that a little embarrassment wouldn't keep them down for long.

"What are you lot doing here?" the General bellows from the raised platform. "We are having a private class! Arran, what is the meaning of this?" He glares at the professor, who smiles in response, smoothing out the non-existent wrinkles on his fine robes.

"I heard that you were doing a weapons test, and my student Braawen said that he wanted to be of assistance. He wishes to spar with Nickolaus to see if he's improved." Professor Arran points to Braawen.

The General glares as he walks off the raised platform. "This is my class, Arran." He turns to Braawen, his eyes narrowed, but then slowly smiles. "But since the Purple class is meant to help those of a lower circle, I shall allow it."

Braawen looks at Nick and smiles.

"This is a weapon test. No shadows allowed," the General states as Braawen passes him, his class cheering him on from behind.

Bhaltair walks off the raised platform and walks over to Nick. "Nick, you've got to win this," he pleads.

Nick nods his head as Malcolm turns to him. "Westmore, you treat him like an enemy soldier or spy. He's not your family," he whispers to Nick, shaking his shoulders and giving him a smile. "Now, go teach this man the might of the spear!" Malcolm yells.

Malcolm's energy seems to resonate with the rest of the weapon assistants and Yellow students as they jump and yell in excitement. Their encouragement gives Nick a new sense of courage and strength as he enters the ring.

When Braawen asks for a sword, the General hands him a practice one.

"This is good practice, boys. I'm sure you know that you will fight against different soldiers with different weapons on the battlefield." He looks at the two young men in front of him and can see the tension between them. *There's history between these two*, he thinks to himself, knowing that it has more behind it than the first fight. "Same rules as last time; knocked down three times or thrown out the ring." The General looks at the two boys, who both nod in response.

Braawen thinks that he's the only one that was on the battlefield, Nick positions himself into a defensive stance.

See him as a soldier. Malcolm's voice floats into his thoughts.

Use your heart less. Laura's advice overlaps Malcolm's.

The General screams for them to go and jumps off the platform as the boys immediately clash their weapons together. Nick puts most of his weight on his legs, not even registering the sudden force as Braawen's sword comes to his chest, almost stabbing him. Nick deflects the blade with his spear, then kicks Braawen in the stomach, which causes the other boy to stumble as Nick moves further away from him, giving himself some space.

Both boys crouch in defensive stances, circling each other, not even registering the cheers of their classmates. The only ones not cheering were the General and the Professor.

"Why are you doing this?" the General asks, though his voice could only be heard by the man beside him.

Arran huffs in response, which almost sounds like a laugh. "My class is just here to help a fellow Yellow."

Though he will never admit it, his class needs something to lighten their moods. The Black Teacher left a sour taste in each of their mouths, and the last thing he needs is his students second-guessing his teaching methods. Seeing a Purple defeat a Yellow will lighten their mood considerably. He remembers the first time Braawen beat the boy, and how happy it made the Purple class.

As the fight continues, he can see that the wretched boy is trying hard against his star pupil. He can even see a touch of fear in the Yellow boy's eyes.

"Ah, yes. It seems that Braawen will teach your pupil another lesson," Arran says with a malicious grin.

However, his smile quickly falls off his face when he hears the General chuckle. "I don't know. I think your pupil is about to learn a hard lesson."

Arran stares at the man as though he's gone mad until he suddenly hears a slap that echoes across the room, silencing the audience. Arran holds in a gasp as he sees Braawen stumble back from the smaller boy, a shocked expression on his face. Braawen's eyes are round underneath a reddening cheek and cut lip.

Everyone slowly turns to the boy who slapped Braawen with the blunt end of his spear, his piercing gaze fixed on Braawen.

As the teachers spoke, fear seeped into Nick's mind as each knock of Braawen's blade pushed him a little farther back. He feared letting everyone down again until he heard a familiar voice.

Breathe, you can do this, the shadows encouraged.

"You can give up," his cousin whispered. Nick heard it over the cheers and the sounds of their weapons clashing. "Pity that your uncle had to teach someone like you. I'm shocked that he didn't get killed for being a coward." Braawen saw the confusion in Nick's eyes. "Running away from battle after his sister died? Guess his sister couldn't protect him anymore." Braawen grinned ferally.

His cousin didn't know that Malcolm had been thrown out by Nick's father. Not only that, the Mountain Clans did not like being called cowards, nor would any mountain warrior allow someone to shame them. Braawen needed a reminder that Nick was from the mountains too.

The first thing Braawen heard from the hit was the sound of disbelief and silence. Then he felt the warmth of his blood on his lip, but it did not come close to the fire that clawed at his cheek. He stumbled, which caused a slight pain in his knee. He touched his lips to see blood on his fingers, and raised his eyes to see the sharp glare of Markus... no, Nick. Braawen almost faltered at the similarity between father and son.

He blinked again and saw Nick, just little Nicky, who finally decided to have a backbone.

Braawen's eyes narrowed, and the grip around his sword tightened. *Time to break his damn spine.*

Everyone is stunned into silence when Nick struck Braawen. The silence breaks with Malcolm's roar, and the Yellow's cheering follows soon after. The General just smiles and claps with Professor Arran gasping.

Nick steadies his heart as Braawen swings at him. He bends his knees to lower his centre of gravity, steadying himself for his attacks. Braawen's swings are fast and long, but Nick remains on the defence and blocks when he can. He notices that Braawen leaves very few openings, which isn't surprising from a boy who fought in the war at age ten. However, Nick notices that Braawen hesitates whenever he moves his left knee.

The arrow. He remembers Braawen's old wound. He doesn't want to injure his cousin too badly; he doesn't want to use his weakness against him. But he glances at his friends and Malcolm cheering him on, believing in him. He can't lose. No, he won't lose. He is tired of losing, kneeling, bending to Braawen's will.

Nick blocks an incoming strike attack with his spear tip. He holds his spear out from his body, knocking the sword towards the ground. He quickly attacks, fiercely striking Braawen's left knee. He can hear Braawen grunt in pain dropping to one knee. Not leaving any room for him to breathe, Nick spins his body while gripping his spear, kicking Braawen across the face.

The whole room goes quiet as Braawen falls off the platform and lands on the ground. The silence is deafening. Braawen forgets how to breathe, unable to believe that he lost.

The silence is broken as Nick jumps off the platform. His feet land on the hardwood floor, echoing around the room like thunder. He looks at his cousin, surprised at the lack of guilt he feels using his weakness against him. His body moves and he offers a hand to his fallen enemy. Braawen looks skeptical but takes his hand. The Purples clap slowly as the Yellows cheer wildly.

"As you can see, I've learned," Nick states and Braawen glares at him venomously.

The General walks over and stands in between the two boys. "Archer," the man states, and Nick almost answers. "You did well. I can see why you survived that long on the battlefield. However, you need medical attention for your knee."

That's when Nick notices that Braawen winces when he puts pressure on his knee. *Maybe I hit too hard*, he thinks.

Emelie and another girl help his cousin hobble away while Professor Arran glares at Nick. "Shouldn't the boy be punished for going so hard on Braawen?" he sneers at the General.

His teacher just grins and grabs Arran's shoulder firmly, his fingers digging into his shoulder. "After the way your boy put my boy in the infirmary the last time? I don't think so." General Herald shakes his head. "Plus, is this not the way you teach your students?" He smiles as the angry professor leaves with his class.

Nick's friends continue to cheer him on until he gets a proud slap on the back from Malcolm. They slap his scars, but Nick is too happy to care.

"You did well, student."

Nick smiles. "You taught me well."

Later that night, he gets a letter from Volodimir, inviting him to the cottage that evening. It isn't their night to practice Shadow magic, but honestly, he's always happy to see Volodimir. He slips out after everyone else goes to bed, knocks on the cottage door, and is surprised to see the table laden with teas and cakes when the door opens.

Sitting in front of the fire in his usual spot, Volodimir sips a cup of tea. He raises his teacup and smiles at Nick. "Good kick."

Chapter 45
Shadow Lands

The next day turns into night; and though most students are asleep, a few are still in their lessons. Braawen and Emelie are in a class all on their own, learning about the country that they believe that they will rule together. Braawen sits at a desk, no longer wincing in pain from his cousin's attack from yesterday. He won't forget it, nor would he forgive Nick for using such a wicked trick.

I never exploited his weaknesses, Braawen sneers inwardly. In his mind, Nick is full of weaknesses. His whole body is a weakness. However, Braawen sees himself as patient and will watch for a chance to strike his cousin where it hurts the most.

If Braawen can't take care of Nick in school, he will take care of him when he rules. He has already imagined the entire scenario for his life after graduating. He will get into Black and be trained personally by the Night Emperor. If he impresses the Emperor enough, the man may even adopt him as a son. Braawen will take Emelie as his Empress and they will rule the Empire together.

As he progresses further in Purple, he can see his goal becoming a reality. Professor Arran has already told him that he and Emelie are improving faster than anyone he has ever seen. Braawen sits patiently at his desk beside his future empress as Professor Arran goes over the history of the current Emperor.

Professor Arran chose this time of night because no one else is really awake. This is a time solely for him and his best students. He can't trust the other teachers to teach them well. They need his personal guidance and skills to unlock their true potential.

"Now, let's talk about something different. This was talked about earlier in the year for students of your age group, but I have no problem speaking about it again." Arran turns to the board and writes 'Shadow Lands' on it with a piece of chalk.

Emelie perks up at the words while Braawen looks on, intrigued. He is interested in the Shadow Lands, but disappointed that they aren't going over the Shadow Weapons. Braawen has only handled weapons one to six. The next level, number seven, is proving to be difficult as it feels like the greedy knife wants all his energy.

"The Shadow Lands are a world different from our own, a world where the shadows take their own forms and where creatures long forgotten exist. We, unlike the other circles, can summon a Shadow Creature." To prove his point, with the drop of his cane, a beast morphs from Professor Arran's shadow and leaps on one of the empty desks, startling the two students.

Braawen is speechless as he sees the dark black fur and looks into the blood-red eyes of the beast.

"A shadow wolf," his teacher states. "Come here," he commands and the beast walks over and sits beside him. "Know this: Shadow Creatures can be summoned by a Purple, but only a true and powerful Purple can tame them. The wolves have seen me as their leader, so I can control their moves and they follow my every command." He pets the wolf, who seems to revel in the attention, more like a giant puppy than a terrifying beast.

"Can we summon a Shadow Creature?" Emelie asks. Her mind flashes to the first person she wants to attack.

"Not yet. One must first speak to the shadows in order to summon or even control a Shadow Beast." Arran sighs. "The only disappointment that I've heard from the Emperor is that none of you can hear them. We will have to work more on that."

"But, professor." Braawen grumbles, "we've been working on it. Nothing is working!"

His teacher narrows his eyes. "Remember, boy, you must remain calm. I would hate for one of the guards to have to hold you down again." Braawen looks to the ground in frustration as his teacher continues speaking. "You are the last relative of the rebel leaders. The Emperor and the Council have their eye on you. They hope you can make it into the Black circle. I have no doubt that you will, but..." He lets the words hang in the air and smiles. "If you fail getting into the Black, well... you may still be able to achieve a high position. Not the highest, especially with your family history. However, second best will have to do for you... if you're lucky."

"I don't want to be second best," Braawen mumbles.

"Sorry? I can't hear you. I thought you were a man, not a child. Speak up!" Arran yells at him.

"I don't want to be second best! I want to be *the* best," Braawen states in a commanding voice.

Arran flashes a cunning smile. "Good. In order to be the best, you must achieve greatness. In order to achieve greatness, you must be willing to give up something great, be it your family, friends, or yourself." The Professor looks at Braawen. "So, what will it be, Archer? Yourself or others?"

"Others," Braawen swiftly replies without hesitation.

Professor Arran just smiles and with a wave of his hands sends the wolf back into his shadow. "Then, if you want to be the best, you will have to summon one of the legendary beasts of the shadow."

"And what beasts are those?" Emelie asks.

Arran smiles widely. "The Phoenix of Night, a bird of black wings and black fire that burns lands to ash. The Great Scorn Wolf, the King of wolves and devourer of beasts and men. The Serpent of Chaos, a powerful beast that can pass through any shadow, with venom deadly enough to kill any man or beast. Legend has it that the last Black wielder who controlled the Serpent of Chaos could read minds and know the darkest desires of anyone.

"Lastly, the Shadow Dragon." Both students sit up straighter at the mention of this great beast. "The current controller of this beast is the Night Emperor. The Dragon is also known as the Dragon of Death, the World Destroyer, and even Wrath itself. The Night Emperor used the Shadow Dragon in his first small campaign to stop a small rebellion, riding on the back of the great beast. The dragon was so enormous that its shadow overtook the sky and its wings changed the course of the winds. The whole army was decimated, and he took over his throne."

"That's the one I want!" Braawen shouts. "I want to control *that* beast."

His teacher chuckles. "It is not an easy thing to control that beast. As the Night Emperor has said, not even he can fully control it. The dragon can choose whether or not to answer his call. The Night Emperor only uses the dragon when needed and doesn't rely solely on the Shadow Dragon; he relies on himself. He uses his own skills and powers to subdue his foes. Why, I've heard that he didn't even have to use his powers to overcome your uncle," he states mockingly.

It takes everything in Braawen not to react. *That's what they want. They want a reaction; they want to see me handled by the guards. The only reason why they haven't killed me yet is because I'm special,* Braawen reminds himself, staying calm.

"I'm not surprised. The Night Emperor is skilled in combat. My uncle was a fool to go up against him. He should have taken the truce when offered the chance," Braawen states as nonchalantly as possible.

His teacher nods his head in agreement. "Yes, he was a fool. The Emperor offered him a truce on three separate occasions, once even before the battle that defeated the rebellion. However, Markus didn't take any of them. Now, you're here and his bones still dangle on the walls of the city. But I digress, back to the Shadow Beasts, I believe that the two of you should continue on trying to listen to the shadows. Then start with a smaller beast."

"What kind of beasts are there?" Emelie asks.

"Any beast that lived once and had a shadow will be in the Shadow Lands. You'll find fish, birds, cows, lions, or even wolves. Some choose a cat or a dog for company, while others wish to have the griffins, the hydras, and the monsters of legends that now no longer exist in our world, but in the Shadow Lands."

She smiles. "I know what beast I want."

"And which beast is that?" the professor asks.

Emelie smiles. "I want the Serpent of Chaos."

I'll learn all your secrets and even the secrets from the Night Emperor. I'll play the sweet follower of Braawen, then I'll take my place on the throne. Royalty runs in my blood. I'm too unique to just be a general or a noble lady. Not even being Queen can satisfy my hunger. No, I want to be the Empress, I will be the Empress, she vows to herself.

Professor Arran nods. "Yes, I believe that the serpent will fit you perfectly."

· ☽ ·

In the light of the moon, a boy holding a spear is hiding behind the trees, Shadow Jumping from one area to the next. Ahead of him is a flag on a hill. He peeks and sees that there is no one there. He jumps, as he exits the tree nearest to the flag. He sees a foot and brings his arms up just in time to get kicked across the snow.

Knowing that Volodimir won't give him a moment to breathe, he moves as soon as he hits the ground and just as he thought, a knife is where his chest would have been a mere second ago. More knives come flying at him and he spins the spear in his hand, blocking each one. He uses a shadow technique, Ghost, for one knife he can't stop, and it phases right through his shoulder leaving a trail of black smoke behind his body.

His teacher appears beside the tree next to him and throws another knife at him. Nick can feel the object approach him, and he sidesteps, dodging it. He sees Volodimir about to launch another attack at him, and he quickly expands his shadow, falling into it and exiting through the tree next to his teacher.

His teacher is quick as he dodges the spear thrust at him, grabbing Nick by his arms. Nick uses Ghost on his hands, allowing him to phase through Volodimir's grip and escape. It's the last time he can use Ghost; he can't use that spell a third time or he'll faint. So, he darts towards the flag, but a tight pull makes him stumble and fall to the ground. He turns to see Volodimir grinning as the black coils of a shadow whip around his ankle. Nick grins and throws a Shadow Slash which Volodimir expertly dodges.

"Should have aimed a little higher, Nico," his teacher drawls sarcastically.

Nick grins. "Wasn't aiming at you!"

His teacher turns to hear the crack and fall of two trees behind him. Volodimir disappears into the shadow of the falling trees, releasing the whip's hold on Nick.

Nick gets up and runs as the tree falls, creating a snow cloud. He runs straight towards the flag, but Volodimir drops in front of him and chucks a dagger at him. Without slowing down, Nick allows the black coils from his shadow to surround him, knocking away the dagger as he Shadow Glimpses behind Volodimir in a matter of seconds to grab the flag.

"Yes!" Nick screams victoriously, jumping in the air. "I did it!" He huffs and looks back to see Volodimir smiling back at him.

"You have done well, Nico. Come, let's get you some tea and cookies to celebrate. Maybe later, we can train more in the Shadow Room. I believe the fifth level would suit you now." Volodimir opens a Shadow Portal to the cottage. As Nick walks in, he can feel the heat enveloping him as he takes his hooded cape off.

He sits down, carefully minding the scars on his back that ache from moving too much and waits as Volodimir puts his coat away. There is a comfortable silence as Nick watches Volodimir make tea. He thinks back to the Shadow Room, he can't wait until he can go into the lower levels soon.

The fifth level! I made it to the fifth level! Nick lets out a sigh of relief.

"I believe you're ready," his teacher states.

"Ready for what?"

His teacher puts the lid on the teapot, letting the tea steep, the cottage filling with the scent of lemons and mint. "To talk more about the advanced levels. Have you been reading the book I gave you?"

Nick smiles. "Yes, I love the book. I didn't even know that Shadow Glimpse could feel so amazing. The General only briefly spoke about it, but one has to experience it to know about it. It reminds me of a faster Shadow Jump with the shadow's black coils acting as a shield."

"Yes, Shadow Walk, Jump, and the next level, Glimpse, are closely related. However, Shadow Glimpse will have you jumping faster and protecting yourself at the same time. Your use of Ghost is supreme, but be careful, that spell will drain your energy quickly. Though, I think you know that and know when to use it. I believe no one will be able to touch you," Volodimir states proudly, crossing his legs in his chair. "How would you like to summon a Shadow Creature later on?"

Nick's jaw drops open and he is thunderstruck for a moment until he gathers his wits. "You think I'm ready for that?"

"Not yet. When you summon one, I want to make sure that you can control it as well. How good are you with animals?"

Nick shrugs. "I've played with a dog a few times."

"Not that good then." His teacher comments as Nick frowns. "However, I believe that working and learning about different animals is the fastest way for you to control them. For example, my teacher was not easy on me and believed that training with tigers was the best way to start." Volodimir spends the next few minutes going into detail about the Shadow Creatures and Shadow Lands. As he speaks, he is proud to see his student's excitement growing.

"The Shadow Lands sound amazing! Can we go there?" Nick asks.

His teacher chuckles. "Only Blacks can go into the Shadow Lands, and they are the only ones to have the chance of taming one of the legendary beasts. Even the Night Emperor has to focus all his attention to get the Shadow Dragon to do as he commands. That is why he opted out on using the dragon during the war, and relied on his own strength and the skills of his men."

He can see his student deflate.

"I said you'll get into Black and I meant it. Now, straighten up. It's time for tea." Volodimir grins, pouring them each a cup of tea and sets one down in front of Nick. He then picks up a spoon and stirs his own cup.

Nick thinks back to the war. *We would have been screwed if he used the dragon.*

"Volodimir, is that the only reason the Emperor didn't use the dragon?"

His teacher freezes for a moment, then sighs. "No," Volodimir states slowly, placing his cup down. "The Night Emperor could lose control of the dragon. Each time the Shadow Dragon kills or destroys, the Emperor can feel the rush of blood going through his veins. He feels what the dragon feels, pleasure, mostly, so he has to keep himself under control as well." He goes back to stirring his tea. "The Emperor was already furious at having to even go to Availa. He was barely keeping his own anger under control. No point in adding a dragon on top of that."

"Would the dragon kill him if he lost control?"

Volodimir pauses and a foreboding silence hangs over the cottage. "Well no," he begins. "The Night Emperor and the dragon, from what he told everyone, have a bond. Everyone else though? Let's just say the Emperor wanted his enemies destroyed, not his own army or the land."

"What does it take to have that kind of power?" Nick asks before he can stop himself.

They both look at each other, shocked by Nick's boldness. Nick wants to take back his words, but sees Volodimir's eyes dance with amusement. "You mean, what does it take to be a Black?" Volodimir asks, smirking.

Barely breathing. Nick nods.

"Learning all the shadow spells from Yellow to Purple, for one. Though another way, I'm sure you've heard is that one must know their own weaknesses and their deepest and darkest thoughts. Harnessing all their negative emotions to fuel their power; anger and even sadness, but not inflicting pain." Volodimir almost spits out the last word.

"Pain is cheap, and it will lead to irrevocable damage. After using your negative emotions, you can move on to other emotions and evolve your powers. However, knowing is half the battle; you can become a Purple with that mentality." Volodimir smiles, but it slowly disappears.

"No, you must accept the weaker part of yourself, accept the mistakes. Then, you must be at peace with it. Let go of your guilt and acknowledge the weakness in your mind. Control your fears to build strength. Once you break through that inner weakness and feel that raw emotion, you can take power by the hand. You must see the truth in both yourself and others in order to achieve greatness." Volodimir looks deep into Nick's eyes. "Are you willing to give up the person you are now to become the person you were meant to be?"

Nick is about to open his mouth but Volodimir stops him. "Many say, 'yes,' of course; the General said it, Professor Arran says it, and everyone says it. However, legends say that to pass into Black, you must go through the unchaining."

"What's that?" Nick leans on the edge of his seat. None of the books talked about that.

"Oh," Volodimir chuckles. "As the Black teacher, I am privy to some Black secrets. One is the unchaining ceremony. To be a Black, you must break through the chains inside you. Chains that hold your power back. To do that, you must accept the past. Embrace the shadows. Change into something great, and sacrifices must be made."

Volodimir chuckles again, leaning back into his seat. "But when people have to make the sacrifice, they stall. All of us will go through a situation that can break us and build us into better people. Many can't make that final step to truly see themselves simply because they don't want to. Many take that step and can't handle what they see. You must become vulnerable and turn it into strength. You must embrace it and not fear the power you are born to wield."

Volodimir sighs. "There are people here who mistake pride for strength, ignoring past pains to not be afflicted by it." He shakes his head. "But that's not what makes you into a Black. A Black user knows their hurt, knows to humble themselves when they are wrong, to embrace the mistakes of the past to make a better future."

They both sit silently for a moment. Nick doesn't like thinking too much on his past and wants to change the subject. As Volodimir finishes his tea, he can't help but remember what his uncle Malcolm told him.

"Volodimir?" His teacher nods his head as he pours them each another cup of tea. "You fought in the war of Availa, right?" His teacher nods again as Nick picks up his cup of tea, cradling it in his hands. "Did the rebel leaders refuse a truce?"

His teacher's cup stops midair from his mouth. "Not a lot of people know about that, but yes." Volodimir takes another sip of his tea. "The rebel leaders were offered a truce. Three times, in fact."

Nick wants to yell and scream, but he pushes down his anger. "We were never told that. They told us that you all came and wanted to take over the kingdom, that it was our duty to protect our independence."

His teacher chuckles "Duty," he sneers, taking another sip of tea. "Nico, a word of advice. If a person must lie to convince you to do something, then maybe their actions aren't as pure as you think. I know that the Archers and the rest of the advisors made the rebellion look like a just cause. However, all I saw was the same system, with a different head."

"How?"

"Tell me, Nico. I heard that the rebellion was meant to bring down the King. Everyone would be treated equally and there would be an elected government, a government for the people, they said." Volodimir chuckles. "However, it was the Emperor who defeated the King."

He takes another sip. "Not only that, was everyone treated equally in the rebel group? Jacques didn't go into detail, but he was surprised that Kaius and Lorcan's people were treated unfairly. Lastly, you all praised the idea of leadership by vote. Did you all vote on who should be leader, or did the people on top decide who should lead what while you all followed like sheep to the slaughter?" Volodimir asks with a small smile.

"Not all of us were blind," Nick snarls.

"Well then, congratulations to those few," his teacher drawls. "But still, too few."

Nick lets out a bark of joyless laughter. "Oh yes, the Emperor and his men 'saved' us. Now, all citizens are second-class. People who didn't join the rebel army were jailed and sent away." *Takara comes to mind.* "People who didn't fight in the rebellion lost their loved ones." *Rohana talking about her father.* "People in the capital lost their jobs and their home." *Bhaltair and Laura.*

Volodimir sits up straighter, controlling his rising anger. "You forgot that people can work their way out. People are able to go and live anywhere in the Empire. Trade has increased, which I'm sure the Mountain clans are happy about. The people who did surrender still own all their lands and titles. They are living better from what I've heard. Overall, the kingdom is doing better," he grits through his teeth.

Nick holds in a scoff. "How am I or any of the children supposed to know? Most of the things we hear are from other students or on the streets!" he snaps. "Of course, it's doing better! We were at war before! But, I'm sure that it's mostly the people who came from your Empire who you're getting the information from. I heard they're making their way to Availa in droves."

Nick leans forward in his chair, challenging his teacher. "Why, I wonder? Do they hate it here so much that they chose my home over yours?"

"Watch it, Nico." His teacher's voice is sharp. "It's not good to be disrespectful when the Empire has been gracious. Remember that you are still a child under—"

"War. I know." Nick leans back into his chair and lets out a sigh of frustration. "I have no citizenship anywhere. I'm at the mercy of the Empire, the Emperor, the school, the teachers, the students..." He gazes at Volodimir. "You." He takes a sip of his tea which is still too hot for him. "Forgive me, I guess I'm being too *treasonous*. As you said, the Empire has been gracious," he drawls sarcastically, fighting not to roll his eyes. "I am healthier than I've ever been. I have no father to yell at me or be ashamed of me."

Nick takes another sip of his tea, gently blowing on it to cool it down. "I can also fight with a spear now. Plus..." He puts the teacup to his lips but lowers it before taking a sip. "I'm at school, receiving an education, making both friends and enemies." He chuckles at that and finishes his tea.

Volodimir watches him. "You don't think this is better for you? You don't feel free at all?"

Nick laughs loudly like Volodimir has told a joke, yet his grip on his cup is firm. "Better? Maybe if it was a damn choice!" His voice rises as he talks. "My home is gone! My family is either dead or missing! Me and the other children, younger ones, were separated from their families and put into schools or other areas of work. The slums are terrible, my people are dying, and the people who are still in Availa have lost their rights. I don't even have a country to call my own!" His voice is hoarse and full of fury as Volodimir stares at him in surprise.

Only the fire's crackles dare to make a sound during the silence that follows Nick's outburst.

"I didn't know that freedom meant chains that rubbed my skin raw, a diseased and dark ship that took me from my home, and soldiers who wouldn't even let me say goodbye to my family!" Nick grits out, his knuckles white from gripping the table.

If this is how the Empire defines freedom, then he will have a lot of work to do when he becomes Emperor.

Once he calms down and remembers where he is, he wipes a stray tear from his eyes. "Free?" They both hear a small crack from the cup Nick's holding. "I wouldn't know what that feels like. Who needs guards when the students here watch us like hawks? Especially when they repeatedly tell us that we lost the war and aren't welcome here. I traded one prison for another." He puts the cracked teacup down. "Freedom?" He chuckles mirthlessly. "My memories don't go that far back."

Volodimir gazes at him, the silence heavy between them.

Nick can hear his heartbeat finally slowing down. His outburst of anger surprises him, yet he feels amazing. Before, he would always wonder what people thought about him. Heck, keeping a good reputation in the school is what's allowing him to survive so far. But there are times when a person just doesn't give a damn. And he can't spare a coin, nor does he care what his teacher thinks. He doesn't care if Volodimir's offended. It's a privilege to be offended and learn about it, instead of experiencing the hardships he's been through!

Volodimir has a voice that seems to be respected, he needs to know that this isn't right. Maybe his teacher can talk to people with more power to make sure this never happens again, but that's wishful thinking.

Nick finds his voice again, though the calm voice seems so foreign to the rage he feels inside. "Honestly, you've made this experience better. I mean... you actually listen to me. You take time out of your busy schedule to train me. So, I'm not ungrateful, especially to you." He puts his cup out for more tea, and Volodimir smiles and pours from the kettle.

"Nico," Volodimir's voice is softer, the softest that Nick's ever heard from him. "I am glad you told me this. Happier that I have made your..." Volodimir looks conflicted at his next words. "...*experience* a little better. I cannot promise you that things will get better, but I want you to know that I am here for you. I will help you whenever I can."

Nick smiles softly at him. Tonight, for the first time in a long time, he feels just a little safer.

Chapter 46
Wolves

The Training Hall only has one class this morning, and it is full of shouting, yelling, and laughter. Nick and his group of friends are practising jumping in between shadows on platforms that the General moves with his shadow. The students are jumping and playing tag; Nick can't remember the last time he played this game. Their teacher told them that this exercise is a great way to move in the shadows while trying to catch a target.

However, Nick is sure that his teacher is just tired. That changes when the General announces it's his turn to catch them. Whoever is caught last would get desserts.

After the 'warm up', they each run their course along the platforms. Everyone does a different course based on their ability. As Nick is about to do his course, the door opens unexpectedly. Walking through the door is Professor Arran and his Purple class again.

Nick looks at his friends and sees that they are stiff. He looks down and sees the General cross his arms, standing tall. No one says anything as the Professor and his students stop and all look towards him. He wonders why they're looking at him, until he follows their eyes and realizes that they are looking at the course that the General has made for him. Seeing that he is not the object of their attention, he's about to make his way down.

"Stay there, Guts. You still have to do your run!" the General shouts at him without turning around. Nick mumbles a few curses as he stands in place, watching everyone from above.

Professor Arran's eyes narrow as he looks at the course that the General constructed for his student. Nick can see Braawen look at the course in confusion. Finally, the professor speaks. "Isn't this too advanced for your pupil?" he asks the General.

The General scoffs. "The boy has talent; he's passed the Yellow, Orange, Red, and Blue courses." The man ignores the Purple's gasps of disbelief. "Naturally, the next phase is the Purple course," the General states as though it's the most obvious thing in the world.

Professor Arran scoffs. "I would like to see that."

The General smiles and turns to Nick, giving him a 'do not fail me boy' look.

I don't do well when people are watching me. Nick gulps, but remembers what the shadows have said to him. *Can't hold back; I've got to try my best.*

323

He looks to the course and sees one particularly large gap, going almost to the other end of the training room. Nick estimates that it must be a good 100 knots.

The General signals and Nick is gone in a blink. He can hear everyone's gasps as he Shadow Jumps past different levels. He sticks to Shadow Walks and Jumps to get more of a challenge. The course is moving quickly, and he has to react fast. One of the blocks disappears under him and he can hear a gleeful laugh from the General. He moves the platform's shadow under him and lands on the next platform, saving him from a nasty fall.

His classmates cheer him on as he focuses on the next round. This is a simple course for him. He's done more challenging runs on the rooftops of the city and the crumbling walls of the slums. This is just another mission to accomplish. He can hear his father's voice telling him to focus on the mission or don't come back home. He can hear Volodimir's voice telling him to trust the shadows.

He trusts the shadows as the final leap comes into view. He knows the wall with the large window is on the other side of the ledge and focuses on how he's going to get there. He knows that this won't be a regular jump, and knows that he will have to reach far into the shadows. Nick grins as he quickens his breathing and feels a burst of excitement and apprehension going from his chest to his legs as he nears the edge. He speeds up, and as he reaches the ledge, he jumps. He pulls up his shadow and is swallowed whole. He sees black and the excitement that he feels as he jumps turns to calm. For some reason, the world seems to slow down.

A normal jump would feel like a doorway. You open one door to get to another room, but this is different. It feels similar to the first time he jumped so far. He's never been in the dark this long. All he sees is black, he's surrounded by darkness, but he keeps moving forward. Then he hears voices, loud and clear, encouraging him. He feels like he's slowing down until a hand on his back pushes him forward, almost sharp to the touch.

"Keep going," a man's voice tells him.

He wants to look back, but like always, he arrives out of the shadow and rolls on the platform.

Nick gets up from his crouching position to see the giant window of his destination. He looks back to see the place he jumped from, then back to the ledge that he's on. He doesn't know why he's shocked that he made it; he's made farther jumps before. On the other hand, doing it in front of an audience and not failing, well… that's amazing.

There's silence due to the sheer disbelief that he made that huge jump. It isn't until Nick looks at his classmates that cheers erupt, and the General gives him a huge smile. He's out of breath as he Shadow Jumps back down to the floor, and seconds later, the arms of Takara and Rohana crush him with hugs, followed by Bhaltair who spins him around.

The General's laugh booms throughout the entire room as he walks towards Nick. His friends make room for him as the General stands beside him, ruffling his hair. He turns to the Purple class with a proud smile. "Guts managed to clear the section that even some of your students can't clear!"

Actually, none of them have. Professor Arran knows this, and turns to Nick, glaring, as his grip on his cane goes white.

That boy is a Yellow. He shouldn't be able to hear the shadows! Arran grumbles inwardly as he puts on a face of indifference. *The boy can't be in the Yellow circle now.* He looks at Braawen, who has a sour look on his face, lips pulled tightly together in a thin line, arms firmly crossed over his chest.

The Professor looks back at Nick and remembers that the small boy went up against his top student and brought him to his knees. There's something different about him. Yes, the boy has changed physically; he is taller and even had a few muscles to actually hold up his bones. He was absolutely worthless before and Arran wonders how the boy had improved so much in just two months.

However, there is still something else, he can feel it. The boy's connection to the shadows has increased. He shouldn't have been able to make that jump; 100 knots is the limit that a person can Shadow Jump. It's a trick that Purple teachers place on their students as their students should be able to know when a jump is too far. For Arran, it's like a second thought that enters him. For others, the shadows give a whisper. Either way, a student should be able to judge by their instincts. That space between the two platforms that the boy jumped is around 150 knots. It wouldn't be a Shadow Jump. It would be a Shadow Portal.

Yellows can't do portals. Arran's thoughts run around trying to remember which circles can do portals. *Only Purples can do portals or...* His heart stops and his eyes go still. There's only one other group. *No!* He refuses to believe it.

The Professor turns to the General as the Yellows make their way back towards them. Arran calms himself and gives a concerned look. "General, even if your student cleared the jump, I think that course was too dangerous. What if the boy had fallen and gotten injured?" Arran gives Nick a condescending smile. "Which means that you refused to use the safety equipment... which leads me to believe that you did not get permission from the Black Teacher?"

The General huffs. "In fact, I did."

Both classes look between their teachers as they have a battle of wills.

"I don't believe that the Black Teacher would be that reckless," Professor Arran answers. "I will go get him."

Everyone in the room looks at Professor Arran. The General puts down his arms. "Arran," the General calls, his voice going cold as stone. This isn't a teacher speaking; this is the army general commanding his troops. "Heed my advice: Volodimir will not be happy to be called away from whatever he's doing just to confirm a course."

Professor Arran scoffs. "What if the students get hurt? What if you're just doing this to get attention?"

The General body stiffens. "Are you calling me a fool? I would never put my students in harm's way. I would push them, but never past their limits. If Guts had fallen, I would have caught him."

"I'm just concerned based on your history on the battlefield. It *was* your reckless behaviour that got you into this position by punishment, wasn't it? Even your wife suffered from your foolishness and had to retire early."

The General looks livid. His voice goes cool, not the outburst that Nick or his classmates are expecting. No, this was something past rage. The General takes a step towards Professor Arran. "Don't you dare bring up my past," he snarls menacingly. "I've done some foolish things, but I would never do what you do to your students. Hurting them. Turning them against each other. You even encourage them to hurt other members of the school, their own teachers."

Nick and his friends process this sudden revelation and gasp.

"You are no teacher," the General continues, stalking closer to Professor Arran as the Purple class gasps in outrage. "I can tell your methods don't bring anything into fruition. My class can all hear the voice of the shadows, even a good percentage of the Blues can. Yet, *none* of your students can hear the shadows." The General's face is inches from Professor Arran's. "The only one harming students here is *you*."

This time Arran's pale cheeks turn bright red. Instead of denying the General's accusations, he grabs his cane and smashes it against his shadow. The crash echoes across the room, and Nick can feel a ripple spread throughout the school and stops as it hits someone. He has to rub the back of his neck as shooting pain erupts from it.

The room gets darker as the entrance door swings open. There, a man's shadow looks like a giant among theirs. He appears to be reading a paper and holds a stack of papers under his arm. Volodimir walks in, not looking up, but Nick can feel the pain go from his neck down to his leg. Volodimir stops beside the General who nods in acknowledgement, yet Volodimir doesn't even answer them, his eyes still scanning the paper.

Professor Arran's face is red and Nick wonders if he would pop.

This lowlife is not even giving me the respect that I deserve. The nerve of the man to not even look at me! Arran thinks to himself. He calms himself; he has to be an example to his students. *There will be people who will think that they are above you. You just need to knock them down and put them in their place.*

"Thank you for coming on such short notice, Black Teacher. However, I had a concern that needed to be brought up. Volodimir, are you the one who approved of this dangerous course?" Professor Arran asks.

Volodimir's eyes continue to scan the paper. His only response is a slight nod.

"Thank you once again, Black Teacher. Please excuse us for calling you on such a trivial matter," the General says, bowing to Volodimir.

Volodimir hums and begins to walk away.

"Wait!" Professor Arran yells. "Are you telling me that a simple Yellow can do the Purple course? I think that you are putting children's lives in danger."

That stops Volodimir and he turns around, his eyes slowly moving from the paper to Professor Arran.

"I have been in this school for ten years and not once have I seen such a disregard for a student's safety. Maybe you shouldn't be in charge of this school," Professor Arran scoffs.

Nick and his friends move back one step as Nick suddenly feels a heavy pressure all over his body.

Volodimir adds the paper he was reading to the pile under his arm. His eyes seem to glow a dull red, but instead of a scowl, he smiles. "You doubt the word of a Black Teacher? Then what do you suggest? Do you believe that your input is better than someone appointed to this position? Appointed by both the Council and Emperor?"

Everyone surreptitiously glances at Professor Arran, who looks startled that the man has the gall to say such a thing. "O-of course not. Yet, let's see if you are still able to guide our school. A simple duel?" He smiles back, covering his stutter.

Everyone quickly turns to look at Volodimir. "I have an interview with another member, but I'll be back here in one hour. See you then, Professor." With that, Volodimir drops into his shadow and disappears.

News travels fast, and all the students, faculty, and cleaning staff—save for Volodimir—are at the Training Hall, waiting for the duel to start. The wall that they thought was made of wood had been unfolded to create rows of raised benches. Nick and his friends are in the centre of the first row, both excited and nervous.

He looks to the four heads standing in the centre of the training area. The raised platform has been removed, along with all the training equipment. Never has the Training Hall looked so clean and bare. Sitting in the balconies across from the benches are the teachers, with another seating area made up of five large chairs, a coloured banner representing each circle behind each one.

Nick feels the excited buzz of all the children, and the faculty seem both fearful and eager. However, the five heads of the school seem to be in a heated argument, mainly the heads from Orange and Red.

"This is madness!" Leia hisses at Arran.

Catherine shakes her head. "Never in all my years has a teacher gone against a fellow teacher! Especially against the Black teacher. Do you not fear the consequences?" She glares at him. "You will put the Emperor's decision at risk, making him look like he made a mistake." She shakes her head in disbelief.

Arran smiles thinly. "It must be done. The man allows students from lower circles to train in areas that are above them."

The two women look unimpressed. "So, you're envious that a student from a lower circle is improving?" Catherine asks. "I've never heard such foolishness in all my years here... Forget that, all my life!"

"But that's what this school was created for!" Leia snaps. "The students are supposed to improve! So, what? I've even let my students do some Red drills with the Black Teacher's permission. There are even some that I have pushed too far, and the Black Teacher has reprimanded me. He does so with all teachers, or have you forgotten how quickly he reacted with Mr. Teslan's science class? The students from Availa have improved tremendously. The General doesn't go above their means. He pushes people, yes, but not into danger!"

Arran just scoffs.

General Herald puts a comforting hand on Leia's shoulders. "Let the man fight." He nods his head with a small smile.

Catherine looks to the General and then Jacques. She smiles at Arran, but not one of her kind ones and gives a firm nod. "If this is what you seek, then I pray to the god of Shadows that you receive your just reward."

Jacques is smiling from ear to ear. As soon as he heard about the duel, he volunteered to be the overseer. He's not surprised that this is happening. In fact, he hoped that it would happen a lot sooner, but it seems that Volodimir has some legendary patience. Today will go down in the history of the school, for as Catherine said, 'No teacher had ever fought against the Black Teacher'. The Black Teacher is the final voice for the

Emperor in terms of education. This will be seen as a clear act against the Night Emperor.

Jacques grins. *Oh you fool, you believe yourself a follower of the Emperor, yet, you think yourself above him. There's a reason why the Night Emperor hasn't appointed you the Black teacher. You would go against his words once you tasted more power.*

The Blue teacher breathes in deeply. *Ah, yes. This will stop anyone from going up against Volodimir again, I'm sure of it*, Jacques thinks.

The entrance doors crash open, causing a hush to fall over the training room. The students and staff peer from their corners to see a shadow expanding, swallowing the five heads. Nick can feel the presence of Volodimir throughout the room. The whole room goes cold, and even Arran pales slightly as Volodimir walks in with a false look of serenity. Nick knows that look; the man is livid. Volodimir's hair is pushed back and he wears all black, not a school emblem in sight. The black seems to absorb all the light. The only thing of colour are his blood-red eyes.

The man's footsteps echo as he walks to the centre of the room, stopping in front of his opponent. Nick takes back what he said about Volodimir not being as muscular as the General. Without his robes, the man looks like he could bring down the old General in an instant. The teachers are silent as Volodimir glares at Arran. The Professor's face, which always seems to wear an arrogant smile, pales even more in return.

"Let's begin this, shall we?" Volodimir's curt voice travels across the room in every shadow so that everyone can hear him clearly.

Professor Arran drags up whatever confidence he has and gives Volodimir a small smile. "Yes, let's get this over with."

The General gives a small bow to Volodimir and he and the other heads, besides Jacques, leave, taking their seats in their respective chairs. To Nick, the chairs almost look like thrones. The General is the only Yellow teacher and he sits proudly, while Catherine looks vexed and Leia is worried.

With a wave of Jacques's hands, his shadows expand into a dark dome which slowly turns invisible, leaving a larger black circle on the floor. The shadow acts as a barrier to protect both the students and faculty members.

"You both know the rules," Jacques begins. "This isn't a duel to the death. However, major injuries may occur. No breaking the barrier or going past the boundary. Staff, students, and faculty members are not to be hurt at all. The use of Shadow Weapons and calling Shadow Beasts is optional." He looks between the stone-faced expression of Volodimir and the arrogant smile of Arran. "Good luck to you and may the god of Shadow favour you both." Jacques ends with a smile.

329

Arran takes his cane and pulls out a sword, while Volodimir takes out a sword from his shadow, the sword with the black blade.

All the students hold their breaths, as Jacques shouts for them to begin. The two lunge at each other and the striking blades cause a ripple of magic to crash against the barrier. Nick wonders if it will hold, as he can feel the raw energy pass through him.

The two continue to fight and parry each other. Arran moves with fluid attacks while Volodimir blocks and remains on the defence. Arran almost hits him and Volodimir jumps back. The professor sends a quick Shadow Slash at him, so fast that Nick is amazed by the speed at which it came. He would comment on Arran's skills if not for what his teacher does next. Volodimir's eyes flash red for a split second as he easily cuts the slash in two, causing people to gasp. Even Arran takes a step back and looks at Volodimir apprehensively.

"Can you do that?" Bhaltair whispers in Nick's ears.

He shrugs in response; he remembers the rules and weaknesses from their first lesson. The General told them that nothing can stop a Shadow Slash. He thinks that he's seeing things, but looking at the faces of the teachers, he knows that he's not the only one who saw that happen.

Arran recovers as Volodimir appears from his shadow and cuts his arm. Arran moves quickly, but Volodimir is always one step ahead of him, as if the man can read his mind. He tries to go through Volodimir's shadow but he can't; his shadow is like a brick wall, which Arran has never experienced before.

Before Arran can react, Volodimir kicks him hard in the stomach, causing the man to fly across the room and smash into the barrier. All the Purple students look on in shock as their teacher lies on the floor gasping for air.

"This shouldn't be happening," Braawen can hear one of the Purples whispers behind him.

"Yeah, he used to easily beat the other Purple teachers," another student whispers.

Braawen looks at the Black Teacher standing confidently above his enemy. He pictures himself as the Black Teacher, standing above Nick on the floor, with his cousin begging for his life. He smiles, which falls as he sees his so-called great teacher pull himself up from the floor.

"Enough of this!" Arran tosses his sword to the side, practically snarling at the man. Volodimir makes his sword disappear back into his shadow. He stands tall, waiting for whatever the professor wants to throw at him.

Nick looks at the two duellists, seeing two very different men. Arran's usually perfectly gelled hair is falling into his face as he growls like a mad dog at the man in front of him. Volodimir's jet-black hair hasn't moved a bit, and he is calm and collected.

Volodimir walks over to the Professor, but Arran's shadow grows and Nick can hear a fierce howl erupt from the shadow. He can't even properly let out a gasp as three huge black wolves form from Arran's shadow. Their howls ring deafeningly across the room, vibrating the stands that the students sit on.

The crowd gasps in amazement at seeing fabled Shadow Beasts. Even Nick has never seen one and is amazed by how similar yet different the shadow wolves are. They are pure black with red eyes, but even larger than the wolves that he'd seen in the mountains. They almost tower over the Professor as he stands, proudly displaying his power. He looks to the Purple class and sees pride flash in their eyes again. They don't seem surprised by their teacher's skills. Nick suddenly remembers that there's a reason why he's the head of Purple; Shadow Beasts are rare to summon and even rarer to control. Professor Arran controlling three of them to fight alongside him as he attacks Volodimir is more than impressive.

"No wonder he's the Purple head," he can hear Takara whisper as Rohana nods in agreement.

Nick just smiles. "Don't count the Black Teacher out yet." They all turn to him and he feels a sense of pride watching Volodimir keeping his own with the wolves, even Shadow Whipping one. "There's a reason why he got appointed as the Black Teacher."

They all stop talking and turn abruptly as they hear one of the wolves whines pitifully.

Volodimir has managed to hurt one of the Shadow Creatures; one of the wolves lays on the ground whining. One of its feet is missing and instead of blood, black smoke pours out of the wound. The other two wolves back away from Volodimir, and even Arran cannot hide his shock. At the sidelines, Jacques's mouth is wide open, unable to make a sound. All but one of the heads stand up in their seats, staring in wonder; General Herald is the only one sitting with a huge grin on his face.

Everyone's attention is on Volodimir. Black veins creep up his right arm, turning his hand black. His nails elongate, like that of a predator; these are claws meant to kill. Nick can feel the pressure pushing down on him strongly enough to make his legs go numb. He can hear the voices of the shadows whisper in his ears, all are saying the same thing.

Watch, friend. Watch and see a true Shadow Wielder.

Nick's head feels heavy as he leans on Bhaltair's shoulder.

Volodimir snaps his fingers and his shadow grows and stands, turning into a circle right behind him. Everyone watches as his shadow grows larger than Arran's, wondering what beast he's about to summon.

It doesn't take very long as a frightening roar pierces everyone's ears as they look to the shadow. Arran drops to his knees, white as a fresh blanket of snow. There, coming out of the shadow is a nose, scaly and black. The more the thing grows, the more Nick can't breathe. The shadow that Volodimir cast almost takes up the height of the room. Only the gigantic head of the creature can come out.

A dragon. A Shadow Dragon with eyes that are red like Volodimir's. It sniffs the air and opens its mouth to bare teeth, each the size of a grown man, and a deadly breath of black smoke that curls around the barrier and heats the entire room. This time, the General stands looking in awe at the dragon while Jacques braces himself against the barrier.

Everyone looks in horror as the dragon eats the wounded wolf; the other two return to Arran's shadow with their tails between their legs. Nick looks as the great beast devours the wolf in one bite. They can all hear the crunching of bones and flesh. Despite the gruesome sight, Nick's attention slowly turns to his teacher whose expression is nothing but pure bliss. Then, he remembers what Volodimir told him about how the Emperor and the feelings of the dragon are connected.

"Oh, we're dead," Nick whispers.

"Good girl," Volodimir smiles. The dragon licks her teeth and gazes around the room; some students faint. "Go back to sleep, I apologize that you had to come here." The dragon purrs, closing her eyes as she returns to Volodimir's shadow.

Volodimir's shadow returns to the form of a man, but his hands remain black. The only sounds are his footsteps approaching Arran, who is still on his knees. Without facing Jacques, Volodimir asks. "Is it not my win?"

Jacques nods as he finds his voice. "The victory goes to the Night Emperor! May his rule be long!" The Blue teacher practically throws himself to the floor.

Nick's heart stops at the announcement. The man who is training him, the person he was beginning to see as a father figure, is the man who killed his father. He was proud of Volodimir winning against Arran, but now all he feels is fear.

Everyone in the room finds the energy to bow. Even the students who have fainted have their real friends bowing their bodies; Nick is sure that it's both out of fear and respect. He bows as well, his mind still going in circles. He can hear the shadows laughing at his dilemma. They are pleased with what Volodimir did, but he can also feel that they are pleased with what he's about to do.

"Rise," Volodimir commands. Everyone stands up. Bhaltair is practically holding Nick up as his legs have given out. The Emperor glares at Professor Arran who is still on his knees, shaking.

Before Arran can beg for forgiveness, the Emperor stops him. "Do you still believe that my judgment is incorrect?" The voice that comes out is both ice cold and with the fury of fire. This time, Nick is sure his eyes glow red. "Tell me why I received a letter urging me to come investigate the cruelty that you inflict on both your students and fellow Purple teachers."

"I—I—" Arran stammers.

The Emperor interrupts him. "I have conducted interviews with all your teachers in Purple and other students. Not only have I seen your teaching from afar, but I've seen how the Purple students have been acting towards their fellow students. They may be in Purple, but it is their duty to help other students reach their potential. All I see are students willing to cripple others so they don't get in their way."

Nick notices that the Purple students stay silent.

The Emperor sighs. "Never have I seen such destructive methods of teaching. Even the Purples in the last two graduations are no match for their predecessors. No wonder there haven't been any Blacks!" he snaps, and Arran flinches like he's been whipped. "There used to be a few of us. Now, I am the only one left. I hope that your teachings haven't stopped them from growing. How is it that I hear that Blue and all of Yellow can hear the shadows? Yellow, to my surprise, can hear the voice of the shadows, but not one," he growls, "not *one* Purple student can hear even a whisper."

The silence in the room is deafening. Though Nick feels like he could pass out at any moment, he tries to keep his breathing to a minimum. However, Arran's breathing is loud and quick and the man looks like he's about to pass out.

"Your transgressions against the students in Purple circle can forfeit your life, but that is not all," Volodimir says, and Nick wonders how there could be more. "There is the added crime of your funding of the school. You blackmailed the previous Lord Gerald Nortshell into making 'generous' donations in your name to hide the fact that you knew of his son's nefarious deeds. When he died, you moved on and blackmailed his son to gather funds. You've used similar tactics with other donors as well. I must say, you do an excellent job at finding and exploiting other people's weaknesses. However, you fail to see your own." Volodimir states coldly, watching Arran pale with each accusation.

The Emperor's smile grows. "I will show everyone the power of the Black circle today."

Nick looks around, confused. *Did he not just show us what Black can do?* he thinks. No one makes a sound.

The impossible happens. With a wave of Volodimir's wrist, Arran's own shadow rises and attacks him. This attack is different from the one on Nortshell. Arran is screaming in pain and Nick can hear the cracking of bone, the tearing of flesh. He has to close his ears as he can hear the shadows; they're either laughing or screaming words that he didn't understand. People around him are gasping, crying, and some more pass out. The teachers look on in both fascination and awe. Nick opens his eyes a crack and sees that even Ms. Joy is fervently writing notes in her journal. The cries only last for a minute and as they subside, he looks to see that Professor Arran is no longer a man. In his place is a small, thin dog made of shadows.

"You say that you love the shadows so much? Now, you can stay in the shadows forever. May your wolves accept you in their pack. Though, I highly doubt it." Volodimir scoffs. The dog whines and the last thing anyone hears is a small yelp as it gets sucked into a shadow.

Jacques can only swallow as he recalls the moment he sent his letter to the Emperor, not actually thinking that the Emperor himself would come. When he first saw the Night Emperor enter through the door and announce to teachers that he was their new Black Teacher, it took everything in him not to get on his knees and bow. When he introduced himself as Volodimir, Jacques knew that he was using his blessed shadow name. It is a common name popularized by him; no one would look twice. Jacques wrote a letter to Abram that very day, cursing him for not telling him that his friend is the Night Emperor! Nothing could have prepared him for this. The Night Emperor taking time out of his busy schedule to personally come to his aid is amazing.

Jacques is living the dream, watching Arran getting his just rewards; utopia.

"Purple teachers," Volodimir's voice echoes. "I would like to speak with all of you concerning the newly opened position of Head of Purple circle. Each of the school heads will go and take their students to their rooms. All classes are cancelled today. Feast meals will be sent to their quarters. Purple students will be guided by their eldest student. No students shall leave their quarters or grounds."

An echo of 'Yes, Emperor' rings out in the room.

With that, Volodimir leaves with the Purple teachers trailing behind him. Nick needs Bhaltair to help him stand as his legs are pins and needles. He watches Volodimir leave; the man gives a quick glance and smile at Nick before walking away.

The General motions for them to follow him, they obey without a word. When they arrive at their quarters, Nick turns to the General.

"Did you know all along that he was the Emperor?" Nick asks. The rest of his friends' crowd behind him, wondering the same thing.

The General smiles. "I've always known who the Black Teacher was and respected him for taking the time to come and fix the problem himself. I'm ashamed that he had to come, but after this is over, he will turn all his attention and duties back to ruling as the Night Emperor. I'm just happy that he no longer has to use a Shadow Clone to go back and forth between the school and the palace. He may be the most powerful user, but even he has limits."

"General," Nick whispers. "Will everything be okay?"

The General turns to see each of his students wearing identical worried expressions. They heard the Emperor's anger, and there's no doubt that he is disappointed in the teachers. Honestly, the General doesn't know what will take place in the cottage. So, with a shrug and a smile, the General walks out of the quarters as his students silently watch him leave.

Soul of Shadows

By: K.L.Alexander

Sneak Peak

Prologue

CONQUEROR

'Yea, though I walk through the valley of the shadow of death, I will fear no evil,'

Psalm 23:4 KJV

In the Purple quarters, Emelie tells everyone that she needs time to process the reveal of the Night Emperor. Thankfully, everyone understands. She glances at Braawen's door, but it's already closed as she heads to her room.

She sits on her bed and sighs. In the silence, a giggle escaped her lips. She laughs at how the Night Emperor, the man who killed her family, had been here all along. She will have to thank him; the fewer people know about her past, the better. She composes herself and walks over to her vanity. Emelie sits on the plush cushion, smiling at her reflection.

"This can still work," she tells herself. "I can still get on the Emperor's good side. Maybe even mention my dear aunt Estelle." Her smile drops when she remembers pale lilac eyes, blood pouring on the floor. She pushes herself away from the vanity, knocking down a hairpin. The hairpin makes a quiet clink as it hits the floor, yet it sounds like a cannon that snaps her from her memory. She shakes her head then quickly picks up the tiny silver accessory. Pale blue eyes unfocused again as she remembers her aunt's hairpin. It had a dragon on it, littered with black stones. And it was sharp.

"It was an accident," she mumbles to herself. She sits down on her bed again and sighs. "Get it together!" She snaps at her reflection in the mirror. "What happened to Estelle was your father's fault. Not yours." She can remember him screaming at Estelle, with her aunt's body littered on the floor.

336

She smiles as she puts the silver pin in her hair. "I'm the only royal blood of Availa. It's my destiny to be an Empress. I'm one of a kind."

Braawen lays on his bed, remembering the fight. He can't help but burst into a mischievous grin at the memory of the sheer strength of the Night Emperor. He knows that the Emperor was probably toying with Arran. He smiles, replaying the event in his mind. This time he is the Emperor, and Nick is the Professor. Then he replaces Nick with Kaius, then with some of the other boys in Purple who needed a good smack. He smiles as he sees his enemies on their knees one by one. Begging for forgiveness. Then he sees the last person he wants to be on their knees the most.

Markus Archer. He sees the man like the day he saw him when they arrived in Andromendor. Braawen doesn't even let Markus beg or apologize. He just cuts off his head.

Braawen sighs and looks at the window, seeing the radiant stars tonight. The Night Emperor is the Black Teacher. The Emperor already knows his skills. Now all he has to do is deal with Uncle Tybalt. The Emperor will surely embrace him if he does this, maybe even as a son. As much as he loved his uncle, if there is one thing on the battlefield he remembers, it's them or him.

"I will always choose me."

Nick doesn't listen as his friends loudly discuss how they can't believe the Night Emperor has been here this whole time.

He just sits in his bed silently pondering today's recent events. Volodimir... he's the Night Emperor. He can't believe it. He thinks back on every interaction he's had with Volodimir.

"I have other duties than being the Black Teacher."

Nick asked him what the Night Emperor would do if he found Markus's son. *"If he was like his cousin with potential, I'd let him live."*

When he asked why the Emperor chose Volodimir to teach, *"Because I'm the only one who can."*

"Only a Black should be the Black Teacher," Nick whispers. He's heard it from the General and Jacques.

The signs were always there. Volodimir's extreme power, the General always showing respect, his aura of authority while shopping, sitting above the nobles in the restaurant and getting the highest view. He remembers what the General told him: no one can use another person's shadow against them except for Black. Yet, Volodimir made Lord Nortshell's own shadow attack himself.

"Nick?" Takara's soft voice brings him out of his mind. "Can you believe the Black Teacher was the Emperor? Good thing we never angered him!" She chuckles.

Nick gives a weak smile back. "Yeah." He looks at his hands and remembers all the times he angered or annoyed Volodimir, only to get a laugh at the end. Volodimir took the time to train him, teach him, and encourage him. Nick clenches his hand.

The deities have given him a huge opportunity. He said he would be their leader, and right now, he is learning from the leader. He smiles, looking at his friends with new determination.

"Guys…" They all look at him, seeing strength. "I believe things are going to change for the better."

Volodimir walks towards the black cottage feeling free and light. Yes, there's still the Tybalt situation, but at least the Arran problem has been dealt with. He sighs and cracks his neck, feeling relief. Then he feels a buzzing on the nape of his neck. The energy in the air has changed. He felt the exact change the day his parents died, the day he won the crown, and on the day he received the letter of the foolish king declaring war. So, he wonders what this night will bring. He doesn't know if it's good or bad, but he knows something will happen before the sun rises to bring in a new day. He's not sure, but he knows he can handle it.

He is already planning Nick's next training regimen as he walks among the trees. He hopes that he and Nick can still have a good relationship after today's reveal. He wanted to tell his apprentice who he is at the Spring Festival, but Arran ruined his plans.

Oh, Emperor of the Night, the shadows call to him. *No longer will you walk in this world alone. Another Black will reveal themselves, and they will succeed in all you have planned. They too shall complete the unchaining ritual. The chains shall break from their hearts. They will be free and reborn.*

Volodimir stops in his tracks. The winds push his cape to the side, the only things that move besides the trees. He can't see the snowy path to the cabin. Instead, he sees a room. He remembers a time when he was at his lowest, when he was betrayed by someone he trusted. He recalls the darkness that enveloped him in the room. A darkness he can never forget, and a clawed hand reaching out to him.

He laughs, and his voice echoes throughout the woods, blending into the shadows. *Is that so shadows?* He chuckles. *Then I cannot wait to have another Black. It's been lonely.*

He wonders if it will be Nick. He knows everyone has high hopes for Braawen and Emelie, the two Purple students. However, he shakes his head. Whether Nick becomes a Black or not, he still has plans for him.

"Nico can handle it," he tells himself. He whistles a tune as he slowly disappears into the shadows welcoming him into the dark.

About the Author

First-time Author who loves God, family, and ramen. Lost my job during covid and decided to write a book to help with the stress of looking for another job. It helped.